C000281352

THE SALAMANDER TREE

THE SALAMANDER TREE

Robert Lipscombe

HAMISH HAMILTON · LONDON

HAMISH HAMILTON LTD
Published by the Penguin Group
27 Wrights Lane, London W8 5TZ, England
Viking Penguin Inc., 375 Hudson Street, New York, New York 10014, USA
Penguin Books Australia Ltd, Ringwood, Victoria, Australia
Penguin Books Canada Ltd, 2801 John Street, Markham, Ontario, Canada L3R 1B4
Penguin Books (NZ) Ltd, 182–190 Wairau Road, Auckland 10, New Zealand

Penguin Books Ltd, Registered Offices: Harmondsworth, Middlesex, England

First published 1990
1 3 5 7 9 10 8 6 4 2

Copyright © Robert Lipscombe, 1990
The Acknowledgements on page vii constitute an extension of this copyright page

The moral right of the author has been asserted

All rights reserved. Without limiting the rights under copyright
reserved above, no part of this publication may be
reproduced, stored in or introduced into a retrieval system,
or transmitted, in any form or by any means (electronic, mechanical,
photocopying, recording or otherwise), without the prior
written permission of both the copyright owner
and the above publisher of this book

Filmset in Monophoto Palatino
Printed in England by Clays Ltd, St Ives plc

A CIP catalogue record for this book is available from the British Library
ISBN 0–241–12795–5

For Fiona, Harriet, and Trish

This book is rightfully dedicated to the late Don Lipscombe –
'Pay your debts, Robert Mark. Always.'

ACKNOWLEDGEMENTS

Lines from 'A Mirror for Poets' from *Fighting Terms* by Thom Gunn reprinted by permission of Faber & Faber Ltd; lines from 'Lessons of War' from *A Map of Verona* reprinted by permission of the Literary Executor of the Estate of the late Henry Reed.

For startling insights into the lives and practices of Renaissance magicians and conjurors of celestial entities, and for translated excerpts from their writings, I am gratefully indebted to D. P. Walker and to Frances A. Yates, and to their respective sources; for material on women writers of the Reformation, and for an excerpt from Marie Dentière's *Epistre très utile . . .*, to Thomas Head, and to Katharina M. Wilson; for news reports of the day, compiled by correspondents of the House of Fugger during the years 1568 and 1605, to Victor von Klarwill and to Pauline De Chary; for alchemical lore, and for extracts from *Theatrum Chemicum* and from *The Vision of Sir George Ripley*, to C. G. Jung, and to Stanislas Klossowski de Rola; for gnostic illuminations and for translated excerpts from gnostic writings, in particular the gnostic codices of Nag Hammadi, to Elaine H. Pagels and to James M. Robinson and fellow contributors to the Coptic Gnostic Library Project; for translated excerpts from works of Goethe and Jean-Jacques Rousseau, to Eva Maria Neumeyer; for lines from Schopenhauer, Kierkegaard and Nietzsche, to E. F. J. Payne, W. Lowrie and W. Kaufmann respectively.

And to my friend and patron, Hubert Poliwoda, a special word of thanks: without your visionary generosity this book could not have been concluded.

PART I

the void is all
it is that which knows itself
it is beginning and end

. . . .

and there came forth from it
hot and wet and dry and cold
forming a cross in the void

and hot and dry grew light
and wet and cold grew dark
and fire came forth and earth

and there were storms in the void
urging creation of the World
which is the hunger of the void

. . . .

earth and fire are substance and form
and the form of earth is being
and the substance of fire is knowing

and chief among the forms of fire
is Naming — which is called Word;
Man is the substance of Naming

Man is called Word

. . . .

what Man knows springs into being
what Man knows becomes real;
the World is Man's fires dancing

Fragments of Lost Cosmogonies: An Anthology of Myths Collected in
the Amazon Basin by Hernando S. Gordon. Translated into English
by J. Millar and D. N. Walters

1

But musical sound by the movement of the air moves the body: by
purified air it excites the aerial spirit which is the bond of body and
soul: by emotion it affects the senses and at the same time the soul:
by meaning it works on the mind ... by the conformity of its
quality it floods us with a wonderful pleasure: by its nature, both
spiritual and material, it at once seizes, and claims for its own, man in
his entirety.

Marsilio Ficino, *Op. Omn.* (Commentary on the *Timaeas*)

On a June afternoon, a little after three, in a sonorous humming as of bees
in the apiary, and coming from Dryfield over Copenhagen, the Halifax
Bombers reached Berlin. Then high above, on Friedrichstrasse, the first of
seventy-six five hundred pounders went crump amongst the tenements.
And just a few hundred metres from where they sat, close to where the
Kongresshalle stands today in the green reaches of Tiergarten Forest,
another bomb went crump and then another, crump, smashing and
kindling: with an odour of singeing in a herbal emporium the pines, oaks
and beeches blazed; among vapours of sap and boiling resins the billowing
crests of flame went whispering to work; and littering the ground where
moments before they had perched on swaying, light-dappled branches,
charred corpses of birds bestowed an absurd and tantalizing relish.

In their fortified shelter and operations room deep below Fuerst-Bismarck Strasse a group of officers and civil servants sat in dismal conference.
They saw how the tiny flakes of plaster drifted from ceiling and from
walls to settle like flour on gleaming medals and expensive suits; and
faces which fear had wetted were whited into stage poltroons in that
easeful shower of particles. But the faces of the military men remained
obscure and darkly complexioned, calmly awaiting the showing of the
film.

In this historical raid it is one aircraft in particular that is of interest
here: ZCZ71BP carried a bomb with a faulty detonator. It fell directly on
to the bunker in Fuerst-Bismarck Strasse where the force of its impact had
the lights flickering but no explosion took place.

And when the sudden storm of plaster had abated there stood revealed upon the dais a tall, round-shouldered man with a bald head and flesh-heavy jowls. He blinked at his audience through thick lenses and as he began to speak his face contorted with the effort of concentration.

'Meine Herrschaften,' he said, 'wir sind nun imstande die ersten Entwicklungen . . .' he spoke with emphasis and with studied clarity in a cadaverous voice that issued like groaning from his chest. 'We are now in a position to present to you the first substantial findings of Project Disko 39. Yes, please, captain. The lights!'

The young SS captain standing at the iron table, his body inclined over the projector, had not distinctly heard the scientist's command. Should he start the film? He found them so nervy, these scientists and civilians.

'Please, captain, the film. If you please!' The voice betrayed a sudden agitation.

In a dry incandescent light the images flickered on the screen. The Reichsadler jerked and settled into place. Then, in response to a new command, the captain switched off the film and the groaning cadaverous voice, now juddering in phase with the drone of bombers, spoke up emphatically in the absolute blackness.

'. . . this short delay, meine Herrschaften. But I must remind you, before we continue with the film, that we have discovered incontrovertible proof of the existence of the Eigenmusikswesen. This momentous discovery will not fail to change the course of history. Ja, bitte, Herr Hauptmann.'

Now the film ran smoothly. A man with a heavy cold spoke precise, objective commentary on a succession of silent images. '. . . And here you see the data collected from continuous observation of the chosen subjects. Each decisional act is recorded according to promptness, rapidity of bodily exertion, pace, and duration of liveliness.'

An ageless man half crouched, naked, on a concrete floor and peered about him with looks of dread. All around him in the experimental chamber were taps and fittings, handles to pull, cords that dangled, switches concealed and prominent, small apertures in the walls. A gleaming wire, snaking down through a hole in the ceiling, was attached by electrodes to the subject's shaven head. His gaze was grim, stricken, furtive.

'When we compared the data across the individual subjects we could at first find no significant patterning. We decided to concentrate intellectual resources on the individual data payloads. For weeks our people applied specialized mathematical tools of the utmost precision to this highly recalcitrant material. The data remained stochastic, that is to say, random, without apparent structure, and then it was remarked that the figures

4

might be construed as rhythmic pulses: yes, beats, meine Herrschaften, beats. It then became clear to us that we were dealing with a hitherto unrecognized musical code. Accordingly we experimented with a variety of different methods of resolution, but in conclusion we favoured a unit of one-sixteenth of a second . . . and on the basis of this unit of time we transformed the data of every subject into a musical notation not unlike that typically encountered in classic musical composition. Our acoustical engineers developed a primitive sound synthesizer and we reduced, in every case, the highly complex signal to its simplest possible form. It was similar, gentlemen, to reducing the orchestral texture of symphonic sound to a simple melodic signature.'

New aircraft had arrived: crump, crump . . . and the earth sighed in its deeps.

'. . . and by this method of analysis the data of each observational subject yielded a certain melody, yes, in its simplest form a melody of a typically musical nature. The melodies of some particular subjects appeared even to possess the qualities of organized personality: a music of the utmost expressiveness. When we played the melody back to the individual subject which had generated it . . .'

Now the gentlemen were agog.

'. . . and as you can see from the film . . .'

In a capacious and otherwise empty chamber a naked man like a willowy stick was rocking on his heels, swinging his gaping thighbones, working his fleshless shoulders; his arms, like slender rods, rhythmically twirled and twisted. In the tight, starved face his lips were drawn back wide in a blissful rictus. He looked very close to death.

As the bombs went crump in the forest a haunting melody trembled in the speakers. Somebody whimpered.

'. . . as you can see, HE DANCES!'

A second five hundred pound bomb landed directly on the ZCZ71BP unexploded bomb, and the two went off together, cracking asunder the reinforced roof of the bunker. And in that irruption of dirt and concrete and the lights going out for ever the original speaker had jumped to his feet and had screamed out to his listeners, that they might take to their deaths a vision of the potency of science, 'The subject dances you see! HE DANCES TO THE EIGENMUSIKSWESEN . . .' The projector crashed to the floor. There were shouts and screams and curses. The bunker became a grave.

And yet, underneath the iron table where he had stood a moment before, the SS captain was alive and unscathed. Careless of the little air left him in that place he called out loudly, 'Is anyone alive?' And from a few feet away he heard the cadaverous voice reply, 'Yes. I am alive. Please help me.'

The captain wormed his way among girders, concrete slabs and other debris of destruction to reach the scientist's side.

'Where is the research station?' he whispered. Without hesitation the scientist gave up the information. The captain was insistent and kind. 'Who else worked with you? What are their names? What is the file name?' The scientist knew that he was dying. It was like a gift, an acknowledgement, to tell that man all that he wanted to know. And he tried to tell the man about his injuries, 'My back . . .' But the man who had come to his side was shouting into the earth-choked semi-darkness, 'Is there anyone else alive?'

In that place of death the SS man brought his elbow hard down on to the nape of the prostrate scientist and heard the subdued crackle of bones. Then he contrived to heave a mass of stonework on to the head of the man he had murdered. Now he worms his way back to the iron table which stands as humble bastion in the ruins. He gropes for the remains of the projector, and finding it, recklessly strikes a flame from his petrol lighter. From the mangled shreds of celluloid he salvages a little strip of film. Only now does Hermann Noltke call for help.

2

Then of the Venom handled thus a Medicine I did make;
Which Venom kills, and saveth such as Venom chance to take:

Sir George Ripley's Vision

At four thousand feet he lay spreadeagled and serenely counted. The night sky screamed and battered at his chest as he fell with blacked up face in rushing pale starlight where nothing grew bigger about him. So calmly did he plummet towards the ground it was as if he had found the balance between falling and ascending, and his precipitous descent had become for him a thing metaphysical, a metaphor only . . . 58, 59, 60 seconds and counting still.

He pulled the cord and all breath went out of him as the parachute snatched him up into the slow sky. Now he knew his weight again, and the hard earth lay below. With clumsy sweepings of his hand he rolled the patch off his dark-adapted eye and stared downwards. Glimmering to the east of him he saw the snaking lines of the railway, leading to Lueneburg, twelve kilometres away . . . 28, 29, 30. The wind was southerly. Confident now of his orientation he tugged at the straps of the 'chute to direct his drift down to earth.

At first, when he had opened his parachute, silence had engulfed him, but he could hear now the fluttering of the canopy above him and the sounds of the terrain below; a gentle whispering of the wind, and the slow surf-like sounds of the leaves of countless trees rose to meet him.

The man in the sky was Captain Dennis Jackson; twenty-four years old, highly trained and battle-hardened, he had been seconded from the Special Air Services to Special Operations. His code-name was Salamander.

Three hundred feet and he was peering down at the heathland terrain. Then it seemed to him he heard female voices. They seemed to be chanting, and then were gone. A copse of low trees loomed below him, was swiftly past him, and he was coming in to land on flat dry heathland. The ground rose suddenly to meet him and now he was running against vigorous kicking earth; he rolled. A sound like a clumsily silenced pistol

7

shot – a terrible pain seized him, he gave a muted shout of rage; like a great ungainly loving bird his parachute flopped down on top of him.

Agony flooded his mind. Something had happened to his leg, to his left leg; then welcoming waves of nausea came for him, beckoning, compelling. He fought to control his breathing, and his hand reached into his jacket for the Browning. His fingers tightened on the familiar stock of the pistol but the wave came rushing, irresistibly broke upon him: he passed out cold. The wind played the sand over him; light puffs of wind blew under the spread of the parachute making soft silk mushroomings, sighing as they expired. Somewhere nearby a nightingale was calling. A hundred yards from where he lay in the balmy summer night a shallow river purled among the rocks.

It was the morning of July 3rd, 1944; and the Salamander had landed in a trap: one of many such traps laid on heathland and in woods and fields all over Europe by starving civilians who hoped to trap a rabbit, a fox, a badger, cat, dog, rat or weasel in the ravished countryside. It was a phenomenon that Intelligence had overlooked, and now the Salamander lay face down in the sand. From his ankle to his thigh the rusting jaws of a hundred-year-old mantrap held him fast in malevolent, mute embrace.

Jackson lay like a breathing stone and blood flowed lightly from his mangled leg. He began to feel the warmth of the sand under his body; he thought he was on the beach at Walton on the Naze. He thought the sun was very hot and red; and then he remembered that it was 0240 hours on Lueneburg Heath and he was injured. He raised his head and turned the upper part of his body so that he could look back and down towards his feet. He probed under the silk of the parachute until his fingers found the iron jaws and the rows of metal teeth. The horror of the injury he kept at bay; there had been other injuries before this night: a bayonet wound in Tripoli, a shrapnel wound on Crete. Wounds came swiftly and slowly disappeared, but the pain he now felt made him curse all creation, and tears of rage were in his eyes.

He issued commands to himself. One: get out from under the chute. Two: tend wounds. He had a twelve-inch stabbing knife hanging in its sheath between his shoulder blades. He drew it out and cut away the swaddling silk that encumbered him. The night air blew on to his brow, cooling him and bringing the smell of the river to him. 'Water, that's right, that's the Luhe.' His fingers found the trap again; how to get it off? He needed to get both hands to it. He couldn't get his hands to it without first turning over, but every effort to do so brought the threatening wave of darkness closer. He lay completely still and forced himself calmly to examine his options.

With the long steel stabbing knife he began to dig. In the sandy soil he

8

scored a shallow trench one foot across and four feet long down the length of his prostrate body. He poked about in his pack and drew out a small implement which was saw, shovel, and axe. Now he patiently dug out the soil to a depth of eight inches. It was difficult work as the soil was loose and he had nothing to shore up the sides.

He reckoned he was ready now; with elbows and fingers, and the hard caps of his boots he held his torso off the ground and dragged his body sideways. Sweat ran into his eyes and the pain stormed him but he dragged himself inch by inch until the trap began to slide into the trench. As ankle and hip took the weight of the trap his pain intensified, but now, at last, yes . . . he swung himself over and lay on his back.

For two minutes he lay still. His right leg quivered with strain and from the several lacerations in his leg the life blood oozed and soundlessly dripped into the warm, infertile sand. He sat up and studied the trap. He had been lucky, for it had not been staked to the ground; but it was obvious that no small animal could drag itself away once those heavy dull jaws held it fast. He saw at once that not even a man could do it.

First he found purchase for his strong, sinewy hands; next he took a deep breath, and then another, despite the onslaught of pain it caused him, and now he applied all the strength in his body. The trap opened, an inch, an inch and a half . . . and he knew that he must not let go, but that he must let go, for his strength was failing: he must use what strength he had to close it gently, ah, gently against the tortured bone, muscle, sinew. The pain grew ever more intense as the heavy steel teeth settled in his flesh and irrevocably compressed it. Jesus . . . Jesus. But the pain grew worse, and still worse. Again he passed out cold.

Jackson lay back and looked at the sky above. It seemed to him that he saw a strange new constellation; it seemed to shine for him alone: a twinkling pillar, a glinting tree of stars.

Eleven minutes later he felt the vibrations of passing footsteps; they were quite light, of a child, or a young woman. Perhaps two? His hand went to the Browning inside his jacket. He thought quickly: if he lay quite still they would probably not see him, and then, if he failed to get the trap off in the dawn light, he would probably die, but if they saw him, or he called their attention to him, would they not inevitably betray him into the hands of the authorities? And later, wouldn't he be glad to die? But it wasn't that simple of course: it wasn't a true dilemma. He remembered the voice of his instructor . . . *a real dilemma's a very rare thing. You'll probably never meet one . . . Don't think too far ahead. Will yourself to win . . . Faced with a trained man civilians are timid. Frighten the buggers. Make them putty in your hands.*

The Salamander groaned aloud. At once he felt the vibrations cease. Just a few yards from where he lay a woman's voice said in German, 'Did you hear that? Did you hear something then?' and another woman's voice hushed her, told her to listen. A moment of silence and then he groaned again.

'Wer ist da?' a woman asked the night. There was fear in the voice, but wonder also. Timing, the Salamander thought to himself. Get the friggin' timing right. He groaned again, then coughed and lay still. As the women approached him he listened very carefully to the vibrations of their footsteps. It was imperative to know exactly how many of them there were. And he must not miss his chance. His command of the situation *must be total.*

It was two, surely only two, and one of them was heavier and slower, but it was the one with the light swift tread who came to him first. He felt the rustle of her skirt and her breath on his face.

'My God!' she said, and she dropped on to her knees beside him. 'He's in the trap, Mother. It's on his leg.'

But Mother, more circumspect, kept her distance. Out of the corner of his eye he saw her eight feet off, a bulky figure standing against the skyline. He pretended to be barely conscious; he gave the occasional groan; he muttered a few words in German, about his leg, about his plane . . . and slowly the older woman came closer until she stood there at his feet, eyeing his mangled leg.

'That's a mess,' she said, in rough country dialect. 'And the bait's all squashed in.' Then she was stooping, peering at the wounds. The daughter was occupied in taking a scarf from her head.

The Salamander sat bolt upright and spoke in a hiss, 'Sit on the ground!' His voice was hard, clear, aggressive. He trained the Browning pistol on the women.

'See what I mean?' said the mother, apparently unperturbed, and she settled herself on her haunches in the dust. His arm snaked out to grasp hold of the young woman. He pulled her roughly towards him. 'You must help me,' he said. And then, as an afterthought, 'Please.'

'Was sind Sie fuer Landsmann?' the older woman asked him.

'I'm a Berliner,' he lied. 'You must help me.' He couldn't tell if she believed him, but he felt her intense scrutiny upon him. Even in the half light he sensed that she had an unmistakable integrity about her, and a penetrating quality, born of considerable life experience. Should he lie to her? It didn't make much difference.

'Take it off me,' he said. 'Take the bloody thing off!' The women did not move. Violently he shook the younger woman, wondering at her slightness of build. With real menace he steadily waved the pistol. 'Do it now.'

'Let me go then,' said the girl, fearful and indignant, and she in turn gave a spirited shake but it was no more than a pitiful spasm. He let go of her arm but he grasped hold of her hair, roughly.

'I'm sorry,' he said, grinning in the dark. 'I'm sorry about that.'

Reluctantly the two women arranged themselves as best they could either side of his body. 'Now, dammit!' His voice was whispered, urgent, sibilant. 'Do it!' The women pulled and wriggled in the dust, kicking up the sand. More, more, more, the mother relentlessly intoned. He felt the darkness coming, sweeping across the heathland to tryst with him; but he held on, and as he ground his teeth he became aware of the creaking in his mouth. The trap snapped open against the earth; he gasped and jerked his leg free of it. His grip on her hair loosened; but his pistol came up to point directly at her head, just a foot from her eyes.

'Don't move,' he remembered he'd said. 'Don't move an inch.'

Jackson's mission was to rendezvous with a local agent at a prearranged location on Lueneburg Heath. He was to make his way to the point of rendezvous (patch) on two consecutive nights. If he failed to make contact with his fellow agent (engage) he was to give a prearranged signal (light-out) so that he could be picked up and flown out. If he succeeded in making contact with his fellow agent he was to rely on that person to send a signal on his behalf. He didn't consider that he had sufficient grounds for aborting the mission, and he calculated that he might, at worst, spend 60 hours without treatment of his wounds. Jackson did not doubt that he could make it to the patch; he was a supremely self-confident man, and by rigorous training and active service in the war zones he was accustomed to making the utmost demands on his physical resources, had learned to treat his body with that same degree of prudential self-interest and ultimate disregard with which the army itself regarded him.

At first, once freed of the trap, and yet coldly apprised of the intransigence of the older woman, Jackson had half inclined to kill them both out of hand; soon, however, he had sensed the strength of their love for each other and knew at once, by instinct, that this was to be his best instrument of coercion. He saw clearly that he must trust one of the women to go in search of medication while he kept the other hostage. The daughter, he was sure, would not fail to follow simple commands to the letter for the sake of her mother's safety; but he doubted that he was yet strong enough, in his present condition, to control the redoubtable

11

mother through the long hours of her hostageship. And more particularly, the lack of experience of the girl would render her a greater security risk when at large. And of course, there were other reasons still for which he greatly preferred the prospect of the younger woman's company.

He saw that he must find the means to impose upon the mother an unquestioning obedience to his wishes. He felt sure that a simple, explicit threat to take the daughter's life would render the mother tractable, but he saw, too, that such a threat must confirm her belief that he was indeed no German, but an enemy spy, a man she could not fail to betray to the authorities. For she was no doubt aware that if she was discovered to be shielding him her penalty would be death, and not only for herself but for her daughter too, and whatever family she had besides. In daylight, he knew it, distant marksmen might easily incapacitate him without actually taking his life; and she might easily persuade herself, he thought, that he would surrender her daughter alive if soldiers arrived to take him away.

It was imperative, he concluded, to keep the mother in a condition of uncertainty as to his true identity. She would be more inclined to obey his commands, he reasoned, if she could not be sure that he was not a loyal soldier of the Reich, entrusted with important but secret objectives, compelled, in the service of the State, to impose his will upon her. And if she could find in this belief a greater assurance of her daughter's ultimate security, would she not more willingly entertain it? But he sensed, oppressively, that to lie to her directly could not suffice, for she had a manifest capacity to see through the appearance of things to the stark truths beneath; there was about her a clarity and truthfulness that promised to confound a falsehood even as he proffered it.

So he must not speak his lie directly; but merely hint to her that he was a German combatant and patriot, entrusted by the highest authority with a secret mission of great importance. He knew that ordinary civilians, in the conditions of terror and uncertainty made commonplace and all-pervading by that catastrophic conflagration, had long been schooled to content themselves with crude improbabilities, with half truths, and sometimes with blatant lies when the war required it of them. Truth was ever difficult; but in Germany, in 1944, it was at best a luxury easily dispensed with, and at worst, a further descent into the interminable nightmare of the times. Since he could not dependably terrorize the women into blind and literal obedience he must deceive and delude them as well. He had said that he was a Prussian, and his German was perfect. He knew their laws and customs almost as well as they did themselves.

12

He would be correct in his manner and authoritative. As long as his leg did not begin to rot or his blood become infected he saw no reason why he should not survive. As the women pored over his wounds and picked from his lacerations the exiguous tidbits of offal, the Salamander mentally prepared himself for this role.

But first he needed to know how well he could walk: with the aid of the women he got to his feet and tottered a few steps. He convinced himself that his leg, although severely lacerated and badly bruised, was not actually broken.

'You must clean and bind the wounds,' the older woman said, 'or you'll die.'

'Will you help me?' he said in reply, settling himself upon the ground.

'Help you?' She seemed impersonal, indifferent. 'Why not?' She was manifestly shrewd; did she really believe that he was German?

'Sit down,' he said to the daughter. 'Here, beside me.' Then turning to the mother he said, politely, 'Your daughter, what is her name?'

'Erna.'

He took firm hold of Erna's arm and said, 'Erna must stay with me. You must clean and bind my leg, do you understand? I need medication. But Erna stays here.'

'Not necessary,' she said. 'Erna must come with me. I'll need her help.'

'Erna stays here!' As he spoke he unconsciously shook the young woman at the end of his arm, and she murmured her resentment. 'Now listen . . . my work is secret. Nobody must know I'm here. You must not speak to anybody about me. Do you understand?'

The older woman looked at him impassively. He could make out her features a little now. She had a round, full face: composed and firm.

He said, 'You must do exactly what I say. But you must do everything in secret, absolutely in secret. If you make a noise, or talk or show yourself . . . many people will suffer. And some people will die. Do you understand me?'

She nodded, but in the pale glimmerings of the dawn her face was expressionless as stone.

'Do it,' said Jackson, 'for the Fatherland.' He looked at her intently but she turned aside and spoke instead to her daughter.

'Don't make a fuss. Whatever he does. Promise me.'

'Yes, Mother,' she replied. 'But when will you come?'

'I'll come at once. Just an hour and I'll be back. Don't you worry now.' She turned to the Salamander who continued to hold the Browning in his free hand. 'There's no food in my house. Just a few vegetables. Do you want some?'

13

'Yes,' he said, 'bring me some potatoes, and something for my leg. You understand.'

'Yes, yes,' she said, with a deep impatience. 'I understand.'

He directed the women to dig a wide, shallow pit in the ground over which they stretched the material from the parachute. They placed stones and earth all round the edges of the awning and strewed the cover with sand and light brushwood. He was satisfied that it would be impossible to spot his den from the air, and all about there was nothing but heathland dotted with scrub and small copses; here and there wild grasses grew thickly. As the mother moved off in the early light he brought the daughter with him into his hole in the ground and tied her hands together with string from his pack. Then he tied another piece of stout string to her arm, a little above the elbow, and attached the free end to his belt buckle inside his jacket. He told her to lie still and keep silent. He must not sleep, he told himself, but it was imperative to relax. He drifted into a half sleep; as his hard, torn body softened in repose it gave up its memories: another time, another sandy place, another girl . . .

On Camber Sands he had loved his girl and afterwards she had cried. Slaked and sinewy and stretched out in the sand he had watched her as she squatted, whimpering, in the sea, washing the grit from inside herself. And basking in the salty, sun-warmed air, he had suddenly grown tired of her and had drawn his heavy eyelids almost closed. Now, through glaring slits he stared, hard-eyed and with a strange, cold delight, directly into the sun. And as she splashed about in the blindness of her tears he counted out his will; inexorable, a dry-eyed man amidst the lonely dunes.

Until the sky seemed to fill with swart wings of sculpted birds rending the midday blue. And now, as he painfully shifted on the earthy sand on Lueneburg Heath, he thought that perhaps he had seen his death that time of a kind of love amongst the dunes; and it seemed to him too that he had shuddered, those years ago, basking in the air's salt embrace. 'You don't love me,' she had cried. 'You don't love me at all.' It was as if the words she had uttered he had spoken himself, like a curse directed on the sand, the sun, the sea. He recalled how he had lain upon her, feeling her breasts against his hard ribs, his hard hands squeezing her thighs. 'You're a horrible lizard,' she had sobbed, 'all cold! I know you don't care for me, I know it!' She had broken off, and her grief had turned furious so that suddenly she had screamed at him, frenziedly, 'You just fuck me!' And she had wept with shame at the deed, and at the words she had used. Her head ached, her skin burned and she hurt down there where the glassy particles cut at her soft inner membrane.

The images were flickering in his mind: the sand of Camber Sands, which was the past; the sandy soil of Lueneberg Heath, which was the present and the future. In 1939 on Camber Sands he had been simply Dennis Jackson, nineteen years old; on Lueneburg Heath, five years on, he was Special Operations Executive, military captain, agent and soldier. The intervening years had been filled with killing, which was the specialty the war had brought him; but nothing much else, it seemed to him, had changed. It was a source of wonder to him that the years had not made him older. The pain he felt from his wound, he knew it was nothing, it was nothing compared to the fierceness of his spirit, his potential, fitful fire-being, watchful and circling all about him.

The German girl was terrified; she lay beside him still and rigid. But the Salamander breathed easily. He tried hard to remember her name, that girl from baked meats at Woolworth's.

'What are you snivelling for? Go on! You know you liked it!' Playfully he had thrown a handful of small stones at her squatting in the sea. She had put her dress back on and the sea was soaking it, all the way up to the waist. Effie. That was her name. Effie had always refused him afterwards, but others had been more willing.

Now it was dawn and the cry of birds was clamorous. A light breeze had become a steady wind and sand was being blown on to the parachute in a light dry rain. His torn leg burned in an arc of flame from his ankle to his upper thigh, sending shivers down his spine.

At half past five in the morning the older woman returned. She had brought little bottles of liquid and small tins of ointment in a bag concealed in her clothing. In her pocket she had a strip of bandage.

'What's all this?' He waved the gun suspiciously at her stores.

'Heilmittel,' she said, bluntly.

'I said I needed medication.'

'Es ist doch Medizin,' she insisted, 'Alles pflanzlich. Es gibt doch nichts anderes fur Leute wie uns.' It was all herbal medication. Plants and stuff. Frig it, he thought. Ignorant old witch. But he believed what she had told him, that there was nothing else to be had, no proper drugs, no proper medicine. Everything was sent to the armies, to the terrible war fronts of the Reich.

'Just get on with it,' he said.

'You'll have to take your trousers off.'

He did as she suggested and she cleaned his wounds. Against the brown of her arm even his good leg looked bluish-grey, like the skin of a half plucked chicken. He couldn't resist a chuckle then; those legs will give me away, he thought.

15

The water was cooling, and slightly astringent.

'What is this stuff?'

'Heilmittel,' she said. She spoke softly to her daughter as she worked. She gave her a potato and asked her if he had been kind to her.

'If you hurt my child,' she said to him, 'I will curse you.'

Now she placed ointment on his wounds and wrapped the bandages round the lacerated flesh.

'Is that right?' said Jackson, coldly challenging her spirit.

'And you will die a terrible death. I swear it.' Her tone made him shudder.

'Sure,' he said, surprised at himself.

She gave him something to drink; he saw at once that it was not pure water.

'You drink first,' he gestured roughly to the young woman, thrusting the bottle towards her lips. With her frightened eyes fixed on her mother's face she tilted the bottle and gulped down a mouthful. 'And you!' he said to the mother, who shrugged and looked at him with contempt.

'There'll be none left then. It cleans the blood and it stops the pain.' She took the bottle from his outstretched hand. 'Go ahead and die if you want to,' she muttered, and she brought the bottle to her mouth. But Jackson snatched it from her and drank it all down.

'What the fuck,' he said. 'You can bury us together, mother, if it's poison.'

And she replied, in that peculiar tone of hers, 'If I wanted you to die, nothing you could do would save you. What do you have to protect you? Only a little gun.'

'What else you got in the bag?' he asked.

'Two apples. One for each of you.'

'Danke, Mutti.'

'Come back tomorrow, an hour before dawn. You're a good woman. A loyal German.'

'Soon it's going to hurt a lot,' she said grimly. 'But the blood will clear and the wounds will close quickly enough.' She handed a second little bottle to him. Jackson examined the yellowish fluid and thought it might be piss. 'Better to drink it now,' she said. He passed the bottle to the young woman.

'Drink half of it.'

When she had drunk her portion he drained the rest dry. He wiped his mouth and passed the bottle back to the mother. She gave a hearty nod,

16

as though she approved of something. She squatted down on the ground and kissed her daughter tenderly.

'My dear little Erna,' she said. 'You'll be all right. I know.'

'Tomorrow morning,' the Salamander said. 'Just before dawn.' He looked at her very intently and his eyes were cold. 'Don't come back before,' he said.

She went away then, with slow purposeful stride, in the clear light of the early morning.

In a cloudless sky the sun climbed towards its zenith; on Lueneburg Heath in the improvised awning it grew hotter, and harder to breathe. Jackson began to sweat heavily; the beads of salty water rolled from his body and collected in the sand. His leg, however, had almost ceased to pain him, and his mind was clear and untroubled. He thought he might sleep a bit, but he knew he should wait for the girl to go to sleep before him; he turned his head and looked at her. Her eyes were shut but he knew that she was awake.

'Erna,' he murmured.

She opened her eyes and looked at the sky. Her eyes were brown, a simple bright brown. Her sunbrowned complexion was fresh and clear, although she was pale with anxiety. Her lips were thin, he noted, but they were beautifully formed, and some strands of her hair, light brown but bleached to pale yellow by the sun, had stuck to the wetness of her brow.

'Alles klar?' he said to her.

She looked directly into his face and he understood that in some strange way she had really seen him in that moment. He had the fleeting but intense impression that somehow, for a moment, the inner architecture of his habits and dispositions had suddenly been made manifest to her. And in that instant he felt a strange, fulsome gratitude; but he snapped his eyes away.

'What were you doing on the heath in the middle of the night?' He was severe, and he knew at once that he had got the initiative again. He was well briefed on the emergency laws that had come into effect in the last few months in Germany. She had flinched, and seemed to shrink back into herself.

'We were looking for herbs,' she said. It was barely more than a whisper.

'What herbs? And why were you looking at three o'clock in the morning? It's very suspicious, I tell you.' He saw her terror clearly; it was as if her face was re-sculpted before his eyes, becoming smaller, paler, sharper.

'Some herbs for medicine,' she replied at last. In a small, anxious voice she said, 'For the people in the village. There aren't any medicines left. We had to pick some herbs before dawn. Before the sap starts to rise. Before the dew dries.'

Jackson lay sleeping. A succession of dreams passed through his mind. They were dreams of intricacy and colour. And at his side the girl slept too. Rabbits played about them, birds flew close overhead and a light breeze ruffled the silken roof of their makeshift pavilion. Jackson's face had relaxed completely, but hers was tense and apprehensive even as she slept. Occasionally the one would wake for a moment and eye the other, almost blind with heat, but sleep would swiftly repossess them.

About midday a thin veil of cloud obscured the sun and Jackson woke to a feeling of raging hunger. He drew a simple ration out of his pack and ate with a sort of controlled fury. As he moved he tugged at the string that was attached to her arm but still she did not stir. After he had eaten he lay awake and listened to the sounds of the heath. Now he was asleep again, and dreamed of the women he had known.

It was late afternoon when Jackson awoke again. He felt well rested and strong. He studied his leg carefully and smelt his wounds. Entirely wholesome. He found too that he was now able to bend the leg and even flex a little the muscles of the calf and thigh without much worse effect than a few sharp twinges. He congratulated himself on his excellent recuperative powers. Turning his attention to the girl beside him he reached out a hand and touched her face. There was a tenderness in the movement which brought a curious sense of alienation to him. She seemed to understand his feeling for she opened her eyes at once and looked at him; to his surprise he saw that she was embarrassed. They stared at each other. She was waiting for him to speak to her, but he had nothing to say; he offered her some of his rations, but she was not hungry; then she begged him for a little water. With something akin to alacrity he took his water bottle from the pack and gave it to her. Tied as she was, and constrained to remain in a lying position, it was difficult for her to drink. He felt a temptation steal over him: why not untie her hands? And then he took account of what had passed through his mind and he felt a moment of alarm. Christ! he thought. What's got into me! But he found himself looking at her wrists, which were puffy, and her hands which were blotchy red from the string that tied her, and he felt uneasy.

'How long,' she said, in a soft, sighing voice, 'shall we be together?'

Her words were like a haze upon his thoughts; there was a wistfulness, a poignancy in her question that caused a wholly unfamiliar sensation in his chest. How strangely she had spoken then, but it struck him immediately afterwards that perhaps she could not have asked her question in any other way without forcing them both to look unflinching into her own unhappy prospects. Jackson reckoned he could look unflinching at anything, anything at all, but he saw that he had every reason to encourage his hostage to be optimistic. And then, an instant later, he heard himself speaking to her in a language that was almost one of youthful love, for it was strangely ardent, yet melancholy.

'We'll be parted from each other,' he said, 'only when it's right . . .'

And she seemed content with that. For a while she lay still beside him and he heard the sound of her breaths. Then, quietly, she asked him to untie her, so that she could relieve herself.

For a time he did not speak.

'Do it here,' he said to her gruffly. 'In the sand.'

She uttered a sound that he thought was probably a sob, or a stifled cry of shame and horror. But as the sound echoed in his mind he seemed to hear in it something more equivocal, as though in forcing her to look to her needs in that unseemly way he had taken a step which somehow served her deeper purposes, and that despite herself she had given herself away.

She had neither stirred nor spoken for some moments and he thought she had probably changed her mind. Again he touched her cheek with his rough finger; but she drew away from him sharply, with a gesture of repugnance. God dammit! he said to himself. She can friggin' well piss here! He was prey to a sullen anger. 'Do it here,' he hissed at her fiercely. 'Or shut up!'

And then obediently, patiently, like an animal, she turned towards him and as her hands went down to the hem of her skirt he moved a little in order to give her more play on the cord. 'Help me,' she whispered to him. 'Help me at the back with my skirt.'

He reached over her slender body and with his long arm he pulled up her skirt at the back. With her own tied hands she adjusted her underclothes as best she could and then she pushed her backside away from him. Here's a bit of fun coming, he told himself.

But when he heard the susurrant flow of her water, something deeply buried within him seemed to dissolve away and he felt his heart shake so that tears were suddenly in his eyes and for the first time since he was a small boy he felt a burning of sorrow and compassion. The soft insistent whisper of her water ran into the sand. With his eyes shut and his head on the crook of his arm he cursed the war which had brought him, until that moment, so much satisfaction, liberty, power. But this unfamiliar wave of energy passed through him all too quickly, and emotional habits which might have held it and taken him deeper towards his higher nature he simply lacked, so that the moment was gone even as it had come; and in its wake he felt an urgency of lust for her.

Jackson was bewildered. Had it been any other moment, any other woman ... the words hung in his mind like burning crusts of earth. He opened his eyes and saw that she was staring directly at him, her face only eighteen inches from his own. And he saw that what was stopping him from making his hard and ravening attack upon her fragile, wasted, defenceless person was a thing both subtle and delicate in his mind; a thing infinitely vulnerable did he but choose to make it so, and yet infinitely stronger than himself. And as he looked at her he found himself smiling; smiling the idiot smile of a kind of love.

'Is that better now, Erna?' he whispered to her.

'But the sand is wet,' she told him. 'It's all wet around me now.'

'Come over this way a bit,' he said, and, placing an arm around her waist, he pulled her gently towards him. Again desire raged at him and fear came into her eyes.

'Please trust me, Erna,' he was pleading with her, 'trust me.' But something in his tone had greatly emboldened her for she turned abruptly from him.

'Lass' mich,' she said, sharply.

All evening he lay quietly and looked at her; he studied the cut and colour of her blue cotton shirt and in his mind he traced the contour of her nape under her straggly, straw-coloured hair. He breathed her natural scent and listened to her breathing, now calm, now troubled. After a time he knew she was sleeping. Then wholly unfamiliar images drew him into a state of entrancement; it was a half-sleep, and she was with him, and his heart was transfixed.

At nine o'clock on the night of July 4th, 1944, Captain Hermann Noltke left his billet in Sargemuender Strasse and drove into the deepening twilight. He chose a road which led out into the countryside and soon his vehicle was the only moving thing on a lonely track on the Heide. He drove steadily for half an hour and then he pulled off the dirt road and parked the vehicle amidst a copse of beech trees. He carefully consulted his map. When he was satisfied he went to the boot of the car and took out a bag. Amongst the trees in the now thickening darkness he changed out of his uniform and into the rough clothes of a country labourer. He placed a battered old felt hat on his head and stowed his uniform away in the bag, which he hoisted up into a tree. For a while he sat and listened to the sounds of the night; then he set off at a brisk walk across the heath. His gait was both blatant and manifestly stealthy; where he considered himself visible to curious eyes he seemed to walk with a swagger, and gave the impression of a slightly drunken man making his way home over uneven, familiar ground. But in those places where the undergrowth lent cover to his progress he moved like a thief, with swift silent caution.

He walked for twenty minutes and then he sank down to the ground and pulled out from under his jacket a compact set of field-glasses. Very circumspectly, painstakingly, he slithered on his belly to the tip of a small natural rise and surveyed the land ahead of him in a slow arc of examination. The moon was a narrow crescent in a furze of cloud. The wind had dropped and all was still. About two hundred yards directly ahead of him there stood a dilapidated farm building that was once, perhaps, a barn or outhouse of a farmstead long since deserted. He saw an owl; he caught a flicker of movement in some bushes a hundred yards away to his left; he heard the authoritative yappings of a dog fox. But nothing else moved in all he surveyed, and nothing seemed other than it should be. With his glasses never far from his eyes he lay in his chosen position at the top of the rise, and waited. His breath was so well controlled it would not have been audible to someone lying directly beside him, and throughout his vigil he remained completely still. Hope he isn't late, he thought to himself.

3

. . . two things have been omitted, and those are important.

The human beings, now: in what direction are they,
And how far away, would you say? And do not forget
There may be dead ground in between.

There may be dead ground in between; and I may not have got
The knack of judging a distance;

Henry Reed, *Lessons of the War*

He had staggered and fallen a half dozen times, but it was more the uneven terrain than any lack of resolution on his part, for he forced himself to walk almost as normal. But the blood was beginning to seep back into the wounds and there was a warm thickening to the sensation of pain that his walking brought him. At first he had taken the girl by the arm, her wrists still tied together and a piece of string attaching from her arm to his belt, but he soon found the arrangement too awkward. And he felt the need to support himself a little. He knew his exertions were speeding his loss of blood; he took a detour into a copse and found himself a stick to serve as a rudimentary crutch. He removed the cord that bound her to him and tied it between her ankles. But it had begun to disturb him, this compulsion to restrain her. He found that if he looked at her in a certain way he was prey to a feeling of disquiet that was close to sadness. He found it necessary to remind himself that she was an encumbering hostage, an instrument only, a means to his survival.

And so they went on through the night, the young woman shuffling like a convict beside her murderous captor, who helped himself along with a stick. 'Get down!' At once she knelt in the sand. 'Lie on the ground,' he breathed into her ear. She did as he commanded. And it seemed to her then that something came between them, a fluttering thing, so that she could easily have imagined them in a different place, in a different time, as enchanted lovers, trembling each towards the other. She had a peculiar sensation in her head, and her body felt hot and restive. She closed her eyes, and her thoughts were like warm-blooded animals swimming in her head. Mother! she said to herself. Mother, what have you done?

The Salamander, not a hundred metres from the punter (local agent in the field), was carefully examining the patch with his own field-glasses. The official directive specified that the rep should be the first to make his way to the patch. Thus the punter, being more sensitively placed and more acutely alert to local dangers, would be free to choose whether or not to make himself known to the visiting agent. This was a sensible practice since the visiting agent would have little or no information about the punter and could not endanger a local network in the event of his capture.

When Noltke spotted two figures moving like bears on the lunar landscape of the heath he was instantly alarmed. His first thought was that sheer ill-fortune had brought illicit lovers to the patch at the worst possible time. And then he reasoned that the look of the man, whom he could see quite well through his glasses, was unmistakably that of a fellow agent. For despite Jackson's limping there was about him a cat-like alertness and aggressive self-confidence. Noltke watched them make their way into the desolate building and then he retraced his footsteps. Moving now with great stealth he followed for a full ten minutes a wide circular path that brought him finally to within twenty paces of the building. He was now convinced that the two had arrived alone. He ran at a crouch to the door, kicked it open, stepped into the sweltering interior and shoved the door to behind him. It was pitch black in the room, but he could sense them, to his right, along the rotting wooden wall.

Speaking slowly and clearly in German he said, 'Don't think I can't see you.'

And the reply came, 'You won't be a mole, then.'

'That's just what I am though,' Noltke retorted. 'Can't see a thing,' he added.

'Just a mo',' said the Salamander, speaking German still. He took off his hat and placed it over the girl's face. 'Look at it,' he said to her roughly, and shone his torch directly into her eyes. 'Keep your eyes shut and your ears closed. Got it?'

'Yes.'

'And don't move.'

But she moved at once, adjusting the weight of her body, trying to make herself comfortable so that she should not later need to disobey him.

'I won't move,' she said. 'I promise.'

23

In the opposite corner the two men allowed themselves a pencil-beam of light to illuminate the transaction. Noltke spoke quickly, in a sibilant whisper, almost directly into Jackson's ear. The latter listened with great concentration, seemed to memorize a few details and then addressed a series of questions to his interlocutor.

'You said Disko 39? What was the name of the camp? "L-u-d-w-i-g-s-l-u-s-t"?'

Erna, in her darkness, imagined herself bathing in the river, where the water ran swift and slow and the river bed was tiled with smooth, flat stones.

'The bastards call it "Heaven",' the German said.

Jackson uttered a short, dry laugh.

'This,' said Noltke, holding out a small package, 'is all I've got. It's just a bit of film and a few documents. I'm still trying to get a whole copy. But the files are completely inaccessible.'

The Salamander took the package and buttoned it into his jacket.

'I'm injured,' he said. 'Fucking mantrap. Get me out tonight.'

'Can't do it,' was the terse reply. 'Tomorrow night earliest. Who's the woman?'

'Forget her,' said Jackson.

For a minute or so the men were silent in the darkness. The wood creaked about them, and the walls gave off the smells of decay. It was very hot in the barn.

'How's Piccadilly?'

'Bombed.'

'And Leicester Square?'

'Bombed.'

'How's things in Bismarckstrasse?'

'Bombed,' said Noltke, with trembling voice.

'Fuck it.'

'I'll give the signal tonight. Where are you going from?'

But the Salamander did not immediately reply.

'You reckon you need to know?' he said at last.

'Yes, I think so,' said Noltke.

'Try for the early one,' said the Salamander. 'It's 4100 3780.'

'Oh,' said the German. 'It's Dulwich Green.'

'That's right.'

'Goodbye then. Give my respects, won't you.'

Then Captain Noltke slipped out into the night; was gone.

And in their time the man and the woman returned to their sandy

24

pavilion. In the aftermath of the rendezvous Jackson was optimistic. Even if I get blood poisoning, he thought, it'll be all right in Blighty. She, too, sensed that a corner had been turned. She wanted to speak to him; it had become urgent that she speak to him, but she was afraid that there was nothing to say. Your leg, how is it? – such things as this, all too quickly exhausted. But when she saw him stumble over a rabbit-hole she went quickly to his side.

'Please, lean on me,' she whispered to him. 'I want you to.'

They were prey to a tenderness of lovers, and it seemed to her a triumph that she could feel so for this man who might have killed her. She could not believe that he would ever wish to harm her now, and she felt a strange alluring solidarity with all his concerns. But she determinedly put from her mind all thought of what his concerns might be. It was enough for her that she was close at his side. She felt a singing in her breast, and she knew that there had awoken within her something akin to love.

The Salamander had no idea that he had been bewitched, beguiled by herbal potions. Nor would it have interested him to know that cause of his feelings for her. For the Salamander, what is, is. But he, too, felt the desire to speak; he wanted to speak to her of his youth, and of his hopes. And he wanted her to redeem his memories for him, to be witness to this miraculous emergence of his tender nature. Look, he wanted to say to her, look, Erna, I have this . . . this fantastic feeling for you.

Erna and Jackson sat on the ground at their makeshift hideaway and breathed the cool night air.

'Tell me about the people who set the trap,' he said.

'It is *our* trap,' she said.

'*Your* trap?'

'I set it two days ago. We were afraid to tell you.'

'But you're not afraid to tell me now?'

'No,' she said softly. 'I'm not afraid any more.' And her voice told him that she trusted him now, and was glad that he had come into her life.

Under a measureless canopy of stars, when the night was thick and still about them, he helped her remove her clothes and with war-calloused hands caressed her skinny body. She smelt of the fields and of the night air. He lay on the cooling sand and she placed herself over him and took him into herself. Then for the first time in his life the Salamander felt joy and sorrow mingle in his heart. His kisses were gifts to her. His strength honoured her. He felt her hunger like his own past, calling for love.

'I wish we were free,' he said to her. 'Free to stay here together. Right here.' He ached to tell her that he was going back, that he would

25

probably never see her again; yet he was glad that everything he had learned in his unforgiving trade forbade him to speak of these things.

'But we can!' she whispered to him. 'We can stay like this until it ends.'

'Erna. Erna! I've never loved . . . never loved any man or woman like I love you now.'

But her reply to him was lost in the high, light cries of her joy. He lifted her a little to one side and they lay with their hearts almost touching through their skins, and she wept for love of him and she laughed for joy as the moon faded from the sky.

At dawn the mother returned. She had brought fresh quantities of herbal medicaments and she immediately began to tend his leg. She berated him for having opened the wounds, but she was pleased with the progress of the healing. She spoke little, and all the while she seemed to be listening to the silences of her daughter. She took from her bag another little bottle of that same yellow liquid that she had given him against the pain.

'There wasn't any pain,' said Jackson.

'This is my masterpiece,' she said, with a grim chuckle. 'You must take some more.'

'Yeah, it's great stuff, Ma.' He reached to take the bottle from her and began to drink it down without a word.

'Stop!' said Erna. 'Me too!' Her voice was urgent. 'Give some to me!' It pleased him then to yield it all up to her, but she insisted that he take the greater measure. It was touching, but the older woman was unmoved.

'What's going to happen?' she asked brusquely.

'Don't come back again,' said Jackson. 'Do you understand? You mustn't come back again.'

'And my Erna? What about my daughter?'

'She'll come home soon.'

'One day,' she said, and her voice had again that quality of in-controvertible fatality, 'when the war is past, you will come to visit us. Erna will tell you where we live.' He saw that he had taken the older woman's hand and had squeezed it between his own. It struck him as odd that he had done so.

'Well. This is it, Mum. Thanks. But just remember! It's not finished yet . . . You mustn't speak to anyone about me. Maybe not ever.'

'I know,' she said. But she said it not as a concession to the truth of his statement, for there was no agreement in her tone. She seemed to be saying only that she had heard and understood him.

'Goodbye, then.'

'Goodbye, Mother. I'll be home soon.'

*

26

They had lain together in each other's arms and the hours of daylight had passed in a moment. They had talked but little, for talk was difficult. She sensed his constraint and was content to lie silent beside him. But when night came again she found him more willing to divulge his thoughts. And when the stars came out and his face was a silvery impression before her eyes she felt she must tell him the truth.

'Our love is not real,' she said. 'Our love is a lie.'

'You're wrong, Erna. This is the only real thing I've ever known.' He'd thought about it all day, the sense that with her he had found a naked, ineluctable reality; it was as real to him as death, and yet more terrible, more wondrous, for it was as a glorious beginning and not the sense of doomful finality that he knew so well. And he had a vivid sense of being wholly alive. 'You've got it the wrong way round,' he said. 'Maybe everything else is crazy. But our love is real.'

And when the time came, they folded up the parachute and buried it. They filled in their shallow trench. These simple and sensible precautions filled her with aching sadness.

'When will you come back to me?' She hated her question, she felt it to be stupid and cruel. She knew it could bring her no possible happiness. Deep within herself she had understood that this man she loved was her country's enemy, and her own; but she could not bring herself to confront that knowledge.

'Don't. Don't do this, Erna.' He refused to lie to her. His training told him to humour her, to take command of her emotions. No, he would not lie to her.

'I . . . just don't ask me anything.'

And she clung to him then and he found her hair in his eyes and in his mouth. He couldn't believe that he could feel such joy in the presence of her, in her nearness such intense, sweet yearning.

They had forded the River Luhe in its sandy shallows and now they went together towards Dulwich Green. In the murmur of the water she had found a sort of comfort so that for a time she had breathed freer and held her head higher as they walked. But soon the grave melancholy descended again upon her, and even though she knew in herself that it would be easy, easy to forget him, she longed for a solution to the hateful puzzle of his going. The Salamander, for his part, grew firmer, clearer, more certain as he drew ever closer to the point of return. It had begun and it must end. He loved her and yet it was war. And he reminded himself repeatedly that both of them might die that very night if he did not show more caution. The demands of his profession drove down on him, and his resoluteness hardened. Should he not send her home? She must not see the plane land; she should not discover the landing zone. But if he sent her away, would she go? And if she went, would she remain faithful to him? He was sure that she knew he was the enemy.

They watched; for twenty minutes he peered all around him. Was she there, the old woman? He sensed that she was there but he could see her nowhere. Did she mean to betray him? Surely he must keep the daughter with him until he reached the Green? Then it seemed to him he had found a solution: he must leave her half a mile from the landing point; blindfolded, gagged, and tied to a tree, or trussed up and abandoned in the bushes. It was the only way.

But as they approached Dulwich Green, the wounded soldier and the girl upon his arm, he found that he could not do that ugly thing. It was not the disgust which filled him at the thought of trussing her like a rabbit and stopping her eyes and her ears that compelled him to turn his face from that course of action; rather it was the irresistible command that arose within him, the command that he trust her completely, or live the rest of his life in horror of his hideous self. So he said to her simply, suppressing the outrage of his habits in this hazardous breach of discipline, 'Erna, you must go now.'

But she could not leave him. She would not find it in herself to go from him then; and he relented for a few more minutes, and then again, until he saw that she must stay with him until the plane had taken him high above the dark land of the heath and her own dear person was but a miniscule shadow moving amidst brushwood on the sandy wastes below.

They laid out the markers. She asked no questions. He made the arrangements to switch them on. She sat with him, oblivious to these operations. She was as a winged creature aloft in the sky of him and knew nothing of plans and procedures. And so the time passed until he heard the drone of a light aircraft distantly circling.

Suddenly there came a crashing from the bushes behind them and a trembling, panting runner burst upon the scene. It was Noltke, clad in the uniform of the SS but with jacket ripped and belt and holster awry.

'For God's sake! Quickly!' In the distance they heard the shouts of men and the baying of dogs; barely half a mile from where they stood lights were flickering.

The plane was low in the sky, searching, circling. Noltke wrenched the apparatus from the Salamander's hands and threw the switch; at once a skeletal runway was visible to the pilot. Already he was turning to make his descent. Then Erna clung to her Salamander and sobbed aloud. A terrible groan came from him, and was repeated. Shuddering he held her to him.

Noltke was yelling, 'You crazy bastard! There's an armed detachment just eight hundred metres away. It's me they're after! Don't let them find her!'

Then the plane came low and its wheels went palping the sandy earth in long, low hops between the lights. 'Bring her, or shoot her!' Noltke shouted, and now he pressed the barrel of his pistol against her slender nape so that its end was lost in her soft yellow hair. Jackson was close to distraction, and a terror that he had never known before took all decision from him.

'Erna!' he shouted, breaking the grip of her embrace. Ferociously he pushed the other man away. 'Erna,' against the racket of the airplane, 'Come with me!' And she looked up into his wild face and the burning question could no longer be evaded.

'Where?' she cried. 'Where are you going?'

'England! To Eng-land!'

He had hardly heard his own voice in the din of the night, amidst the firing of shots, the blowing of whistles, the barking of dogs, the rattlings of the incoming airplane. But she had understood; had had no need even to hear the word.

'No, no, no!' and with a cry of grief and horror she had thrown herself back from him so that she stumbled and fell to the ground. And now the plane was rolling to a stop just thirty yards away. Noltke's pistol followed her scrambling and his finger tightened on the trigger. He fired one shot; it missed. And the Salamander had hurled himself on to him and with a wild, bellowing cry had struck him with clenched fist a little below the ear. The pistol went off again, but Noltke was out cold.

'Erna!' he shouted, breathlessly. 'My God, Erna!' But she had scrambled up and was running into the bushes. 'Erna! For Christ's sake run like fuck!' he screamed, but he did not know any more who it was he shouted at, for he was with her then, even as she ran from him, swallowed up in the darkness. He scooped up the body of his fellow agent and with his face now running with sweat and tears he tossed the gangly body across his shoulder and went sprinting for the plane. His wounds tore open and the blood was spurting down his leg. But the pain he felt was in his spirit, in his heart.

'Tally ho scallywags!' the pilot hallooed, and his tallowed face and wildly shaking voice were a parody of bravura.

'Go go go!' screamed the Salamander, and with the door banging at his heel the plane lurched into motion and the shooting intensified as the first of the soldiers began running towards them a hundred and fifty yards away. The plane was quickly airborne. And twenty minutes later their escort appeared in the sky above them: two Spitfires, which stayed with them all the way to Folkestone.

Jackson never again saw his Erna alive, but he saw her photograph, which her mother had swiftly cut from a larger family portrait and had positioned in prominence on the mantelpiece; and he touched the cheek of the body laid out on the great oak table, dressed in her Sunday best for the grave. That was in April of the following year, just about the time when the victorious armies of East and West met in jubilation at the River Elbe. At Westergellersen, not twenty miles from the Elbe river, in that sunny kitchen by the mill-stream, Erna's mother sat impassive in her rocking-chair while Major Jackson, stock-still in regular uniform, with swagger-stick under his arm, stared and stared about him. For a time his gaze rested on the harrowed form of the older woman, for she had saved his life on Lueneburg Heath and had bewitched him with a herbal potion; thence it shifted to the body on the table. Erna, he thought, Erna really loved me . . . and then, I suppose, his pain was at its height; only lastly did his gaze come to rest on me, gurgling in my cot upon the window-sill, blameless and tiny and bathed in the sunlight of that spring.

'Give me . . .' he said hoarsely, 'I want . . . something to remember her by.'

And when the old woman rose from her chair and offered him a tiny, needle-pointed pair of sewing scissors beautifully crafted in the shape of a stork, and in the dear exertion of speech mammered to him 'take a lock of her hair, then,' the soldier turned abruptly, violently, to face an inner darkness of his own and ground his whitening fist into his eye.

He said to her, gruffly, 'Leave it. Leave her hair alone.'

Jackson left her hair alone, but he took from her then a memento to which he lacked all title at the time; and it caused her mother much pain to see it. It was indeed a theft of sorts, when he took it from them, but in the course of his later years he made it truly his own; let me be witness to this: he truly earned it and he made it his own. What matter that he had already given it away by then? For the act of giving had been for him a further memento, a decisive, intent remembering of Erna, his trysting bride of a scrap of heathland of the soul; and he loved her, I believe, through all his years to come.

PART II

the beings of fire went mad and their madness was a dragon;
it flew hither and thither in the madness of itself
it did not know it was mad with thirst;
it roamed the great emptiness
it ruled the world

then the dragon lured the children of Man
into the great emptiness;
they wandered in the dead forests
by the black rivers of stars
and the new-born of Man were mad and blind

. . . .

then Earth rose from sleep and became a great tree;
her hair flowed like branches through the skies
and her roots were in heaven and in earth;
Earth caught the dragon in the tangle of her hair
and it raged and burned in her roots and branches.

From *Fragments of Lost Cosmogonies: An Anthology of Myths Collected
in the Amazon Basin* by Hernando S. Gordon

4

I never knew my father or my mother; and we do not, of course,
until we have grown to be worldly in the forming place of family
life, and by the means they have bestowed upon us we learn to see
them as they are. And yet long before we are ever ourselves we are
our own mother–father, our *Matropater* as the gnostics would have
it: radiant, eternal, illimitable, and earthed in the transient twin
towers of the flesh ... Today, in the vigour of my adult life, it
behoves me to celebrate those strangers who were me: I celebrate
my mother in the rhythms of prose; my father in the range of love's intensity.

Conjuring with Magicians, or The Author's Meditations on a Sixteenth-
Century Gnostic

My name is Robert Mark Clare though most people call me Mark, not
least, I suppose, because I have always been somewhat marginal – at
school I was considered something of a freak; and some people call me
Robert, of course. I dwell on names quite a lot these days: among the
many other meanings of the name I carry, the following appropriate
referents are listed in the Oxford English Dictionary: 'boundary, frontier,
limit; the common land of a village community; sign, token, indication; to
take note, to keep watch, to ascertain by observation'. Futile, you think?
A pointless activity – looking at definitions to find out about oneself? But
the language, you know, it *winks* at us.

Two years ago my whole life changed, not overnight but in the course of
the six months of the events of The Commission ... Yes, The Commission
broke up what was darkly, densely packed; and those intimate forces
which I had hitherto been ignorant of, all that had shaped my life seemed
then to loosen up, to become detached and gently to lift away to orbit
round a centre that was suddenly void; and myself, well, my self just was
all of it – all the twinklings and signallings of the named known things of
my life, each at its proper distance, all lawfully revolving, yet bound in
the laws of harmony so that pattern was evident. The patterns and
materials of life: that's what we're all about, all right.

*

I'm thirty-nine years old; hair, dark brown; eyes, dark blue; somewhat short of stature — well, five feet and four inches to be exact; wiry of build, and of complexion rather dark so that often enough I have been taken for Indian, which in fact I am not. Add to that a love of English sentences, a tendency to philosophize and to get into trouble, and a healthy disregard for team sports. As I say, at school they thought me a freak.

It was my mother in fact who determined that I should be called Robert, and long before I was born; but it was the good people who adopted me who wished to name me Mark, and in their gentle desire to compromise took me to church and christened me Robert Mark Clare. I honour them for their love, for their generosity, and for the name they gave me. And I send them my love.

I live in the cathedral city of Canterbury, in a small, narrow house, in a narrow street not far from the old city wall. On certain days the wind brings the sound of chanting in at my window, but I cannot see the cathedral spires from any room in the house. My garden is a small patch of green—grey grass, bounded on three sides by a brick wall five feet high. In the spring, shimmering blue speedwell carpets that scrap of grass and there blooms, always rather late, a clump of daffodils and a few straggly sprays of bugloss. In the summer months aromatic herbs grow in profusion all along the wall.

I work as a part-time lecturer at the College of Further Education but I like to think of myself as a writer; some years ago I had a piece of luck, for a book I had written enjoyed a moderate success and I was able to put down the deposit on the house. I undertake occasional translation work, too, as I have good knowledge of German, and I write the occasional review. When money is tight I take a lodger.

But it's time I told you about The Commission, which would never have come about if the agent sent to Lueneberg Heath to rendezvous with Noltke had not been Dennis Jackson. 'The bastards call it "Heaven"',' Noltke had said at their rendezvous; and just a few days after his visit to Westergellersen Major Dennis Jackson carried out his most memorable wartime mission: barely fifteen hours before the Russians came, the Salamander liberated Heaven.

But he was travelling in a Wehrmacht staff car and wore the uniform of a colonel of the Waffen-SS, complete with death's head insignia and Iron Cross, and had much in common with the angel of death when he arrived at the gates of Heaven. His platoon of British soldiers, similarly attired, manned two armoured vehicles and drove three sealed trucks. They had

34

no difficulty gaining access to the top secret establishment at Ludwigslust; the camp personnel were severely demoralized and were expecting the Russians within forty-eight hours. Jackson was iron-willed, purposive, and unquestionably authoritative; perhaps the detachment of camp guards saw in him their adventitious saviour. Certainly the camp commandant, who was nearly in tears at his arrival, proved more than eager to co-operate. And the scientists themselves were like children who had suddenly discovered that their moral leaders were no longer leaders, and no longer moral.

During the course of a confidential interview with the camp commandant the Salamander shot that person dead and arranged his corpse in the lineaments of suicide. In the ensuing confusion the invaders disarmed the camp guards and herded them into the camp's experimental chambers. The leading scientists and a few dozen of the remaining experimental subjects who could be of interest to his masters, the resourceful imposter rounded up and loaded into his trucks. He blew the safes open and packed documents into boxes, and with the sounds of Russian tank shells exploding only a few kilometres away he drove at speed towards the Elbe, which he had crossed the night before under cover of darkness.

Contrary to his orders, however, the resourceful major did not purvey his charges back to 8th Army Headquarters at Lueneburg on the Heath, no sir: Major Jackson liberated Heaven and handed over his job lot of tormentors and their victims to the more market-oriented Americans, who paid him an undisclosed sum of money and airlifted out scientists, subjects, boxes of documents and Dennis Jackson himself. They flew from a meadow by the Elbe direct to the east coast of the States, and thence, after a short refuelling stop, direct to Dallas. And for forty odd years Jackson was never seen again by his former colleagues in British Military Intelligence. But he was destined, you might say, to return to Europe; and so to The Commission.

About eighteen months ago, in March of 1983, just a few days after my thirty-seventh birthday, I received an unlooked-for letter; it was an A4 size envelope, thick and buff-coloured and franked with Dutch postage stamps featuring the sort of water-craft you see in a certain genre of Dutch painting. Opening that envelope was the single most critical decision I can remember ever having taken.

Robert Mark Clare Esq.,
10, The Friar's Walk,
Canterbury

Dear Mr Clare,

You have been selected from a list of over four hundred contemporary writers as our preferred candidate for the award of a commission to produce a written document in narrative form, subject to specific conditions as listed below. The commissioned writings shall relate to aspects of the biography of an individual, henceforth referred to as the Subject. Payment for this work shall be in the form of a monthly consideration of 5,000 Dutch guilders payable on the twenty-eighth day of each consecutive month for a period of not less than twelve months. We are pleased to place under offer to you the privilege of effectuating this work, henceforth to be titled The Commission.

Please find enclosed three sheets of A4 paper comprising Subject's Documentary pages 1, 2 and 3 (copies), and Bank Draft S.D. 01/March 1983, to the value of 5,000 Dutch guilders, payable to yourself and drawable on any British clearing bank. The enclosed A4 sheets are duplicate excerpts of 104 such pages including appendices, held at present in a file relating to the life of the Subject and eponymously named, see above. You will incorporate into your written narrative all the details contained in the Subject's Documentary as and when despatched to you in the course of your work.

If you enter into contract with us you will forthwith receive delivery of word processing facilities, which you will use to accomplish The Commission.

Please study without delay our terms of contract, which subject to execution are legally binding. Please note in particular Items 5, 7 and 8. We look forward to your early reply.

Yours sincerely,

T. E. Visse
Secretary to the Interested Parties

I accepted The Commission in spite of the conditions, most notable of which were the following: if I failed to complete the written Commission within the 'three calendar months following the last monthly payment, I would be required to submit to controlled seclusion in premises chosen by the Interested Parties, with full normal comforts and facilities supplied, for as long as I would need to complete the work. The undertones were undeniably sinister, but I tended to view this as justified caution on their part given the notorious dilatoriness of commissioned authors. Item 5 stipulated that I alone could decide when the written work was complete, but that once I had done so I would not be allowed to make the slightest alteration to the finished document. Item 7 stipulated that my work on The Commission was at all times the exclusive property of the Interested Parties, even before I had written it, and I was to have no claim

36

whatsoever on the document or its contents, neither during the period of 'effectuation' nor at any other time. Item 8 expressly forbade me to speak of The Commission to any unauthorized person in any case whatsoever, or to show any writings taken from it or relating to it to any other party. This condition would come into effect from the moment I cashed the bank draft and would be *retroactive!* What this meant, of course, was that I could only discuss the offer with anybody else if I had already decided not to accept it. Furthermore they gave me only three working days to make up my mind. I did not consult a lawyer for two reasons: I was leery of Item 8, and I didn't want to be dissuaded from accepting The Commission. The thing thrilled, delighted and terrified me; I easily convinced myself that having once undertaken The Commission, if I felt compelled to be free of it, for whatever reason, I could easily churn out some second-rate work and pronounce it complete.

The astute reader will no doubt observe that I am in breach of contract with regard to the above conditions; to which charge I would answer that this book is as much an experiment in freedom of information as it is indisputably the product of a breach of contract. And notwithstanding the customary waivers, I should like to make absolutely clear that the facts I lay before you are true, real and barely disclosable. And I invite the reader to share in this experiment by reading on; for who knows but when the book may be withdrawn from circulation.

The letter from the Interested Parties coincided with the arrival of rates bill, water bill and telephone bill. I cannot doubt that freedom of the will actually exists, for if the will were not free why should circumstances crowd together, as on this occasion, to compel us, by dint of argument, to follow a previously determined path? And so it was, that very afternoon, that I went down to the bank, clutching my bank draft for 5,000 Dutch guilders, worth at the time a little over £1,000, and opened a business account, which, obviously enough, I titled Draft Account.

The following morning I took delivery of the word processing facility and spent the rest of the day familiarizing myself with the functions. The computer was linked to a telephone line, and the technician who installed the thing informed me that everything I wrote into the machine could be read at will by the suppliers of it, of whom, he assured me, he knew nothing. I typed out a few experimental sentences, rather severely at first, but I soon relaxed and almost forgot that I probably had an audience. However, when I went off to make a pot of tea and found myself prey to the idea that I had been somehow discourteous not to excuse myself from my electronic listeners I felt the first stirrings of alienation. I could only assume that I was myself some kind of experimental subject; but what the true purpose of the experiment was, or what might be expected of me, I could not say. I went back to the gleaming screen and typed in . . .

Is there anybody there?
Please declare yourself.

Neither the screen nor the additional telephone they had installed gave any answer. I read again the sample sheets they had sent me from the Subject's Documentary.

When a woman forgets her love, when she unlearns her love a chasm has opened; it is unaccountable, incomprehensible, insupportable. To those who are witness to it, it is a savage enlightenment.

If you can't forgive you know nothing, you understand nothing. At best you trace idle patterns in the dust of things. But it is hard to forgive those you do not love, and harder still those you do. Is it true that a human being should forgive again and again, past all counting, must learn to forgive eternally? And for what? And what is there to forgive? And to what end, forgive? And what can be left, after such forgiveness?

He concentrated hard on these questions. The machines worried the dirt from the cheap underwear, the threadbare sheets, the exhausted towels. A spinner hummed and effortlessly took water. The dryer groaned and shuddered. Shirts and sheets and towels writhed and twirled in the drum. He flopped down on the stained plastic seat. He pondered and strove.

He remembered the spring day when they had stood together on a humpbacked bridge on the Isle of Seil. It was early morning. They had watched the green tons of water rush down the narrow gulley and out to sea. Submerged weeds, tall as tall men, black and green, lank as drowned men's locks, strained at their roots, taut and straight in the awesome tide. It had thrilled and horrified him. The channel was narrow, barely five feet wide, and for much of the day it was dry so that children played among the weeds and rubbed their feet in the scouring sand. But the sea would return; old grey Atlantic shaking her marble spears would fill that channel with ocean. And turning at last would make it a place for drowning armies. He shuddered to remember that awesome power, so close, so narrowly contained. And he remembered how she had loved him then. In his memory, in his imagining he held her and hugged her close. At his roots he strained in the current of her.

He trembled and got to his feet. His drying was not yet done. He paced to the window and looked out. Across the ill-lit street the sea beat at the promenade and threw dark spray high into the air. Under the street lights the wind took droves of whitening spray and threw them away. Should he ring her?

What is forgiveness for? It's for giveness. That's what it is. Forgiveness is for giving. Forgive.

He knew that already he could and did forgive her. He knew too that there was nothing for giveness, there was nothing to forgive. He thought to himself, this is perhaps why we all have this strong sense of grievance, one against the other, in order that we may at least have something, some forgiving, for giving in a life. I love her, he thought, but I have nothing to give her because there's nothing she wants from me any more. All I have is a sense of grievance for giving her. Her. The sound was a breath, made flesh.

He saw that his error lay in a certain immanence of the self. He was prey to introspection and maddened by desire. He said, 'The road to the light lies in the outward.' And with this realization there came to him glimmering moments of hope. He tried to write it down. To hold it down against the flow of time. He sat at the typewriter and cajoled that inwardness outward. He must concentrate like someone hunched in an ingle, attentively exerted in making a fire. At first he simply milked himself with clumsy off-mark words that came like harried messengers from the incomprehensible chaos. Slowly, however, he quieted, and made his peace with the lingering possible truth. Gently, gently he closed on it. It was ever beckoning, ever intimate, resonant. He closed on it, at first with astonishment, and then with love. And sometimes thereafter his wife was gone from his mind, but her presence pervaded all the landscape of his thought, still breathed upon his thought, clothed all his sentences with love.

Next week Paris. Must borrow some money for the fare.

I felt the writing was rather too good for a bona fide diary, and probably a touch too self-conscious; furthermore, I thought it was an unlikely diarist who referred to himself in the third person. But neither could I comfortably assume that the pages in front of me were mere fictive sketchwork, for the emotions expressed in the writing struck me as true and real; in fact, the thing was rather touching, almost painful to read. I assumed, since these were pages one through three of the Subject's Documentary, that this must be the beginning of the relevant writings of the Subject. I was soon to discover, however, that the page numbering of the Subject's Documentary, although not destructive of the coherence of the text, nevertheless did not reflect the true chronology of events. And with the exception of the initial contractual letter, as quoted above, the Subject's writings were sent to me quite randomly, a fact which struck me as a clear directive from the Interested Parties that I should order the material only as I myself thought fit.

Early that evening Lucia turned up. At the time I nursed the secret hope that she might one day consent to become my wife. Actually, I wasn't at all sure what she saw in me; but I certainly wasn't going to dwell on that question. You take what joys you find and you celebrate.

'Ooh!' she said. 'You've got a new computer. It's splendid.'

She tugged at her hat as she sat down; she slipped the hat cord over her shapely, rather pointed chin, and up over her nose, which is slightly retroussé; she pulled her long, beautiful fingers through her hair as she removed the hat, and for an unforgettable moment the dark blue velvet rim perfectly framed her face. Lucia has the most beautiful eyes, a soft brown delicately tinged with green, and a wide pleasure-loving mouth. Her hair is dark brown but with red highlights, giving her the sort of glow you see in a pre-autumnal sunset. She peeled off her gloves and placed them in her lap.

'What other goodies have you got?' she asked. 'I love surprises.'

'I've got a big story,' I said.

'You sound like a reporter with a scoop!' She sat back and closed her eyes. Lucia always closes her eyes when she's not using them or being paid to keep them open. In this way she hopes to retain their beauty.

I said, 'I can't tell you.' I must have sounded quite serious, for she opened her eyes and stared at me. Of course, I should have known that something was not right between us when she failed then, signally, to show curiosity.

That night I dreamed I was dead behind a wall; but it was only my body that was dead, and the wall was not made of bricks, or concrete blocks, but of nothingness, so that my knowledge of the corpse that lay on the other side of it, and was myself, seemed to me, even as I dreamed, a sort of miracle. And then I was a great city in the darkness but so much better lit on one side than on the other; here I could see bright illuminations and coloured neon signs, but over there on the other side all was dim, densely-shadowed weavings, and so much more threatening and powerful. I felt the energy of this city, its people, its traffic, in the nerves of my sleeping body. And then I became a great continent and felt the weight of mountains and the hollows of valleys and ravines and then I was alive again in my body behind the wall. I awoke, feeling my way along the wall which had been transformed into the elegant back and buttocks of Lucia, who stirred now beside me.

'Are you going too?' she murmured. Her words struck me as odd even then in my half-sleep state of terror.

'This dream,' I muttered. Then I was fully awake and on the instant I felt the presence of the computer in the study. I nudged her, 'Wake up, will you.'

'Better take something,' she murmured. 'That rich food.'

'What?'

'Upset tummy. Rich food!' Mounting exasperation came through the mantle of her sleep. She pulled the sheet over her head and was gone.

In my study I sat crouching before the computer screen. The coal-black glassy rectangle showed me a slightly altered version of myself amidst the golden slats of light from the standard lamp. The dream had faded, but in its aftermath I felt a clawing fertility, an exaggerated emptiness, a frightening sense of hope.

Within a fortnight or so it had become clear that there was another, quite distinctive side to the Subject's writings; increasingly in the pages of the Subject's Documentary I encountered a confessional tendency, a poetic self-searching that seemed to be directly related to some posters:

> I am a mirror warped and dirtied. Others' words, others' selves fashioned by still others' selves have wrought this deformity. And now in the betrayed market of tongues a deformed thing gives back a hero's image.
>
> But I am a river, too, wrinkled with the currents of the world. And I am a compass, a matrix of forces. I am a cross in the void.

And elsewhere still the Subject writes:

> What self I have is knowable only under the opaque mantle of words. I am a tree of others' attributions, hung with their fruit, their blighted flowers. My own fruit too hangs there on this stuffless stick, this totem self in its faceless dark forming its own ill-favoured intimations.

Indeed there was so much of this singular, confessional-type writing that I became convinced that the Subject had something important to divulge, or more significantly, to confess, but could not find the means, or feared to be too blatant.

> . . . child prostitution, − slavery, − abuse: collective starvation, − terroriza-tion, − dehumanization: deception, inveiglement, collusion: exploitation, toxification, destruction . . .
>
> NB Adam Smith's conception of 'natural liberty' accords with the best interests of all men but will not be realized if government is entrusted to, or heeds, 'the mean rapacity, the monopolizing spirit of merchants and manufacturers, who neither are, nor ought to be, the rulers of mankind.'
>
> Why then did I put my strength, my youth, into these posters? Into a mere business? Why am I in this drowning pool?

. . . .

41

Am making regular contact with Bruedelmann, but have had no further contact with God.

In the following extract I began to discern the nature of the business experience the Subject is bemoaning:

How foolish of me to imagine that I know what I'm doing. How foolish of me to think that my intentions and my reasons actually cause and define what I think I go on to do. What is it that really prompts me? Who is it doing what I do? Am I trying to make something clear to myself? . . . like a player who is destined to discover as the play unfolds, the play in which he takes the centre stage, that he himself is its author . . . and the whole point of the play is to show how it is possible to change the author for the better, and the agent of change is just the author himself and his instrument is the play . . . At some point the play and the author must merge and be one; and the actor must be one with the part he plays . . . and since he is the agent of the self, he must betray and betray to be one with the author of the play.

I am phrasal verb man talking to himself about the particles he's made of, about the particles the world is made of, about the particles he's made of the world . . . and about the particles of language which particle men use to particularize the fertile void cosmos . . . Yes, that's why I did the posters. I'm phrasal verb man, telling himself . . . of himself and of the world.

But I can't drop it; but it won't work. There's only one way out of it, then: I have to make the poster business the instrument of a new project; I shall learn how to be a man who is good at doing business and is good at the business of doing good . . . I'll redeem myself and my business.

Easy does it though: let me be wise as the serpent and innocent as the dove.

Some weeks had passed and I was becoming disturbed at the nature of the material. One morning I logged in and sent a note to the Interested Parties:

MEMORANDUM

FROM : Robert Mark Clare
TO : The Interested Parties
SUBJECT : Reconstruction by Infictifaction of Subject's Documentary.

This material gives me no purchase on the basics. I must have something more substantial if I am to make a start. Please send me something catalytic.

*

Finding me in particularly low mood Lucia took me along to Sarah's birthday party. Sarah, who is Lucia's sister, is nine years younger; at the party she was surrounded by loud, aggressive young men. As a birthday present to herself she had had her beautiful blonde hair violently striated with fluorescent orange. Her boyfriend, sullen as ever, had dark-blue spiky hair that evening, and his head closely resembled a medieval bludgeon.

'Hello Mark,' said Sarah, and she threw out an arm that slowly encircled my waist in a languid, sea-creaturely fashion. She has a melodious, caressing tone, very healing, but a shade overbearing at times.

'How are you getting on with Hitler?' I asked her.

'I finished Hitler at the end of March,' she said.

'A March you stole on the Allies,' I said.

'Hitler,' she said, ignoring my remark, 'was just one manifestation of a general tendency.' Sternly she added. 'There is nothing to laugh about.'

'Who's laughing?' I said.

'In the last year of his life,' she continued, 'he looked more like a concentration camp victim than the author of the Final Solution. He dribbled all the time and was almost blind. He used to drag himself along and every other step he had to sit down. And he wobbled all the time.'

In fact I was more interested to note that Sarah's pink mouth, which is small and decidedly oval, was equally bedewed from the effort of her speech. She is a well built girl yet dainty of foot. Her face is full and round, her forehead high, her nose rather small and slightly snub like her sister's. Her eyes, too, are like her sister's, hazel, and tinged with green, and her hair then was long, reaching half way down her back and worn in a thickly braided tail. She has a strong neck and fleshy hands, with carefully tended fingernails for her classical guitar playing. She is ever so slightly knock-kneed.

'Actually,' she said, looking rather intently at my complexion, 'he suffered from a funny discoloration of the skin.'

'Mmn,' I said.

'But if you want to know what *I* think . . .'

'Yes?'

'I think it was general psychological breakdown. His mind was falling apart and his body was too. It's very interesting, Mark . . . some people believe that what made him so beastly was the fact that he was a delegate for his parents. It's called heroic reconciliation. Did you know that?'

'Oh come on Sarah,' said her boyfriend and he tugged on her arm.

'Wait a moment, can't you!' she very emphatically protested. Her boyfriend, who is a foot taller than she, sulkily hung his heavy jowls.

'Mark,' she said, in a tone of voice which implied that I might be expected to have special insight, 'what do *you* think about Hitler?'

'Monorchidistic,' I said. 'Isn't there some popular connection with the Albert Hall?'

'What?' She screwed up her face in annoyance. 'How silly!' She was very disapproving. 'I ought to tell you,' she said, and now she allowed her disconsolate beau to lead her away into the mêlée, 'that you do look just the teensiest bit like him, you know. Before he got into trouble, of course.'

'I bet that boyfriend of hers has got fascist tendencies,' I said to Lucia. 'I think she may be attracted to the type.'

'You should have heard her the other morning', Lucia replied. She was talking about Hitler's nephew. "I bet you didn't know," she said, "Adolf Hitler had a nephew called Patrick"!'

'Nothing strange about that,' I said.

'Well, this Mr Patrick Hitler,' she was giggling through her dazzling, perfect teeth, 'tried to blackmail his Uncle Adolf in 1930 about his grandmama because she . . . can you guess?'

'She was Jewish?'

'That's right! Anyway, Hitler got his secret policemen to investigate the matter and they concluded there was no proof.'

'Surprise, surprise.'

'Yes, I thought so too,' said Lucia. 'But that's not the end of the story. You see there's a dear little village in Austria, I mean there *was*, and in 1938 Hitler made them turn it into an artillery range for the infantry or whatever.'

'What little village?' I asked, but this was only to please her. My gloom was deepening.

'Oh, Dollershome or something. I expect it was pulverized, along with the village cemetery where the old lady was buried.'

'I shouldn't think she was a lady,' I observed. 'She probably had to work as a maid all her life.'

'Well anyway,' she gaily concluded, 'by then she was a box of bones. And blown to smithereens.'

A little later I saw an improbable party-goer approach Sarah and her crowd of male friends. He was waving a stick like a blind man but his walk was confident and sure. He was very tall and thin, and his hair was lank, and silvery-grey, and rather long. His clothes were slovenly and ill-maintained yet he seemed entirely self-possessed and full of presence. Perhaps the most striking feature of all were his dark glasses, which were small, round, green lenses held in a fragile gold frame. As soon as she caught sight of him Sarah turned away from her friends and went to speak to him very cordially. I moved closer and heard her say, 'Oh . . . I really am so glad you've come, Herman! Do you want me to introduce you to anybody?'

'Perhaps not quite at the moment.' He spoke with a precious clarity. I had the funny idea that he had a trained voice. It was surprisingly deep and powerful, and seemed ten years younger than the man himself. I took him to be about sixty.

'I'd like to mention something to you, my dear Sarah. *Unter vier Augen.*' His hand gently guided her away from her friends.

'Nudge nudge, yessss?' It was Sarah's boyfriend who hissed so. 'That German then? *Inter-fere-a-gain*? German?' The boyfriend was clearly very angry; his blue spikes wavered and shook with it.

'"Unter vier Augen" is German, yes,' the man replied. His tone was one of such abject humility that it pained me to hear it. 'It means "please allow us to speak privately". Do you very much mind?'

'Yes. I bloody well do,' the boyfriend retorted. 'I don't want you to speak to her.'

'Don't worry, silly,' said Sarah, with a blitheness that would have been out of place had it not been for the slightly sinister appearance of the interloper. 'I shall be back in a moment.' With a sort of dramatic flourish she gave the man her arm and they moved away together.

'Strange man,' I said, to no one in particular.

Lucia told me that the man had been living in Canterbury for about a year and that Sarah wrote letters for him. He suffered from very poor vision and didn't venture out much.

I watched them for a moment, as they stood in conversation on the other side of the room; spirited, colourful Sarah – theatrical and slightly plump, and the lank-haired man with the stick. He seemed to be talking to her without moving his lips; she seemed enrapt.

'What's his name?' I asked.

'N.', said the boyfriend, as you might utter a threat.

'N.?'

'Mark,' Lucia was offended. 'Aren't you listening to me?'

'Yes,' I said quickly. 'Of course I am. I'm sorry, Luce. Let's dance, shall we?'

And although I do not strictly dance, so much as conform to the ill-perceived commands of the music, and in that sorry way I always use to conform to commands, I mean uncertainly, doubtingly, and with a natural resistance springing from I know not what within me, Lucia at least was

45

glad of my suggestion. But we had barely begun to dance when a rumpus started in the next room. And through the open doorway I saw Sarah's boyfriend sprawl to the ground a little way in front of the character with the stick. A beer-glass flew through the air and crashed against the wall. Some screams ensued, and some shouting. Then the whole thing quietened down. A girl started to laugh hysterically.

'I think he was trying to trip him up.'

'Who?'

'The old chap with the stick. That lout of a boyfriend tried to trip him up. I swear it.'

'Oh, that reminds me,' she said, inconsequentially. 'When he was a very young man . . .'

'Who?'

'That man.'

'Oh.'

'Well, anyway, when he was about fifteen or something, according to Sarah, and she won't supply any details, he had his cheek patted by the *most* charismatic politician.'

Lady of Grace, eternal, on the indefectible waters of time they have rowed
your white-boned barque in stillness and in light.

This comment was circled in red ink. They had sent me more sheets from the Subject's Documentary. The entry was dated October 26th, 1982. There followed numerous drawings of aspects of a cathedral, in ink mainly, but some were pencil sketchings over half-completed ink lines. One aspect in particular seemed to have obsessed the diarist for he had assayed the same drawing at least four times. I thought it might be the north-eastern view of Notre Dame de Paris. I reckoned the 'white-boned barque' of the writer's description was a reference to that building's celebrated flying buttresses. On my writing desk in front of me I had spread out the twenty-odd photostat sheets that I had so far received of the Subject's Documentary, and, in addition, the typed version they had sent me. Compared with the handwritten pages, which teemed with corrections, the typed sheets seemed almost a mockery of the original. At times the handwriting seemed to pulse with energy, at times it was barely legible, barely meaningful when readable, so sluggish and despairing did it seem. In the coils of words the diarist's spirit seemed to vanish and re-emerge. I could have done so much more with the actual diary, assuming such a thing existed. I wondered what its status might be; perhaps it lay in a safe somewhere, or in a locked filing cabinet in an office. Was it a commodity to be auctioned off? A secret? Such silly thoughts as these gave energy to my efforts as I struggled in those early days to fulfil the terms of The Commission. I needed a manifold, a plot against which the personal feelings and experiences of the diarist could function as a sort of counterpoint. In vain, too, I sought a voice, a framework of beliefs and expectations by means of which I might make sense of the diarist's incandescent prose.

Another week had passed and I had had no response to my despairing memorandum; but I had solved my problem, provisionally, by imagining that I was myself the Subject of the Subject's Documentary and thus both reader and author of it. This imaginative device enabled me to write truthfully about my own feelings and experiences as they occurred in direct response to the material sent to me by the Interested Parties, and lent a dramatic poignancy, I hoped, to the situation of the diarist. However, I still faced the problem of explaining how a diarist should find himself reading his own diary writings in that condition of bewilderment, suspicion and doubt that I myself was prey to since taking up The Commission.

I pictured to myself a victim of some form of memory default: a person about whom so little documentary or anecdotal evidence is available that it is necessary to create his past as though he had never had it, as though, in fact, it did not yet exist; a man who has become aware that he knows nothing of any past, who is compelled to reconstruct it for himself, by means of logic where possible, by imaginative insight otherwise. Thus, to make his story, or if you will, to make history of his own identity, he studies his diaries, his letters, his notebooks, his love letters, his business memoranda; he reads all that he can find to aid him in this quest to construct the person that is himself. And as he grows in knowledge and understanding he makes important discoveries: perhaps he learns that he and his wife have separated, but he cannot yet discover the cause – nor can he bring himself to ask her, preferring to find out for himself, or perhaps not at all. He hopes, imprecisely, that illuminations will come to him in his dreams, where he might act out again the past realities of his existence, could he but remember them on waking, and, remembering them, be able to understand. Perhaps too, as he slowly takes piecemeal possession of the identity of the diarist and correspondent that was himself, he is prey to a growing moral disquiet.

Thus I solved the puzzle of The Commission by imagining that it did not really exist; and having transformed it into a fiction I was able to make it real again by placing myself at the heart of its mystery; and in making of myself the real subject of its fictive embrace, I set myself to find me amidst the mysteries of my own existence, and I immersed the narrator, successfully I thought, in the very weather of the self.

I had written some sketchy narrative along these lines and was rewarded, it seemed to me, by a sudden shortfall in incoming documentary material; I had the distinct impression that the Interested Parties were mulling it over. It struck me then that a good way to provoke them into sending me 'something more substantial' was to keep inventing new scenarios; even if the Interested Parties failed to send me something 'catalytic' it would at least give me the opportunity to examine their reactions. And they would be compelled, in time, to respond to my changes in a way that would determine my further responses. Realizing that I was much like the laboratory rat in his dealings with the experimental psychologist, I introduced a new development into my scenario of the amnesiac subject: I let fall a hint of my growing inclination to investigate the Interested Parties.

Three days later I received from the Interested Parties a weighty batch of documents, amongst which one item in particular caught my eye.

Included in the packet of papers there was a letter addressed to 'mon ami', written in French on the headed notepaper of a Spanish countess living in Paris. It was dated February 11th, 1982, and addressed to a person (name crossed out but presumed to be the Subject) who had formerly lived over a petrol station in the town of Lippstadt, Westphalia. On careful examination of the document I found that it was possible to read the sender's name and address, which caused me considerable happiness.

At once I resolved to take a trip to Paris. And from that time onwards the factual details of the Subject's real life began to crowd in upon me. They cast their shadows over the diary and the reports, and over the taped conversations and everything else that was sent to me afterwards. And like a ritual traveller I passed from the escapable world of the fictively real into the unending labyrinth, where nothing is so real as the writing on its walls.

5

For gnosis is to know . . . 'who we were, and what we have become; where we were . . . whither we are hastening; from what we are being released; what birth is, and what is rebirth.'

Theodotus

I caught the morning boat from Dover. A cold wind came in rough blasts across the point but I lingered on deck to watch the crewmen casting off. The April air was keen, and salt; the steel decks delicately thrummed underfoot; in a rush of raincoats and brightly coloured bags a crowd of school-kids clattered off the bulkhead into the lounge.

Sarah, whose French is far better than mine, had kindly translated the countess's letter for me.

'Do you want me to read it all to you? Every word?'

'I would prefer that, Sarah. Please.'

She had been embarrassed. I had explained that I needed a thorough knowledge of the correspondence of a certain writer for a review I was doing. One of the unfortunate aspects of The Commission was that it was turning me into a liar.

'But this has got . . . Well, it's a bit personal in places,' she had said, her mouth falling open as she had looked away.

The gist of it, according to Sarah's rather coy interpretation, was that the man to whom the letter was addressed had left some posters in the countess's cellar and she wanted them removed. Apparently a bookshop man had been pestering her for more copies.

'Ah,' I had said, and I had felt sure then that the addressee of the letter was indeed the Subject of the Subject's Documentary. 'Posters, you say? Excellent. What else does she say?'

'She's complaining because he hasn't been in touch. She's disillusioned. Disappointed,' Sarah had continued. 'She means disappointed, of course. Because he hasn't written. She says if every woman cared for him as much as she does he would be the most adored man in the world.'

But at the countess's house I had been sent away by the concierge;

Madame was in Spain, for three months, yes; her apartments were closed. I had tried then, in tortuous unwarrantable French, to gain access to her cellar, only to be ushered away. It was a poor beginning. Afterwards, by dint of some rudimentary detective work, I had found my way to a bookshop in the Latin Quarter.

In the window of the shop I caught a glimpse of an enormous, faded poster. I pushed the door open and went in. At the back of the shop a lugubrious, portly individual with dark, brooding eyes looked up from a work desk and gave a perfunctory nod. I looked briefly at the shelves of English Language teaching books, audio-cassettes, glossy work-books, flimsy packs of notes on grammar, and such like.

I said, 'I'm actually looking for the phrasal verb posters.'

'Sold out,' he promptly replied, and put his pen behind his ear. Now he watched me, thoughtfully. He had thick, black, curly hair and his large, heavy head seemed to nod a little as he spoke; his eyes were round and mournful but his chin and mouth were delicate, and full of wry good humour.

'There is only the poster in the window,' the bookshop man continued. 'It is one of the set.'

'I'd very much like to have a closer look at it, if you are agreeable, Mr ... uh ...'

'O'Bleaghnaulty. The name is O'Bleaghnaulty.'

'Ah,' I said, very congenially, 'you're Irish, I take it?'

'Half French, half Irish,' he replied.

He showed me a point where I could put aside a screen and subject the poster to closer scrutiny. The first thing I looked for was the copyright mark; and there it was, at the bottom of the poster, complete with the author's name and date: *1981 Hugo Thayer.* As I scanned the story which the poster told, my scalp prickled and I experienced a moment's intense melancholia.

A childless English couple had adopted an infant boy found abandoned amongst refuse in the streets of Calcutta and had brought him up in a middle-class English household. But in his teens the small, wiry, dark-skinned child began to ask questions: 'Who am I?' he asked of his parents, and for answer they told him his English adopted name; so he asked again, and they could not say. Then he asked of them, 'Who made me?' and they, being Christians, answered, 'God made you; God Who is the Father of Jesus, He made you.' But the Muslim children, and the Hindu children, and the Buddhist children at his school, he knew, had different answers to this question, and so, with a feeling of great sadness, he disbelieved what his parents told him. Then he went to the science master in his school and asked him, 'Who really made me, please, Mr Simpith?' And Mr Simpith said, 'You are your genes, boy. They are a sort of colony, a co-operative of makers and organizers of human cells who have come together in order to survive. So you see, nobody made you, or they did.'

The boy went away and thought about this very hard, and believed that he was a colony, a place where things called genes ruled in their own way and for their own selfish purposes a foreign country which was him, and purely because it suited them to do so. Then he grew very sad indeed. And his adoptive parents, who loved him, said, 'V. J. darling, we love you, what can we do?' And he, thinking there was still a chance, said, 'I want to find my real mum and dad.' And they told him that it was completely impossible, that no one could help him do that, that he was an abandoned baby, found in a dump in a slum. And now his adoptive mother was weeping and his adoptive father was getting very cross indeed. And his next question was 'Where do I come from?' to which they replied, 'From the backstreets of Calcutta.' And he said, 'I want to go home.' 'Home?' said his mother, and she had to sit down; then his adoptive father took him for a walk in the park and begged him to be patient, because they loved him like a real mum and dad, maybe even more than that, and they could not bear to see him suffer, and besides, he was killing his mother with his questions. And later his parents promised to go with him to Calcutta if he would only wait a little while and do his 'A' levels first; he was studying geography, English, biology and history.

He finished his 'A' levels and then he went to Calcutta and wandered around by himself. A few weeks later he returned to his adoptive mum and dad, who were over the moon to see him again. He said to them 'We've nothing in common, Mum and Dad, but love and language – this English culture that we share. I love you both and yet I am a stranger. I know I am only a colony of genes, but I've realized that genes are like letters and letters can make words and so I'm going to be a writer. I will use language to free the colony; I will use words to take back what has been taken away; I will have words for genes, for blood mother and blood father, and I will create a future where nobody cares any more who they were made by. Then everybody in the world will be part of the family.' And his mum hugged and kissed him and told him that she understood and that she loved him even more now if it was possible, and his dad said, 'Come on, let's go and buy a word processor. Might as well start today.'

*

In its original form on the poster this story was cleverly reduced to short, simple sentences accompanying some thirty full-colour images. The text below each image was larger, and was in narrative form; above each image there was a text in smaller print which took the form of dialogue, or supplementary observations. Not the least remarkable thing about it was that the whole story was couched in English phrasal verbs.

'I wonder,' I said to the bookshop man, 'what kind of man would write such a story in a language teaching aid? The man who holds the copyright, Mr uh, Mr Hugo Thayer ... did you ever by any chance meet him?'

The bookshop man looked at me very acutely, sizing me up, no doubt, and probably suspicious of my chattiness.

'He said to me once that traders have no souls. He was wrong, you know.'

My pulse quickened; my readings of the excerpts in the Subject's Documentary clearly indicated the type of man who said such things in a business environment.

'Good Heavens,' I said, mildly.

'He was in the wrong business, too,' said the bookshop man, whose voice was pleasantly deep but supple. 'He was rude to everyone. He did not respect our way of doing business. He was a very eccentric person and a most unlikely businessman.'

'Well,' I said, 'I'd be fascinated to talk to him about his posters. I share his interest in phrasal verbs. Could I ask you . . .?'

'It's hopeless,' he said. 'I've not seen him for six months. He has not communicated with me in any way. I cannot get any more of the posters. I think he has probably given it up.'

I gave expression to my entirely genuine disappointment and wondered what I should do next. And then, by chance, my gaze fell upon a shelf of English readers; and there, among the books on the bizarre was one I recognized all too well.

'Excuse me, please,' I said, and on impulse I walked across the shop, reached up to the book in question and plucked it down from the shelf. It was the original hardback, still in its dust-jacket; and there on the back, untouched by time's attritions, was my own sweet face of yore: smiling, self-confident, full of hope. I put on a somewhat woebegone look and passed it to Mr O'Bleaghnaulty.

'Ah,' said the bookshop man, turning the book over and over in his hands. 'It is a good photograph,' he said. 'But you have changed a little, I think.'

'Well,' I said, 'that photograph is eight years old.'

The book was the product of ten years spent practising martial arts and five years reading in related subjects. It attempted to show that there was an interesting connection between the functions of the mind, the disposition of the bodily limbs, and the structure of reality. The book was hackneyed from start to finish, poorly researched and rather silly. But it bought me a house.

Mr O'Bleaghnaulty talked at length about the soul and about its struggle with the passions. He was amicable and eloquent. After a few minutes it became apparent that he expected me to buy my little book from him.

'Actually,' I said, grimly shaking the hardback as I held it clasped in my right hand, 'I rather think I'll take this . . .' And keeping a tight smile for a good three seconds, I said, 'For old time's sake. How much is it anyway?'

He rubbed his cheeks with long, expressive fingers and now there was a cynical glint in his eye; pretending to overlook my question he went on to say, 'Just yesterday afternoon, funnily, I sold the last full set of Mr Thayer's posters. If you like I can ring up the customer and ask him if you could look at the material. He's a very accommodating person.'

'That would be terrific,' I said. And now I casually put down the book on a shelf behind and waited for O'Bleaghnaulty to pick up the telephone. But he seemed to have fallen to musing. I waited.

'Now Mr Thayer,' he said, thoughtfully, 'he was much given to hard thinking. He was forever talking about Darwin. About the theory of survival of the fittest, and about the genes. He said to me once that he could not understand how he had survived, in his business you understand, because he could not lie, or cheat.'

'Mr O'Bleaghnaulty,' I said, for I was now convinced that Hugo Thayer was the Subject of the Subject's Documentary, 'could we try that customer you mentioned, Mr O'Bleaghnaulty?' I was deferential, but pressing. I hoped it would do the trick.

'Oh, but he was a fox if I ever met one, was Hugo,' said the bookshop man, and now he was shifting about at his desk, pushing papers around, moving books.

'How much is my book, anyway? Reluctantly I had picked it up again from where I had laid it down in hope. He craned his neck and hooked his princely, tapering finger under the flyleaf; but it was clear he wasn't looking for the price mark: he was assessing how much I would be prepared to pay for it.

'Well,' he said, 'you know, I am not so sure any more.'

'But of course,' I said, brightly, 'you'll be giving me a discount. After all, I wrote it. I mean, I'm trade, aren't I?' and I gave him a soulless smile.

We struck a price and then he made the telephone call to the buyer of the last full set of Hugo Thayer's posters. As a result I received an invitation to a vernissage that very evening. O'Bleaghnaulty scribbled down the address in the flyleaf of my book. The purchaser was a Mr Georges Bruedelmann, proprietor of an art gallery in the Marais quarter.

'I don't suppose you'd like to sell me that poster in the window,' I said to O'Bleaghnaulty as a parting shot. He had followed me out on to the street and for a moment we stood together and looked at the sun-bleached, wrinkled poster, of which glimpses of images and story-line were visible through odd arrangements of books and other scrolls of paper, a dozen or so casually disposed audio-cassettes, language workbooks and similar materials, a map, I noticed, and a small plastic globe.

'No,' he said, 'I would not.' He gazed at me out of the deep sad wells of his eyes as if looking for someone he recognized. 'I like this poster,' he said. 'It speaks to me, you understand. Mr Thayer and I used to have drinks together. For a time we were friends. But he said to me once: "O'Bleaghnaulty," he said, "I can never forget that we must always continue to lie to each other because if we stop lying everything will stop. And if we cannot bear to lie any longer we must make the effort to deceive ourselves as to our lying. Either we must pretend to be sick, or we must believe that we do not lie." Now tell me, won't you, Mr Clare, how is a man supposed to answer that? I ask you now, how on heaven's earth are we to change the rules of the game?'

'I'm not sure I follow that,' I said, all ears, but dull.

'Hugo said that his posters didn't work,' Mr O'Bleaghnaulty continued. 'But he had to keep selling them because of his commitments. It worried him a lot that his language had become a commodity for him. What can it forebode, he used to ask, that those who love it best have brought it to market?'

It was a long, low-ceilinged gallery with generous windows which looked out on to a small, quiet square; at the centre of the square, on a flat patch of dust among scrubby trees, a group of old men were playing boule. The gallery was split level, and since I am short of stature and was, in any case, a somewhat marginal viewer there, I sought the higher ground at the back of the shop. A 'vernissage', I soon realized, was merely a preview of an artist's work; sophisticated people with distracted, concentrated faces exchanged intricate gestures, elaborate as arabesques, and odd-looking characters with large, silver trays wandered about serving chilled wine. One of these persons wore a sleeveless leather jerkin over his bare torso, from which a tuft of reddish hair sprouted at the neck. His head was completely bald-shaven and he wore a gem in his ear-lobe. In the hard, white light it sparkled brilliantly. At odd places in the gallery were small groups of chairs where persons of privilege sat very still, their limbs composed. The place was crowded, stuffy, and rather too warm. I confess I don't speak much French — a fact which shames me; but I got the distinct impression that nobody was discussing art.

I was standing in front of what appeared to my inexpert gaze to be an original Antoine Watteau oil painting. There was a piece of paper tucked into the corner of the picture frame with a scribbled note on it. I was about to inspect that note more carefully when a woman's voice beside me said in English,

'It's very sinister, don't you think?'

She was a gat-toothed English girl with swept-back auburn hair, trimmed to a downy furze across her nape; her eyes were pale brown, her face a delicate oval but full like a child's, her chin sensuous and vulnerable. She wore a thin green cotton dress with a wide, ornately elasticated belt which accentuated the curves of her hips.

'Yes I suppose it is, rather,' I said, coming across like a poorly staged Englishman. 'Does it have a title?'

'A friend of ours,' she said, with a sort of wide, coy gaiety, 'calls it the "Lichterfelder Fête Galante".'

The Lichterfelder Fête Galante depicts a group of revellers, richly dressed yet moderate in their pleasures, enjoying music, dance and feasting amidst overhanging bowers: here the satiny funsters make to walk, as in a dance, and here, demurely in this restful shade, a sober, more somnolent group repose on the stonework of a ruinous classical monument. All enrich their talk with gestures both classic and discreet, and while away the beautiful hours. But for all this grace, this mild exuberance, there is a chastening mood upon the company: it is as though they trembled in their souls at the proximity of brutal murders, carried out wholesale in that same shaded, woody spot where they had chanced to walk. And in the depiction of the revellers themselves there are discernibly pornographic elements; these convey a sense of giddying sexuality, roused not by life but by death's stark imminence.

'I'm Tara,' she said, extending her plump, slightly moist palm.

'It's very strange,' I said, slowly forming my ideas, 'but this painting has something almost Gothic about it.'

'Oh, do you really think so?' she said, and her enthusiasm was such that I thought her either insincere, or genuinely impressed by some as yet

55

still unidentified achievement of mine. 'You must remember to tell Georges that.'

'Georges?' I said, wondering if she meant the man who had invited me there.

'And you must be Mr Clare,' said a richly baritone voice at my back. And, turning, I found myself dwarfed by that Austrian emigré and man of parts, visionary, reformed racketeer and avid collector of occult artefacts; Schorsch Bruedelmann, but I must call him Georges for he insists on the French version of his name, was soon to become my friend.

He wore a dark blue velvet suit with ample lapels and deep side vents. His shirt, of silk, was the colour of damson wine, and round his neck he wore a tightly wound scarf of stark ebony. It was magnificently fluffed up and fluffed out, and pinning it to his shirt-front was a small, bright artefact of necromantic aspect, studded with tiny jewels; they shimmered as he moved.

He carried a fine mahogany walking-stick with a large, polished silver bob in the shape of a lion's head. His hands, which were disproportionately large even for such a heavy-boned man, were cluttered with rings of great value and variety. His leathery yachtsman's skin was the colour of dark gold. His bald head and hairless face shone with vigour. Indeed, the man had such richness of impact that my senses were momentarily flooded: I gawped. And Tara, smiling very brightly, placed her sensuous fingers on his heavy forearm. 'What were you talking about, my dear?' he asked her. His voice was baritone and yet rich with subtle intonations, as though he had perfected in it not a mere speaking tube but an instrument for musics that he himself invented.

'We were talking,' she said, 'about spies and actors.'

'We were not!' I said, and I felt horribly tainted and compromised. 'We were talking about this painting here.' And as I turned to the Lichterfelder Fête Galante and raised my hand, almost to prove my innocence, Tara, without a word, slipped away from Bruedelmann's side and disappeared into the throng.

'I found her,' said Bruedelmann, 'in Sagres.'

If you should address a remark to Georges Bruedelmann, he will give you his full attention and will weigh up the substance of your communication while searching sympathetically for the underlying fact. And you will feel, when he addresses you in his turn, that the intention of his communication is almost palpable. He has a nature so eclectic and so compounded that for a long time I could not agreeably respond to it, until by chance, some months ago in Torremolinos on the southern coast of Spain, I had an an experience which helped me to comprehend in unity my several and disparate impressions of this highly complex individual. I was walking along the promenade at twelve o'clock at night and stopped to observe the scene in a sprawling over-lit bar. A Spaniard in tight pink trousers and shimmering black jacket strummed a small guitar which he contrived to hold by the neck high up on his chest while his clever fingers found their way nimbly about the fret-board. A little behind him and to his left, a smaller, more sombre version of himself played, with a degree of small-stage melancholy, a stately, gilded harp. The bar, which was essentially a rudimentary counter with primitive cooking facilities under a large striped awning providing shelter from wind and weather to a dozen round plastic tables, was a shrine to all that is kitsch in the world; there were plastic madonnas and decorated ashtrays in the form of cheerful sea-creatures, and colourful arrays of artificial flowers. The place was further decorated with large full-colour photographs of egg and chips, and calamari, and cans of coke that sizzled with freshness. In a small space between the doleful tables a man who could have been Georges Bruedelmann's own twin brother was dancing a boisterous waltz with a small slatternly draggletail who laughed raucously as they lumbered about. He held her at arm's length, with wonderful vitality and self-confidence, and his heavy womanish hips and the curving bones of his arms seemed imbued with the significance of art, and his bald head and long sensitive fingers seemed to glow with life. He was foreign and yet cultured, eccentric and yet alien. In that moment I understood at last that what marked out Georges Bruedelmann and set him apart was his foreignness of spirit; it was this that made him at home in every society, and yet truly at home in none.

'I don't know much about art prices,' I said, pointing at the Watteau before us, 'but I suppose this work is worth a small fortune.'

'It is amusing,' said Bruedelmann, 'to listen to the opinions of experts on this matter. If you examine the figures in this composition you will find that they are all to be found in Monsieur Watteau's personal collection of red chalk studies. There is, additionally, documentary evidence to suggest that the work was executed during the summer of 1720, in London, when the painter was visiting the renowned Dr Mead, who later became physician to George II. But you know, he could not cure poor Monsieur Watteau's tuberculosis, and within a year the painter was dead.'

'Really?' It was a bit too much to take in. 'Do you mean to say that some experts have pronounced it a forgery?'

'Quite the contrary, Mr Clare. When Monsieur Watteau was admitted to the French Academy in 1712 he was registered as a painter of "fêtes galantes". Is this not a fête galante?' He waved his hand at the painting. 'And do you know,' he said confidingly, 'that you will find in the pigments of this work a characteristic degeneration which is common to many of Watteau's oil paintings?'

'Oh yes?' I didn't know at the time that Bruedelmann never makes pointless remarks.

'Oh yes! Monsieur Watteau was too impatient, do you see? He was wont to paint too quickly ... He spread the oil too thickly on his brush ...'

'So it's definitely not a fake, then?'

'Ah! My dear Mr Clare, I must tell you that Watteau oils are notoriously difficult to authenticate. It is true that this particular work is not to be found in the *Recueil Jullienne*, a contemporary catalogue of the painter's works, but neither will you find there certain other works by Watteau, among them the most celebrated oils: "Embarcation pour l'Île de Cythère" of the Louvre, and the popular "Pierrot".' The man's big, shiny sun-bronzed face hung before my eyes like a Byzantine icon, and there was about him then a frightening, uncanny knowingness. 'Ah, Pierrot, pauvre Pierrot ... that guileless unfortunate from whom nothing is hidden! It is interesting to note, in the light of what is to come, that the Pierrot of the latter work, affectionately known as "Gilles", bears the selfsame face of the village curate of Nogent, for whom the master painted a Christ on the Cross during the last few days of his life.'

What did he mean? What was the man insinuating? I winced to hear of Pierrot's guilelessness, his perspicacity, his singular lack of fortune.

'But that is not all, Mr Clare,' he continued. 'Not at all! This painting has a morbid stillness, does it not?'

'Absolutely.'

'There is an undisputed Watteau original entitled "The Dream of the Painter" which used to hang in the dressing room of Lady Walpole at 10 Downing Street. It has the same unmistakable quality as the Lichterfelder Fête Galante.'

'Presumably he painted that one, too, in the summer of 1720 ...'

But Bruedelmann ignored my remark. He leaned forward and whispered at me. 'It was painted by a Jew, Mr Clare! Yes, a *Jew* painted the Lichterfelder Fête Galante, in the time of the glorious Third Empire of France. But it is an *original*, you know.' He shook his head firmly in a big, almost comic display. 'No, Mr Clare, you may be sure it is not a fake.'

And then, as though his will had drawn me to it, I found myself looking hard at the little piece of paper tucked into the frame of the painting. It was a scrawled note: *This is the rightful property of Lothar Reh of Lichterfelder Ring, 1000 Berlin 45, and should be returned to him at the first opportunity. H.T.*

It was this urgent injunction to the reader, so flimsy and creased the strip of notepaper, so alarmingly shaky the handwritten English, that impressed me far more than the astonishing virtuosity of the forger of the work, for I had already recognized the handwriting on that note. I was certain that it was the same handwriting that I had been studying these past four weeks in the photostat pages of the Subject's Documentary. 'H. T.' I thought: who else but Hugo Thayer? The hairs prickled on the nape of my neck.

'Do you know,' I said, and I was suddenly gabbling, as though in the grip of a superior force, 'I was once on holiday in the South of France. It was the mid-seventies, in the area of Nice, and there were some young German drop-outs around. They were barely clothed and showed complete disregard for the passer-by, I mean they pissed and shat among the rocks which they had made their home. This painting here, this blighted vision of amusement, brings those kids to mind just as a smudge calls for something cleansing and astringent. Those German kids, it was as if they wanted to purge themselves, but in the astringent innocence of filth . . .'

Bruedelmann studied me for a full ten seconds; he was puzzled, or pretending to be so. I was reminded that Tara had said we'd been talking about spies and actors; in the silence of his intense scrutiny of me I felt wrapped around with layers of complexity and folly.

'That is very astute of you, Mr Clare,' he said at last. 'I too believe the artist had a vision. But what he saw was so monstrous in its time that he could not directly depict it; it was a vision of culture so deeply compromised that it was possible to address it only indirectly, by means of a deadly irony, an oblique glance, if you like, into an abyss that history had not yet opened in the European mind.'

'I suppose Lichterfelde is a suburb of Berlin?' I casually inquired. 'Is it because Lothar Reh lives there that the painting is called the Lichterfelder Fête Galante?' I wanted Bruedelmann to understand that I hoped the painting would soon be returned to its rightful owner; I am afraid I have always had this streak of sanctimoniousness.

'That is another story,' said Bruedelmann, briskly dismissing my unbidden piety.

He asked me what had brought me to Paris and I explained that I was here to research a writer, but that I had chanced to see Hugo Thayer's poster in a bookshop window . . . etc. He ignored my reference to Thayer and his posters, which were the cause, after all, of my being at the gallery, and remarked instead that Paris was a good place for research of all kinds; but how sad it was, he observed, that I was not here to research myself. To which I replied, in lambent mode, that it was not so easy to find payment for such work. He smiled. It pained him, he said, that so very few were able to research themselves, and yet the whole world depended on it; if we did not know ourselves we could not know what we did, and if we did not know what we did then we were no better than the playthings of unknown forces.

'May I see your book?' he asked, politely indicating the book I had bought from the bookshop man. With the greatest reluctance I passed it to him. In my anxiety to distance myself from it, I said, egregiously,

'This, actually, is not a reflection of how I am or how I think, but it is, ironically, along with my passport, my only means of self-identification.'

'Well ... exactly, Mr Clare,' said Bruedelmann; and now, suddenly, inexplicably, I felt that he and I were very much *on the same side.* He cursorily scanned a few pages at random and then studied for a moment the anachronistic photograph on the back of the dust-jacket.

'But my dear Mr Clare,' he said, and his eyes were sparkling with amusement, it is my duty to tell you that you do not even *look* like yourself.'

I took this in good part, and showed some appreciation of his wittiness. 'I find,' he said, handing the book to me, 'that the problem in writing well, as in living well, is precisely the dualistic nature of experience. There is process, which is flux and flow and is ceaselessly in time, and there is form, which is static and timeless. Our ways of thinking, our sciences and our arts are forms which we have wrenched from the flux of life. But vitality, the spirit, the mystery of being, all these remain in the flux, wouldn't you say so?'

'It doesn't sound as if you have a problem at all,' I remarked, impressed with his view of things, and astonished at his fluency in English.

'But we have language,' he continued, and he smiled graciously. 'Language, which is surely our greatest treasure, for it redeems us, and resolves the paradox of flux and form.'

'Really? How so?'

'Language is flexible, and sinuous. It is like a snake. And yet it is hollow. It binds the flux and it gives form; it lifts us out of time and still it remains in flux, in process, for it moves and changes its shapes in time. It expands its coils, or contracts its widths, here more transparently, there perhaps less so, and endlessly it turns and it turns upon itself until it is impossible to say where it ends and where it begins. And what flows in its hollow cavities is the very flux of life. It is vital, don't you think, it is the very life of culture itself to safeguard the hollowness of language.'

'Gosh, yes.' I was quite fascinated.

'Tyrants, of course, whether spiritual, political, cultural or economic, clog up that sacred hollowness. They bring death to all of us. But he who kills the snake of language is a killer in a deeper sense than he could ever imagine. And yet you may be sure, in his wicked heart he knows what he does.'

'I assure you,' I said, 'that I shall always endeavour to safeguard the hollowness of language.'

It was a congenial moment, and Bruedelmann and I exchanged a few chuckles.

But this confidential mood was shattered when Bruedelmann suggested, with ironic mien, that if I wished to research myself I should write a novel. I was instantly alerted to the undercurrents of our talk: what did he know about me, this man? Was he involved in The Commission? Or did he read minds, or what? He was saying, '. . . For the novel resists the flux of time and yet it gives form to our experiences within it. Because it is written and read in time it is process, Mr Clare. But when it is completed, or is not being read, it acquires a quality of timelessness, and this is form. And as it grows less important it slowly re-enters time and it becomes process again. But let us not forget that novels are reconstructions of ourselves; we should be mindful of the patterns that we make as we move in and out of time, making form of process and process of form.

And then, quite without rhyme or reason, he launched into the telling of a brief but harrowing tale of a certain 'New World' tribe of rain forest Indians and of one 'little Indian' in particular. But Bruedelmann's manner of narration was both *telling* and *knowing*, if I may make so bold with the language, and I felt extremely ill at ease as he spoke . . .

They had been children of the Sacred, who were the tribe's religious and cultural leaders, both man and woman, and they had learned the hallowed rites. Then there came from the living forest men with metal bodies, who bore dead trees for arms, which ate the flesh of humans with lightning. The metal men stole from the tribe its most sacrosanct possession, which was a chalcedony figure of polished petrified wood no bigger than a woman's breast; and scored upon it were the sacred lines which revealed the mysteries of Heaven and Earth, and proved the existence of other worlds and showed the paths which the spirits must seek in order to reach everlasting life. Two years passed of this new time, and then, out of the green, living forest the metal men came again.

They carried off young women. And when the women had died of the new deaths the metal men demanded that all the tribe's young women should be brought to their stockade. The Sacred men and women met in conference; the women must go to the metal men, but they should first treat their womens' parts with deadly poison, for only thus could the violations be brought to an end. And to safeguard their lives the young women should imbibe a protective preparation, so that death should come only to violators. Thus the young women prepared themselves; and being prepared they went to the stockade. Soon there were many deaths. Then the conquistadores resolved to avenge the deaths of their Christian brethren: in great force they fell upon the savages in their quiet village. They brought a great metal trunk which spewed forth fire and flying teeth which chewed trees into small parts; they ravished the children; they slaughtered everything that moved or breathed; they razed the village to the ground. Then they prayed to their fierce God, crossed themselves, and ate white leaves. And afterwards they made a great fire and burned all the bodies of their victims. Only when they had scooped up the ashes of the dead and had thrown them into the river did the metal men depart, and took with them their forest of killing trees.

The little Indian was then in retreat in the forest, in company with a girl-child of the same age. When they returned to where once their village had stood they found nothing but churned, blood-slaked earth. They fled into the living forest and took refuge among the trees. And they came to believe, these sacred children of the ravished tribe, that they had been chosen to restore the world that was lost; and to this end they must seek out the men with metal bodies and follow them to their own world, there to retrieve the sacred object inscribed with the sacred paths of everlasting life.

They surrendered themselves to a soldier of fortune; the new master sold the girl to buy a pack mule for his plunder, but he took the boy to Spain for he had realized that here was a trained healer who knew the lore of plants and herbs. He meant to make a fortune out of his 'littel Indyan' in the curing of rich, moribund Spaniards.

The boy, who was half dead with shock, saw in this man his own necessary, fateful guide and surrendered humbly to his will. He knew he must travel to the world of the metal men, where even the living were in the grip of death, and there retrieve the sacred object of the tribe. Some days passed and then his master took him aboard a ship, a thing he had never seen before, and brought him to a river so vast that time had no meaning between its banks. The boy then knew that his sense of mission was confirmed, and he trusted deeply that he would be guided, that he would find what he sought in the metal world.

In Spain his master set him to work, but kept him in ignorance of the language, and prospered and grew rich from the boy's labours, for his cures were efficacious and uncommonly benign. They came one day to a great house in Zaragoza where the little Indian treated for syphilis a famous nobleman and patron of New World explorers. In this house they were very kind to him, and fed him well, but the day came when they caught the little Indian in an act of theft; his hands had closed about a chalcedony artefact which the noble master of that house had got from the New World. They demanded an explanation, but he would give none. They commanded that he prostrate himself and beg for mercy, but he would not move. They begged him to confess his crime so that they might forgive him like good Christian men, but he would not speak. They were sorry, they said, but they felt moved to punish him severely, for he would not release his plunder; then they severed the tendon in his wrist and wrenched from his useless hand what they had stolen in the first place, and to remind him forever of his offence both to God and to Christian Spain, they took a hot iron and burned a hole in his tongue. And when this justice had been done they threw master and servant out into the road, where the master, now gravely disabused, beat his boy nearly to death, and abandoned him.

He did not know where he was, nor could he speak his woe; he was maimed, and entirely alone; home no longer existed, for it lay in another world and had been destroyed. If he had had a fleet of ships and as many unconquerable armies, and a thousand fortunes in gold, he could not have known where to go, nor how to find again the burned earth that was his cherished Amazonian world. But he did not die by the roadside of a grief beyond the comprehension of ordinary men. He resolved, instead, to live, and to learn the tongues of the beings about him, and to learn to read the strange figures which they drew on leaves, and to discover what to do with a map and how to make sense of it, and through its power to learn where he had come from and how to return there. And when he had found this knowledge he would seek the means to retrieve the sacred object, which he had found again in Zaragoza, and he would bring it with him to his Amazonian home. This was his duty and his life's work; it was the highest and best thing in the world.

'What was this Indian chap's sacred duty anyway?' I inquired of Mr Bruedelmann when it was clear that he was done with the telling.

'It was to do with a tree, Mr Clare. Have you ever noticed, I wonder, the strange, vertical symmetry of trees? Above the ground they are rooted in air and fed by light, and below the ground they have branches in the earth and are fed by matter. The earth is dark and full of riches, and it is where the dead live. And heaven is light and full of riches, and it is where the dead live.'

'You know,' I said, cutting right across his flow of thought, 'if this person had had his misfortune in the twentieth century he could have solved his problem by bringing in the services of a professional anthropologist.'

'You think so?' He smiled patiently. 'I think it would be difficult to find an anthropologist who knew himself, don't you? And if we do not know ourselves, what can we know?'

Bruedelmann talked for quite a while in similar vein, but I have scant memory of it. I remember that I became more and more fascinated by that artefact he was wearing on his shirt front. Perhaps there was a lack of oxygen in that overcrowded gallery but I seemed to fall under a kind of spell. I think it must have been during our conversation that Bruedelmann may have played some manner of psychological trick on me. As I got to know him better in the weeks to come he virtually admitted it.

I became aware of an endless procession of people coming up to Bruedelmann to take their leave of him. When the chance came I asked him if I could perhaps borrow his set of Hugo Thayer's posters. By all means, he told me, but on two conditions: that I returned them to him in person when he should have need of them again; and that I should read some papers, which, he assured me, identified with the matter.

'Please don't be offended,' he said to me, as I was myself taking leave of him, 'but it is very clear to me that you are not as you appear. But what is more interesting is that you are also not as you appear to yourself. We must remember, Mr Clare, that the mind has laws not unlike those of mirrors, and the falsities by which we live, and on which we ground our experience, are fated to be reversed and inverted in the events of our days. The more layers of delusion we have, the more complex and ironic will be our reverses.'

Well: first there was the matter of the delusory hotel. I took the metro from close by the gallery and got out at Hôtel de Ville, in itself an apparently reasonable thing to do; but in fact I was in the grip of language alone, for my decision had no real purchase on the world. You see, my hotel was actually close to Gare du Nord, a long way from where I now walked, confidently, past the Tour St Jacques with its howling, derisory gargoyles. For a time I gave no consideration to my surroundings; and then, quite suddenly, as though a house of cards had collapsed, my convictions entirely deserted me. I stood on a pavement in the midnight dark and I was prey to an overwhelming perplexity. *I had no hotel to go to;* or rather, I had to ask myself, *where in fact was I going, so assuredly; where was the true location of my hotel?* And what was I doing at Hôtel de Ville? Worse still, I had walked down a back street and into a seeming labyrinth of such streets beyond it. I tried the door of a cafe that seemed to be serving still, but it was locked. And then I seemed to remember that it had been my intention as the train had pulled into the station at Gare du Nord to book into a hotel in its environs. But this was a remembrance that I could place no confidence in, for it had about it an induced quality, and one that I was loath to credit.

Damn! Now what do I do? I had the sudden thought that my delusion was an early symptom of severe food poisoning. I remembered the early lunch I had eaten on the train: perhaps I was even now on the verge of collapse. That very nearly had me panicking; if I pass out on the pavement, I told myself, I will probably die there. And then my hand, which had been foraging in all my pockets, found Bruedelmann's visiting card. I looked about for a public telephone. There was none. I resolved to seek out a taxi; but there was none to be seen.

I hurried along a silent, ill-lit street and heard only my own footsteps. Then there floated into my mind an intensely clear picture of Georges Bruedelmann, and the gat-toothed girl on his arm. It was an impression made unpleasant by its very vividness. A few minutes later I emerged on to a grand boulevard. There were cars and people, and lights from shops and bars. I waved down a taxi.

'Hotel, any hotel. Une chambre,' I said, and quite automatically I gave him the card that Bruedelmann had passed to me at the vernissage. Barely three minutes later we stopped outside a hotel, *which, for whatever reason, I seemed to recognize.* It was the Hôtel Vienne. I wondered, as I went in . . . would I be recognized? Did I already have a room?

At the reception a well-groomed young man with flamboyant air-ace moustaches offered me a room with a shower and a toilet. I said to him in English,

'Do you know if I have a room here already?'

I thought he understood my words but he didn't seem to make any sense of my question. No doubt he saw in my face confusion, fatigue and not a little anxiety. He shrugged his shoulders and gently smiled.

'Kindly follow,' he said.

I dreamt that night of Lucia: she was carrying a glorious light, or was it her eyes that filled my dreaming awareness with celestial radiance. I grew aware that I was demanding something of someone and then it seemed she had plucked out her eyes and had given them to me. And in the same instant everything seemed to slant as if the horizontal plane was jerkily rising to become a slope under our feet and then everything went black. I awoke in the early hours and it came to me clearly and incontrovertibly that I had indeed checked into a hotel quite close to the Gare du Nord and there I had deposited my suitcase. This was confirmed in the morning when I found in my wallet the hotel receipt for the payment I had made in advance.

I also discovered, in the welcome light of the morning, that my room overlooked the river, and about three hundred yards to my right was Notre Dame. In the spring sunlight the cathedral was unforgettably beautiful: it was indeed a stately barque about whose prow the dark blue waters of the Seine swirled heavily. The slender white flying buttresses bestowed upon the structure a gracefulness that was undeniably spiritual; the twin towers, decorated with saints and gargoyles, stood like sentinels to the west; and in the robust April breeze the surface of the river was royal blue with tiny white crests of foam.

This was very like the view of the cathedral that the diarist had sought to capture in his drawings. I was almost inclined to believe that the Subject had studied it from this very window. Upon more careful consideration, however, I reckoned that a view given from a point of vantage somewhat closer to ground level and a little to the west of my own position would perfectly match the one that had obsessed the Subject. I found just the place on the Ile St Louis, which lay directly before and below me. On the western promontory of that island, where it tapered to a narrow point, there was a solitary tree, a bench, and a railing. I thought I would stroll over there after breakfast and put my calculations to the test. On my way to the dining room I stopped, on impulse, at reception.

'Telephone?' I said.

'Pour Angleterre, monsieur?' said the girl behind the desk.

'Yes, for England.'

'Veuillez prendre celui-ci.' She was a gentle girl, solicitous and kind. But she looked at me in silence, rather dolefully. I took the phone and dialled.

Lucia's flat was empty, or she wasn't answering the phone. I tried her parents' house. Sarah answered.

'Sarah, it's Mark. I'm ringing from Paris. Is Lucia there by any chance?'

'Lucia? No, she's not. She's away, remember?'

'Away?'

'She's in Wales. She must have told you she'd be away. They're doing some filming . . .'

As I replaced the receiver the girl at the reception said something to me in French. I shook my head and showed her the palms of my hands. I watched her working out her sentence in English. It was all so trying.

I said, 'Breakfast?'

'Oui oui,' she said gladly, pointing the way to the dining room.

They brought me a wide low basket full of cold croissants and some expensive little rectangles of butter with fleurs de lis on the wrapper. With cheerful mien I said to the waiter, 'Boiled eggs?' and he brought me a basketful of cold hard-boiled eggs. He smiled. Soon afterwards he brought me a bill for 98 French francs. What? Ah, room included.

'I stay,' I said to the waiter and gave him back the bill he had brought me. 'I rester,' I said again. 'You payer.' It was my little joke.

'Très bien,' he said, and whisked it away, along with the hard-boiled eggs.

I sat and reflected. I felt furious with Lucia. How could she not tell me she would be away? And then I had the thought that perhaps she had told me and I had forgotten.

The young man with the air-ace moustaches came in very smoothly like a glider. He explained to me in English that they would have to put me in a room without a shower if I wished to stay. He said that they were always booked up at this time of year.

'It is Notre Dame,' he said, and raised his eyebrows apologetically.

And then, promptly and with elegance, he placed his own personal shower at my disposal.

'That is very good of you,' I said, and got up from my table to shake his hand.

'With the compliments of the proprietor, Monsieur Clare.'

It was an uplifting conclusion to the paltry breakfast.

I devoted some time that day to a careful examination of Hugo Thayer's posters, and then I took a long, circuitous, touristic stroll through the streets of Paris in the environs of the hotel. Lucia was greatly on my mind; so much so that I seemed to encounter her look-alikes at every turn. But I realized soon enough that of the figures and faces that so appeared to resemble her, few actually did so in markedly physical ways. It was rather that I was prey to a compulsion to discover her in every proximate female form. I began to wonder if I wasn't going mad.

It was probably because of this general disorientation and bewilderment of the senses that I decided to buy a book of French phrases; although I had no intention of attempting to read aloud from it, I thought I might hold it under the noses of necessitous interlocutors in the event of harrowing incommunications. I noted that I had fallen into a condition of some considerable disquiet, brought on, no doubt, by the trying events of the last twelve hours.

At regular intervals throughout the day I inquired of the hotel reception staff whether *une demoiselle anglaise* had rung me from Wales. I was a pitiable tourist; and I didn't know the French for Wales, so that I was compelled to say England where I meant a quite different country – until I had combed through the book of French phrases – and for this I sincerely beg pardon of all Welsh persons.

Lucia rang me that same evening; I was in the bar at the time, disaffectedly watching a rugby match on French television. I rushed into the cabinet and picked up the receiver.

She had been a little breathless, as though she had been running; it was strange to think of her, standing in a telephone box somewhere in a Welsh valley, surrounded by the pitchy night, while I spoke to her from a telephone cabinet in a Parisian hotel bar. Across the room, through the high, wide windows and bathed in white floodlighting at a distance of a few hundred metres from where I stood, the cathedral was a numinous ornament of the night, scattering its secrets on to glimmering dark river waters. I tried hard to imagine what Lucia could see from her phone box in the valley. No sooner had I spoken to her than she instructed me to ring her back; I dashed to reception and bothered and bullied the thoroughly compliant young woman at the desk. At last. *At last . . .*

'Lucia,' I said, 'why didn't you tell me you'd be away?'

'There's something I have to tell you, Mark.' She was businesslike. Was she an hour ahead in Wales, or an hour behind? It was 8.35 p.m. in Paris. I suddenly began to sweat. 'I think we should stop seeing each other,' she said. A shout of laughter went up. 'Are you there? What's that noise?'

'It's a rugby match,' I said. I felt giddy and hot. I said, 'I don't understand, Luce. I mean, we'll have to talk it over of course. I don't think we should stop.'

'I don't see that there's anything to talk about, actually.' Her voice had the singular detachment of law. I wondered if it was very cold in her telephone box.

Gravely she said, 'There's someone with me.'

'Please Luce,' I said, 'please . . .' Then I paused and took a grip on myself; it was pitiful to fall into long-distance pleading. 'We must talk about it though, don't you think?'

I found out that she would be staying in the valley two or three more days, depending on the weather conditions. I immediately decided to travel to Wales the very next day. She clearly wanted to hang up. I went so far as to tell her that I wouldn't contemplate letting go until I saw in her eyes that she really meant us to part. And then I remembered that in my dream she had taken her eyes out of their sockets and had passed them to me on a plate . . .

Ten minutes later I was ready to leave. There were things of far greater importance to me that day than Hugo Thayer and his posters, or the whole damned enigma of The Commission. As I was settling my bill the man with the air-ace moustaches handed me a letter in a sealed envelope, and a sheaf of A4 papers in a transparent plastic folder. Scanning the cover page I found myself reading:

> Beinge the work of Your humble servant John Pike in dedycation to my sometime master Sir Francis Walsingham in this yeare 1589 of Our Lorde Jesu Christus and relatynge to the historie of Bartholomew of Gaillac, sometime clerke, wanderer, botaniste, agent of spyinge, and skryer of celestial entities.

And this, I told myself somewhat bemused, *identifies with the matter*? For it was, of course, from Georges Bruedelmann, along with the letter in the sealed envelope, which I read in the taxi on the way to that hotel near Gare du Nord where I had left my suitcase the day before. In fact I had pointlessly lugged it from Canterbury to Paris, and now I was about to lug it all the way back again. The letter read:

Dear Mr Clare,

I hope you found my hotel to your liking. Certainly I am confident that you experienced no difficulty in finding it. A propos, sir, I must tell you that I saw at once that you were spying, but you do not know who you are spying for, nor even why you are doing it; you are a man who pretends to be adrift just so that he can shirk his true responsibilities. You are a little Indian who reads strange books not because he wishes to return to himself, nor because he wishes to change the world, but because he wishes merely to appease it. I feel duty-bound to remark upon this habit you possess and which perspicuously cloaks your mind. You know where your home is, but you pretend to yourself that you cannot find your way back to it, that you have lost it perhaps for ever. Perhaps too you are so bold as to tell yourself that it does not exist! You do this so that you can enjoy a freedom which is only given to those who take responsibility for being free. I lay these facts before you only because yours is an exile that is even worse than his.

Please try to remember me with kindness, for I set you adrift quite close to my hotel, and took care to provide you with my card. You see, Mr Clare, mine is a half-way house, and I welcome your return to it, for I am fully confident that we shall meet again quite soon. Indeed, I look forward to it.

Georges Bruedelmann

6

For we ought not, any more than men, hide and bury within the
earth that which God has revealed to us women.

Marie Dentière, *Epistre très utile* . . . (to Queen Marguerite of
Navarre), 1539

Master John Pike, formerly a soldier and subsequent secretary to Sir
Herbert Kittlesleigh of Noke, records in his arduous prose many of the
conversations he had with Bartholomew, both on their way to Lippstadt
in the late spring of 1581, and on the occasion of their meeting some two
years later at La Rochelle on the western coast of France. In addition to
such partially verbatim records there exist the narrative reports which
Pike sent back to England in the course of the Lippstadt Mission, and the
final report on its unsatisfactory conclusion penned soon after his return
to London. There are also some official commentaries appended to these
documents which give insight into the organization of Sir Francis Walsingham's spying operations and the structure and administration of his
projects. And there is a detailed line drawing of Bartholomew himself, in
enduring black ink, unsigned but dated December 2nd, 1572 and stamped
'Offys of Defense'. It portrays a man with short-cropped hair, which is
listed as black, wavy and thick. Alongside the identifying portrait there
are fragments of sketches on a larger scale showing the man's arms and
the form of his fingers and his feet, from which it appears that Bartholomew was slenderly built. But his constitution was robust and he had
excellent health. He weighed one hundred and thirty pounds and was five
feet and four inches tall. He had dark brown eyes of a very shiny quality,
and a bulbous nose. His mouth was wide and his lips somewhat ill-
formed. His face lacked symmetry so that he would always appear to be
looking away to the side, and his left ear was higher than his right by
about half an inch, and bigger too, and more rounded in the lobe. Two
special distinguishing marks are noted: he had a small scar across the
bridge of his nose; and under his chin he had a large mole measuring half
an inch across and sprouting five white hairs. But these were hidden
characteristics for he had a swarthy Mediterranean complexion and by

custom he wore a beard. On a separate sheet of paper glued to the back of the drawing are written the following words:

Qualitys:
In speech; mild and courteous and in manner and disposytion amenable.
Of intelligence; spirited and quick, ingenious, of Catholyck lerning, having five languages and much science and knowledge of antiquities.
In what manner specially skilled; in herbalistic and medicinal science, in Cabbalistic and magical lore, in alchymical experymentation, and in resource-ful purveying of tricks.
Of temperament; bold and venturesome.
In religious inclinaytion; God-fearing but having no allegiance to any church.
In his secret person; rebellious and much critical of his masters.

It was on the road to Lippstadt that Bartholomew related to John Pike something of his early life, and told how he had come to dwell in a Benedictine monastery having been born a peasant child. In the following account it is Bartholomew who speaks and John Pike is his interlocutor:

'My father died about the time I was old enough to gather wood alone. And my mother was taken from this world in the hour of my birth. He laid her death to my account and left me for the wolves to take. I lay all day by the slow river. Whispering reeds swayed over me and the willows creaked. I was not my father's son. But my mother's mother came and bade the hawks watch over me, and bade the wind bend the long stalks of the reeds that the sun might not burn me. And at evening when the sand was cooling and the reeds were turning from green to blue she came again and brought me home. She was my grandmama, but she was younger then than I am now. Grandmère was all my family then. She was a wise good woman.'

'How so, a wise woman?'

'One day she took herbs and bade me piss into a bowl. She strewed seeds and leaves over the water. She told me to sit quiet while she warmed my water over the fire. And when steam arose from the bowl she began to sing. They were words I had never heard before, nor ever heard again. And when she stopped her singing and closed her eyes I thought she slept, but I was awake still, and fearful. Then I saw dancers of shadowy form, even in our hut. By their motions they made me sleep, or I seemed to sleep, but I thought I was awake. Yet a voice told me I dreamed. Grandmère spoke to me. "They will come for me," she said, "and put me to the fire." And I heard my own small voice, like a reed piping, "And me? Will they put me to the fire, Grandmère?" She

71

answered, "You will run into the wild, my son, and run until your body burns of its own fire and when you fall you will sleep, and when you wake you will run again like the wind. Hawks will guide you to the stream where the great beech has fallen among stones of an ancient house. You will hide there, my little Bartholomé, and be silent as the fish that time will show you beneath the drinking leaves." I slept. And when I woke I had no remembrance of what we had done . . .'

'How can this be, Bartholomew? For you plainly remember now.'

'. . . until a day came when she took me to walk with her in the fields. She showed me then the blue—green hills to the north and told me I should have my eyes upon them ever as I ran when the day was come for me to flee my home. "And I will give you five stones, my child, and when you sleep in that place where you have fallen you shall place these stones about you, two stones on the left side, two stones on the right side and the one dark stone is for the head. And when you wake you must run again to the hills." "What shall I do with the stones, Grandmère?" "Three times only you may rest with the stones about you, and then you must cast them as far as your strength will make them fly, and with each stone you must call my name. Be sure to cast each stone in a new direction and forget not my name." Then we went to the river shore and we took smooth stones and we practised these things together. Many times I lay down and made to sleep with the stones about me just as Grandmère showed me. And always, after the third sleep, I threw them far from me. And after each stone . . . I called her name . . . Aye, aye. Grandmère. I called her name. And I wept for the sadness of the stones and for her name which I had cast away so many times. Then Grandmère took me in her arms. She rocked me in her arms and wept with me. First her cry was thin and dry like a goat's cry, then it changed to a flowing sound, sweet and deep . . .'

'What's this man? Are you snivelling?'

'Her soul was singing.'

'Her soul? A-singing?'

'When I was a boy I slept by the slow river in Grandmère's arms. And I dreamed I had my home in a great tree that grew beside a river half as wide as the sea.'

'A blasphemous old crone. A pagan ceremony. I warrant she was a witch.'

'Did I not tell you she was wise, and good?'

The following record of Bartholomew's rabbit supper and the promise he gave that night comes later in Pike's account. It is extremely improbable that Bartholomew would have confided such compromising information about himself while still in Walsingham's employ.

'When I was still a small child a man came at evening and shouted. Like a drunkard calling for ale he called for my grandmother in a fierce voice, and she went out to him. He carried a stick, and had a rabbit by the hind legs. He shook blood from the carcass and his speech was harsh. Then Grandmère called for me to show myself. My knees shook and my heart pounded in my chest but I went out to him. Grandmère told me to be wise, and then she went away down the hill in the dusk. I wanted to run after her but I kept still. I walked with him into Grandmère's house. I wanted to be brave.

"You like rabbit pot, boy?"

His eyes were yellow as flame and he smelt of sweat and horse-shit. His arms were bare and I saw strong sinews and manly thews like knots of wood. He gazed upon me wildly and I felt fear. He threw stick and rabbit to the floor and plucked me up and smelt my face and told me to breathe on him. He smelt my chest and he smelt my stomach and then he put me down. I knew he was sad then.

"Give me your hand, little boy."

His hand was hard and full of strength. I asked him, "Are you my father?"

"No."

"Are we going to cook rabbit pot for Grandmère?"

"Old women need no meat. This rabbit is ours, boy."

"I will give her some of mine," I said. We skinned the rabbit and threw into the street the parts we would not eat. Then we cooked it in the pot and late that night we ate.

"Why are we eating rabbit together? Don't you have a house?"

"We are eating rabbit to remember your mother. I have no house but roots of trees, holes in the ground. But once I lived at the château. With the horses."

I was wonder-struck. "You have seen the Seigneur?"

A strange dark look was in his eye. He grasped me at the shoulder and shook me like a dog.

"Are you going to beat me?" I cried. But he clasped me to his chest. "Are you my father now?"

"How should I be your father, boy?"

I had no answer. I felt how he was sharp and sour inside, and I felt his sorrow pass into me. It seemed to go into my body, so that I was angered against him. I shouted then, "Why are we eating rabbit?"

"Stay, little boy." I fought his embrace but he was like rope about me. "Don't you remember your mother?"

No. I knew it was a fault. But I knew not how I had done this wrong. Had I been asleep? I began to cry.

"Now, now. Put tears away. You don't remember her, and that's no sin. She died when you were born."

"I think I remember now," I said. But I was full of doubt.

"Not you, little boy, but I remember her, I. You have forgot your mother but she has not forgotten you. She is with you. I can see her. She is in you, I feel her." He was silent then for a long while. With hot rabbit supper in my belly I fell asleep. And when I awoke he was carrying me through the night and I saw the bright stars like thorns above his head. I heard an owl calling, and the air was thick with the sound of the cicadas. We stopped among alder trees and he put me down.

"Here it was I last saw her alive. Here your mother kissed me. She said she would love me for ever. Feel the night, boy. Smell the night. Like a black flower."

But I found it hard to be wakeful. I lay on the soft ground under the alders and a sleep was upon me.

"She and me. We were to be man and wife but two days away. Don't you sleep now, boy." He shook me and pulled my ears until my eyes were wide open. "You must listen. You must remember. Later you will understand." And I was thinking then, this man is my father, and he has come to find me and to tell me what I need to know. He is my father and I am not to know it. This is his will. I said to him . . .

"You are not my father."

"That's true," he said. But he spoke again, hard into my ear. "Would you like to be my son?"

"Yes, yes!"

"Listen to me!" His breath hissed and he breathed into my ear. "If you will be my son then you must hate them for ever. And when you are a man you must fight them in every way you can. Until you have brought them down. Those bastards who live on our backs and rape our women. The ones who treat us like dogs, nay worse than dogs. D'you hear, d'you hear me, boy?" He shook me like the wind scattering embers. Terror and confusion overwhelmed me. I howled into the night.

"Shsh! Be still! Be still, my son!" He thrust my head under his jerkin and I heard his heart beating. The man's chest was stained with wine and my hair stuck fast to his skin. Sweat and wine and a scalded spirit. This was my father and yet was not.

74

"Who are they, Father, the ones I must hate? I will hate them, Father, I promise it."

"The masters, my son. That damned Seigneur!" '

'This was dire misfortune, Bartholomew. But I have not understood you. Tell me again. Were you the child of this man? I fear he was a vagrant. A desperate one.'

'He took me home to Grandmère, and he spoke not a word, but peered about him as we went through the fields. At our door he clasped me to him. Goodbye, my son. I have never seen him since that time.'

'And he was your father, Bartholomew?'

'He was, and yet he was not. But I have more to speak of, John. Before the seasons had come round again my grandmother was taken. But she knew the day, and she placed in my hand the little bag of stones and bade me run. *Vite, vite! Cours Bartholomé!*" I ran and ran.'

Lucia was filming in a valley some three miles outside Dinas Mawddwy. According to the Ordnance Survey map, the telephone box stood at a fork in a winding farm road which threaded the length of the valley. A chapel stood opposite the phone box, and there was a bridge over a stream about fifty yards beyond.

There was a complete standstill on the M25, and suddenly there was snow: big flocks of it, like morsels of fresh white bread across the windscreen. In that slowly churning, harrying whiteness I could barely make out the rows of stationary cars about me. I switched on the windscreen wipers. Slow regular sweeps; so patiently they wipe across.

Underfoot, the snow was crisp on Mansfield Road; precarious cyclists came arduously out of the gloom. I had reluctantly decided to spend the night in Oxford, about half-way to Dinas Mawddwy. I walked towards the Bodleian Library where I planned to sit, think, and thaw out. I thought incessantly of Lucia. And I thought of my fear of losing her; it filled my mind, insistent as the road, as the wild white weather.

The custodian at the Bodleian took a look at my old reader's card and told me to apply for a new one: 'It's white plastic, sir. Last you forever.' I thanked him and walked up three flights of ancient wooden stairs into the Upper Reading Room. It was packed with readers. Old memories flooded back: the interminable shuffling of feet and rustling of paper; the sniffing and coughing, and the sighing. I remembered the frustration: intellectual, but substantially sexual too; the despair: intellectual, but substantially social too; the anxiety: free-floating. Most unsettling of all, from my own point of view, was the occasional glimpse of some astonishingly beautiful woman. You might be reading linguistics, or Pope, or be immersed in the watery depths of the novel, when one such being would chance to pass within the compass of your gaze. Don't look up! Too late! Ah, fatal, fatal quickness!

I moved through the great high-ceilinged Upper Reading Room and looked about at the readers. Time had transposed the lank-haired seers of my day. Now the close-cropped Troiluses of a youth unemployment movement stormed the paper garrisons and threw old heirlooms in the air; in their sharp faces there were vague shadowings. I found an empty place and sank down against the hard, curved back of the chair. In front of me, in the little cubicle of space, a half dozen books lay open. I leaned forward casually and chose one at random; I started to read, idly, as one does.

> ... and this relationship is nowhere more evident than in this little known work of Piet Goris, minor master of the seventeenth century. The esoteric practice under discussion is clearly revealed to us here: we see that the process of applying paint to canvas is an intense, concentrated act of the mind in which there are invoked a number of geometrical forms of a mandalaesque significance, whose everyday representational qualities, far from serving the main point of the work, make immediate sense out of magic in an entirely fortuitous way. We come away with the irresistible impression that those elements of the painting which are for us the very real objects of our daily experience merely subsist for the artist; they are the jetsam of a dream coincidentally redeemed ...

I studied the photograph of the painting under discussion. The compositional elements were highly characteristic of Dutch painting of the period, with its unsentimental attention to detail, its peculiarly practical cast of light, its obvious relish for pots and pans and everyday objects of work and provender. Studying it then I seemed to understand how a people had been liberated from the oppressive baroque of the Roman Catholic Church, and a nation forged through the sheer commercial appeal of tubs and barrels. And I recalled, too, the stamps on envelopes sent to me by the Interested Parties.

> There are other exciting examples of the genre to be found in 'Art and the Esoteric Science' 1978, Roar Rasmussen; 'Occultist Traditions in Western Art' 1947, Eduard Schaffer; and 'Geometry, Gematria and the Golden Section' 1967, Frans van der Wee.
>   ... happily however, as with all traditions which are deeply rooted and

which serve to give form and expression to energies deriving from dissatisfaction with prevailing and oppressive orthodoxies, occult art continues to thrive in our modern age, as does its critical history in the discipline of art occultism. For a lively and astute discussion of contemporary trends the reader is referred to S. Bruedelmann's monograph in 'Art Occultism' No. 146 pp. 67–102.

'Do you mind?' a soft voice sounded close to my ear. I whipped round and looked up into the face of a woman of about 25. It was a thoughtful face, and kind, adorned with blue tortoise-shell spectacles that seemed to sink into the flesh. I saw buoyant dark-brown hair and pale, greyish-blue eyes. She was wearing a shapeless smock in blue needlecord, displaying at the open neck the exquisite lacework of a blouse of white silk.

'Sorry!' I whispered. 'Is this your seat?'

She gave a forceful nod, but her manner was not unfriendly.

I hurriedly whispered, 'Can I just make a note of something?' I scrabbled for the yellow tickets. As I wrote down the reference for Bruedelmann's monograph she peered over my shoulder.

'Are you interested in the subject?' She sounded enthusiastic and I gave a vigorous nod. She said. 'You won't find the Bruedelmann monograph I'm afraid.'

'Why not?'

'Pinched,' she murmured. She continued, 'But if you're really interested I've got a photocopy of the whole thing.'

'Gosh!' I said. 'Do you think . . .?' My voice had risen to speaking level and I became aware of an elaborate display of baleful glances from other readers. 'Do you think I could have a look at it?' My new friend blushed, nodded, took a yellow ticket and scribbled down her name and phone number.

'I haven't got it with me,' she said. 'You'd better give me a ring. I usually don't get back till late.'

I thanked her warmly and then crept away. There was a quality to the encounter . . . As I walked down the wooden stairs I knew I would see this woman again.

At the height of the lambing, blizzards were sweeping the country; it became clear that my trip to Wales must be abandoned. It was not even certain that I would be able to return to Canterbury without considerable difficulty and delay. I organized a bed for the night and then, on impulse, I rang the number of the telephone box. It was half past six in the evening and I thought it must be pitchy night in the snow-filled valley near Dinas Mawddwy . . . but I was desperate to speak to Lucia. I listened to the ringing tone; did the phone ring stridently, compelling in its wilderness? I found that I was counting the rings. After three minutes I was even more determined to wait there for as long as need be . . . then somebody answered. A male voice spoke a few words in Welsh. In English I asked if the photographers were still at the Williams's cottage.

'Oh yes,' he said, speaking now in English. 'The photographers are in the cottage, yes.'

I introduced myself and told him that I needed to get a message to the photographers; could he possibly carry it for me? He promised to do so at once, whereupon I thanked him profusely, passed on the message, told him I would wait by the telephone for the reply, ensured that he first wrote down my number . . . and hung up. He was a very gentle soul, and I had pressed him, but . . .

Twenty minutes later Lucia rang me.

'Well,' I said, immensely relieved to speak to her, 'how are you?'

'Fine,' she said, with a voice of glass. 'Why are you ringing me, Mark?'

'How's the filming going, Luce?'

'We've had a few problems. You know . . . the weather mainly.' She spoke mechanically. 'But it's nice being here. The valley's lovely.' It pained me intensely to hear her speak like that. 'Look Mark, I'm not coming back to Canterbury.'

'What?'

'I'm probably going to America. I've reached a decision, Mark.' Her tone of voice suggested that my bad behaviour had at last become intolerable. It's no good apologizing, her voice implied. My chest constricted and I held my breath.

'I'll just hang around,' I said, forcing the words, 'it'll blow over.'

'Oh Mark,' she said, 'what's the point? Nobody even knows who you are. I mean you clearly don't, do you?'

'What?' Now I fought to speak. 'That? That's a reason for ditching me? Know thyself! That's the culminating pronouncement of the Appollonian Oracle, and you blame me for finding it problematic! Christ, Lucie, that's grotesque. You think just any block of wood knows what it is, let alone a *person*! You think you know who *you* are, Lucia? Jesus wept!'

I stared into an inner wilderness. Was he with her? Did she have someone there?

'I'm coming up to Wales,' I said. 'I'm coming to see you.'

'Don't,' she said, and her voice was full of terrible warning. 'I'll never forgive you.'

'The female,' I said, 'can be unbelievably hard. She can push the runt to the wall . . . she can . . .'

'The female can do what has to be done,' she finished for me. Suddenly her teeth had begun to chatter.

I said, like a caring robot, 'Lucy, love, you're cold . . .'

She replied, on a wave of mustered affections, 'Mark, I'm so sorry . . . I have a grand impulse to change my life . . . I'm so sorry underneath. But I know it's for the best. For you too, I know it. Honestly, I promise. I really do love you, you know.'

I was thickly buttoned up and walking; it was four or five degrees below and there were deep drifts of snow beside the road, and all about me the hills were solemn and glittering white. I couldn't see a light anywhere. The car had died on me and I had abandoned it. I was heading for a bed and breakfast I had spotted a mile or two back along the way. The night was preternaturally still, and the sounds of my own ice-wracked progress seemed to fill the world. I was unnerved, frightened even, by the unreality of it. My coat felt bulky, wooden, cumbersome; I fell over. Some way behind me I heard a car approaching. I turned where I sat and saw its lights. I struggled up, and waved. How cold I was, suddenly!

It was a Volkswagen beetle, driven by a woman. She was a very self-possessed individual and didn't seem at all reluctant to stop for me in that desolate night-ridden place. I spoke to her through the open window of the car but I could not make out her face. She said she would gladly take me further along my road, and I was effusive in my thanks. My teeth were chattering in my head and my hands were numb as I clambered unadroitly into the car. She was disinclined to talk and I quickly fell into a doze.

Some time later I heard a scratching at the roof of the car. At first I took it to be a low-hanging branch that had scraped us as we passed, but the sound persisted so I asked the driver what she thought it might be. She said it was a creature of the night.

'What sort of creature of the night?' I inquired, courteous as ever. In fact I longed to sleep.

She replied, 'They are countless as the stars. Some are as tall as a tower and as wide as a road, and some are a hundred times smaller than a single grain of salt.'

And now, in the near distance, I could see a light shining in a window, and a sign that welcomed the traveller.

'It is waiting,' she said. There was something very strange about her voice. 'Waiting for your soul to fly away.'

And then it seemed the damn thing was banging on my cheeks and shining a glaring eye. I tried to brush it away. I wanted to poke my finger into its brilliant round eye.

It said, 'Hey! Wake up! You must wake up!' And then it started to pull my hair.

'Drink this brandy,' it said. I was certain now that it wasn't a creature of the night but an ordinary man. He was standing over me, trying to persuade me to get up. A few feet away I saw a car. The interior light was on and the headlamps were shining. There was a steaming drizzle all around.

'What?'

'Are you all right? You were lying in the road!'

'I'm freezing,' I said.

'Was that your car up the road?'

I nodded.

He helped me into his car and together we drove to a house with a big bed and breakfast sign hanging ten feet above the roadside. I felt awful, as if I'd had a terrible shock but couldn't remember what had caused it.

'Now you'll be all right!' said the man.

'Who are you?' I asked.

'I'm Hugo Thayer,' he said.

Then I knew it must be a dream and I struggled to wake from it. There was a film over my eyes and my body was heavily cloaked and swaddled. At last I awoke and switched on the bedside lamp. I was roasting, and gasping for a drink. My fingers were hot, red and tingling and my body surfaces itched from head to foot. As I gulped down water from the tap I discovered that I was wearing all my clothes; I was bewildered and half asleep. *It was a dream, all right*, I said to myself, *but why am I fully clothed?*

I discovered that it was ten fifteen in the evening; I had slept for at least two hours. On impulse I rang the number of the woman I had met in the Bodleian Library. Dammit, I thought, dammit all . . . let's get back to work.

Victoria's house is dark, cramped and in Jericho; it has five rooms in all, and a tiny back garden foreshortened by Oxford's gloomy canal. The place has an atmosphere of dispirited eroticism probably engendered by the sexual antics of former student tenants. The garden is full of snails, and in the morning, Vicky relates with a sort of zealous horror, there are silvery trails on the kitchen floor from the patient foraging of slugs, 'This is England,' she cries, and claps her hands.

She is five foot four inches tall and weighs about 120 pounds. She tends to wear loosely flowing one-piece dresses of cotton or velvet; her hair is dark and curly and got up in heavy Romantic tresses; her eyes are changeable in expression and a quiet grey—blue in colour; a slightly sour scent emanates from her when she moves suddenly. Most strikingly, she is a very good listener and seems to draw words out of her interlocutor, taking them deep into herself as though they had entered another element.

She led me into her cosy front room, which is gently lit and lovingly draped with shawls and curtains.

'Ma and Pa live in Great Yarmouth in a huge old house with Gothic turrets. Pa's a bit of a tyrant really. It's because he's surrounded by females. Helen, that's my sister, she's twenty-eight, she's a nurse. She works in the local hospital so that she can visit them easily. Ma's got this compulsion to do jigsaw puzzles. By the way, I'm half Welsh, can you see it? She does a bit of gardening, too, of course, and some needlework. I used to think she lived entirely for Papa, but I don't know any more. You can never tell with mothers and fathers. Don't you think?'

While she talked she watched my face intently. She seemed to be saying, 'I'd never allow myself to bore anyone, you know.'

'Of course we all love him dreadfully, or we think we do. That's what we tell each other anyway. He's like the sun in our lives, well, less so now. A bit bloody, though, and red and blurred. He likes to think he guides our lives and you'd think he did it with complete indifference, as though we were all totally foolish anyway so we could never really follow his advice, even if we could see its value! So we all tend to bungle things for Daddy. It's like a gift I suppose. We all love him, don't we.'

'What sort of things do you bungle?' I asked her. We were drinking a dry white German wine, which seemed an outlandish drink in the raw, clinging cold of that Oxford evening. I had the impression that she was showing me only her weaknesses, but not so that I wouldn't otherwise be frightened away; rather she seemed to be implying to me, subtly, that her weaknesses were actually her strength.

'The intellectual life, of course,' she answered. 'What else? I'm supposed to be half-way through a degree in art at the Ruskin but I took a year off because I got side-tracked by this art-occultism. And before I came to the Ruskin I was studying natural sciences at London.

'Sounds . . .' I searched for the word, '. . . pretty eclectic. A great life, if you can afford it.'

'Pa keeps shelling out for me. He bought this house. He takes responsibility for *everything*.'

I took a sip of wine and had a momentary vision of Lucia; her eyes glittered like the peaks of a snow-capped mountain in Wales.

Victoria seemed to slip into a private sadness. Her left hand came up and she pushed her hair back. Her forearm was white and lightly shaded with fine, dark hairs. She had a slim blue watch strap that made her wrist puffy. Her hands were small, her fingers short and pointed, her palm and thumb were pulpy. She shot me a quick sidelong glance and saw that I was staring.

'Are you hungry?' she asked.

'I thought we might go out and have a meal somewhere,' I suggested mildly. 'If you can spare the time.'

'I'd like that,' she answered.

We went to an Indian restaurant on the Cowley Road. It didn't surprise me that she opted for a hot, spicy curry; I chose milder foods and bathed them in yoghourt and graced them with delicate cool slices of cucumber. She continued to talk about her father, so much so that I felt she was waving the idea of him before me, almost as though she was testing a possible lover. I learned that he was connected with various government offices and agencies, that he had been involved in parapsychological warfare techniques during the war, and that he was a passionate and gifted inventor.

I studied her while she ate; even her way of taking food into her body was erotic. I found myself thinking about her inner organs, the coiling intestine, the liver. There was about her a quality of dank fertility. And despite the forwardness of her conversation I sensed that she was a highly introspective individual.

'I'm sorry,' I said, for she had caught me staring again, '. . . I was miles away.' But she gave me a look that intimated, on the contrary, that I had been very close indeed.

Remembering my purpose, and my present woe, and suddenly tiring of this mild flirtation, I asked her about her interest in art-occultism. She told me that she had attended a lecture on the subject, quite by chance, one evening about a year earlier, and her interest had developed from that beginning. The lecturer, who was a middle-aged Czechoslovakian woman, had looked every inch a witch.

'Her hair was full of henna, but it was obviously so black anyway that the effect was a sort of black crimson, if you can imagine that! She had very long hair, all the way down to the waist. She wore it quite naturally. And she had all sorts of talismans and bangles. But every bit of her clothing was natural.'

After the lecture Victoria had gone up to the platform to ask the speaker for a reading list. She noticed that the woman had a very strange smell about her.

'Like iron,' she said, 'that's been left immersed in water for a very long time. But the strangest thing about her was that when I was speaking to her I became incredibly alert. But I was totally relaxed too. And everything was suddenly intensely vivid, and sort of new, really, as if it had only just come into existence and hadn't had time to run down ... And in the college bar afterwards I noticed that people were looking at me strangely, as though something had been added. Or taken away, possibly.'

'Are you still in touch with this woman?'

'Oh yes. She lives near Celle, in West Germany.'

'Celle? What's the nearest big town?'

'Hannover. But I think she's planning to go back to Czechoslovakia. To Prague, I think. They're making difficulties for her though, the authorities, I mean. Georges Bruedelmann is helping her. He's a wonderful man. Herta, oh Herta's her name ... she lives in a funny little house just outside Bergen.'

'Bergen?'

'It's where they had the camp. It's just a short walk through the birch woods.'

'The camp?'

'Oh ... the death camp. You know ... Belsen.'

As we drove back to Jericho she started to hum; at first I thought I was hearing things, for the sound was not a melody so much as a signal of some kind. When I became aware that it was my passenger making the sound I found it quite unnerving.

'What *is* that?' I asked her.

'Oh,' she replied, casually, 'it's just an energizing technique.'

'For energizing what?'

'The whole being,' she said.

'Well,' I said, 'you'll be interested to know, and I gave her a sly, sidelong glance, 'it's also energizing me.'

'Well of course it is,' was her prompt reply.

We had returned to Vicky's Jericho house and it was nearly midnight. I hadn't wanted to compromise the romantic atmosphere of the evening by asking her to put me up, nor did I wish to find myself out on the street with nowhere to go at twelve at night. It had been too easy, in the last few hours, to flow along in the current of things, but now it was necessary to decide. She had left the room for a moment and I was browsing in her bookshelves; there was an equal distribution of books on art and art history on the one hand, and natural sciences on the other. In addition there were a number of books on the New Physics and a couple of dozen novels. On the bottom shelf I found books on the healing powers of plants, on acupuncture, some astrological reference books, and an assortment of theosophical writings including Blavatsky, Gurdjieff, Ouspensky and some German-sounding writers that I had only vaguely heard of. Suddenly I had the quite distinct impression that Vicky was standing immediately behind me. I started to say something to her but when I looked round I was alone in the room.

'I'll be right down,' she called to me from above.

I sat on the dismantleable block-foam sofa and put my hands behind my head.

'I couldn't hear you from upstairs,' she said as she entered the room. She was wearing a flowing silken nightrobe. She had done something to her hair and her throat was uncovered. It seemed whiter than ever. She bent down towards the coffee table in front of me and an exquisite scent wafted towards me from her breasts. I noticed that she wore an amulet on a thin silver cord around her neck. She coolly, deliberately breathed into my face and I saw in her eyes and around her mouth a self-confidence that was almost rapacious.

'Do you like me?' she murmured, and there was a wild, suppressed delight in her voice.

'Yes. Yes I do,' I answered.

She sat down beside me and her head went back and then rolled towards me slightly; her lips parted, her tongue waited.

'Are you sure?' she asked, and her breath came in short gasps so that all her fragrances played upon me.

'Well, actually,' I said, thinking it only fair to warn her in advance, 'I'm a bit depressed at the moment . . .'

'You don't have to worry about that,' she said, and now her sexual self-confidence released in me the most extraordinary rush of desire. I went to kiss her but she placed her palm flat on my lips. There was a cool majesty in her eyes.

'Come,' she said. 'Come upstairs with me.'

Sex, like art, I've always thought, is best practised only by those with an aptitude for it; otherwise it can be embarrassing, even life-diminishing, where what is hoped of it fails. Myself, I confess it, I've always been somewhat inept in making love, and have thought myself all the more English for it; but that was before I met Vicky the witch.

In the event it was like falling into the torrent only to discover that I could float, swim for ever, merge with the mass of energies and make it mine, even as it drew me into dissolution.

Vicky my love: I thought you'd be a little too plump for me under your flowing nightgown, but you were curving, tense, rounding, of urgent female proportion, fragrant and sulphurous like bread, like earth, and endlessly moist, and hard and soft, and wide and strait and sonorous. I kissed her kind sweet mouth and found her mind there, waiting; and I kissed her in between her soft, rounding thighs and met that presence there that she was all expression of, dark oceanic, humid flower.

Her touch was imperious and supplicant, sustaining, empowering; her fingers, palms, lips, tongue were instruments of love's intelligence. She talked to my body in her own rich language of caressings, sighs, yearnings and made of it a copious herdswoman's banquet; I have never known such ease, such luxury of unselfconscious revelling . . . spirit, mind, body of love.

Shuddering, her body seemed to take me up to another plane; and I was like water then, in runnels of sand by the great motile ocean.

My sleep that night was deep and dreamless, and I awoke next morning refreshed and full of hope. I was alone in the bed, but on the violet pillow beside me a piece of violet notepaper lay pinned; it bore a blue scrawl of handwriting, as though she had written in pen directly on to the pillow-slip.

It read:

> *Hello.*
> *Back very soon.*
> *Don't go.*
> *Vicky.*
>
> *P.S. You are not allowed to touch anything!*
> *P.P.S. Wasn't last night lovely!*

Indeed it was; and it had amazed and delighted me that I had so been able to make love to her, ardently and with terrific pleasure, when all day long thoughts of Lucia had been weighing upon my heart. No doubt, I thought with considerable satisfaction as I easefully reposed in Vicky's bed, no doubt she's bewitched me. Two years on, and looking back, I really think she had.

It was a delightful little room: the curtains were pale yellow and green, and the wallpaper was patterned with cheerful little homes. It had the most remarkable atmosphere, which had no doubt contributed to my excellent sleep. And in a glass frame on the wall above the bed was a passage from the Bible. It was from the King James Authorised Version, based on William Tyndale's exquisite translation, for which he paid with his life.

When I was a child, I spake as a child, I understood as a child, I thought as a child: but when I became a man, I put away childish things. For now we see through a glass, darkly; but then face to face: now I know in part; but then shall I know even as also I am known. And now abideth faith, hope, charity, these three; but the greatest of these is charity.

A little while later, when I was up and about and looking for breakfast, Vicky returned. She was bearing a sheaf of papers which she thrust into my hands. 'That's your copy of Bruedelmann's monograph,' she said, with glistening eyes.

I flicked through the pages of the monograph, casually scanning its sentences. The work contained five separate sections: Section 1 was entitled 'An Introduction'; Section 2, 'Representational Occult Art'; Section 3, 'Invocational Occult Art'; Section 4, 'Occult Art as Spiritual Practice'; Section 5, 'The Occult Painting: Enchantment or Spell?'

Locks and keys are contraptions of containment but also guardians of form. Our notions of time and place are locks and keys by means of which we determine our more concrete lives. In our dealings with the material world we pare off and divide, we determine and designate how things are to be ordered. It is work best secured by means of locks and keys, but inevitably we forge in the mind the locks and keys of our spiritual lives and then it is our wiser selves that beckon to us from the thicket of complex things. It is not for nothing that we love mysteries; in the contemplation of works of art we shake our keys in their locks and wonder what may be revealed.
. . . . .
. . . Of particular interest to the art-occultist is the function of occult forms of art to encode in esoteric images certain irrepressible aberrations of spiritual doctrine, and more frequently in modern times, dangerous dissent from state ideologies. We find countless instances of doctrines specifically proscribed which have found complete expression not in futile public utterance from people's pulpit and public square, but upon canvas, and on wooden boards, hewn and prepared to decorate an altar.

. . . It is a further belief of the art-occultist that where no such channel of expression is kept open there must inevitably ensue severe disruption at the material level: despots and tyrants, know that the beloved countries of

86

your depredations, those lands and people that you plunder and torment, under your perverse ministrations grow unnatured and ever more prey to catastrophe. Earthquake, flood, landslide, plague, mass psychoses and deadly contaminations of the air — these will come inevitably from the evil that you do.

. . . . .

... but art-occultism is not a science, nor is it an art; yet it draws its strength and inspiration from all domains of human investigation, and it applies in its disquisitions the tools of the scientist where experiments are to be performed, and the methods of the artist where what is to be revealed has greater consonance with the phenomena of the spirit. As art-occultists we require of ourselves a blend of intellect, intuition, vision and good judgement. Our goal is a greater and more beneficial understanding of the spiritual nature of man. The immediate subject of our researches is his art.

Occult art grows more potent the more it works for the good. Its true object is illumination, and right-mindedness; its counterforce is hateful ideology. Thus, quite contrary to ill-informed opinion, far from being the ground of occult art the vileness of man is in truth its natural enemy. And what has given such art its malefic reputation is not the purported traffic with evil, for such is a frequently heard charge against it, but the irony that is to be found at its heart.

. . . . .

It was chiefly in Holland during the sixteenth and seventeenth centuries that the practice of occult art found its most favourable market conditions. The reasons for this are complex and for a clear account of them the reader is referred to 'Art, Economics and the Esoteric Science'. Today, as much as then, where despotism and cruelty oppress the spirit of men and women, the practitioners of occult art carry on the great tradition. And today, as then, it is essential that the resources and practices of this tradition remain secret, for it is a curious paradox that the oppressor, wherever he be found, blindly destroys those forms of art which speak out against him, even though their very existence assuages much of the hatred that is directed upon him. Occult art is not revolutionary, nor is it destructive; there is no violence or ill-will in it. It is, in the strictest sense, a secret teaching, a message of gentleness. Often it is the communication of love.

'Georges Bruedelmann,' said Vicky, 'is a jolly interesting man.'

I replied, evasively, 'I'm not sure I can take this stuff altogether seriously.' She gave me a look then that made me blush. 'I ... do you know him very well?'

'I've only met him a couple of times,' she said, and took a mouthful of toast. 'If you have the chance, Mark, you should get to know Georges

Bruedelmann just as well as you can. That sort of person can really change your life.'

I saw my opportunity and said, 'Vicky, did you ever meet anybody called Hugo Thayer through Georges Bruedelmann?'

She looked at me with wide blue–grey eyes. 'Hugo?' she said. 'Isn't he the guy who went mad?'

'Hugo Thayer *went mad*?'

'Well, I don't suppose he's a raving lunatic,' she said. 'But I heard from Herta that he'd cracked up. Probably had a nervous breakdown. Hugo Thayer? Yes, I'm sure it was him. Why? Is he a friend of yours?'

'No,' I said, truthfully. 'But he was a publisher of English language teaching materials and I've seen some of his stuff.'

'Oh, you mean his posters?'

'Yes. Do you know anything about them . . . specifically?'

'Only that Georges Bruedelmann took quite an interest in them.'

'Does Bruedelmann have students, as such, do you know?'

'Oh yes,' she said, 'he's got a whole school of them. They're usually youngish.'

'And I suppose he teaches art . . . art-occultism to them?'

'Well, yes, I suppose so. But he's got all sorts of projects running. If you get to know him a bit he'll probably invite you to one of his gatherings.'

'Gatherings?'

'He's got a beautiful château in Normandy. People go down there for the weekend. All sorts of things can happen there.'

7

Within the infant rind of this small flower
Poison hath residence, and medicine power:

William Shakespeare

Two days and a night Bartholomew ran on skinny legs through changing countryside; he ran with all speed, and with childlike devotion because it was an act of love. And after he had slept for the third time he took the five stones and cast each one away and into the wilderness he called her name. 'Grandmère. Grandmère.' All her life she had carried the stones in a little bag around her neck; the stones he cast away, but the little bag he kept for thirty years, until at La Rochelle his inquisitors tore it from him and declared it proof of his pact with Evil. The child Bartholomew wept for the stones, and for Grandmama, and for himself; and then ran on, with bruised and burning feet.

And when he could run no more, had quite forgotten why he ran, no longer cared to run, not for himself, not for Grandmère, not for anyone, there was suddenly before him the ruined house that Grandmère had foretold. And there, its trunk athwart a stream and with leaves of dark red and gold, lay a great uprooted beech tree. He crawled along the trunk and hid himself amongst the branches. But he searched in vain in the sunlight-dappled waters of the stream for the silent fish that Grandmère had seen on the day of her dreaming prophecy. And then, through the leaves that fluttered all about him, the boy saw horsemen slowly riding downwards to the stream.

A proud young man with yellow hair rode foremost on a palfrey. His clothes were very fine; Bartholomew knew he was the master of the party. A little way behind him came a scholar, of melancholic mien, who read from a book as he rode. And two soldiers rode at the rear, each with a helmet, a spear and a sword. The man with the yellow hair was noble of limb, and he sang a noble song: it spoke of his love for his lady, whose hair was long and brown and braided, whose skin was white as milk and softer than the softest leaf of spring, her voice like the murmuring stream ... And he must leave his love and betake him to the war, for his honour calls him. The riders came closer, descending to the stream, and Bartholomew forgot his cares and his hunger. Then a flicker of light drew his attention downward; and now, below him, amidst trembling lattice of light and shadow, small speckled fish were sporting.

A hawk was hovering; Bartholomew saw it. It hovered in the sky just thrice the length of a man above the head of the pale-haired songster. On the steep slope the horse trod warily among rocks and jagged blocks of stone. The young man swayed from side to side and abandoned his singing.

The hawk swooped. The soldiers shouted a warning. The rider looked about him, forgot his seat, remembered it again and jerked back in the saddle. His hands flew up to save his eyes but the winging storm and gouging talons, sparing the rider, slashed instead the muzzle of the horse, making tatters of velvet skin; then flew on. Up, up on a rock the horse had shied, on her hind legs kicked at the sky and scrambled away again. With clatter of hooves and skittering stones the palfrey bolted down the slope; enraged and terrified she spattered the ground with blood-flecked foam.

In the felled beech the wide-eyed boy saw the rider thrown from the saddle and hard upon the stones. The scholar clamoured, tossed his book into a lilac tree, leapt from his horse and ran to the thrown man, whose outstretched arm dangled pale, fine fingers in the stream.

The man with the yellow hair made not the least sound. The scholar knelt by his prostrate lord and fetched up two or three great sighs. Slowly the soldiers dismounted, strolled over, waited, stared. One of them, sharp-faced and scowling, couldn't find the right face. He looked about, slyly, smiling, put hand to mouth. But the scholar, who lacked the strength to lift poor Master's head from the mud-wet grass, was openly weeping.

'Looks dead to me, sir,' said the scowling one, and wiped his face on his sleeve.

'Enough of that, bumpkin!' the sergeant said, and boxed him a blow that staggered him. 'You just help us lift him!' and he raised his fist again.

'Praise God! My lord still breathes!'

'Fetch some water, you hear me!'

They called to their master, each uttered distant, respectful halloos. But he did not heed them. The scholar laid his head upon his master's breast.

'Be quick with the water!'

He took a bright cloth from his pocket and wiped the soiled face and the fine yellow hair.

'We must make a halt then,' said the sergeant. The scholar wiped his eye.

*

90

On a slab of stone the soldiers played at dice; cursed and laughed in low voice. In the bushes of the slope the scholar searched for his book.

'Sun's going down,' said the sergeant.

'Best eat then,' the scholar said. And he took out bread and meat from a sack of victuals in a saddle-bag. The soldiers, too, took what they had of provisions; squatting on the rich turf they ate their supper in a cloud of stinging midges. In the red light the horses cropped the grass, and swinging their heavy heads they blew hot breaths into the ground.

Scrawny diminutive Bartholomew, bright of eye and nine years old, liked best the sergeant, whose face was patient and composed; feared the younger soldier, of dumb torment and hapless days; was awed by the scholar, who was close to a distraction of midges and his master's woes. Bartholomew, with a nose that promised to be bulbous, smelling their food, longed to eat meat and bread with the men on the bank, longed to be their friend, but couldn't think what to do. Grandmère had saved him, cared for, loved him, had taught him much of what she knew. He remembered about nettles, how Grandmère had used them to help the women make milk in their breasts; with celery seed and dandelion had eased the pain in fingers that would bend no more; he remembered burdock that cured the rash and the scale, and how the women loved chamomile and cranberry when the moon hurt them; and Grandmère had given him valerian after his father had gone away and the bad news had come; and to those whose heads burst with lightning there was yarrow water to ease the suffering; and garlic for everything, and mixed with onion for the summer sneezes which came from the hay. Much that Grandmère had taught him Bartholomew had forgotten; and yet there was much he knew which he had not got from Grandmère, nor did he know that he knew it, for no one had ever told it to him. It was Nature had whispered it to him, in his blood had made the gift of her wisdom. He could act upon instinct, and he heard the inner promptings when they moved him. It was Nature that prompted him now.

The men stared to see a boy emerge from a fallen tree in that isolated spot; and now he stood before them, a filthy peasant child. His arms were red with bramble cuts, and grazed by countless falls; his knees were scabby. Shoes he had none. In his stinking smock with the stains of the goat's udder and the smell of child earth upon it, and the precious string tied around the middle, the valiant hungry boy stood his ground and stared at the men. He was glad that the sergeant had eyes like Grandmère. He liked the sergeant best. But the other soldier was a sharp-faced youth with a skin inflamed by pimples. A wispy furze grew on his cheeks and his teeth were set all at odd angles. He took a sharp bite of his bread and looked at Bartholomew, and then he looked about, and his eyes were dull and cruel. But the scholar was quizzical. He laid down his book.

'Do you know a wise woman, boy? This is a lord's son.'

'I am a wise woman's boy, sir,' said Bartholomew, merrily piping.

'Do you say so? Then get you gone and fetch your mother, fast as you can. What! Still here! There's a coin for her when she's done.'

'Mother's gone. Grandmère's gone.'

'Gone where, boy?'

'Gone, sir, I hope . . . to heaven.' Speaking his sorrow made the boy weep. But he didn't want to weep now.

'It's . . . I'm . . . I'm alone sir.' He wiped his tears on his arm and took a deep breath. And now, more boldly, he looked up again and said, 'But I have some woman's wisdom, sir. In my head.' And Bartholomew's small finger went pointing at his crown. 'If it please you I can help him, sir. I can.'

'Best set to,' said the scholar. 'Here's your man. Wake him first. Then heal him. Afterwards we'll take him home.'

No doubt but Grandmère would have made good use of what Nature had disposed in that place; there were bushes of hawthorn twined with bryony, and an alder, and the toppled beech tree. Some way off there stood a copse of slender birch, and a hundred paces up the stream there grew a willow. Along the banks there bloomed valerian, and stately woundwort of the pale pink flowers, and small verdant fountains of freshest green and yellow, blessed St John's wort. There was horsetail and the blue-flowered skullcap, and water mint, and comfrey. In the fields about grew yarrow, and chamomile and poppies, and scarlet pimpernel; and much else besides for one who knew.

Bartholomew fussed and fingered grasses, pinched at leaves, sniffed at sprays, pulled up plants by the roots, knowingly nodding his head; took pebbles and herbs in his hand and crushed things together, held pungent handfuls to his nose; he inhaled and coughed, spluttered, sneezed. He asked the scholar to hold this here, if it please you sir, just under the nose; then, against the patient's temples, he rubbed a whole new leaf; and again on the pale, blue-veined wrists, more vigorously, for there lies the pulse. And he asked them to fetch more water, and to make a fire, please.

'A fire?'

'Water must warm. I'll make a drink with leaves, and this yellow flower. Like feathers, sir. 'Tis meadowsweet.'

Inhaling that earth of crushed growing things, the patient first shuddered, then twitched his arm, groaned, coughed, and awoke. Then his servants saw that one arm was broken, and one wrist sprained, and two ribs were fractured. Master had a gash on his head, too, and his chest was bruised where he had fallen on the stones. Bartholomew went to pick St John's wort and the blue-flowered woundwort in the stream ... but the sergeant came and laid a heavy hand upon him.

'Master's wounds hurt him. You must stop the pain, boy.'

'Why ... Why then, sir, I'll fetch him belladonna, sir.' He darted away, up the bank and into the fields ... where's belladonna? ... Oh! There is none? Shall I take mandrake then? Satan's apple? No, not that one! It's full of terror for the picker. Then ... then ... what then shall I take him? Ah, henbane! Is there no henbane here?

The boy ran about like a chicken when the fox has come. And on a mound of broken earth he found henbane growing, and from its foul bed plucked up the whole plant. And running back to the stream he kept the giddying fumes from him as he went, for he knew the power of them.

Bartholomew plucked leaves of henbane and placed some in a helmet; steeped them in red wine. Others he crushed on a stone and strewed the parts on the bruises of the nobleman. He took the wine-soaked leaves and placed them on the pale brows, whence the wine, in fine red runnels, ran into the yellow hair.

'Sleep you, my lord, sir. Please it you, sleep now.'

Running about, gabbling his skills, the boy looked to his patient's needs; and while he was thus at his work the youth with the sour eye took up the henbane and sniffed the stem and the leaves. Then his head swam. He staggered, giddied and nauseous; his legs gave under him.

'Let go o' that, numbskull!' said the sergeant, and snatched it from him.

The soldier lay on the ground and watched the sky. It turned slowly about him. And slowly he turned his scowling face to the ground and he retched his supper out of him.

Bartholomew returned.

'No moss for a poultice, sirs. I must use bread.'

They gave him some. First he chewed the bread, as Grandmère had showed him, but he could not resist the taste of it and gulped a mouthful. The men looked on with hard stares. In haste and trembling the boy spat out a half-chewed morsel and patted it flat in his hand; then wrapped it in woundwort and comfrey leaf and laid it on the wound.

'Do you see?' the scholar said. 'He chews it first! That's a rare trick from a peasant boy.'

Full twice as rare as that, thought the wise old soldier with the kindly eye. This boy's starving.

'Take some food, boy,' said he, and offered a piece of cheese from his pocket.

The boy's quick hand took it. 'Thank you, sir.' Hiccough. Bolted and gone.

'Here's a hunk of bread from me,' the scholar said.

Bolted.

And wonder of wonders . . . a wing of succulent chicken. On the instant the flesh is stripped off, gone.

Hiccough. Hiccough.

Said the wry scholar, 'The boy's had a wolf for his supper. Wolves must feed or they howl.'

'Or they howl! Ha ha! 'Tis a howling we had from him first of all,' said the scowling youth, and he hurled a stone into the stream.

Two o'clock in the morning and the patient woke screaming. Instantly the scholar was by him, murmuring comforting words; but the patient wanted a remedy. His screams tore the darkness and the horses grew fearful. Befuddled, exhausted, the shaking boy tended him. More henbane. More wine.

Dawn, and the soldiers pissed in the stream while Master lay moaning. Sergeant sent Jacques to fetch a wagon. Bartholomew changed the dressing on the torn crown and made a drink of meadowsweet.

'To make the heart merry, sir.'

Bartholomew found a comfrey root for his breakfast. But Master was not content with the meadowsweet and must have more of the other thing. Bartholomew grew fearful. The scholar was pleading.

'Too much will kill, or make him mad,' the boy said.

But the sergeant commanded him, so he obeyed. Then Master sighed, grew still and slept again.

Jacques returned with the wagon; they lined the boards with clumps of turf and prepared to ride away.

'What about the boy?' the sergeant said.

The scholar shrugged his shoulders. 'Why,' he said, 'we'll leave him.'

'Give him money, sir, at least.'

'Money for him! There's nothing to be had. What'll he spend it on? You give him some.'

'You know I have none.'

'Please sir,' said Bartholomew, who scarce could stand or walk this morning, 'please take me with you.'

The sergeant spat, and searching in his pockets, found nothing.

'Nothing to give you, son.'

He spurred his horse and the men rode off. Two minutes passed and the sergeant came back again and threw the boy a small bag of oats.

'From my horse, boy, who has more to give than I can. God keep you, son.'

*

Beyond the slope on the rutted track the wagon jolted and Master awoke. He began to rave.

'Ha! That boy . . . he's a monk! And there's devils in the house, d'you see? D'you see?'

'What should I see? Sweet lord, no monk is hereabouts.'

'Look, look there! He'll dance with a maid! What a pickle he's in . . . the devil! The devil's advancing! Oh, d'you see! Dancing in a monastery! Catch him! Catch him for me!'

'My lord, my dear lord!' The scholar tried hard to wake the woken noble-man.

'His eyes are open but he sleeps,' the sergeant said, wondering.

'Hee, hee, hee!' said the scowling youth. ''Tis that stinky henbane. He'll puke soon.'

'Not a monk but a spy! . . . An English devil! Oh fetch me a priest if you love me . . . Ah but the soul, 'tis sick to death. What's his name, what's his name? Ah, me . . . took in a tree, took in a tree that's all aflame. Oh help me! I die . . .'

The scholar cried out, 'Fetch us that boy here!' And the sergeant, who needed no spurring, went like the wind across the meadow.

Where the fallen beech tree lay across the stream the sergeant strode up and down, shouting. He stooped and peered, prodded his spear haft into holes.

'Hola there, boy! It's me! Jesus, he's gone!'

Aboard his ship, a beech athwart a stream, Bartholomew lay hidden and trembling. Has the pale lord died of the hog's bean? But Nature prompted him again.

He cried then, 'Here I am!'

'Mother of Jesus but I'm glad, son. Come quick, come sharply! Hola, hoop . . .'

Full five feet hauled into the air Bartholomew sat suddenly a-horse. Never had he done such a thing. He shook with joy, and feared for his life.

'What's your name, boy?'

'Oh, Oh, Bar—Bartholomew.'

'We'll put you in the wagon. Come midday we'll eat at the inn. How's that to you?'

'Oh, oh I th—thank you, sir. I'mmm g—glad. But the m—master, sir. M—must have onions. Or g—garlic in w—w—wine.'

Prancing shy of the slope the mare took dancing strides along the bank. In the saddle Bartholomew bounced and fretted, wildly swayed. 'Hold steady now,' the sergeant said. 'What's that you say?' He spurred his horse and the child's thin voice was a warbling in his ear.

'At the inn, sir. Or the s—same to be drunk in goat's m—milk. 'Tis the same. Or we must p—put pine kernels in sweet wine. Against the fever that comes from the hog's b—bean.'

'Hold tight to me, Bartholomew, d'you hear me now? And hold your tongue.'

Because of a hawk and a fall and the poisonous henbane, bringer, in the first, of prophecies and dreams, and death by stupour in the last, Bartholomew came to dwell within a château; and not bare-footed on rough, dangerous ways, and starving as he came, but chewing on a chicken bone, and with his legs outstretched for ease, and cushioned on straw in the back of a haywain.

They put him to work in the kitchens. In the warm months of the year he slept in the stables, and when the frost came he slept on straw in a corner of the kitchen and shared leavings and fleas with the household dogs. He showed his skills in full measure: for those who suffered from fungus of the skin he made a salve of marigold; to soothe the teats of suckling women he made a salve of herbs in smooth pig fat; against contagion he made potions of angelica; for lice and scabies a rinse of alder buckthorn. He showed how the smoke of hog's bean and devil's apple eased toothache and asthma, and to those infested with the worm he gave a purge of bitterest wormwood. Most favoured of all was his remedy for winter coughing: a linctus of sweet violet, coltsfoot and honey. And for the baron to sip in the morning when his kidneys ailed him, he made a bitter tea from the bark and leaves of the silver birch tree.

At first, for he was small and friendless, he ate as the dogs ate and did no better than they; in time he found his place at the servant's table, after the masters had eaten.

For an orphaned boy from a peasant's hovel in a nameless hamlet on the Tarn, this was a life of privilege. Grandmère had had to beg for food when none had need of her potions, but Bartholomew saw good foods in liberal measure. Often he tasted the smell of ox on a spit, saw meat every day, himself bore heavy chargers, laden with garnished pork, lamb, beef, duck, goose and chicken up the steep steps from the kitchen. And the dogs loved him and licked his wounds when he was beaten. And the boy knew his good fortune. When he gathered herbs in the fields he saw the peasants labouring: the sun burned them, the plough deformed them, in winter they went in rags, bent and shivering. And yet, in his twelfth year, he grew melancholy; in vain the baron sent a servant to speak with him, and to bring him the good tidings that the master was pleased with him, and that he might stay a little longer in the château; in vain he had seen so much of the wide world, for he had left his home, gone out of his own country, travelled in a wagon and eaten chicken, had lived in a château. In vain, it seemed to him, he had eaten beef in a great hall and had seen the travelling players, who regaled the baron with tales of Athens, and another place called Rome, and of Olympus, where gods lived, who were not like God at all. These beings of passion bore names of fire and metal, hatched plots and swore, were cruel, vain, hungry for power, lustful, ruthless, deceiving; some too, the players showed it, were friends of justice, gentle, kind, loving. It became a matter of the utmost importance to the boy to discover where they lived, these gods, who were not as Jesus was, who lived with His Father in Heaven ... And still a greater question preyed upon his mind: these gods, the boy told himself, they are as men; I see these gods in all men's faces ... but no men or women I ever met, save perhaps my grandmama, were ever like Jesus.

The players had stolen the boy's heart and had awoken in him an urge to possess he knew not what, but it was not land, or a castle, or even the power of the baron to whip, or starve, or pay coin to whom he will. It was learning he wanted, but he did not know what learning was, nor even that he wanted it. Once, early in the morning, upon some errand about the castle, he had chanced to lose his way. He found himself in the library, where great books lay upon the table, and hundreds were stowed on the shelves. The bold child looked, and saw the strange shapes on the vellum; like weeds springing from the soil, they filled the line from end to end, and wonder of wonders! the illuminations — glimmering and holy. Filled with passion he stole away and did not dare to speak of it to anyone; nor could he put a name to the great blocks of wood with their strange broad leaves all of the same dimension, and on the skin of the leaf the rows of fine blue flowering lines. He knew there was magic in them, that they had power to change men and matter; but was it a magic of such power, he wondered, that it might change the very nature of the gods?

Book! It was called book, he learned it from a stable boy. And since this thing was book, then that which he had seen within its covers was sure to be writing, which needs to be read by readers; and readers are not ordinary men, but look like the scholar, or wear the robes of the priest. So the boy yearned to read. But it was dangerous to stray too close to the library, so he read instead the book of the seasons: this must be my reading, he said, and he noted the phases of the moon, studied the signs of flower- and fruit-bearing in plant and animal, listened for meaning in all natural sounds. He heard the phrasing of the wind, saw the wind write mystery on corn, on water, on bending reed. And when he was more skilled he measured the progress of shadows by scratching thin lines in the dust of a window sill. And by means of placing coloured stones among lines drawn in the dust he found means to remind himself of songs he had heard, sung by the baron's son. He grew ever more secretive; and all the while he gathered herbs, as Grandmère had shown him, and studied the ways of men and women, and thought he could see how sun, moon and the stars affected moods, manners, the bearing of men and women. And sometimes it seemed revealed to him that plants and planets and the gods of Olympus all were bound under one natural law. As the months passed into seasons and the seasons changed the years, Bartholomew grew more restless, disaffected, yearning.

The day came when the baron was stricken; he lay like a corpse in the great bed and gave forth pestilential gusts of wind, filling chamber and hall with intimations of his death. And while noble Master bellowed, writhing for the torment in his bowels, the harried maids, laden with their steaming pails, went scurrying to midden with Master's putrid excrements. Two days passed thus and the dogs sickened; then the baron, blubbering and fearful for his soul, commanded on pain of death that none in the house should eat, and hoped by this penitence to win a pardon from God; but his servants grew too weak to tend him so he relented, permitting a thin soup to be served in the evenings. He bade the priests read prayers and chant psalms, and beseeched his wife, who loathed him, to count the rosary for him; putrefying, stinking, he stroked his shiny breviary with fat, listless fingers.

Joyful news came that was proof of God's proximate Hand; a great physician from Paris, one that tended the King, a doctor of wondrous skill and renown, would disembark at Bordeaux port next Wednesday morn. To lure the goodly doctor out of his way the secretary sent a troupe of soldiers lugging a box of coin.

The physician was handsome; he was a tall man, and his hair was grey and silver. What dignity he had, what bearing! He was a cause of wonder among us, and we went in awe of him. Great doctor was very rude to everyone except the baron; him too he roundly scolded when he saw that Master was weak unto death and craven in his noble bed. He upbraided the master's son for eating too much of food that was hot and wet; we saw that this was a very superior man. Often he said to us, 'in all the nineteen years I have studied medicine . . .' and this affected us deeply.

The baron's son, ever mindful of pleasures yet to come, ordered that

Bartholomew should witness the healing, that he might learn things of note; but they hid him behind a curtain, lest the sight of him offend the virtuous physician.

The doctor looks twice at the baron in his bed, scans those assembled in the room; then he peers at the wood panelling, tuts, puts hand to chin and goes pensive; next he hauls his great leather bag to him and draws a sharp knife, putting the baron into trembling. Now he cuts the baron's toe-nails!

'Ingrowing toe-nails,' says he, and repeats as much in the Latin, 'make cripples of great men!'

Upon deep consideration the doctor prescribes a letting; there are calls for letting bowls and leeches. Stable-boy spends ten hours in the stream to keep the supply. Two days and a night fresh leeches, hungry at first, now gorged on the blood of a baron, drop into the letting bowl, sink to the bottom. And in the hours between the doctor is at work in the library, where he examines all the serving girls, one by one, some say for strangury. Put your trust in God, little women. And in the godly physician.

And now good doctor returns to the sickroom. But how his labours have tired him; he is short of breath, his eye is bleary, he is pale of complexion. Now he examines the baron, all grey and shiny in his bed; now he demands more money. And now he bespeaks his wisdom.

'I have done, here in this room, what medicine can. What medicine knows I have done for the baron, and with all skill known to man.'

The company are awed, yet full of dread. Will the doctor pronounce great Master's doom? Or shall a greater tragedy befall them?

'But God hath greater skill than I,' the doctor said to them. And there were some in the chamber who so revered that consummate physician that they wished to gainsay the great man, but feared to address a doctor without permission, and feared, too, that God might be offended by it.

'Be still, good people. Pray listen. God's mighty Hand doth hold the balance now. If God hath no need of him urgently, my medicine shall save the noble baron. This is my considered opinion, of which I am absolutely assured, beyond all dispute or doubting. But if God will have him presently ... why then, if it were possible to know more of human frailty and the sicknesses that flesh will fall to than I have learned these nineteen years past, 'twould not avail him. I pray you now, good people, let me have my convoy presently. The King awaits his consultation!'

At three in the morning the baron made rattlings in his throat; the secretary drew near.

99

'My lord?'

'Bring me Bartholomew.'

Small, scarred, ragged boy is run into the chamber. With wild eyes glistening he stares at the sombre face above him. To the great bed they bring him and down on his knees he goes, the wretched low-born peasant child, who is valued no higher in the demesne than a sickly pig in farrow. A groaning issues from the great seigneurial bed.

'My lord?'

'Heal me, Bartholomew. Damn you. Begin.'

'It was Nature again that prompted me. And good fortune attended. I tell you, Pike, that worthy physician aided me.'

'How aided you, Bartholomew?'

'I do not think the baron was dying. The physician was unneeded, his time wasted. But his attendance brought the baron to a crisis.'

'Of health, d'you mean?'

'Of fear of death. And wasting by leeches. For three days I attended him. I calmed him, and soothed him with my preparations. I strengthened him so that he slept well. And while he slept so, God cured him.'

On the fourth morning the baron wakes and calls for his bursar and his secretary. 'Give me a reckoning,' says he, 'of monies paid to that damnable dog physician.'

'A damnable dog, my lord?' The bursar, trembling, hands him the reckoning sheet.

'So much gold coin? I am robbed!'

'My lord,' says the bursar, fearful for his post, 'I praise God for that good physician. He has made our master well.'

'It is true, my lord,' the secretary declares. 'Nineteen years of aught but bloody leeching. Blood from bodies, gold from coffers, the man goes his way. A leech and a lecher.'

'Bring Bartholomew to me.'

Amidst chamber pots and sprays of goose-down Bartholomew is dozing under the master's bed.

'My lord?'

'What shall I give you?'

'Why sir, give me . . .? Why b—books, if it please you . . .'

'Learning?'

'And reading too, my lord. If it please . . .'

'Have a care, Bartholomew . . .'

'Then sir, please sir, if it please you, my lord . . .'

'Speak boy.'

'Won't you send me to a monastery instead?'

So Bartholomew came to dwell in St Benedict's House at Montauban; it was the sergeant that brought him to the gate, who hugged him close and said to him then, 'Goodbye, son, and God be with you.'

Claviceps purpurea, purple fungus of wheat and rye, which unwitting millers ground into meal, which bakers baked into bread, induced Bartholomew's expulsion from St Benedict's House at Montauban; and it was the slaughter of Huguenots on his namesake's day in 1572, far to the north in the city of Paris, which drove him into service for Francis Walsingham, spymaster of Elizabeth of England. If Bartholomew had lived out his days secure in the body of his Mother Church he would doubtless have produced such herbals as to assure his perpetual remembrance; and the mysterious painting he is said to have commissioned, and all that came after it in respect of cults and visions, and his fatal notoriety as black magician of turbulent times, might never have been.

But the stigmas of the flowers of rye were showered one year with spores, and the tiny threads grew down into the ovaries, and what should have nourished there the grain of rye quickened a parasitic growth so that there came, in time, to the rough-hewn tables in the hovels, the toxins of ergot in the poisoned bread; ravenous mouths then gulped it down for there was little else to eat. And there followed the gamut of ghastly symptoms: in a tide of blood the pregnant women of those hamlets in Garogne aborted blue-bodied, half-formed foetuses; some froze like statues, others ran screaming and burning and tearing at their flesh, or suddenly imbued with diabolic strength, raged through the villages; many died of gangrene. And hellish visions beset the victims: devils and goblins tormented them with irons, and with loathsome antics and rasping cries they preyed on the harrowed villagers and made them stark mad. It was *ignis sacer*, called St Anthony's Fire.

In the monastery at Montauban in south-west France Bartholomew had lived ten happy years and was a lay brother of St Benedict's Order, which was just, humane and friendly to learning. And as the boy was possessed of skills in the healing powers of plants and was diligent and virtuous, the abbot encouraged him to dedicate his arts to God. By his twentieth year he had long had his own chamber, in which to hang his plants and mix his preparations, and small plots of land in the monastic holdings had

101

been given over to his use. The abbot, who loved him, bought for him phials and bottles complete with stoppers and seals to preserve his medicines against the contagion of the air, for many were the youth's attainments in the invigoration of the sickly and the feeble. And he was much admired in the villages thereabouts; but it was known too that the boy was an experimenter, and some of his cures had seemed inspired so that there were folk who were jealous of his gifts, and some even doubted his Christian faith. But the boy was pious; he seldom spoke and kept his eyes downcast.

The boy mixed herbs and tasted potions, counted his pulse, examined his urine and his stool, scrutinized the colour of his eye-ball. He measured his sweats in the bottles and made experiment with his bodily exudations; he inflicted wounds upon his skin and rubbed his tinctures into the lacerations, and wrote in his book, in the Latin and Greek that the Church had taught him, all manner of observations: how this drink caused strange changes of mood, how that brought on a coldness, and with this potion here – mauve in its colour and sharp to taste – he quickly grew insensible to pain, how with the swart tincture safely stowed in the phial there he might hear the moon calling and know the thoughts of birds in the fruit trees in the garden. A wonder that he did not put himself into his grave by his twentieth year; but he read widely and ardently and he knew the wisdom of Pliny the Elder, and of Dioscorides, and all the ancient herbals. He read too the modern ones that came from the presses in Basle and Freiburg. He compared the drawings from the several books and to the conceptions therein he added his own experience so that he became so skilled in judgement that a visiting savant said of him, 'Our good Bartholomew knows the real form of a herb better even than Master Plato!' And he did not fear to mix new potions and assay rare cures: sometimes he saved a mule, or this man's horse or that man's favourite dog; he grew, in his successes, so knowledgeable that ever more people were disposed to fear him, thinking him a natural magician.

One day in spring, when the light was sharp and pale and there was bloom on the apple trees, Bartholomew was at work in his officinarium. Then two or three brothers brought to him a woman from the village; she was weary unto death but her flesh pricked and burned so that she scratched at herself with cool sharp stones and could not sit still and was ever twitching and prancing. She was sad, and full of foreboding.

'Je suis lasse! Tellement lasse, Bartholomé . . . et tant ça fourmille!'

'Sit down, poor thing, sit down. Does it hurt here? The burning? And cold, you say, and like ants biting?'

Bartholomew questioned her with kind simple words and the girl, for she was barely fifteen years, scrawny but well-formed, twitched and quivered on the stool and answered him as best she could in the coarse tongue of the villages. The brothers looked on and admired her arms, gazed at her long black hair, at her broad, flat, sunburned feet that never yet felt a pair of shoes; and all the while dark dread was mounting within her until, on a sudden, she uttered a shriek and leapt from the stool. A stream of lewd, hateful curses flowed from her lips; next she was on the flagstone floor, writhing and flexing, now whimpering, now grimacing, uttering all the while such pregnant malice that none could doubt that a devil was in her. She bared herself and tore her skin with her nails; then the brothers, tempted, and fearful for their souls, huddled together and murmured. Now her head jerked back and she flung out her arms, shuddered all over and leaped up again; now issuing harrowing screams she kicked about her with long brown legs. With billowing habits and babbling prayers the white-faced brothers fled; now she whirled un-hindered, swept a dozen bottles to the floor shattering them there; and from the drying bundles on the beam she struck with her wild hands a shivering rain of seeds and shimmering leaves and slower sepals and fading petals, and Bartholomew, fallen to his knees upon the flagstones, scrabbled to save what liquids, seeds, unguents and tinctures. Then her sunbrowned feet came stamping near the shards of glass and he, with bare, bloodied hands, swept them from her path, and the shards like needles lodged in his fingers: blood, mixtures, petals, seeds all besmeared his palms. He clambered to his feet and the stricken girl threw herself into his arms, her face convulsed with horror, her eyes tormented, beseeching him, entreating pity, her tongue extruded to the uttermost. And his heart swelled and he cried out for sorrow and clamped his arms about her as the half-starved girl at last began to rave: of the abysmal pit of death all heaped with offal, and a multitude of demons, all shit-encrusted, awaiting the tidbit that was her own precious soul to be shared among them all.

Lord God help us! Bartholomew shouted to heaven, sobbed to not let her die, Lord! And he held her fast and they wrestled, but he would not let go.

'Blood!' cried the brothers from out the door. 'Blood on her shoulder, and there on her arms! See the silvery needles? She is cut, cut!'

In a litter of herbs and phials she and Bartholomew danced like bears and the blood flowed from her arms where his hands held her, cutting into her flesh. At last, for Bartholomew prayed aloud and beseeched them to help him with her, the brothers, emboldened, entered the chamber, laid hands upon her and brought her forth as she spat her terror. And there where the scents of rue and hissop tinged their breaths with sharp, sour

103

melancholy airs the girl grew quieter and at last lay still. And some minutes later she opened her eyes and smiled at him who did not dare touch her for the blood that ran from his hands, and she spoke to him with love and gratitude, and the brothers heard her words.

'God bless you, Bartholomé,' she whispered. 'You have chased out the devils and I am well.'

Amongst scattered seedlings and shards of glass, and paling petals, and faded florets like miniature brooms, and the flux of potions spilled on uneven flooring, Bartholomew had chanced to mix a cure. Was it not a plain miracle? It provoked dark mutterings from the gathering crowd of anxious brothers, for this was the time of the French religious wars and deeds of terror were done in that region, always in the name of God: Huguenot clashed with Papist, sword and dagger; in their soiled frocks hanged priests dangled from sycamores; lay communities burned to the ground. In Languedoc, Gascony and Guyenne, where once the heresies of Albi had flourished, where once whole cities of man, woman and child had been done to death by the bishops' men, there was open rebellion among the Huguenots. The brothers saw the danger: would not the heretics seize upon this chance to accuse the Benedictines of satanic practices? The peasants would hammer at the door, brandishing flame and iron, demanding food and silver. And for those who had sheltered the devilish experimenter what guerdon but sudden, violent death? Had he not restored to life the great black dog that was sick almost to death, against all belief and expectation? Aye, aye, the devil would pay in kind. *Let him quit the house forthwith! Bartholomew must be gone!*

Before that day was out, and much against his will, the abbot sent Bartholomew away. This kindly man, who had taught his pupil Greek and Latin and Hebrew, and a little courtly French, turned him out at the door. But he did not abandon him wholly to fate for he gave his once-favoured pupil a letter of introduction, with highest recommendation, to carry with him to Paris. Circumspect in phrase and in parts encoded it commended the youthful bearer to the erudite master of a prosperous house; this same man, Antoine de la Minerie, formerly a student friend of the abbot at Montauban, was now a wealthy merchant and diplomat, a widely respected humanist scholar.

Benumbed, haunted by memories of his childhood, Bartholomew passed through the narrow doorway in the monastery wall and out into the world. As he walked away it seemed to him that the world was a silent place, for he could not hear the rasping of his boots on the stony surface of the road nor the calling of the living creatures in the fields through which he passed; his eyes were full of tears and despite his best efforts his chin, with its fluffy wisps of beard, was puckered up like a babe's. He carried a small bag of sacking in which he had stowed a cheese, a loaf, a skin of milk, and a sponge. He wore the simple clothes of the local artisan, and all who encountered him on the road thought him a troubled craftsman for his tense looks and his gaze betokening horror at the world. He had walked but a short distance when he heard a whispering from among the trees to his left.

'Bartholomé! Bartholomé, viens!'

He walked off the road and made towards the sound. Who was it calling him? And when he had wandered into a dense copse of trees there appeared a little way before him the figure of a woman, who smiled and beckoned. *Bartholomew*, she seemed to say to him then, *I am yours and you are mine. I shall be with you always.* And she threw back her long black hair and advanced towards him. Her face was filled with a dark shining and her limbs spoke voluptuous promise to him. *I am yours*, she said to him again, *and you are mine.* Then Bartholomew, fearful of death and filled with shame, stumbled from her outstretched arm and fled away.

Monsieur de la Minerie, paragon of his circle, was master of a collection of books which woke the wonder even of the King. And to his celebrated library in the city of Paris came emissaries from all the courts of Europe: Turk and Russian, Moor, Venetian, Dane, grandee from Spain; great and distinguished men might sit there reading. And those who did not browse among the tomes discussed the affairs of the day with the high-born, and with certain renowned thinkers of the schools of the Sorbonne. In that celebrated household Bartholomew found a welcome and a home, and soon became assistant to one of the many secretaries of that man.

PART III

the eyes of the dragon were hot and red
the scales of the dragon were as stones burning;
but Earth bathed the dragon in the water of herself
and the heat of the dragon was mist in the emptiness
hot and wet and dry and cold

Earth bathed the dragon and cooled the burning scales
and the scales turned to leaves on the tree of Earth
and the quenching of the dragon's thirst was dew;
it lay upon the leaves and was a clear light
it was a temperate fire that filled the world

and the dragon's eyes were fruit on the tree of Earth
and the tail of the dragon was a creeper hanging;
it rooted in a hole in the trunk of Earth
and the dragon was one with The Tree of Earth
and root is branch, cool fire warm earth

From *Fragments of Lost Cosmogonies: An Anthology of Myths
Collected in the Amazon Basin* by Hernando S. Gordon.

8

It was a violent time. Wheels, racks and fires
In every writer's mouth, and not mere rant.
Certain shrewd herdsmen, between twisted wires
Of penalty folding the realm, were thanked
For organising spies and secret police
By richness in the flock, which they could fleece.

. . . . .

Above all swayed the diseased and doubtful queen:
Her state canopied by the glamour of pain.

Thom Gunn, *A Mirror for Poets*

Q: What do you know of demons?

R: I have seen demons . . .

Q: Where?

R: In a goblet of strong wine. In a privy in a bordel. In the face of certain merchants and moneylenders, sir.

Q: Have you the means to expel a demon?

R: I think I have. Once, in a monastery at Montauban, I banished a demon from the body of a girl.

Bartholomew's induction into the burgeoning ranks of Francis Walsingham's spying service took place in October, 1572. I have discovered that 'Q' in the text designates the anonymous interviewer by virtue of the Latin expression 'quaeritur': similarly, 'R', which represents 'respondetur', designates the interrogated party. It is astonishing to note that the officials who were at pains to exhaust and record those aspects of Bartholomew's knowledge to which the organization could attach some value, required three full days to do so; in a peasant boy of twenty who first learnt to read at the age of twelve this was signal erudition.

Although his early years were not neglected by his questioner(s), it was not until Bartholomew began to recount the details of his life in the Benedictine monastery, and in particular told of his fellow brothers in that house, that his interviewer(s) began to take careful note and record. And

109

once he had described his miraculous cure of the girl afflicted with St Anthony's Fire it must have been clear to Bartholomew that they wanted to know everything about him thereafter: whom he had met and where and when and what had transpired and why . . .

Q: Why were you in the house of M. de la Minerie on the day of August 24th of this year?

R: I was in that gentleman's library, where I had my desk. I was the assistant to that gentleman's amanuensis.

Q: Why did you go to the house of the English ambassador on that day?

R: I went there to save my life. In haste with my master and his young ward, the Mlle Floriot.

Q: Why did you think your life was threatened?

R: It was the day of the massacre. They killed three thousand Huguenots and Protestant sympathizers. There were naked corpses in the Seine. The gutters were full of gore. There were hacked limbs strewn about the streets.

Q: But were you not a cleric in a Benedictine house, at Montauban? Surely your own life was safe?

R: My master was a humanist. His opinions were widely noted. Many powerful servants of the State knew him for a Protestant. The Admiral Coligny was his personal friend.

Q: Why was your life endangered?

R: I was my master's servant.

Q: Have you no other answer? Consider carefully.

R: I think, sir, my life was threatened because by natural inclination I am a Protestant.

Q: Good!

Q: At the house of M. de la Minerie — what was discussed? And who attended?

R: I saw many different gentlemen. Some two or three used to frequent the Lyceum of Leo Suavius . . .

Q: Jacques Gohorry, who studies plants?

R: The same.

Q: Does he, in your knowledge, practise magia naturalis?

R: I think he does.

Q: What other gentlemen frequented your master's house?

R: I met there a philosopher from the University, and a student of La Boderie.

Q: Tell me of these men.

110

R: They sing Platonic hymns, sir, in Gohorry's garden. He keeps a music school for sacred singing.

Q: To what end?

R: Gohorry, La Boderie, and Tyard, sir, practise to improve men's souls by sacred rites of music and singing. Tyard believes in the magical powers of words, but repudiates the doctrines of celestial music. La Boderie swears that the bards of ancient Gaul were the source of all true music, and all poetry and philosophy, too. The Bards of Gaul, he says, were the first to expound the harmonic composition of The Soul of the World.

Q: Surely this is Master Plato's doctrine . . .

R: As you say, sir, it is in the *Timaeus*. But La Boderie propounds that Master Plato learned it from the Gauls.

Q: Master Plato learned it from the Gauls? This is the famous vanity of the French! Do they say so much? The Gauls taught Plato? 'Tis as ripe as one of their cheeses.

Q: What are the languages you speak?

R: English, which I learned in the monastery from poor Richard, who was expelled from Glastonbury when he was a novice. And French, my mother tongue, of which I know the learned and the courtly. And I know Latin, sir, and Greek, some Hebrew also. In my master's house in Paris I got the rudiments of Spanish. Of late I have studied German too.

Q: German? To what purpose?

R: To read the books of Paracelsus, who wrote in vernacular German.

Q: He is a trouble-maker. A sower of discontent. But what do you know of the original language?

R: Master Plato spoke of it in the Cratylus. It was the tongue, sir, that Adam used to name all things. It is rerum essentia rendered into words. But I think it is chiefly the Hebrew that has the power.

Q: What power is that? But tell me first, what is the rerum essentia, in your opinion?

R: It is the immaterial formative intelligence, sir, it guides developments, both of living bodies and events.

Q: And as to the power you spoke of?

R: Rerum essentia, sir, informs the world; but man may influence it.

Q: Change it to his will?

R: To some degree I think it possible. But chiefly by language, sir, which may draw the rerum essentia into itself.

Q: And what of characters, seals and figures?

111

R: I think they may be very efficacious.

Q: Do you have personal experience of such powers?

R: Not I, sir. And the gentlemen in Paris were very cautious. There are many among them who seek to bring their Plato to an honoured place in the Roman Church. But this is a dangerous project to espouse for they are as like to put Lord Jesus in the school at Athens as get Master Plato into Rome.

Q: How's that?

R: I mean, sir, there's much in Plato's doctrines that makes more sense to honest Christian men than the teachings of the cardinals and patristic fathers.

Q: But this is heretical talk.

R: I do not practise, sir, I do but report.

Q: What do you know of the old abbot of Sponheim?

R: Of codes, sir, and crypta?

Q: Proceed.

R: The abbot of Sponheim, Johannes Trithemius, was a man of towering genius who learned as much in a week as your clever scholars can learn in a month. He wrote on the methods of secret messages and their despatch, and some say he had concourse with demons.

Q: What do you know of his cryptographic methods?

R: He said he could communicate his thoughts by fire, sir, to any place inside a hundred miles.

Q: Do you think he meant the use of mirrors?

R: I do not. He says an unknown visitor came and advised him. I think his method, sir, was revelation.

Q: What nature of revelation?

R: I do not understand it, but I think he had got the secret to call to mind, *to illuminate* at will certain chosen aspects of that formative intelligence I spoke of, such that his intended confidant, be he a hundred miles distant, might see them too.

Q: *See* them? See them *where*? And what are *they* that they may be seen?

R: Items of rerum essentia, sir. I think of fields.

Q: *Fields?* Such as things do grow in?

R: It is a figure of speech, sir. I mean fields of such stuff which is wholly insubstantial, yet is in the world; and man may know it, perchance even change it. Fields of light perhaps, in which all living things are formally prefigured; fields, in which all worldly forms are first determined and defined, from which the substances and forms of all known things inexhaustibly emerge.

Q: This is dangerous talk. And yet we may proceed with it. You said Trithemius had got the means to *illuminate aspects* of your light fields? How is that?

R: What is a field, sir, but a plane in which collective things enjoy more favourable conditions? But you may prefer to think of these fields as a structure, as of glass, if you will. Imagine a sphere, sir, that was all of glass.

Q: A sphere that was all of glass?

R: Indeed, sir, and painted and stained at every point so that every thing that ever could exist, all objects known and yet unknown, all events, all possible things to come, were somehow there prefigured . . .

Q: Like images on a window in a church? A stained glass window and yet spheroid?

R: Just so. And our world stands at the centre of this sphere just as a man might stand in a cathedral all of glass; and yet the glass, the fields of light are very close . . . for I think this sphere, and I think it exists, sir, even as I describe it, has its centre everywhere . . .

Q: Then its centre is also in ourselves, in each of us severally? The sphere of glass has its centre in our world? The cathedral, then, is in the man?

R: Its centre, yes, and he is also at the margins . . .

Q: I have lost the thread . . .

R: Rerum essentia, sir, and how it may be rendered into thought and language. My fields, sir, your sphere of glass . . .

Q: Quite so.

R: . . . and yet stained with an infinity of images, like a multitude of cathedrals, yet perfectly round, and with its centre everywhere and its circumference never to be found . . . Shall I continue?

Q: Do so.

R: On the sphere of glass which I have described to you, and yet I think it is not glass, sir, but *light* . . . on this sphere of light, whose centre is everywhere and whose circumference is nowhere, populous with images of all possible things, a man might read a sequence of images which imparts the intelligence of the sender.

Q: A sequence of images? And made of light? How so? It is insubstantial stuff your sphere, your globe of light. How should a man see images upon it?

R: By mental practice, sir, one might direct one's inner eye upon it. But to the crude optic in the head, I mean the standard eye, my globe of light all stained with images would by daylight seem but grey and blue, very like the sky, sir, and in the night . . . in the night it would be black, and yet . . .

113

Q: And yet?

R: Methinks it might twinkle, sir, in its mystery.

Q: It would be black like the sky, and yet it might twinkle?

R: I think so.

Q: Faith, I do not see why it should twinkle.

R: In truth, sir, nor I. Trithemius had got a trick, I warrant, to catch at certain several images in the fields of light and bring them to mind both in himself and in his correspondent. Thus conjuring . . .

Q: Do you say *conjuring*?

R: I mean, sir, *calling to mind*. In the dark of the mind's night, or in the blue of its daylight, he might call to mind his chosen objects, perhaps, too, sequences of events . . . I mean a sequence of images, sir, one swiftly following on the one before and followed swiftly by the next . . . but seen in an instant . . . and thereby tell a tale in the field of the mind.

Q: And might he not also make it come about? Your insubstantial images are rerum essentia, which man may influence. Did you not say so much?

R: I think it not impossible.

Q: And what of he to whom this message is communicated?

R: In that same plane or field of the mind he would perceive a shimmering cryptographic message. That sir, is *revelation*.

Q: You are a clever young fellow. But I find you melancholy. I note your complexion is tainted.

R: Facies nigra, sir. Saturn's black bile afflicts me now and then.

Q: Indeed, 'tis so. Are you inspired? You learned to read when you were twelve years old. So much learned in these eight years! How can it be?

R: When I was in the monastery I saw how ignorant I was. Accordingly I sought a means to make full use of what little I knew already so that I might speed the learning of what I was ignorant of.

Q: Pray explain yourself.

R: All I knew, sir, was herbs and flowers, and the change of seasons. And I knew men's faces, sir, from studying my masters.

Q: The better to know their desires and so retain their favour?

R: I did not say so. I devised a method, a mnemotechnic system.

Q: What's that?

R: A memory aid. Trithemius taught a system of memory, compounded with steganographic means.

Q: Come, come . . . Tell me of this, I mean your system for remembering.

R: It drew upon my knowledge of herbs and my understanding of men's faces.

114

Q: Was it efficient, this system of yours?

R: It served my purposes.

Q: Could you use your system to encode messages?

R: In one single image, sir, in a painting, I could encode the knowledge in those hundred books.

Q: You are mad to say so.

R: There is much to read, sir, in the human face, or in a flower.

Q: Explain yourself.

R: I mean, sir, each herb has its proper stature. Its leaves and stems, and its flowers too, each according to its pattern; all lawfully shaped and ordered. For every part of a herb we may examine its arrangement: what is above and what below it, what is before it and what precedes it, what it is contained in and what it excludes, whether it stands upright, or creeps along, or twirls about . . .

Q: Quite so. This is natural philosophy you speak of. But I cannot yet see how a plant might impart intelligence.

R: Any departure, sir, from the expected form and colour, yields information. The bloom of a rose when set on a lily stem, yet having the leaves of the woundwort, may impart considerable intelligence if one knew the code. And we have not yet chosen our colours for the bloom, the stem, the leaf. Think of a half dozen of such flowers, yet each one different in some degree, and all arranged according to a pattern. Such an image, sir, to one who knew the code . . . would speak these volumes to the viewer.

Q: But how could another man 'read' what you had set down there, in your image? Could you write it all down, your method, so that another man could learn it?

R: I could sir, indeed, but it would take a man six months or more to master it.

Q: I think it would serve no purpose. Why think, man, to send me information you would have to despatch a painting. I think it nonsense.

R: Not a painting, sir, but a mere number, which a fool could memorize, and carry to you even in his head.

Q: You over-reach. How should a number encode an image?

R: By means of the division of the image, sir, into squares of equal size. Each square will have its number; each number will encode that colour which the square contains. Bring your several numbers into a series, and there is your message; which then must be transferred again to squares, and so to colours to reconstruct the image. Then, if you know the code to the image, sir, your message may be read.

115

Q: I see it, yes! ... Now let me rehearse it: the number encodes the image, the image encodes ...

R: The word, sir.

Q: The word! But tell me, young man ... this must be a large number indeed. How should I remember it; or if you will, how should I encode it?

R: I think, sir ... I think you might encode the number as a dance.

Q: A dance? Ah me, a dance!

Q: And to remember things by your method? Is it difficult?

R: Now that I am master of my method I need to read a thing but once only and on the instant I find means to remember it for ever.

Q: Do not vaunt yourself, for we can test your claims most stringently. Better be more than you appear than fall but one jot short of what you promise.

R: I must review all that I know twice each year. As to my claims, sir, I submit to your tests when it shall please you to make them.

Q: And how long does it take you to review what you know?

R: If the books are to hand, then I can do it in nine days. But each review takes longer than the last.

Q: Is it so? You grow the more forgetful as you grow older?

R: No, sir. I learn more.

In a cryptic little note penned to one of the pages quoted above, there is the following information:

Barth. left P. in the train of Ph.S. in the charge of Dr Wtsn. as that good man's servant. Entrd England September 28th and dwells at prsnt. in my lord's house annexe. Soon to be snt to Oxfrd.

My research has confirmed that Francis Walsingham was the English ambassador in Paris at the time of the St Bartholomew's Day massacre of Huguenots. At about that time, Walsingham's master, the Earl of Leicester, had sent his nephew to Paris to visit him. His nephew was a much admired young man of whom it had been said that he was *lumen familiae suae*, and of whom Ben Jonson himself declared that 'all the muses met' at his great birth. And the Earl of Essex on his death-bed, where men speak true and breaths are short, saw fit to extol that same young man with a long sentence, saying of him, 'he will be as famous and worthy a gentleman as ever England bred'. It must have been edifying for the peasant boy Bartholomew, raised in a hovel in Garogne, to travel in the company of the young man in question, whose name, I am certain, was Philip Sidney, one of the great Elizabethans. Celebrated for his perfect gentleness, his soldierly heroism, his book of sonnets and his *Defence of Poesie*, Philip Sidney later entertained the Italian philosopher Giordano Bruno, and heard first hand from that ingenious and visionary man, forerunner of modern science, the reasons why the earth does indeed move round the sun and why the cosmos is compounded of an infinite number of worlds. Perhaps in the course of their shared journey Sidney and Bartholomew spoke together of the heliocentric universe. But they shared, too, something more subtle and more immediate; Bartholomew, I think, looked to Walsingham almost as a son looks to his father, and Philip Sidney, three years before he died, married Frances, who was Walsingham's own daughter. In a sense they were brothers, Sidney and Bartholomew: they were contrapart twins of paradox; two images of the pattern of their times.

9

What did we do when we unchained this earth from its sun? Whither is it moving now? Whither are we moving now? Away from all suns? Are we not plunging continually? Backwards, sidewards, forwards, in all directions? Is there any up or down left?

Nietzsche, *The Gay Science*

It was something of an anti-climax to return to Canterbury, where the more wearisome aspects of The Commission awaited me. Besides, I now had a further difficulty to contend with: in the course of my recent journeys I had learned quite a lot about the Subject of the Subject's Documentary, and, courtesy of Georges Bruedelmann, I now had a set of his posters to study. Therein lay my difficulty: I had begun, belatedly, to feel anxiety about Hugo Thayer; had begun, indeed, to take a morally responsible attitude towards the man whose private papers were sent to me by parties unknown in regular batches through the post. And Vicky's remark, to the effect that Thayer had had a nervous breakdown, was sufficient to induce in me the beginnings of a mild paranoia.

Sarah rang me soon after my return; she wanted to know if I remembered her friend N.

'That chap at the party,' I said. 'The tall fellow with the stick.'

'Well,' she went on, 'he asked me to be sure to tell you that he's giving a demonstration at the University next Monday night. He said he hoped you would be there.'

Somewhat mystified I told her that I had never actually met the man. 'I think he's confusing me with somebody else, or you are, Sarah.'

'No I'm not,' she said emphatically. 'He calls you "that fellow Clare, the writer".'

It struck me that N. might have some connection with the Interested Parties. 'What demonstration?' I said. 'What's it all about?'

'He's a T'ai Chi master,' Sarah replied.

For the rest of that day I was prey to faintly lunatic paranoid imaginings; how did N. know that as a younger man I had practised martial arts, unless he was somehow involved in The Commission? But if this was so why did he not simply contact me by telephone, or send me a letter? Was it that 'they' deemed me to be misbehaving and planned for me a masterly, light drubbing? Lately, however, it has occurred to me that N.'s skill in T'ai Chi was to be deployed by the Interested Parties as a means to test my knowledge of Disko 39. But of course at the time I had never heard of the thing; it will easily be imagined, therefore, that I did not go lightly to N.'s demonstration.

I removed my shoes and entered the dojo; a short, powerfully built individual who wore a black belt so frayed and ragged as to be unadorned white in places moved among a dozen or so sparring pairs of students. The white belts faced each other grimly; they slowly hurtled one against the other, and with their faces full of fear they plied their stiffened limbs like unwieldy spars. The man with the faded black belt walked among them, calming them, directing them, ensuring that they did not hurt themselves. Then he ordered his brown belt assistant, who was a straight-limbed youth with the beatific looks of a choirboy, to spar with another man, a taller, much heavier individual with a brown belt of a lower grade. They sparred alertly, and with circumspection: blocked each other's blows. Even though they guarded themselves conscientiously, each found improbable openings in the defences of the other. And they attacked swiftly, and lightly, and yet with tremendous onslaught. With each fierce attack their bodies touched and touched again but there was no injury done. With a terse acknowledgement the sensei dismissed them; the class members chose new partners and began to spar again. But they all sparred exactly as they had done before.

N.'s demonstration was wondrous and comic; and slightly chilling too, for not once in his long, thin face outlandishly tinted by the light which fell across his lenses did I detect the least trace of feeling or consideration for his audience of students. Again and again he reduced his attackers to confusion. He was somehow able to control and direct his energies beyond the limits of his physical body. If there was a point to his appearance that evening before a karate class it was, I suppose, to impress upon his fit and martial listeners that the physical element in their training was purely a preparation, a preliminary conditioning process which related ultimately only to the mind. 'You could just as easily have learned a highly complex set of dance moves,' he told them. 'The difference is that you have trained yourselves to spread yourselves outwards, to become outward-turned. But a dance is an inner experience. The dancer seeks the centre within. In karate of course you look for the centre *out there*. Difficult things to talk about . . .'

119

As I was leaving the dojo at the end of the lesson I felt a bony but very solid hand descend on to my shoulder. Turning, I found myself staring into those round green lenses.

'Mr Clare?' said N. 'I would rather like to talk to you . . .'

'By all means,' I said. 'I'd be delighted. Your demonstration was fascinating.'

'About The Commission.' He took a card from his bag and passed it to me. 'Why don't you drop in on me later this evening?'

And so I had my first inconclusive but revelatory chat with N. It must be said that I felt highly ill at ease with him. It was clear that he had inside knowledge of my role in The Commission, and he told me that the fact that he himself lived in Canterbury was a resource which his superiors wished to exploit. He said it was his personal responsibility to feed information to me; but in regard to the timing and the type of information he chose to pass to me, he was required, he said, to use his discretion.

'May I take it,' I asked him, 'that you are one of the Interested Parties?'

'Not exactly,' he said. 'But you may be sure that I am very interested in the project and am a party to it.'

'Why don't they just send me the necessary information all in one go?'

'But that is precisely,' he said, 'what makes this project unusual. It is highly experimental, and rather ahead of its time.'

'Well, what precisely is the project?'

'I have only the broadest of guidelines in this matter. And even if I knew, I couldn't tell you. As I understand it, the project is an open experiment. It involves individuals, each following his own private destiny.'

'To what end?' I inquired. 'I mean, what's the point? And why have I been commissioned to write about Hugo Thayer?'

'Ah! So you've got that far, I see.'

'Do you know where Hugo Thayer is?'

'Not exactly.'

'But you know that he is . . . well, all right?'

'He's under surveillance, actually.'

'Under surveillance? In what sense? I mean, that could mean he's being spied on or . . .'

'Or?'

'Or that he's in hospital or something.'

'Quite correct,' said N.

'Well what's it all about?'

'The point of the project,' said N., choosing his words with great care, 'is to ascertain whether individual lives may hold secrets which are accessible to certain novel kinds of investigation.'

'Novel? How do you mean, exactly? Are you talking about spying? Or about writing?'

'Too many questions I think. Let's just say observation, shall we?'

Throughout our 'chat' N. sat very still in a tan leather armchair with a chrome frame. He had laid his stick across the arm rests so that it lay before him and between us like a sinister barrier. It was impossible to see his eyes and his head hardly moved at all, even when he spoke. I noticed that he worked his lips very hard; it was as though his words took invisible, concrete shape on the humid pliant flesh.

'What it is hoped may be discovered,' he was saying, 'are *secrets*, if you wish, which relate to the everyday world of practical realities as well as to the world of the esoteric. I mean pneuma, and psyche – what you might call the otherworldly. As to the methods of investigation – these are still in the process of discovery.'

'OK,' I said, 'what information are you prepared to give me?'

'Firstly, that you have been chosen for this work for very specific and pertinent reasons which have little to do with your literary practice, or whatever craft you may possess.'

'Could you tell me a bit more about that?'

'Your uncertain origins, in the first case. In the second case, your psychological profile.'

I waited for him to go on.

'We know that your true parentage is unknown, and that you were found abandoned. We know where and we know when. There are, however, some relatively uncontroversial beliefs entertained regarding the identity of your parents . . .'

'Really?' I was suddenly very interested indeed.

'Strictly confidential, I'm afraid.'

I felt a moment of hatred for him then. He sat in his tan leather armchair, secure behind his round green glasses, perfectly still, perfectly complacent, and addressed me in knowing tones about the parents I had never met and could not identify. I had the thought that he was a ruined oracle; it unnerved me that I could not see his eyes. I couldn't even be sure that he could see.

'But I may tell you,' he said, 'that you were left in the back of a British military vehicle one evening in April 1945.'

'I know all that,' I said, sharply.

'And the place too? You know it was . . .'

121

'Westergellersen.' I nodded.

'On Lueneburg Heath. The ATS driver who found you was encouraged to make a fuss on your behalf. Most unusually, she won the right to adopt you into her family. They gave her seven days' compassionate leave to bring you back to England where she left you in the hands of her sister and brother-in-law. And then, of course, her plane went down with no survivors. Over the North Sea.'

'And what's this got to do with The Commission?'

'That very much depends on how you look at it. I can't go any further at present. You see, I'm not permitted to influence the course of your actions. Unless I have a clear inner prompting . . .'

'What?'

'. . . that the time is right so to do.'

'"Inner prompting"? In that case,' I said, but I was talking off the top of my head, simply making difficulties for them, 'I shall have to insist on a meeting with Hugo Thayer.'

'You can tell that to the machine.'

He offered me a drink, which I accepted; then he sat in silence for nearly four minutes, and I permitted myself to examine my surroundings. The room was bare, almost ascetic in its lack of decoration, yet mounted on all four walls were small glass photograph holders each in a wooden frame; but each little frame was empty so that only the unpapered wall, unchanging in texture and of the colour of blankness, showed through the glass. Finally, and purely for the sake of conversation, I asked him how it was that he knew Sarah.

'Through her father's shop,' he said. 'I buy my music there.'

And then, quite suddenly, the conversation took a turn for the worse, by which I mean to say that I came seriously to doubt his sanity by the end of it. He started by asking me if I was 'au fait' with modern theoretical physics, specifically quantum theory. I told him I was not. He expressed satisfaction at my avowed ignorance. Then he started to talk about wickedness, and about *personal baggage*. 'Do you think it possible,' he asked, 'that the evil things which people have done could leave a recognizable mark upon them so that another person, who was trained in such things, might recognize this mark and actually identify the evil in question?'

'Well . . . uhm, possibly, yes.' I shifted uncomfortably in my seat.

'And do you think that it might be possible to remove this mark from oneself by certain types of psychological practice? I don't mean psychoanalysis, although I can see that this might contribute to that end.'

'Well,' I said, wondering all the while where this was leading us, 'I don't doubt that practices such as prayer, or yoga, or meditation can have a healing effect on one's person.'

'Yes, yes,' he said. 'Nobody seriously doubts that . . . Do you believe that by pursuing a certain course of action one might get shot of all one's baggage? By writing a series of letters, for example?'

'A series of letters? Why yes . . . well, why not?' Lucia, I remembered, had told me that Sarah wrote letters for this man. My flesh crawled.

'Do tell me more,' he said.

'Well,' I said, and now I didn't know how to go on . . . 'didn't Machiavelli write letters to the dead? I mean, that is to say . . .'

'Yes, Mr Clare?' I could feel a cold stream of baleful energy coming from the man.

I said, grittily, 'Well, take Machiavelli . . . writing to the dead brings detachment, wouldn't you think?' And warming to my theme I added, 'A sort of otherworldly transparency is brought into a life . . .'

'A most interesting and pertinent observation, Mr Clare,' the man replied. 'I find you very intuitive,' he added; and now I felt stirring about him a dark, sinister intensity. 'I may tell you,' he continued, 'that a certain person once proposed to me that I should write a series of letters. I feel a compulsion to write such letters, even though I am not convinced that they serve any purpose. But there is no question that I have done evil things in my life, and those evil things are with me still.'

He waved his arm at the rows of empty photograph frames. 'The letters in question I write to the dead. To all the people I killed in Poland.'

As I went down the hall he was saying, 'You know where I am. I'll be expecting you. I'm in the book, you know. Under Nolton.'

'So that's your real name, then.'

And then, on impulse, I turned in the doorway and said to him, boldly, 'You know, Mr Nolton, I'd very much like to know who you really are.'

'You'd like to know who I really am?' Nolton's face was tinged with a greenish hue, and his smile had changed from the ironic to the sickly. 'That is something that I too would like to know. It used to be a dream of mine. *Amor vincit omnia*, Mr Clare.'

My conversation with N. had thoroughly shaken my confidence in the innocence of my role within The Commission. I lay awake that night and thought about what he had said; the only connection I could find between Hugo Thayer, observation or surveillance, modern physics, and Nolton's letters were the *particles* that Hugo Thayer had listed in Poster 5.

I vaguely remembered books I had read about particle physics, and about the problems involved in observing such particles, but I could discern no connection between the particles of Hugo Thayer's phrasal verbs and the world of particle physics. It was something that worried me, however, for I had had the suspicion all along that there was more to Poster 5 than I was able to identify.

Poster 5 of Hugo Thayer's posters contained an elucidation of the grammar and logic of English phrasal verbs. And since this linguistic phenomenon is not without significance, particularly for Hugo Thayer, I devote four paragraphs to a short discussion of it.

A phrasal verb is a combination of two distinct linguistic elements: a verb, and one or more particles. The verb 'go' when combined with the particle 'on', or 'away', or any of the other twenty or so particles, is a typical example of a phrasal verb. Particles in phrasal verbs usually function as adverbs, and far more rarely, as prepositions: the former lend a sort of commentary to the verb and define its scope, as in 'run away', 'come along', 'move aside'; the latter do not relate to the verb at all but serve to signal the presence of another independent object and establish locational connection between this other object and the respective subject or object of the verb, as in 'Humpty Dumpty fell off the wall', or 'they pushed poor Humpty off that wall'. Such verb particle combinations, where the particle has a purely prepositional function, are not true phrasal verbs.

Prepositional particles relate to ideas of position and situation; adverbial particles relate to ideas of movement or orientation. Phrasal verbs may be transitive, or intransitive, and they may have two or three quite different meanings. Thus a driver of a bus can 'take on' a peaceful passenger, can 'take on' a vandal in the sense of standing up to that person, and can 'take on' that person to the local police station — even if he 'takes on' about it. As this example indicates, some phrasal verbs have both literal and figurative meanings, as in 'take up the breakfast' and 'take up the offer of the breakfast'; some have only one or the other, but the great majority have both. The phenomenon is further complicated by the fact that phrasal verbs may have more than one particle so that further shades of meaning are thereby often added, viz, 'get on', and 'get on with'. Furthermore the particles need not both be adverbial.

Finally, depending on whether the particle is adverbial or prepositional, there are certain grammatical rules relating to word order and to the pronunciation of stressed syllables, which it is necessary to master in order to avoid ambiguity and grammatical incorrectness. These rules are important because the great majority of verb forms used in everyday spoken English are phrasal verbs. Thus, to borrow an example from Hugo Thayer, if a still-life artist chooses to paint in a rose at the centre of his study of a vase of flowers, he will probably paint *in red*, not blue. We may say then, 'he paints it in in red', but not 'he paints in it in red', which is to say rather different things. Indeed, if additionally we choose to employ the adjective 'rose' to stand in for 'red' we can see that the seas of language will rise a little higher still; in the inscribed sentence 'he painted in rose' we may find that we are hard put to choose between the prepositional and the adverbial interpretations, even though they mean quite different things; of course, 'he painted in roses', and 'he painted in a rose', do not tease our minds to anything like the same degree.

It is thus true to say that phrasal verbs are potently meaningful linguistic entities which organize the world into our recognized patterns: they describe the behaviours of bodies in space, and in relation; they are tiered and shingled and swiftly communicative; as bearers of meaning and form they are as abstract and as concrete as a dance; they lie at the heart of our language's capacity to unify position and movement, which are contradictory conceptions. Phrasal verbs have the power to describe movement *with* position, for when they describe movement they also imply relations of position, as in 'head off'; and when they accentuate relations of location, they convey too the sense of movement, as in 'run round'. I could see, at a pinch, that they might conceivably prove as interesting to a linguistician as quantum particles to a modern physicist.

Hugo Thayer, who has a very special relationship with phrasal verbs, and calls himself Gnostic Phrasal Verb Man, declares that phrasal verbs are *quite transparent with regard to objects and yet they are primary pattern-makers by means of which we make our world*. He says, too, that phrasal verbs, closely examined, *prove the world empty, and dimensionless*. He says they are *mentalistic devices that conjure forms in nothingness*, and in the very moment of conjuration not only the world springs into being, but also the very person of the phrasal verb user himself.

The reader will conclude that for Hugo Thayer, at least, the phrasal verb is a numinous, ontological force hidden away in a particle of language. *Phrasal verbs are archons*, he says. But he has seen them for what they are, and has spoken their name, and by this means he has freed himself of their power.

And now, at last, I had begun seriously to concern myself with the welfare of Hugo Thayer. N., or Mr Nolton, for I did indeed find his number in the telephone book, had implied that Hugo was being detained, if only in the medical sense; but I had detected in that information a more sinister drift of sense. And I saw now that the oppressive terms of The Commission could not fail to awaken in me intimations of clandestine, dishonourable, perhaps even criminal concerns; concerns to which I was myself a party, mainly for reasons of money. An image came to haunt me then: a phrasal verb expert, a man who had identified the nature of his actions and who knew the name of action as it were, was now at the mercy of unknown manipulators and had become a sort of object-for-others; and all his movements, directed by unseen hands, were phrasal verbal in form. It was an image from which I could not shake free, and an intimation of pathetic irony. And although there was no shortage of new material from the Subject's Documentary, including school reports, university essays, and various business records, I found I could not use it. I went to the computer and typed:

MEMORANDUM
10th May, 1983

FROM: Robert Mark Clare
TO: The Interested Parties
SUBJECT: Reconstruction by Infictifaction of Subject's Documentary

I feel that it is impossible for me to continue with The Commission until I have had the opportunity to meet and talk with Mr Hugo Thayer. Please make arrangements for such a meeting as soon as possible.

For ten years Bartholomew plied his trade in the service of Queen Elizabeth of England. His adventures, however, which were many and varied, are not, for the main part, of concern to us here. Suffice to say that he spent a year at Oxford, where he advanced his knowledge of the great doctrines of the time and spied on Catholics and scholars. And he mastered the complexities of the English language as he went about his business. Thereafter he spent some years in Holland, where he furthered the cause of the Dutch rebels against their Spanish overlord. Much of his time he was deployed to seek out Catholic plots against the Queen's life — a line of work in which he proved himself exceptionally skilled. Indeed, so well did he serve that he was rewarded in November 1579, in a way that was to bear fatefully on his death: from a trunk of New World herbal preparations lately plundered from a Spanish merchantman he was invited freely to help himself. But he did not tell his masters that during his years in Paris he had read and learned by rote the *Herbal of Badianus,* which was a book of New World herbal preparations complete with careful descriptions of herbal medicines, stimulants, narcotics, and hallucinogenic agents. This remarkable work contained the herbal lore of a tribe of New World Indians and was dedicated by its author, himself an Indian shaman, doctor, and priest, to the Jesuit God of his Christian conversion. No doubt but that the herbs and spices in the plundered trunk had figured in its pages, and were quite as familiar to Bartholomew as they were foreign to anyone else in England; on the basis of his prior knowledge he was able to undertake a series of experiments which made him perhaps a unique virtuoso of herbal and plant-based magical lore. But it was a prowess that was to be tragically curtailed, for just three years afterwards, and in consequence of the Mark-Rietenburg project, Bartholomew met the standard fate of more venturesome and brilliant Renaissance magicians.

It is the Mark-Rietenburg project which concerns us here, and for brevity's sake I call it the Lippstadt Mission. My source text is Bruedelmann's own modernized version; however, where the period flavour of the writings is noticeably diluted I am myself at times to blame, for I too have made some small adjustments to Pike's account. There is much in his reports that is prolix, and it is to be remembered that he was first and foremost a soldier by trade. He had acquired the arts of reading and writing somewhat late in life, and aped the phrasing of his masters to ill effect. It is John Pike's thinking, however, which I faithfully convey in the following account.

The Lippstadt Mission, May, 1581

The project was founded upon intelligence gathered in Lippstadt, Westphalia, by one Adolphus Kremer, a burgher of that town and sometime merchant with trading interests in the Baltic. Kremer had become an informant for Walsingham as a consequence of his strong Protestant convictions and his unswerving belief that Protestant interests in the North German states were broadly allied with the interests of English foreign policy. The state of England was an established power, equipped with a strong navy and regular men at arms, and Elizabeth's foreign policy was anti-Roman and hostile to staunchly Catholic Spain; this is not to be wondered at in view of Pope Pius V's Interdict of 1570, which 'released' all her subjects from their allegiances to 'Elizabeth, the Pretended Queen of England'. In January, 1581 Kremer sent a brief to Sir Francis Walsingham, the spymaster of Queen Elizabeth. Kremer's report is pasted into the Book of Bartholomew, and I have summarized its contents as follows:

County Mark-Rietenburg lies south-west of Hannover and north-east of Imperial Dortmund. By the census of 1574 some 40,000 persons live there. The Dukes of Kaunitz rule the territory, but they are absent landlords who reside in Prague and Vienna at the courts of the Holy Roman Emperor. The county is administered by their servant, the Count Bernhard von Halle, who is resident Landdrost in the Schloss at Rietburg. The territory confers upon the Dukes as holders of its title the privilege of Reichsunmittelbarkeit, which bestows the status of kings and the right to sit on all the Emperor's councils. By virtue of this eminence the Dukes hold dear their title to Mark-Rietenburg and their rule is mild.

The House of Kaunitz is Roman Catholic as is the Emperor Rudolf II, the military champion of that Church. The heresies of Luther and Calvin are proscribed in Mark-Rietenburg, and yet there are many Protestants in the county. Some say more than half the population follow heresies. But the Dukes, for reasons of policy and statecraft, fear to provoke rebellion, and the Catholic observance is not enforced. And yet they fear too the accusations of intriguers at the Imperial courts. They constantly enjoin the count both to administer the county with benign, enlightened will, and still to suppress all instances of heresy. This task is impossible.

Lutherans and Calvinists proselytize at markets and it is rumoured that the Anabaptist heresies of Muenster, a town some thirty miles distant to the north-west, attract the disaffected. Nor have Counter-Reformational agents failed to establish themselves here: from the Catholic bishoprics of Muenster and Paderborn, teams of Jesuits make their way into our towns and villages. These men are organized. They have great skill and are trained in the arts of the Counter-Reformation. Petrus Faber, who was active here in the forties, has written down his methods of reconversion: *show them a large-hearted charity and high esteem, win their heads through friendly intercourse, discussing in an amicable spirit, without any rancour, about things over which there is no dissension. Begin not with what separates hearts in discord but with all that draws them closer together. Start with good works and an exemplary life just because the Lutherans despise good works and deny the possibility of enduring hardship for the love of God.* A notorious Dutch Jesuit, one Peter de Houdt, called Canisius, followed these methods in Augsburg and in a three-year period doubled the congregation of Catholic worshippers there.

To the north lie the lands of Tecklenburg, of the Nassau dynasty, whose head is the glorious Protestant revolutionary, the illustrious Duke of Orange; to the east lies Protestant Saxony. The southernmost part of the territory has been alienated and is ungovernable being at this time in the hands of the rulers of Hesse, the great Protestant champions of North Germany. The term of the loan expires in 1602; it is certain that the Kaunitz family will repossess their territory as soon as the law permits, but for twenty more years this area, being not less than twenty square mile, affords an ingress for Protestants, Calvinists and all manner of mischievous spies and religious wanderers.

Mark-Rietenburg is flat, sandy and chiefly barren in its northern parts, but more hilly and wooded in its centre. In the southern parts it is sparsely wooded and partially flooded for much of the year, by cause of the several tributaries of the Rivers Lippe, Alme and Emmer. Access to the territory and to the Schloss at Rietburg is best achieved via Dortmund, Soest and Lippstadt. There is much traffic on the Lippe, which joins the Rhine at Wesel, a town at present controlled by the States-General.

Count Bernhard von Halle, Landdrost of Mark-Rietenburg, is much embroiled and entangled. His task demands of him contradictory allegiances and his health fails. The man is known to vacillate in policy and is a figure by turns tragical and comic. Yet the people love him so long as he pleases them. He is borne up by one Adalbert Stremel, his secretary of ten years, whom many think unscrupulous and opportunist. Stremel, it is rumoured, stands in league with Jesuit missionaries on the promise of political advancement. In addition he has business interests with Lutheran burghers in the towns. The count has but one child, an idiot son, who is heir to his father's lands and title. The Countess von Halle, who is never seen, is an invalid and keeps to her bed. There is no prospect of further propagation of the line, for the count fell from his horse and was rendered sterile. Some say the secretary entertains ambitions beyond his station and exploits the unsettled spirit of his master, for the count still grieves the death of his first-born son, who died in Vienna but nine months ago. There is a cloud of intrigue all about this death; some say the boy was poisoned. Count Bernhard travelled to Vienna to visit the grave of his son and grew so troubled that he sought relief from local physicians. One of those who treated him is Henricus Wykzo, an outstandingly skilful and compassionate man, and Wykzo is now favoured with the friendship and the confidence of the count. In Vienna he was known to be an alchemist, who had suffered calumny at Rudolf's court in Prague and was forced to flee. In that dangerous court he still enjoys considerable renown among the learned.

The count brought Wykzo to Rietburg and gave him chambers, laboratory, and library. The 'chemist is now secure and honoured. In exchange Wykzo contracted to discover what means he could both to restore the propagative powers that the count had lost and also to speed the development of the idiot son. With Wykzo came his daughter, Magdalene, in the autumn of 1580. They have dwelt there since.

Three additional matters merit your consideration: in the first place, the alchemist is a Jew, although not proven so. In the second, the nature of Wykzo's contract with the count is not as it appears: a former servant at the castle has shown me proof that Wykzo's commission is to explore some chemical or other means to advantageously affect the course of war. The count wants a means to get victory speedily, with fewer casualties. In the third place, the count has sworn, in return, to marry his idiot son to Wykzo's daughter. The 'chemist craves this union as he craves an untroubled autumn to his life.

The Book of Bartholomew is more a portfolio of papers than a simple biography of Bartholomew de Gaillac. Here and there, affixed to the pages of the narrative, are additional sheets, in Pike's own hand, containing highly confidential reports on Bartholomew's demeanour and performance. Their tone and content reveal John Pike to be less Bartholomew's companion and friend than his secret monitor and potential assassin. There are, too, a number of further papers, as for example the above report from Kremer, written in a quite different hand; and some others of an altogether different status, which evaluate and pass cryptic comment on what is written elsewhere. I counted at least six different styles of handwriting in this category: their authors, whose scrawled and barely legible initiallings safeguard their anonymity, cast long shadows over the tragic events to follow.

Penned to the bottom of the last page of Kremer's analysis is the following persuasive summary in an elegant, diminutive hand:

1. M-R is favourably located to disrupt the Calvinist expansion; both southward across the North Sea from the Scottish consistories via the Low Lands, and northward from Geneva.
2. Political instability, partial alienation, absent rulers and weak administrators: the Landdrost will be courted by other powers. If he is to fall under influence let it be our own.
3. The expansionist policies of Sweden, the perennial opportunism of France, the intensifying effort of the Counter-Reformation, the proximity of the revolution in the Netherlands cannot but lead to war in north Europe. M-R could not fail to be of strategic advantage to our State.
4. Henricus Wykzo is ambitious, resourceful, industrious, timorous and vain. His researches cannot prove wholly fruitless. Whether as Jew or not he fears his German hosts. He knows small territories may be engulfed. At this time of unrest let him be courted by our great State.

Conclusion: a mission to Mark-Rietenburg should urgently be funded. Following advantages may accrue: appropriation of novel means to expedite victory in war; close ties with a foreign territory in a sensitive region; close intelligence of Counter-Reformational activities.

Proposal: send agents to M-R to prise the alchemist loose from Count von Halle and to bring the latter under our influence, by means of pecuniary interest, or motives of power, or whatever sentimental weaknesses may prove manipulable.

This proposal was accepted. Soon afterwards a team was sent to carry out the mission. It comprised John Pike, plain Bartholomew as he was at the time, and a twenty-eight inch high midget named Flink Hudson. On May seventh 1581, the three men left London. Much of the time Hudson was concealed in a trunk, for such a little man, so proven in spying, was no mean secret weapon of the time; in his trunk, however, courtesy of his master and by way of compensation, Flink Hudson sprawled on a pillow of velvet, and like a modern voyager slumbered as he travelled the rough, uncertain ways.

10

Several English Jesuits, who had come from Rouen to London, and, at the behest of the Pope, were trying to convert the people to the faith, were taken prisoner in London. Three were hanged, and two were quartered. A further sixteen of them are to be executed.

September, 1581, from a letter to Augsburg, *The Fugger News-Letters*
1568–1605

Six days after my memorandum of May 10th I had my first full-blooded encounter with the Interested Parties. I was reading something on Christian symbolism which Bruedelmann had discussed in his monograph when I heard a loud banging at the door. No sooner had I pulled the door open than my visitor, a large man, had placed one heavily booted foot in my hallway and had put all his weight down upon it. By way of experiment I pushed the door against his foot and the door bent alarmingly. My visitor, who was plainly amused, looked like everybody's idea of the burly policeman, now retired and working for a security firm. But he was younger, probably only about forty, and his demeanour was more overtly aggressive. He had an overgrown military haircut and wore an imitation suede car-coat in the style of the mid-seventies. He placed one big fleshy hand on my front door, reminding me irresistibly of a piece of pork with fingers, and with the other hand he flashed a card at my face. But it was no sooner before my eyes than he had withdrawn it from my inspection.

'Mr Clare, I presume.' He placed his other, irresistible foot upon the threshold and now he was standing over me in the hallway. He had very clear eyes, I noticed, but around the mouth and at the corners of the eyes his skin was flecked with broken veins giving a sickly ruddiness to his otherwise pallid countenance.

'Steady on,' I said, my pulse rate taking a jump, but I was already retreating down the hall. He placed another large piece of pork on the door and shut out the world of Friar's Walk.

'Have you got a moment, sir?'

I took a deep breath and invited him into the front room. He was at least fifteen stone and a good nine inches taller than me; he sat down heavily on my little sofa . . .

'What do you want?' I said.

'It's about The Commission.' He placed his hands on his knees.

'OK.'

'But it's not OK is it though, Mr Clare?'

'Isn't it?'

Whatever prejudices this man had it was clear that I fitted the bill. He looked at me then like someone who is about to beat a dog. There was a set to his jaw and his eyes glinted.

'You,' he said, 'have taken on a contract, and you have taken our money . . .'

'*Our* money?'

'And now you think you're going to start calling the tune.'

'Do you want me to explain what I put in my memorandum?'

'Fuck your bleeding memorandum,' he said. 'Just get on with the job. I have been instructed,' he said, 'by the Int —'

'. . . terested Parties,' I chimed in.

'Parties, to kindly request of you a guarantee that you are going to get back to work.'

'Right,' I said briskly. 'That's fine, then. I've got that.'

'So let's have it. If you please.'

'I'm sorry,' I said, my heart in my mouth, 'I thought I made it clear that I can't carry on with The Commission until you accord with my request.'

He made loud tutting noises and gave himself up to a slow unmannerly scrutiny of the objects in the room. He seemed to find the books particularly interesting.

'Intellectuals,' he said, sorrowfully. 'You'd be surprised. Nobody really likes them. Nobody really wants them,' he said. 'Not in our country.'

'I'm not an intellectual,' I retorted, truthfully.

'The great British people,' he said, and he started to heave himself up off the sofa, 'don't give a fuck for intellectuals.'

He gave me a sober, threatening look and took a large step forward. Suddenly a great pork finger hung in the air before my face. 'I want a guarantee from you.'

I went quickly to the front door and opened it wide. From the end of the hall I called out to him, 'I would like you to leave now, please.' Then I heard the sound of drawers opening and I strode back into the room. Schooling my courage I said, 'I didn't realize that I was working for a criminal organization!'

His face had gone slack, but his jaws were working. The flesh seemed to hang off his face, red and blue as the flag.

'You know,' he said, and his face was a loathsome parody of quizzical earnest, 'I think you might just be a teensy bit of a nig-nog, Mr Clare.'

'Christ,' I said, 'before this country can ever hold high its head all the people like you are going to have to get educated.'

In a friendly way he said then, 'You used to do karate.'

'What of it?'

'Karate,' he said mildly. 'We don't believe in it, back at the office.' He peered into the drawer. He said, 'Try this then, son,' and lunged at me with an extended knuckle; I stepped to the side and pushed his hand away.

'Good,' he said, unconvincingly. And then he did some kind of judo hold on me and as I felt myself leaving the ground I thrust with my hand and grasped hold of his truss, squeezed. He grunted and froze, my heels rocked back on to the carpet.

'Easy does it,' I said.

His huge hand came up my back and wrapped itself round my jaw, then he started to pull. I knew at once that he could easily break my neck.

'Hold it,' I shouted, spraying spittle between his porcine fingers. He froze again. I said, with difficulty, 'A stalemate. Another inch and I'll tear them off.'

'You haven't got the blimmin' strength, though,' said the man.

'Desperation,' I huffed and spluttered, 'is strength.'

And so we stood there, locked in unarmed combat, that large man and myself; and this is perhaps as it should be, I thought, the writer and the State, one to one, pent and challenged, at the very brink of radical violence.

No, but seriously, you're quite right of course; that last little bit isn't true. I made it up, I couldn't resist the opportunity. In fact he did both threaten me and lay a hand upon my person, and by way of retort it was my foot that spoke to him, for it came up smartly and tapped him with my toes, lightly, in the balls. I confess it is shameful and repugnant, and I would not report it here if it did not have its consequences in this text; however, I should say in my defence that although I am not a soldier, or a guardian of the peace or of the people, and therefore lack the customary, unwritten title to this kind of treatment of my fellow man, and nor am I by nature a criminally violent type — some of us, now and then, have a chance, perhaps even a duty, to let it be known that we are still there, we the weaponless, thinking populace. And that, I suppose, is what I did then, for in my prepossessing visitor that afternoon I had sensed the palpable presence of the State.

*

Afterwards I hurried to see Nolton, for who else could I turn to? I explained to him, possibly untruthfully, that I would never have carried out such a cowardly assault if I had not been convinced that the man had been about to strike me again. And I expressed the hope that my visitor, whose name I later learned was Pearson, was a professional criminal rather than a policeman, for I had decided, in the shaky calm that followed his departure, that it was preferable to be at loggerheads with villains since their unlawful treatment of me, I believed, would be something which I might fight in court with at least a modicum of hope. N. wanted to know why, if I thought Mr Pearson was going to hit me again, I had not begged for mercy, or simply given in to his demands, *just like any other civilized person.* 'You don't come across as a yobbo,' he said.

He told me that I had 'done well'. In his view I had no cause to give the matter any further thought. He was of the opinion that 'they' had tried to intimidate me not because they wished me to toe the line but in order to test my mettle. Had I unwittingly entered the Great Chariot Race, I begged to know? And who were these shadowy monitors of my less respectable talents? But Nolton was evasive, and asked me instead why I was spending so much of my time hanging about in Canterbury. I should do better, he told me, to betake myself off to France. Now he wished to meditate, he said, and sent me away.

14 May, 1581

This night we stayed at Holsterhausen on the Muenster road. The keeper of the tavern is Christian Rotbart called Stahlgriff for his strong grip.

At Stahlgriff's house we chanced upon an Englishman, said he was a sea captain bound for Gelsenkirchen to visit the mother of his mate that died at sea. He asked our destination. We said our road lay in the north-easterly compass, for which he was much relieved. He spoke of a band of notorious free-booters, all Dutchmen, who preyed on travellers in that country. He said they hate all Englishmen for that their leader had got some grievance against us through the Spanish Wars. This wicked man, said he, knew but one phrase of English: 'I can tell you!' he says, and then he cuts the throat of his victims. 'I can tell you!' said our sea captain, "tis his motto!' and he quaffed his ale with relish. We invited him to travel with us in our convoy. 'I go to Gelsenkirchen,' he said in a mighty voice. 'Tis south.' Next he asked our purpose in that country. '*Diplomatic*' said I. He winked and put his finger to his eye.

We bought him ale. He said he knew a German in Augsburg who owned a whole town of 30,000 working men. And women too. 'This is

135

surely a great lord,' said I. He shook his head and spit on the floor. 'A miner of silver ore,' said he. 'A mole in the ground.' I supposed it was the Fuggers he spoke of but he swore it was not them. Thereafter he grew abusive; soon he wished us all dead and went off into the night.

15 May, 1581

Bartholomew groaned all night and was sick this morning on the road. Talks much of his early life, seeks quarrels with God, is forever tasting powders. I never knew him complain so much. Not in seven years. It is the powders, I warrant, that he got from the New World.

About noon we pass through Wulfen by wagon. Three scholars travel with us, and a troupe of actors. The scholars are disputatious, melancholy men and much given to fantastical witticisms more tiresome than poor comedy. Such men as these, who cannot find a post at the university, tramp the roads and make a motley school of logic under the skies. They enter the towns only to talk with scholars, or to seek out masters of their schools. They are surly folk and not to be trusted.

We follow the road that keeps sight of the River Lippe. This region is unwholesome, being marshy and very flat. The farmers are not friendly hereabouts.

Six actors in the troupe: sweet singers and players. These folk love to entertain and possess thrasonic skills in great measure. When we halt they perform their numbers for our pleasure. I fear they will ask me for money as I am the best clad among the company — thanks to my good master.

About sunset on the same day:

We had a dire adventure on the road and I cannot say if it was Providence that saved us or Bartholomew's cunning. We had made a noon-day halt in the shade of an oak tree thirty yards from the road. One among the actors, Raymondo, a graceful Neapolitan, would have us believe he was a *Chinese tyger*. A tyger I never saw, nor a Chinaman neither. It was a dance he did for us, one that was flowing and full of power. I never saw such a thing for he needs no music to show him the pulse of it but proceeds like a man who walks in his sleep, most silent and intent, and you'd think he prays as he goes. Nor does he care a fig if it pleases us or no. Like a man magicked in a trance, or a river that knows no hindrance he goes his way. Said he had been to China! Spoke some words in that tongue. To my ear it was like the shouts of children heard from a distance. Six years, he said, *six years he spent in a cage at a crossroads in the mountains*. Here's a claim for a Neapolitan! But the scholars believed him so I lent my ear. His tale was a strange one.

Ten years ago he quit the town of Naples, which saw him born, and went to Genoa where he contracted to serve a young Jesuit missionary, who had travelled from Paris. His master embarked for China and so did Raymondo. They travelled first to the Portuguese island of Macao, and thence, in time, to the great mainland. But his master, who was much possessed of his vocation, offended an official in that country and was flayed to death for impertinence. His man, being lowly, was beaten black and blue and thrown into a cage at a crossroads in the mountains. There they left him to perish.

Three days he raved and beat at the bars of his prison but none heeded him. Water he had enough, for rain was plenteous on the mountain and nothing stood above his head but the sky itself and some bars of iron. 'But the clouds,' says he, 'contained no victuals.' On the fourth day he grew quiet and looked forth but little from his cage. But in his mind's eye, he said, death came slowly up the winding road to greet him.

On the fifth day in the evening he saw an aged man approaching. Is it death so soon? thought he; but death brought not oblivion but a bowl of food and pushed it into his cage. *Rice and raw vegetables!* And thereafter his benefactor came each day in the evening, and for six years, if we please to believe him, and always with a little food. It was a small, thin man that helped him, and very lined in the face. 'But when he moved,' says Raymondo, and how craftily he told his tale! 'When he moved he had the way of a cat in its full strength and prime. And when he came near me in the dark I felt him like a cool fire or the pull of a lodestone. Every evening he showed me his dancing and made signs to me that I should do even as he. He taught me the dance of the tyger, and the dance of the *crane.*' Which is a noble bird of that country.

Raymondo said it was the dancing that saved him. Made his mind calm through the summers that burned him and proved his body against winter frosts and spring rain. Two thousand days passed! At last a troop of soldiers came for him and trussed him up and put him in a sack across a horse. What's now? Is it my execution? But they brought him to a river and so by degrees to the sea where they found him passage on a ship bound for Siam. And in the kingdom of Siam, at a trading post of the sometime Emperor Charles V, he made his reunion with Christian men.

Raymondo performed for us the dance of the tyger and next he began the dance of the crane . . .

And in that instant they were upon us, some eight or nine brigands. Some bore pistols, some had swords only. Among their party was a giant who carried a great axe all crusted with blood. I turned my head and looked into the very muzzle of a snaphance pistol with a double barrel.

And the man that held this weapon to my head was that same English sea captain that was bound for Gelsenkirchen!

'I can tell you!' cried he, his face all twisted in devilry, 'I can tell you!'

This was dire to tell, for my pistols were in the wagon and my sword lay on the ground.

'Tell me,' said he, 'tell me why I should not on the instant blow out your brains? I can tell you!' he cried, 'I can tell you!' and he threw back his head and blasted in my face a wind of his pestilential breath. 'Why,' I said, but I grew pale then, 'why,' said I. But in truth I knew not why.

'I can *tell you*,' said Bartholomew. And straight he launched into his tale: 'Look at this gentleman's doublet,' said he, and pointed to my habit, 'pray look at his hose!' Then the brigand poked his bloody fingers into my doublet and let out a whistle for he saw it was lined with silk and of very good quality, as befits its provenance for it was bestowed upon me from my gracious good master's own wardrobe.

'This gentleman,' says Bartholomew, sober and grand, "twere best you molest him not, for he is befriended among the very great. Were he to die on the road 'twould not go well with the captain and his shipmates!' And he gave that rogue a sly wink so that the villains roared with laughter at it. 'And what profit lies in it?' says Bartholomew, his tongue as silver, quick as mercury. 'The gentleman carries no coin with him. Go search the wagon. As for the rest, they are but poor mendicant actors and starveling scholars with scarce provision for the morrow.'

Now this soy-disant sea captain has not by the grace of God one bauble of wit in his head but must think very hard before he'll understand a word of it. He twists his beard and takes into his mouth a wisp of his greasy moustaches and gnaws on himself awhile.

'If he be great . . .' says he, '. . . where is his retinue? Where is his soldiery?' And now he looks about, half in triumph yet half in fear, and seeing no hidden soldiery puts himself to laughing. But his eyes are murderous cold.

'It is my lord's conceit,' Bartholomew replies, 'to travel this great distance without convoy. It is *diplomacy*,' says he, and he gives the brute a cunning nod and it wins at once a stupid mean sly look from the murderous dolt. What a creature was this! Fit for the gallows on his birthday! I looked about. Some brigands were plundering the wagon, others searched our company. A snaphance pistol pointed at my heart.

'There is a certain high-born gentleman, and one of the very great,' says good Bartholomew, 'who counts himself friend and confidant of the Lord High Chancellor of England. And this same high-born personage assured his Grace that the dukedom where now we stand is exceeding well-ordered.'

'What's that to me?' cries the brigand. And now his eyes are black as hot pitch in the cauldron. 'What's him to me? Or this or that? Or that or this or that?' the creature shouts, slavering all the while like one possessed.

'It is this to thee,' says Bartholomew, 'and pray mark it well: *I can tell you, good reckless mariner* that this same high-born personage is selfsame cousin and kinsman of the Prince of Westphalia himself. Hearken to me, captain ... hearken. To this same kinsman of the prince, and to the lord he serves, mark you well, it is a matter of great honour and import of state that my good master here may so depend upon the prince to keep an ordered realm that he needs bring not a single soldier with him yet suffer not the least harm on the road to Muenster. That, sir, is *diplomatic*.'

Now the ruffian thinks it out ...

'So if I should kill him now, then they must seek me out, for their honours' sakes,' says he, ruminating still, and chewing on his beard.

'You have it,' says Bartholomew. 'Most clearly perceived. And I have still more powerful argument to sway you from that dangerous course.'

'Speak it, good sir!' the dolt replies, but the swagger has gone out of him.

'Think man,' says Bartholomew, pressing to keep the advantage, 'if this good gentleman make mention at the court that he was rudely harried on the road past Wulfen, think on the consequence. The cousin of the prince shall not escape dishonour by this report, for does it not give the lie to his promise? And it will shake, too, the standing of the Lord High Chancellor himself. And this being so, why think, good captain, the Queen of England herself must be tainted by the breath of it. Why tainted? She? For that her Lord High Chancellor consorts with a vaunting liar. And think, sir, think what dishonour it shall do the Prince of Westphalia. Come, come *good captain*, think hard on it. Know you not 'tis past madness to shake thus the honour of the very great? Put out more sail, sir, and pass on! This is a ship must sink you in the taking!'

Now there is silence. The sea captain chews hard. The sun is under a cloud.

'Let us now part company,' says sweet Bartholomew, reasonable as an angel. 'Let us part company, sir, and live long, like wise men.'

'Not yet, good sir. If you please, not yet!' Now the rogue starts muttering, squats on the ground and frets his cankers, confers in low voice with his *shipmates*. Methought their conference was over-long. I prepared myself for desperate action.

A great shout was heard and a brigand cried in triumph, 'Here's one!' A scream went up among the actors. Is it a woman? 'And here's another!

Here's two pretty women!' By this unhappy means did we discover that women travelled with the troupe, but dressed in manly habit to preserve themselves from such a handling as they now had to suffer. Luckless creatures! These pirates had commanded the members of the troupe to remove their breeches. A woman cried out in desperate voice, 'Help me, Raymondo!' And I commanded, in thunderous voice, 'For God's sake touch them not!' Whereupon their captain leapt to his feet . . . but *mirabile dictu*, as swiftly fell clubbed to the ground! And where he had meant to stand and do what violence he would, stands now the Chinese tyger! And he holds to the throat of the captain a long narrow pin of sharpened steel, which is called a *stiletto*. A very convenable weapon. 'Call them away or I stick you,' says he! So soft his voice yet spirited, and fierce as a Chinese tyger!

Nobody moved. The brigands were bewildered; their leader was down and close to having his throat stuck through, and yet they had the numbers and the weapons by, more than enough to kill us all and carry off the women. I would that Bartholomew might be persuaded to carry a sword.

'I'll stick you,' says the tyger, like he was singing to the rogue.

'No,' our sea captain roars then. 'Don't kill me!' And he calls out to his men, 'Dierik, Slasher, Mickie! Set free the women!' But there is a musket trained on the tyger, and a pistol in my back, and Bartholomew stands close by that blood-encrusted axe of the giant brigand.

I know not how it would have ended. We stood in a tableau, and the time passed, and each was alone in the sphere of his thought. A full minute passed thus. And then we heard the shouts of men moving in the brake. Our relief, or certain doom? The brigand called out to welcome them. 'Here!' he cried, 'Quick!' and on the instant the tyger stabbed him in the throat and his life-blood flowed into the air, a full yard. I threw myself to the ground and snatched up my sword, but think what relief was ours, for even then the villains took to their heels. And there burst forth from the brake not brigands but soldiery, well armed and bearing the colours of a local lord.

19 May, 1581

We concluded our business in Muenster and took to horse. Hudson has gone to Paderborn and will meet us in Lippstadt. We are one day's ride from Soest.

In the early morn we passed through a town where they burned a witch. A girl of fourteen years. We rode across the square as they

140

brought her from the Hexenhaus, which is a witch's prison. The press of citizens was great about her and the guards half carried her to the place of execution. We reined our horses some way back and watched the proceedings from over the heads of the townfolk.

As we rode on to Lippstadt Bartholomew cursed and wept. These New World herbs undo the man. I fear he will be useless to us.

20 May, 1581

Last night we passed into Lippstadt and put up at the inn. Hudson sought us out and brought K.'s man with him, who took us to his master. We were welcomed, and got fresh intelligence of the count. K. counselled us to seek contact with the count's retainers. Two Wednesdays in the month his soldiers come to Lippstadt to fetch the accountant who keeps the books. It was Monday then, near twelve midnight.

22 May, 1581

The soldiers did not come. We heard in the inn that the accountant has fever and is abed. We wrote a message to the count and by inquiry in the Wirtshaus found means to despatch it. Now we wait. Hudson is amenable and very patient. During daylight hours he lies concealed in the trunk, for we must expect to have eyes upon us at all times. When we go forth we must lock him up in it: and so we learn to make small matter of our dangers, for in Flink Hudson it is evident that great fortitude has but small mass. This is Bartholomew's conceit, which I find both fair and apt.

24 May, 1581

About nine o'clock this morning four of the count's retainers alighted at the inn. Demanded to speak with us. 'Which one is the magician?' The count is well served; the man who spoke to us thus was bold, very powerful of build and shrewd. Bartholomew presented himself, and me, in a pretty speech both humble and splendid. He denied he was a *magician*, for magic was not an art for a good Christian man to practise. Rather he was a *scientist*, who sought to uncover the infinite riches of this world which God in his wisdom had laid before our sense but sometime concealed in the flow of time and events. The count's man knew not a whit about it but was not a jot out of countenance neither. He bowed to us, and I did not much like the expression in his face, and told us that his gracious master, the Count Bernhard von Halle, was pleased to see us that very day. Did we agree to go presently in his convoy to the Schloss at Rietburg? We did. Thereupon the captain, for he led the troop, sent word before to herald our arrival and then sat down at table with his soldiers. While we gathered our effects, they drank five jugs of ale and ate some sausage.

At ten we set off. These were taciturn soldiery. In a ride of two hours, on very bad roads, they spoke barely a word. B. and I talked at length of our lives at the University. It was for their ears we gossiped thus but I think they did not heed us. Besides, we spoke in English.

If it seems to me today that I have travelled a certain distance in the spirit and find myself now within reach of a New World, then it should be said that in the period of early summer of that year of The Commission I found myself becalmed, in the doldrums if you like, somewhere south of the Azores. And it was Georges Bruedelmann who rescued me and took me out of those dog days, for a day or so after my little tussle with the State in the narrow confines of my living room, I received from him an invitation to a weekend at his Normandy château; he also requested the return of Hugo Thayer's posters.

And now the phone was ringing.

'Mr Clare?' It was a cultured voice, male, about forty.

'Yes indeed.'

'We'd like you to plug in and switch on . . . got that have you?'

'Eh? What? Oh . . . yes, the machine, right.'

'Jolly good. There's something coming through for you. Just sit tight, now, and when you see the question mark flashing then you can reply.'

The phone went dead.

I sat in front of the word processor staring at the screen; there was something faintly lunatic . . . heart-stirring, my pulse rate was high. Suddenly the words were appearing before my eyes . . .

'Hocus-pocus,' the machine told me, 'is the bastard child of the new technologies. More particularly of the new physics. We are the wide-eyed ingenus of the after-revolution. Now take this little thing we've got with you. We know you're a bit of a one for hocus-pocus. We've read your book, of course.'

'?'

'I was a bit younger then.'

'The rehabilitation of hocus-pocus was caused by the war, and not by your tender years.'

'This meeting,' I asked it, 'is this an example of hocus-pocus?'

'It's hardly drear quotidian,' the machine told me. 'To the matter: any questions?'

'Yes,' I typed in, swift enough to be witty at the keyboard, 'I want to know what the matter is.'

'It is yourself that is the matter with us. The project in hand, of which The Commission makes up a significant part, is the queerest thing. It is intricate, of course, and most unusually, it is open-ended. Its objectives are quite possibly chimerical, and its assumptions are probably unsound. Not least of all, it is very much in a state of flux.'

'?' said the machine, to which I replied in kind, '?'

'Mr Clare, we have difficulties enough to contend with without your getting up on your high horse. You have, after all, undertaken a contractual obligation. We should like you to get on with it, and no more tergiversations if you please.'

'I've requested to meet Hugo Thayer,' I replied, 'because my ability to do the job depends on the outcome of that meeting.'

'Now what on earth can he mean?' the machine appeared to ask itself.

'If,' I wrote, 'I have cause to fear that I'm participating in something immoral when I write, then I can no longer write. For me, writing is a grave, solemn, moral activity.'

'On the face of it,' the machine continued, 'it is a most unlikely alliance; ourselves and yourself. We are, however, in quite complementary relation. So often, Mr Clare, we are at pains to contain what it is our writers, albeit investigative journalists in the main, are at pains to reveal. It is seldom the case that we find ourselves at pains to divulge what our writers seem at pains to contain. It is our concern, Mr Clare, to encourage you to write, while being compelled in the same moment to discourage you from going too quickly to the heart of the matter.'

'?'

'?' I retorted.

'We are at pains to reveal, through your good offices, what it is we have determined to reveal. And here we have a commissioned writer who is more tight-lipped, more secretive, dare we say it, than we ourselves. We do so wish you'd co-operate.'

'Look,' I told the screen in four quick jabs, and it was apposite, I note, 'I'm normally a man of my word.'

'Scrupulously,' the machine observed.

'But I can't be sure that you're not doing something that goes against

my principles. I'm not prepared to continue with work that serves . . .
immoral ends.

'You seem to be saying that because we are discreet, because we do
not brief the local papers on a day to day basis, we are in the wrong? Do
I interpret you correctly?'

Did the screen look offended? I hadn't the time to decide. I replied,
'You secretively entrust to me the task of divulging information about a
person whom you secretively keep from any contact with me. You send
racist louts to threaten me. No matter how you paint it the facts are
suspect.'

'Why do you wish to meet Mr Thayer?'

'To satisfy myself that he is not being harmed in any way. Or discom-
moded.'

'What is done secretly, quite unlike what is done secretively, is not
necessarily wrong. Indeed, agents of the most charitable acts invariably
do not divulge their behaviours, is that not so?'

'Yes,' I said, 'but . . .'

'Are you not able to envisage good things flowing from behaviour that
is not in itself transparently good?'

'Yes, I am, as a matter of fact.'

'We knew that you have this compulsion to be a good chap. We took
it into account. We even embraced it. I mean to say, would we deliberately
encourage a good sort to get himself involved in a bad business?' It was
cheery now, and plausible, that green machine.

'You still expect me to proceed in good faith,' I argued. 'You can't
reasonably expect that.'

'Oh but we can, and we do. In a democracy this is entirely what we do.
We expect you to proceed in good faith. And if you refuse to proceed, or
if you are shaken by too much doubt, we can help you along a little.'

'?'

I typed in at last, 'I suppose you're threatening me again. Like the other
chap you sent.'

'We needed to know how you respond to that sort of thing. Actually
we thought you were quite good. You'll be pleased to know that I
predicted your behaviour most accurately.'

'So when am I going to meet Hugo Thayer?'

'You must understand, Mr Clare, that once we allow you to start
dictating terms, and to start arranging interviews through our good
offices, the whole object of the thing will be lost. You will simply have to
trust us.'

'Then I think you're going to have to find another writer.' And now my hands were trembling quite badly.

'Has it not struck you that you might be the second or even the third writer who has undertaken The Commission, and that the others might be . . . ah . . . otherwise detained?'

No, that thought had not struck me. 'Then you'll never get your damn book written,' I rejoined, inwardly lamenting the lack of a Gothic type-face.

'Has it not also struck you,' the machine was relentless, 'that some of us don't want the damn thing to be written?'

The sheer novelty of this consideration threw me into confusion. But I saw the need to keep talking.

'If you'll just let me meet Hugo Thayer,' I quickly replied, 'you'll get a better book. I'll finish The Commission just as quickly as you please. Or as slowly. Or not at all, if that's what you want.'

'I conclude then,' it concluded, suavely, 'that you believe, after all, that the project is unexceptionable. You have therefore removed the need for such an act of goodwill on our part. The alternative,' it continued, 'is that you are lying.'

'?'

But I had nothing to say; and I was resting my hands on my knees.

'What a pity it is, Mr Clare, that we can't depend on you to do the decent thing.'

'How horribly sanctimonious,' I typed with my teeth gritted. The machine then calmly pointed out to me that it was I who was being sanctimonious. All this nonsense about doing nasty things to people; it was pure pretext. I was finding the work difficult and I didn't want to do it. That's why I was rocking the boat. 'So let us not strike attitudes, Mr Clare.'

'?'

'Another bloody stalemate,' I remarked, at last.

'Funnily enough,' the machine replied, 'Hugo said you would do this.'

'Hugo did?'

'Oh just a while back. I think his words were: *You'll find he'll need tension from the outside. Otherwise he won't write. When the outside is slack there's nothing but turbulence and chaos.*'

'Hugo Thayer said that?'

'I'm not sure I understand him entirely. Clever chap though, our Hugo. After all, it was his idea in the first place.'

'What was his idea?'

'The Commission of course.'

I couldn't credit it, although strictly speaking I was in no position either to believe or disbelieve what I had just been told. What caused me the most difficulty, I suppose, was the fact that I might have to rearrange my categories: Hugo Thayer, whom I had begun to see as a victim, as an observed object of systematic but unspecified abuse, had suddenly become a participant; more than that — an abetter, a co-operant. I felt quite giddy with it.

'?'

'I'll tell you what,' the machine rejoined. 'We'll have him send you a message. I have in mind a video communication. Got a video have you?'

'Much will depend, though,' I replied, 'on how he comes across.'

'Truncheon marks, the cowed spirit, that sort of thing? He'll be as right as rain, you see if he won't. He's edgy, mind you. And he's got rather a sharp tongue.'

'?'

I was trying to work it out: had it only just been decided to meet my request, or had it been intended all along? I remembered something that Nolton had said about 'inner promptings'. Was it really so 'open-ended', so contingent, this Commission project?

'But you really don't trust us at all, Mr Clare.'

'I can assure you,' I tiredly and somewhat dispiritedly typed, 'that nothing would please me more than to have complete confidence in you. I'm sure,' I added, more confidently, 'that I speak for the entire population.'

'Pshaw,' the machine observed. 'And before you switch off, old chap, there are just two other little matters.'

'Yes?' I responded, suspiciously.

'I want you to watch your step with Mr B.'

'Mr B?'

'That art dealer chappie in Paris. Calls himself an occultist.'

'Georges Bruedelmann? What's wrong with him?'

'You'll be interested to know that a few weeks of exposure to that particular individual had an unfortunate effect on poor Mr Thayer, whom you seem to care so very much about. He was quite out of his wits when we picked him up. I shouldn't go spending too many days cooped up with him, if you'll take my advice.'

'Why are you interested in Georges Bruedelmann?'

'Now, before you go, I'd like you to have this little photo here. You'll need to know what he looks like. Before my eyes a face was generated on the screen, and then was gone.'

'Who was that?'

'Who but Hugo?' the machine retorted. 'There's Thayer for you. You'll get it in tomorrow's post.'

11

Je ne cherche pas, je trouve.

Picasso

In that section entitled 'Invocational Occult Art' Georges Bruedelmann had written:

The canvas is the void, the eternal emptiness, and the artist paints upon it with magical, form-bringing resins. Beings and biographies are conjured and sustained not in the paint but in the minds of the onlookers . . .

In the painting reproduced in fig. 3 we see people who are talking and waving and calling to each other but we cannot hear their laughter, and their speech remains unheard: a film of colour on the surface of emptiness. We can see the crude fact of the canvas, the cake of pigment, the wooden frame with its flaking gilt, and yet we feel that we know these people; how is this possible? The artist knows that his canvas is not a fact of his painting; it is only the backcloth of imaginings, it is death in life: the stiller and blacker it is, the more brightly and fully does life show forth. And yet we do not look at this painting and say to ourselves, 'look at these brush-stroke persons'; nor do we say that these persons are smears of pigment on a canvas, for it is no more true that they are smears of pigment than it is true that these persons are forever and inescapably immured in a bounded abstract field. This is a form of magic, of a most rudimentary kind.

Since we cannot say that the persons in this painting look like persons who are not in a painting, what then can we say of them; that they are painting-persons? We must address this question: in what way, and in what degree do they differ from persons we encounter in our everyday life? And we would answer that the latter persons are real, that we could reach out and touch them if we did but want to, that we could enter into their lives. The persons we encounter in our everyday lives are real, we say, just because they exist. We may, however, for a fruitful moment, assume that all such persons are as painting-persons, and as such it is for us to make them real; this we do by the process of ascribing to them firstly physical characteristics, and secondly, those essentially human qualities of motives, reasons, emotions and beliefs. It is a process of discovery, this process of

147

creation of other-persons for ourselves. It is a making-real of an element in our own phenomenology and as such it is closely related to the magical practice of spirit-invocation by means of images.

Just as the artist paints upon the void, just so, in a sense, do we live our lives; our deaths run along beside us, are always with us like a roll of canvas, and as we live our phenomenologies we paint upon our deaths with magical form-bringing resins. For the void is death both in occult art and in the human mind. It is the fertile, placid darkness at the root of all experience; the more we are aware of death, the more vivid, the more real will be our phenomenological representations. And just as the artist is free to choose his forms and his colours so we too are free to make of this world what we will. It is an occult process, this conjuration of painting-persons who sleep in our phenomenologies; and by similar and extended means the magician creates extraordinary forces in our lives.

Bruedelmann's Normandy château is located on a small country road which skirts a picturesque village some two hours' train ride from Paris. A first view of the place is of the high wall that protects it from the public gaze. The wall is two hundred metres long either side of the imposing wrought iron gates through which the driveway, of dull red cinder, gives access to the grounds and leads, in leisurely semicircular fashion, to the great façade of the house.

I climbed the five extended shallow steps that led up to the massive oaken door and turned to survey my progress. The cinder driveway bounds a well-tended lawn of oval aspect at the centre of which there presides, in mottled and mouldering stone, an imposing and yet disquieting statue of Pan. His legs are shagged with fur which descends like breeches to his knees, and he has cloven hooves, and is all in motion, as if he wheels about on hard, dainty feet. His torso, arms and head are human, and well defined in all their features; he is athletic but not heroic, and he holds a horn to his lips, but I could not decide whether he drinks from it or intends gustily to blow it. His face has a look of ecstasy, and his lips are parted; but his is not the bestial, giddisome delight of the satyr — it is arcadian, rather, almost beatific, so that my thoughts were torn between profane and sacred, brutish and divine. His tail, thick as rope, arches back in a proud upward curve; but his organ of generation nests modestly, like a small bird, in the thatch of his lower belly.

I grasped the door knocker, which was a large bronze disc in the form of Helios with a chevelure of bolts of fire, and rapped sharply three times on the metal plate beneath. A satisfying summons boomed within. Two minutes passed and the door was opened to me by a man attired in eighteenth century livery. He led me along a narrow passage of beautiful parquet flooring, up a spiral stairway of grey–blue marble and along a second, much plainer corridor to my room: a simple iron bed complete with stuffed mattress, a plain chair beside it, and in the corner a diminutive wardrobe. The ceiling, however, was decorated in green and blue, and peopled with the swirling forms of plumpish, lightly-clad ladies cavorting by a natural pool amidst dreary-exotic flora. On the pillow there lay a printed card: it welcomed me to the château and reminded me that costumed dress was to be worn for the seven o'clock cocktails. I went off to the wardrobe room.

I chose a tunic of dark red leather, silk-lined and slashed at the sleeves, and an undershirt that fitted well across the shoulders but was rather baggy at the backside. I dispensed with the headgear, however, which was low, soft and round like a new loaf. The shoes were delightful: soft leather, light brown in colour and as tight-fitting as dancers' wear, no heels to speak of. They hugged my feet right up to the ankle where they widened in a casual efflorescence of even finer material. I slipped the tunic on. It was actually too tight for me, but no matter.

As I considered myself in the mirror there came a light, insistent tapping. I crossed the room and pulled the door open . . . to find myself face to face with a noble lady. From the first moment, it seemed to me, that I clapped eyes on her I had an overwhelming sense of *déjà vu*, and indeed, a poignant sense of *déjà aimé*. It seemed to me that I knew her scent; I felt it in my chest and in my vitals. Her eyes were deep Arabian blue, the colour of the waters of the Gulf in the swift twilight, tinged with chaste violet crystals. As I gaped at her I seemed to remember, to recall in all my senses, unsurpassable nights of love; and she too, stared.

She wore a pale blue dress that seemed to be one continuous piece of material from her shoulders, where it was embroidered with floral motifs, to her feet, where the cloth lay around her in graceful folds and furrows. From her slender shoulders down to a little way above her hips the material hugged the outline of her body, and then it grew capacious about her. At her wrists the satiny material fell away, and her trailing cuffs merged with the pool of material at her feet, seeming to bathe her in a visionary fountain of colour and texture. Her hair was long, almost to her elbow, and of a lustrous gold, and around her forehead she wore a headband of pale blue with an inlay of amethysts.

If I had known then that the apparition before me was all too human flesh and blood, and was, to boot, the erstwhile lover of the Salamander himself now sent to look me over, I suppose her magical presence — for she stood there silent and wondering before me — would have seemed to me all art; in my innocence, however, I found her occult, even mystical can you believe. And such is Bruedelmann's castle.

'But it's too small for you,' she said. Her voice was American, and this, I suppose, brought me back to my senses. I struggled to find my tongue. 'But it's surely you,' she added.

'And this,' I said, vaguely gesturing, 'is surely an enchanted château.' I stepped forward, and she gave me her hand; at once I did not know what to do with it. I wanted to squeeze it, but I wasn't sure that I might not do better to kiss it. She laughed, and the sound gave clear indication that she was a woman of considerable, nay formidable life experience.

'I'm Marilyn,' she said. 'Marilyn Moore.'

We looked at each other and the sense of a magical recognition was already melting into the air.

'I was actually looking for the library,' she said.

'I'm afraid I can't help you,' I replied, joyous and playfully soulful. 'I'm a complete stranger to the house.'

'But I feel,' she said, 'you know I really feel that we met before.' There was puzzlement in her voice and something exquisitely cordial so that I felt my pulse quicken.

'I too,' said I, 'have that same impression. Very strongly.'

She stepped back a pace, and then she said, 'But I feel as if I've hurt you. Do you get that feeling too?' She was suddenly grave, and perfectly still. In her enchanting dress she was quite otherworldly.

'No,' I said. 'No, I don't.' But I was not going to have to disappoint her with a flat rejoinder, for I felt, in a curious way, as if it had been the other way round; and I told her so.

'Well,' she said, and she was full of quiet good humour. Her hands went wriggling into the sleeves of her dress.

'That gesture,' I murmured, 'it's so you.'

She looked up and smiled. And then, with a light sweeping sound, she walked from the room. I pictured the slippers on her feet. I imagined her toes.

At seven o'clock, as I made my way to the cocktails salon, I encountered some half a dozen other guests, mysteriously attired, who silently emerged from modest doorways, or chanced upon me at ill-lit corners of interminable panelled corridors. I saw a woman in a buoyant, stately crinoline who fanned her face as I passed her in the hall; another, as Oscar Wilde, in velvet coat, satin knee breeches and silk stockings. And there emerged, in a frou-frou of fine fabrics from a doorway a few steps before me, a pale, serene young woman in Amelia Bloomer's eponymous dress: under her full, knee-length gown her satin bloomers swished about her ankles. And I found myself closely followed by a man of towering stature who was dressed in the manner of a nineteenth-century gentleman prize-fighter. What was most striking in each case was not the comedy of costume but the impression conveyed that each person I met had somehow chanced to slip away, so that the obscure realities of period dress were like opened stained-glass windows pointing to more enigmatic absences. Marching self-consciously towards the salon I felt I encountered phantoms; nobody spoke so much as a word, and an uncanny mood was upon us.

In the salon, where elegant French windows opened on to the patio, affording a striking and romantic view of the grounds, our host was ubiquitous and presiding. He moved amongst his guests, congratulating, remarking, expatiating with great virtuosity. He was thoroughly Byzantine in a richly decorated gown that covered his body from head to foot. On his head he wore something not unlike a fez in shape but lower and wider. In its centre was a darkling jewel of night-blue lustre.

'Ah,' he said, as I entered the salon. 'Here is my English friend,' and he gave me a light good-humoured wave.

I was one of fifteen or so people in the room, at each end of which was a bar. One of the bars was tended by the man who had shown me to my room, but he now wore a rugby shirt and jeans; at the other bar a slender young woman of very intelligent mien graciously served me a cocktail. She wore a South-East Asian national costume, and she told me her name was Kwee. I made my way across the room towards Marilyn Moore, who was talking quietly with the tall, powerfully built man attired like a gentleman prize-fighter. I observed, with some disappointment, that they behaved very familiarly towards each other. They chatted coolly, without hesitation or effort of any kind, and all the while they looked around the room: now at the paintings on the wall, now at the three spectacular chandeliers suspended from the decorated ceiling.

'Hello again,' I said to her.

'Ah, but you're different than before,' she replied, glancing at the prize-fighter. 'Mr Robert Mark Clare,' she said, 'Mr Burt Munker.'

He was about two hundred and fifty pounds of bone and muscle, his handshake more a warning than a greeting.

'Hi.' He had an open honest face, a square jaw and very small ears. His hair was distinctly institutional in cut.

'D'you know,' I said, very politely, 'that you look exactly like an early nineteenth-century prize-fighter?'

'Is that a fact?' he said. 'I guess I chose what I could get into.'

I asked, with a grin, 'Is that what you're into?'

'Excuse me?' For all his puzzlement he was self-possessed to the point of being offensive. I had the impression that underneath his entirely contingent politeness lay a chaos of arrested development.

'Well,' I said, sensing that this was no place for me, 'I'll be on my way.'

. 'Just hold on there will you, Robert Mark,' said Burt Munker. 'I sure'd like to talk to you. Shall we go over here?' I found that my elbow and forearm lay like offerings upon the shovel-like palm of his hand. Thus disposed we walked out briskly and on to the patio.

'We know about your work and we want to make a proposal,' he said squarely.

'What?'

He twitched his shoulders. 'We need evidence,' he said. 'Evidence that Mr Bruedelmann here has been smuggling art works into the States.'

'What?'

'Sure,' he said. 'We particularly want to know about some paintings that he brought in illegally way back in the tail end of the forties.'

'He's just over there,' I said, finding my voice. 'Why don't you ask him yourself?'

'Oh boy,' he said. He spoke as though someone had just told him that a lion was loose in the building. But he had a flame-thrower, and some light canon. 'Oh boy.'

'Look Mr Munker,' I said, 'I'm not going to tell tales on my host, you know. You're a guest here too, I take it?'

'Unwelcome guest.' He had reached into his frock coat before remembering that he wasn't wearing his suit. 'Shit,' he said. 'Just hold on. You just stay right there.' And he strode off back into the salon. A moment later he returned and showed me a photograph. In the great palm of his hand it was a tiny, poignant thing: it looked like nothing I had ever encountered.

'This is an artist's impression,' said Burt Munker, 'of the painting we want to hear about. It was commissioned way back in 1583. Guy by the name of Bartholomew. Some kind of political freak.'

'Who?'

'And take a look at this guy,' he continued, placing in my hand a small passport photograph of a total stranger. 'Recognize him?'

I felt a curious pressure coming from him, as though what was happening then was a purely formal preliminary to a more blatantly physical interrogation.

'No. No, I don't.' I was staggered. Could he be serious? But Munker's comportment made nonsense of that question: 'This is for real' his neck seemed to tell the world; and his shoulders concurred.

'Play ball,' he said, 'and you get to meet him.'

'I don't know that I want to,' I said.

'Sure you do. Guy's your father.'

'Guy is my father?'

'Your old man,' he explained at speed. 'This guy here. He's your biological parent. Here's the phone number of your contact in Paris. On the back there. OK?'

'Why, Georges, you great big cuddly bear!' Marilyn Moore made a loud, squameous kissing noise.

'Stick them in your pocket pal,' said Munker. I was quick to oblige. He turned from me and walked back into the salon.

'Do I get to use your phone, Bruedelmann?' I heard him ask. And then he was gone.

'My dear Mr Clare,' said my host as he came to greet me, 'won't you come back inside now? I need you to be where we can see you.'

'Oh?' I nervously responded. 'Why's that?'

'It is all a matter of preparing the ground,' he said confidingly. 'I seek patterns, spectacles; I like to stage little fêtes. You know, we often find that something uncanny may supervene upon our gathering and envelop us in its mystery.'

'Since you mention it,' I said, struggling to regain the initiative, 'I've just had the most amazing sense of déjà vu.'

'Of course. Of course.'

'Why "of course"?' I asked him.

'But of course you feel it,' he replied, adjusting his heavy gown; I saw that he wore sandals, the thongs of which were decorated with tiny precious stones. His feet were large and very brown. 'There is something in the air, don't you think so? Some people find when they come to my gatherings that they experience their unconscious states as intensely personal memories inexplicably recalled. Yes, Mr Clare, much of what happens to you this evening will come to you suddenly with a haunting sense of heightened familiarity like something long forgotten but at last recalled. And the same is true of what lies before you, for even the future may haunt you in this château. Indeed,' he concluded, patting me somewhat heavily on my back, 'if we attend, we find we may discover a great deal about ourselves.'

'Your American visitors,' I said, 'they've disappeared.'

'Such a short appearance. But they were kind to dress themselves up for us, wouldn't you say so? You see, Mr Clare, our costumes are magical.'

'Magical?'

'Yes! You will find, Mr Clare, that your costume tonight will simplify your inner world. Meaning is not within; truth is not inside. These things

153

are the product of all of us, of each of us individually contributing, existentially participating in a process which will resolve itself, I assure you, into a striking coherence, a pageant of colour and form.'

There had been a wonderful change in the atmosphere of the party. Not that it was any the less uncanny, for it was more so; but people had evidently shed their inhibitions, and the earlier straggling sequence of scattered groups had merged into a mass of persons all congregating in the centre of the room. There was shouting, laughing, and loud expostulations; and there was a rhythm to the gathering, an unmistakable swing. It welcomed me, drew me into its unity.

I found myself talking volubly to a French woman of about thirty. She was dressed in the ostentatious fashion of the late seventeenth century; on her head she wore a fabulous hat with an enormous pink feather in the hat band. She made great play with her lacquered fan, which was decorated in Chinese motifs, and she took immense delight in her shoes. She twice drew up her skirt to present them to me.

'You know what I really love,' she said breathlessly, 'what I really love about this dress?'

'The ribbons?' I said.

'The underwear!' she replied, and giggled deliciously. As I strove to decipher her remark a man who looked just like Danton, both in face and dress, came up behind her and left me in no doubt as to her prior amative commitment. And I recalled then a story that Lucia once told me on the subject of ladies' underwear: according to the memoirs of the Comte de Gramont, translated into English by Horace Walpole, a certain Miss Churchill, who was very ugly, won the heart and hand of a duke. Her good fortune was occasioned by a violent fall from her horse which left her temporarily stunned and her garment in such disarray that those who came to her assistance, and among their number was the duke himself, 'could hardly believe that limbs of such exquisite beauty could belong to a face like Miss Churchill's.' And so it was that a conspicuous absence of underclothes led to a very fine match. This incident took place in the early years of the seventeenth century, at which time, according to Lucia, who had become quite an expert on the subject, ladies seldom wore knickers of any kind. And marriage-brokers, presumably, ran stables.

At the dinner table that night there was much talk of history, and art, and metaphor, and of personal identity, and being. I recall very little, however, of the several and complex conversations that occurred. But I remember very well how we sat at table, each in a distinct and historical costume, and, for my part at least, uncomfortably prey to the idea that we were somehow strangely uniform. And of course, being costumed we were somewhat at odds with our inner selves so that we thought a great deal about truth and illusion, and about self-expression, and about the meaning of signs. Much of the time I had nothing to say, and no wish to speak, for my encounter with Marilyn Moore, and later with Burt Munker, had awoken in me feelings of intense excitement not unmixed with foreboding. My costume, too, I found disorienting. Very quickly I got rather drunk.

'This costume is just talk, a speech with various elements.'

'Sure, but the elements refer to . . .'

'Sets of metaphors, not facts.'

'But that's just how I see history.'

'Something on your back?'

. . . And such like, and so, and thus.

There was a weave of voices, and running through the fabric of talk the threads seemed ever unbroken; my head felt heavy and I was flushed in the face.

A harmonious tinkling of voices delicately stilled the intricate conversations; two Vietnamese girls of five or six years of age had come tripping into the room, their hands held high by Kwee. The little girls were solemn, and graceful as ballet dancers, and yet astonishingly joyful. And each was the very picture of her sibling; we looked agog from one to the other, and saw the same round moon face, and dark eyes shining, the tiny ears, the same straight black hair. The twins were dressed, however, in one-piece suits of quite different colours: one red, one blue. We learned that every week the colours were exchanged, and the new arrangement was carefully recorded in a ledger! Kwee brought the twins to the table, and Bruedelmann, with a grin of comic proportions, set them upon his knees. He spoke to them in French, each in turn, and they uttered a chorus of remarks and observations, and clambered about on his knees and thighs in their little blue and red shoes. Then he gave them each a kiss on the cheek and wished them good night. And they, in disorderly unison, excitedly and at very great speed, uttered short, deft phrases of French as they kissed his yachtsman's leathery skin and as if on the order, burst into giggles; their faces filled with mirth and rocked on their slender shoulders. Under the guidance of their mother? nanny? governess? the little girls went skipping from the room.

Kwee, Georges Bruedelmann informed us, was the older sister of the two little girls and their only living relative. The other members of their family, including their father, mother and brothers, had perished in an open boat on the China Sea. 'When I contemplate my dear little Viet-namese twins of tragedy,' he said with great solemnity, 'I am reminded of the order of the day. *We must find ourselves in each other,*' he said. '*That is the challenge of our time.*' Then he started talking about children.

The door opened and a young woman came into the dining room. She had golden reddish hair and was clad in a long loose robe of white muslin. On her broad, high forehead she wore a narrow headband of black velvet, and on her feet she wore dainty silk slippers with woven motifs. On seeing the newcomer enter our midst, Catherine, who had talked to me earlier about her underwear, delightedly clapped her hands together and cried out, 'Madame Récamier!' But Madame Récamier, I discovered, was not the name of the latecomer to our party, but the subject of a famous sitter of Jacques-Louis David at about the time of Napoleon's accession to the Empire. She was a lovely and courageous Parisian socialite of the day, and the person who had brought her now to life was Hugo Thayer's Harriet.

'My dear Harriet,' said Bruedelmann, raising himself from the table and taking her outstretched hand, 'how delighted I am to see you!' Leading her gracefully to her place at the feast he inclined towards her and said, with a sort of murmuring politeness, 'I think you know none of my guests tonight.' But Harriet looked unhurriedly round the table at us, and smiled warmly, and nodded to herself.

'Yes,' she said, in a beautiful heavy voice, 'I don't know anyone.' She seemed to reach out to us then, as though she were singing the opening bars of a love song. 'Hello everybody.' Her eyes shone like amber. And when she saw that she had quite stolen the initiative from Bruedelmann her hand flew to her mouth revealing the beautiful cool lines of her wrist and her long graceful fingers. 'Oh! I'm sorry Georges!' Then she laughed, with enchanting, operatic exuberance; and we all laughed with her. People were calling out their names; she seemed to take them all in as she sat there with her elbows on the table and her hands cupped under her chin. I noticed particularly that her eyes were strikingly alert and lively. Then, with a light, tripping tone she ran through our names, and faltered only once. It was my own name that seemed to confuse her, but not because she could not choose between Robert and Mark, for she called both Edward, who sat beside me, and myself, 'Robert Mark'. Everybody laughed.

Several conversations were going on at the same time. But questions of language, or signs in general, and the topic of self-expression came up again and again.

And then I found myself loudly defending somebody else's ideas, and at just the time, I soon discovered, when I could have made best use of silence. 'I think it's plain wrong-headed,' I was saying, 'this talk of inside and outside; having something that needs to be expressed is not at all like having something to show someone. When people talk about expressing themselves they tend to think that there is "some thing" actually inside them, perhaps an idea, or a need, or a belief, and that this "thing" needs to find some external means of expression.'

'Yes, it's much more likely that . . .'

'I think it's a blind merging. Intelligent but basically blind. A merging. When we express something, when we say something about our feelings, for example, there are two elements in a single process: one of them is a sort of semi-cultural intendingness which is formless, meaningless, ungraspable; and the other is an already existent sign in some external, public code. It could be a word, a gesture, a phrase of music, or even a little dance.'

'Is it possible,' someone asked me, 'for your "blind intendingness" to hit on a sign that is actually a poor choice?'

'Yes, I suppose so. But I think the criteria for assessing a given choice as "poor" don't exist independently of the choice. They are conjured into existence by the very act of making the choice. That of course is how art develops. I believe that if the person doing the expressing had the right feeling, the right craft, and was in the right frame of mind at the time of the merging, then it is most likely that the sign chosen or "hit on" in that instant would become as though carved in stone in its unchangeable rightness.'

'*And how is Hugo?*' Georges Bruedelmann asked Harriet. Notwithstanding the complexities of the discussion, as soon as I heard the name I was somehow certain that it was Hugo Thayer who was intended. My ears pricked up and I strained to hear what was said.

'*He sleeps a lot,*' Harriet replied. '*But he talks much more now. Especially he talks about you. But they don't like that. They think it makes him agitated.*'

Bruedelmann nodded but said nothing. '*I told him,*' she continued, '*that I would come here on my way back to England.*'

'*Was that wise, my dear?*'

'Is that why you think there could not, properly speaking, be a match between the inner cultural intendingness, as you called it, and the external chosen sign?'

'Yes, I . . . What?'

'*He wanted me to tell you something.*' She paused; looking pointedly, I thought, in my direction, she said, '*But can I tell you later?*'

'*Of course.*' He patted her elegant forearm.

'I mean,' I said, vigorously taking up the thread, 'in what sense could there ever be a match? Would the chosen external sign be a picture of the thing-to-be-expressed? How could that be? How could we be sure? What is a painting a picture of? Are Cézanne's apples true pictures of something else, something which isn't apples? I don't think it even makes sense to ask.'

'That's precisely what art's all about!' someone shouted inconsequentially, and in triumph.

As our feast drew to its close Bruedelmann talked about his life. I had the impression that everything he said was calculated in its effect; it was as though he was at pains to forge something in our very heads. He talked about Sephardic Jews, the Franco-Prussian War, political cartoons in Charivari, picture-restoring in pre-War Vienna, the Nazi death camps, Seine bouquinistes, the post-War Berlin black markets and the Lichterfelder Fête Galante, which reminded me not a little of the libidinous gat-toothed Tara, whom I had met in his gallery in Paris. I think what impressed me most in what he said that night was his claim to have been taught as a child by a world-famous twentieth-century philosopher . . .

Somebody had asked him if he didn't feel that his childhood nature had been ruined and his adult psychological condition irredeemably doomed by the fact that he had lived his childhood in the Nazi era.

'I was saved,' he said, 'even as a child, because I chanced to be placed in the hands of teachers of the highest moral character. Even before I became apprenticed to my master in Vienna I had been exposed to what is highest and best in human nature. You see, I was a schoolboy at a tiny village school in Otterthal in Lower Austria. There I had a teacher, only a young man, who had a commitment to truth that was so powerful we feared him like the devil, but we loved him like a father. He was handsome, and fine, and he seemed to us like a German knight from the Middle Ages. He was so gifted in music and had a remarkable memory for it. He used to whistle whole passages from Beethoven's concertos. He always said to us that knowing truth is not so important . . . *first be the truth*, he used to say to us, *and only then must you try to think it. Nothing else will do*. The authorities, of course, as you can imagine, detested him.

'Who was he?' we asked.

Georges Bruedelmann replied, 'His name was Ludwig Wittgenstein.'

12

Discussion, however, is rife amongst some of this city's philosophers as to whether Mamugnano, the illustrious alchemist, can renew the material wherewith he had made gold, once it is used up.

January 1590, from a letter from Vienna, *The Fugger News-Letters*
1568—1605

About noon we came to the Schloss at Rietburg. It is not well-fortified but it is impregnable: the house stands on a rocky isle at the centre of a deep lake. It is built four-square with high, sheer walls and has four towers, one at each cardinal point. There are some sixty rooms, and from tower to tower the passage measures twenty paces. The courtyard within the walls is square and partly paved. At the rear of the house and without its walls are convenient outlying buildings, these being: the brewery, the bakehouse and the stables, to which there is access via a gateway in the courtyard. And there is a small pleasure garden in that place, bounded by a few solitary pines, and some vegetable plots. I warrant there is some secret, underground access to the outlying buildings. Hudson shall find it out.

Count Bernhard von Halle met us in the great hall and bade us welcome. This is a nobleman of *dignitas*. Magnificently attired in furs and fine cloths he bears himself very straight and is slow to turn his head. 'Pray attend me at your leisure,' he said. 'We shall have audience.' He commended us to his secretary, Herr Stremel, who had greeted us at the gate. This secretary has hair of a silver hue, fine-spun like silk, and a very long nose. His eyes are set a little uneven in his head. Bartholomew says there is naught but cunning in him and great mischief. At all times he carries with him his leather case, which is stuffed with papers. He insists he knows no English so we conversed with him in Latin, in French and in German. He has a voice like honey, but a cruel lip. B. says his mouth is hungry. I know not what he means by it, save that the man is ambitious.

*

25 May, 1581

We have been thirty hours in the castle and still no audience with the count. We are lodged in the west tower at the top of the house and fully eighty feet above the ground. The waters of the lake lap at the stones of the outer wall. Fine views provide a recreation of the eye. But poor Hudson must stay in his trunk from dawn to midnight. I do not doubt but some hidden passage gives clandestine intelligence of us, and I fear this discourteous trend of the count. Bartholomew grows quarrelsome. Spends long hours in the library, which fills the towers and the passageway on the floor which runs north to west below us. More than two thousand books are stored there. Bartholomew has befriended the count's librarian, one Doktor Pedelspur, and they converse at length, of herbals, and of efficient causes, and a host of antiquities, sometimes in Greek, sometimes in Latin. No word yet of the alchemist.

26 May, 1581

This morning at breakfast we were interrupted. The secretary told us the count would see us this day at four of the clock.

Last night I stood in the northerly tower and watched the evening. I had a view over the pleasure garden and chanced to see the alchemist's daughter. I think it was she. First a slender shadow passed between the pines. Two seconds after there came a truly giant figure. This was surely the Saxon, her protector. This same Saxon who guards her night and day once killed a bull with a fist blow to the head. Whatever be the truth of it this man's sense is keen. As he went his way he stared about intently and cast his gaze upward to where I stood.

With Stremel in attendance we had our meeting with the count. Bernhard von Halle sat in a great oaken chair. It is carved with woodland monsters and upholstered in red velvet, and is very padded. I thought the man ambitious by it. B. says he has piles. He rested his hand on a writing-table of great proportions strewn with letters, reports and sundry dispositions. Bartholomew interprets thus: they wished to signal to us that the count is ever preoccupied with the cares of his high office. It was subtle and conciliatory, he says, as befits the delay we suffered.

The count spoke German, French, and Latin with us. He showed great interest in the affairs of Oxford University. It is well we were briefed for he asked most searching questions, but generally, both of the administration and the individual doctors' reputations. He said it was his lifelong ambition to found his own university and he wished to build one in

Mark-Rietenburg. This I did not believe, and nor did Bartholomew, and yet it was fair-seeming. He mentioned by name some dozen of the most illustrious scholars of our age. Spoke, too, in learned detail of the books they have written! No doubt but he foregathered this information intending to test us, which might explain the delaying of the audience. Bartholomew answered fluently and well. The secretary, Stremel, who stood three feet behind his master's chair, never spoke a word. I thought he had no interest in us and affected only to listen to us. Bartholomew says he only affected *to affect to listen*, but studied us most intently all the while. 'This man listens deeply,' said he, 'and thinks far ahead. His thoughts,' he said, 'are like those who forage for an army: ranging wide and far ahead.'

Bartholomew and I were seated on low stools with our trunk of books laid open beside us and Hudson stowed in the false bottom thereof. I spoke at last of the beauty of the castle. Whereupon the count, who is most courteous in conversation, inquired if I was a lover of the new architecture. Bartholomew said that we Englishmen were at best *dilettantes* of that art. And straight engaged the count in talk of views and *vistas*. Begged the count to show him some places where he might profitably ride for pleasure. Whereupon we all went to the windows and scanned the countryside. 'Our journey eastward hastens the sunrise,' said I, and dropped some books which I had lugged to the windows. This was our signal to Hudson. Swift and silent as a falling stone he escaped the trunk and stowed himself in the bookshelf. And all the while Bartholomew's talk flowed and flowed, ravishing his listeners. The secretary, too, must smile at his eloquence but it was more *deliberate*, methought, than cordial. Then a horseman appeared on the brow of a low hill and rode at the gallop through meadowland down towards the lake. I thought it was a boy of fifteen or so. He hooted as he rode and swept off his cap and waved it in the air like a lunatic. Birds flew about him, which was very strange. 'It is my one remaining son,' the count said. Whereupon Bartholomew drew him out on it: the count informed us of the death of his first-born, of which we knew from K.'s briefing. He spoke with heavy voice of a beautiful young man, of soldierly spirit yet very keen of wit, and blessed with good judgement withal, and of high moral character. There were no more sons of his line, he told us, and no more progeny to come. He said he had fractured his *os pubis* when his horse had thrown him and this had robbed him of his generative powers. Bartholomew spoke simple and great lines from a Greek tragedian. The count deigned to reply in that same tongue. Bartholomew says his words were apposite and from the same work.

By and by to the purpose of our visit: we had heard, we said, that

Doktor Henricus Wykzo, much admired by certain scholars at Oxford, had lately travelled from Vienna to dwell in Mark—Rietenburg where he was blessed with the favour of the high born. On behalf of the Schools we looked for an interview with him. The count professed himself surprised that learned gentlemen had travelled from Oxford, full three hundred and fifty miles, to meet his servant and friend when few beyond Bohemia's borders knew of him. We protested, most courteously, that Doktor Wykzo's books were much admired by certain doctors of Cambridge, Oxford, and London. What works were they? the count inquired. Then Bartholomew expounded on Wykzo's book of mathematical studies printed ten years past in Basle, and also of his lectures on Prima Materia, which were read at Augsburg, and the celebrated 'notes' on the transubstantiation of minerals. And then he asked the count if perchance our reports were false: whereupon the count affirmed that Wykzo dwelt in this very house under his own protection and had his laboratory in an experimental chamber without the walls. This was a measure of safety, he said, in case of explosion. We voiced our approval and our delight. But why, the count asked us, had we not written directly to Doktor Wykzo? To which we replied that we had feared to offend his noble patron, and besides, since we had business in Helmstedt we had not found it incommodious to journey first to Mark-Rietenburg. I thought these answers satisfied the count. Bartholomew was doubtful.

Next he wants to know what we purpose with the alchemist. We drew our letters from the trunk and showed him our brief of instructions from the Committee of Schools. It was our task, we said, to inquire into the nature of Doktor Wykzo's present researches, and to ask some scientific questions of him, and perchance to commission him to write a book for the library of Sir Thomas Merton. We showed him a paper by means of which Doktor Wykzo might make his application for an honorary stipendium. We said there were many in Oxford who would gladly hear him lecture, too. The count said not a word to this but passed our papers to the secretary who put them to scrutiny unashamedly. And while the master pondered we sat and waited.

Henricus Wykzo, he said, was a solitary man whom adverse fortune had made distrustful. The count next proposed we make our way to Helmstedt and from there send word to Rietburg when our business was concluded. He would endeavour, he said, for the occasion of our return from Helmstedt, to fix a meeting with the Doktor. We expressed dismay. We planned to take ship, we said, at Cuxhaven, and would much prefer to wait in Lippstadt, or at an inn near the castle, until we might meet with the doctor. The count looked hard at us. Bartholomew requested permission to pen a note to good Doktor Wykzo. 'To what end?' the count inquired. 'To inform the man of our high regard for his work, and to communicate our good intentions,' Bartholomew replied, saying, too, that we hoped this might dispose the doctor to meet with us. (This was well done.) The count looked to the secretary, who seemed to nod. Whereupon the count invited us to prolong our stay in his house until the day after the morrow, when he might have better news for us. It was his custom, he said, to speak with Henricus for a short time each evening. He would not fail, he said, to discuss our suit with his servant and friend, and would request him to permit his guests to pen him a note. He warned us to expect no progress in the matter for a full day, and twice enjoined our patience. The audience was concluded.

Late in the night Hudson returned with substantial intelligence. His adventure: having hidden himself in the bookshelf he placed a cloth over his face, for it was very dusty, and lay still as a corpse. After we had departed, B. and I, for full five minutes there was no word spoken in the chamber. The count sat brooding at his desk, the secretary walked up and down at the window. At last the master spoke:

'I cannot trust these men. I sense some hidden purpose in their visit. The one is dull of speech yet strangely knowing. The other . . .'

'The priest, sir?'

'Ha! Do you say a priest, Stremel?'

'An erstwhile priest, sir. A fallen one.'

'That's true, very like. What brings them here? I would I knew it.'

'I would I knew their provenance, my lord, more than their purposes.'

'Have you not studied the letters they brought? Written by the masters of Oxford. Their persons are commended to us, their bona fides guaranteed. Even their purpose is named.'

The master fidgeted at his desk, the secretary read over the letters.

'If the letters are genuine, secretary, then so are the scholars.'

'The letters are genuine, my lord.'

'Ha!'

'I mean, sir, the letters are written upon some genuine authority in that place, but I doubt these messengers are scholars. Great influence upholds their purpose. Will my lord permit them to meet with the 'chemist?'

'Stremel, I shall not.'

'My lord is wise. To hold them separate is policy most prudent. For the present.'

'For the present only? I did not say so much. They shall not meet my friend.'

'I would I knew how long my lord plans to keep them in his house.'

163

'Until I have sure knowledge of their true intentions.'

'Shall we set a spy on them, sir?'

'We shall.'

'I fear that policy, my lord.'

'Fear it? Why fear it, Stremel?'

'My lord does not trust them and neither do I. This makes them very likely false. And false men who are plausible of face and speech must be very cunning and well prepared. Who knows what craft of thieves or spies is theirs? I fear it would show them the colour of our thoughts to set a spy on them, sir.'

'How's that, Stremel? I do not see that.'

'Would they not be swift, sir, to spy on him? These men sleep with open eyes. But if my lord will give them freedom they will grow in confidence and come the quicker to their purpose. My lord's servants are everywhere in the castle. Let them in their ordinary tasks keep intelligence of these men's doings. And by and by we'll find the means to read through their letters.'

The count held his peace. He scratched his eyebrow, and his nose. Hudson swears the master does not love the servant, nor the servant the master.

'You said we should keep them separate for the present only. You said this to me. I tell you now, I would not have them meet the alchemist at any time.'

'My lord, we must let them think they dupe us.'

'Must let 'em meet the 'chemist?'

'We must make promises, my lord. Yet we must protract and then prorogue, but not delay too much neither, lest they should move out of our supervision. Let us obstruct their purpose but not so far that they will grow stealthy and dangerous. Let them think we are deceived, sir, but ponderous in policy, and cautious. They will be more patient for it. And we shall have the occasion to catch at their letters.'

The count gave thought to the secretary's words.

'Good. I'll have them write the letter.'

'That's good, my lord. 'Tis very good.'

'They should name their purposes therein. And they should plainly state what actions they intend. Let 'em set down what experiments interest them, and they must give proof of esoteric learning. They must do all this before they get their audience with Henricus. Is this not good, Stremel?'

'For his time is precious, and his labours press him, sir.'

'You will find means to intercept their letters?'

'With your permission, sir, I shall. But first we must give them matter, sir.'

'Matter?'

'Something of substance, and to the point, and of a scale to their true purposes. We must induce them to write a letter for despatch to their true masters. Be they never so cautious we'll get some savour of their purposes by it. And perchance we shall discover their true provenance.'

'Then we shall have the measure of their lying . . . in the one hand, their written statement of intent, and in the other, their letter to their masters. It is good, Stremel.'

The count thinks hard at his desk. The secretary watches him, his long finger curled about the crooked bridge of his nose.

'Will you propose some matter, Stremel, whereof they shall be tempted to discover themselves?'

'Most gladly, my lord. Tell them there is soon to be a wedding.'

'A wedding?'

'A marriage, sir, of my lord's son to Wykzo's daughter. That'll shake them. If the object of their interest is the alchemist, sir, this news must bear on their hidden purposes. It will change the complexion of their hopes, my lord, it will unsettle their policy.'

'I do not like this proposal, secretary.'

'My lord?'

'Henricus Wykzo is my friend. I would not play tricks with his daughter's name, nor with his hopes.'

'A friend, sir? We thought him no better than ourselves. I crave your pardon. I had quite failed to note his singular favour, sir.'

'I will speak with my friend. And I will think on your proposal. I pray you, go now, Stremel. At breakfast you shall give our guests some news. But let them have none tonight.'

The secretary bowed and left the chamber. The count sat at his desk and rubbed his face with his hands. He groaned aloud and threw down his papers. He uttered curses, rose again and went to the window. All the while he mumbled to himself, but Hudson could not make it out. At last he returned to his desk and wrote for an hour. Then he laid his head among his papers and slept for five minutes. Awaking, he took up his sheets and quit the chamber.

Hudson crept from concealment and read over the papers on the desk. Husbandry and households: naught but local matters. When it was very dark he snuffed the candles and stole to the door, and hearing a guard in the passage he mewed like a cat, then hid himself. When the guard entered the chamber Hudson slipped away.

We commended him for this excellent intelligence. And now we saw we had a difficult path and our hopes sank. Did Stremel not know of the intended marriage? Was K. falsely informed? Bartholomew said the secretary's nature was our surest pointer: Stremel, he said, had no love for his master and would grasp an occasion to embarrass the count if it could be done without risk of blame. From this he concluded firstly that the marriage promise had occurred as K. had stated, secondly that Stremel was excluded from that information, thirdly that Stremel had discovered it for himself, and fourthly that Stremel had his own spies. As to our policy in the light of Hudson's report: we would affect a great trial of our patience, and yet would place a firm date on our departure. This to put an edge to our host's deliberations.

27 May, 1581

This morning at breakfast in the hall: Stremel came and brought with him in attendance a young woman whom he did not present to us. And five paces behind her there strode an enormous Saxon, whose name is Juergen. I never saw a man so large. His arms are as another man's legs in girth and he is a full head taller than myself. As the giant passed with slow tread and much creaking of floorboards, the secretary whispered to us, 'Soon to wed, good gentlemen.' We inquired who she was. 'Why,' said he, ''tis Magdalene Wykzo, daughter of Wykzo the alchemist.' And who is she to wed? 'My lord's son,' said he, 'shall have her for his bride.' That same one that was on the horse? 'The same,' said he. He wished us good-day and left the hall. Three minutes passed and then he returned to us again and reminded us of the letter we should write. We should name our purposes, etc. therein, just as Hudson had reported. He urged us, as though he served our interests in the matter, to write the letter at our earliest convenience as we could not hope to get an audience until the doctor had had occasion to peruse it. And protocol required, he said, that we address the letter both to his Excellence the count, and to Wykzo the alchemist. Next he told us that a man rode with the post at mid-morning and at six in the evening. If we wished to send letters abroad we should place our mail with the guard at the gatehouse. We thanked him for this courteous attendance and informed him of our firm intention to depart the castle on the 30th day of the month, if it pleased our host. He bowed, smiled, and departed.

Bartholomew took pen to paper and crafted Wykzo's letter which we sent to the secretary. Then we went walking round the lake. Two soldiers came with us but showed no interest in our talk and stayed some thirty paces off.

We examined our position: B. says the count is melancholy and given to fits of dread. This makes him both over-cautious and yet suddenly careless in policy and decision. The secretary, Herr Stremel, is cold, phlegmatic and full of craft and measure. Is more dangerous than the master, but less powerful, and the count likes him not. In this game of waiting we are not without advantage. And so to the question of the 'matter of substance' that Stremel spoke of: should we send a letter to Oxford, or to London? Bartholomew said we should not write to either place except we got clear and certain profit from it, such as would promote our cause. I proposed we should write to Oxford, giving news of the forthcoming marriage, making some comment on that union's influence on our hopes. But B. said we would get no meeting with Wykzo except the count could see some profit in it *for himself*. We should be dismissed from the castle, he said, with our hopes dashed if our letter was too innocent. We concluded: a letter must be sent to the University at Oxford, and we must put some 'savour' in it, something to catch the interests of the count. Videlicet: our text would *hint at our ulterior purpose*, and *intimate* our desire to reveal this purpose to our noble host, and yet imply a doubt *as to the timeliness*. Thus we contrived that our host should discern in us a need, which was not yet grown ripe, to divulge to him a secret matter of notable interest to himself. And our letter should prove us to be prudent men, and of good judgement, who watched events, were not skittish, but kept close counsel. So and thus we practised to whet their appetites, knowing their intention to snatch at our mail. And Bartholomew swore by this means to inflame their curiosities and yet frustrate their desires, and to win us time, and yet exhaust our host's intransigence.

Upon our return Hudson told us our chamber had been searched. By good fortune our tiny man was out, a-spying in a hidden corridor which he had chanced on in the night. And so he spied on those who spied on us, and heard a man say that Stremel the secretary had ordered the search, and *not* the count. 'Slowly it comes to a head' said I. Upon returning to our chamber we sat down straight and wrote the letter to Oxford, which I took to the gatehouse a *little after the post had gone*. To give our noble host the time to read it, Bartholomew said. It did not please me though, how he said it.

28 May, 1581

Not yet dawn. The best news yet. Hudson returned at three in the morning. Very excited. Said he'd found access, by drain or culvert, direct to the foundations below Wykzo's laboratorium. He lay there hid last night; some two hours and a half he listened to Wykzo himself, muttering and groaning at his work. H. says he *sensed* the presence of Magdalene ... How can this be? The man is half out of his wits with his story: Wykzo kept muttering about *the light*. H. said the 'chemist spoke strange words in a very foreign tongue. We pressed him to utter some and by and by he pronounced some garbled syllables. Then B. supplied some words of Hebrew and H. confirmed some half a dozen sounds, whereupon Bartholomew declared he had *forgot* their meaning! Half asleep and drugged as ever ... Hudson said he dozed a while but woke with a start when a heavy receptacle smashed on the boards above his head and Wykzo screamed out 'The light! The light!' or perhaps 'My light! Oh my precious light!' and in that instant, where Hudson had fixed his upward gaze through ill-joined floor boards, there came a *silver–golden rain* and *sparkling bright as diamonds*. Hudson swears it passed *straight through the wood, and passed straight through poor Hudson's flesh, even down through his feet. He swears he saw it pass through his knee and out his heels!* The stout-hearted fellow fell to the ground and scrabbled to take it up, droplets he said, *but dry as dust*, or *not there at all*! And even as he scrabbled there, this precious substance, *bright as the sun*, seemed to grow dark and sombre as he looked at it. Hudson was awed. Said he never saw *such evil*! He said *it was as if it lived, and it knew him*! So Hudson, fearing for his wits, leapt back ... and the stuff grew bright as gold again, then swiftly *passed into the solid flagstones like gold coin thrown into the blackness of a well, yet lighting itself as it fell*. And Wykzo starts praying, more foreign gibberish, weeping and cursing his fate. 'Oh my fields of light!' or some such utterance. A half an hour later all was quiet.

Daylight has brought only idleness and speculation. Hudson says this house is peopled with sombre presences. A very bad house, says he. But he'll out again tonight, stout fellow, and try his luck for Queen and country. Bartholomew remarked to me how strange poor Hudson appeared today in the sunlight. Like a man drained of his strength, he said, or one who has fought a mortal illness all his life. I concurred: but in his strength of purpose we found him more solid than ever. Hudson has the spirit. An excellent comrade.

After supper Stremel brings word that we are invited tomorrow night to dine with the count and with his servant Henricus Wykzo. Here's welcome relief at last.

A strange night. Bartholomew cried out in his sleep. Walked about the chamber *crying for his mother*. By Heaven if I must I'll toss his potions in the lake. He would not heed my exclamations and when I left my bed to grapple with him I found he was fast asleep. He woke in my arms with a wild, mad shout and said to me 'Good Pike, have you one mind tonight?' and 'What but it all grows trammelled,' or some such phrase. At half past three our Flink came in and fell into the trunk. Said he wished he was home in Cheapside and hated all foreigners. And your father, said I, that German tinker. What of him? We had a drink on it. I must keep up morale. These men oscillate. Is it this castle that brings it on us?

29 May, 1581

Have come from dining with the count etc. Also in the party were Henricus Wykzo, his daughter Magdalene and the accountant from Lippstadt whose name is Beutelsmann. This fellow was most convivial at table and made great play on his own name, which means 'he who keeps the purse'.

Doktor Wykzo is a man of small stature and very thin. Bartholomew says he is fearful for his soul. In part I agree. We thought him a man haunted by some secret of which he is ashamed. He is about sixty years old. Hair white; eyes yellowy and bloodshot; complexion shiny and a little green. He walks with difficulty, and carries a stick to help him about. But he is a man much stronger than he looks, if Bartholomew has rightly measured him, for great ambition fires his blood and drives his endeavours. I think he works like a Trojan. Has an insatiable lust for knowledge and when he speaks of his *Kabbala* and his *gnosis* he is quite transformed. B. says he has true genius. I found him astute, and yet there is something of the child about him too. I think him vain, but B. says he is *naive*. Whatever be its name it is a quality that lends him to exploitation. And still more to the purpose, he loves his daughter almost beyond the natural love of a father. God's name is ever on his lips, uttered in great reverence. He wears a heavy German cloak that reaches to his feet and he wears a hat of fur. Yet it was a warm night. I think him very infirm.

Magdalene Wykzo: a maid of eighteen years and beauteous in proportion. Has a rare sweetness of expression, such I have seen only in religious paintings. Her *demeanour* is very spiritual. Her smile surpasses all smiles I have known, and she has good teeth, which is exceeding rare. Her brow is high, her skin is very pale and smooth like Mutterperle, her eyes violet, which I never saw in any other person. It is her eyes that mark her out: sometimes she looks about her wildly and there comes into her face a look of such terror it freezes the blood. I took this for the inner drama of unreason. B. says she looks about her as one who searched for demons in the dark. A sinister conceit.

169

This child is burdened with misfortune. She came in silence into this world, being born deaf and dumb. And so cruel the traverse it carried off her mother even as it brought her in. She cannot speak, but some portion of what she meets with she seems to understand. Her gaze is somewhat deficient: yet it happens, myself I saw it twice last night, this wildness in her face, this terror in her gaze give place to an other-worldly quietude and the darkling grows clear. Then sweetest reason, almost of angelic orders, seems to light her up, and what compassion, what knowledge she appears to possess in that instant. It chastens a man to behold. Bartholomew, I saw, was deeply affected. I never knew him take such note of a woman. I warrant it is the common tragedy of their births. But her eyes and lips, her hair, I must record it, the girl is beautiful indeed.

After she had eaten she sat to the side and did some needlework, although the light was rather dim. Methought she saw with her very fingers, which are long and fine. Great Juergen the Saxon sat by her then and picked up the thread if it rolled away, or held one end of her work as she plied her fingers through it. The maid is very confident with him, and very gentle. But not so gentle as he with her when he brings her to her chair, or helps her from table! She sits in his care like a madonna on her throne. Bartholomew watched her all evening. I would he had hearkened half as much to her dad.

Henricus Wykzo spoke of his life in Prague and Vienna, but of little else, save God and his daughter. Said he would not speak of his present researches at the dinner table. To this contumacious reticence the count gave full support. Wykzo said that all God's creatures point to Him that made them. His grace is manifest. What creature is there higher than a man in all the gross, material world? He talked half the night about Count Pico, the Florentine Kabbalist of Mirandola. B. knows well what he spoke of, from the famous oration on the dignity of man: *Medium te mundi posui, ut circumspiceres inde commodius quicquid est in mundo. Nec te caelestem neque terrenum, neque mortalem neque immortalem fecimus, ut tui ipsius quasi arbitrarius honorariusque plastes et fictor, in quam malueris tute formam effingas.* Which is to say that man must make what he will of himself, must sculpt and paint himself into what image he will, and being at the world's centre, neither celestial, nor truly of the earth, and not mortal, nor immortal neither, he is wholly free. For my part I found it vaunting talk in a man so small and sickly withal. And herein lies, methinks, the measure of the alchemist's ambition. I would I knew what he does with his *light*, which Hudson saw, or where he got it from. He boasts that his daughter is his *bright lantern*, and *lights his way for him*, which I find unwholesome. Nor, he declares, by virtue of her want of faculties, can the world get

170

purchase on her soul and so corrupt her. He holds her up, he says, that he may see what the world is. I think it pitiful a creature so delicate, I mean the daughter, and withal so beautiful, must marry a paltry boy whose wits are gone. Doubtless but the count's son must treat her roughly for how should he know the value of her soul? And there was much talk of the coming marriage, for it is a prospect which greatly pleases Wykzo. Yet how does this sit with his love, that he spends his daughter on a feeble-minded lunatic boy? 'Tis piteous. We take it as sure proof of his fearfulness, which we may turn to our purpose yet; and proof too of his lust for security of rank and tenure, which we may yet manipulate.

Doktor Beutelsmann, the accountant, that same citizen of Lippstadt who was ill last week but is now come to draw up the books: about thirty-five years, refined and yet very cordial, and much travelled. He is well-disposed to Englishmen. Five year ago he lived for eighteen month in London and studied the flow of sterling silver in the market. Likes to speak English. I set myself to make a friend of him, which was easy work and pleasurable. I commend him to my masters: such a man might do *sterling* service to the Crown.

Wykzo said he would see us tomorrow for discussions. Said he was impressed with the letter we sent him. But I think it was the letter we sent to Oxford that wrought this change in his master's disposition. When should we declare a postponement of our intended departure, which falls due tomorrow? And upon what ground?

30 May, 1581

Stremel came. Said Wykzo had changed his mind and could not see us that day! Galling. And we are thickly in it. Bartholomew construed it thus: the count wants to know our secret first, before we divulge it to the 'chemist.

Hudson, who slips in and out of the count's chamber by night, has so far failed to lay hand on the secret letters from the House of Kaunitz, nor the count's replies. And no fresh news of the alchemist's nightly labours. Bartholomew has taken to his bed and *will not speak to us*.

31 May, 1581

We grow slack of purpose and dispirited. Bartholomew lay in his bed, said he had a fever, would not move nor discuss policy, not so much as a word.

I walked in the woods with two wood-faced soldiers for company.

171

I fear we have played it poorly. I pressed Bartholomew for counsel: should we divulge our true provenance to the count? Bartholomew studied the wall. I laid my hand upon him and shook him lightly. Then he called me dolt and turned away again. I nearly struck him for it. Such is our morale.

Surely this castle weighs upon the spirit. There is a something *in the very air*. It is this, I fear, that keeps Bartholomew abed. I informed the secretary of B.'s indisposition, and later in the day we had a letter from the count. He expressed his *condolences* and extended the hospitality of his house. I fear these men will prove too clever for us.

Late this evening I returned from riding (ever with two soldiers for company) and found Bartholomew gone. He returned two hours after sundown. He was pale in the face and sweat hung on his brow. When I spoke to him he shook like a girl. Said he had a fever and had walked while he slumbered. He threw himself upon his bed and on the instant fell asleep.

1 June, 1581

June begins and nothing is accomplished yet. Bartholomew is better today. Makes all manner of teas out of his trunk of powders. I wished to discuss our policy with him but he could not concentrate his mind. Next he gives way to sighing and laughing. His behaviour is very strange. I fear he is more sick than he knows.

Hudson very surly. Pressed me for some chance to walk in the sunshine. Says he grows melancholy in his cache-hole. A house of dark spirits, he said, for the tenth time.

I fear we lose this game of waiting. We must review our policy for it is certain our credibility suffers. But there is nothing to be done. Hudson must wait for sunshine. And I must wait for Bartholomew to be well.

In the afternoon of the same day:

Events have outstripped us; a great change. I cannot say yet if it be to our advantage. About five o'clock I stood in the library window and saw below some four or five soldiers come running. And there, in a corner of the yard like a stag at bay stood Juergen the Saxon. With a great staff he flung off the soldiers as they rushed upon him. I never saw such formidable fighting skills as this giant showed: with utmost resolution and precision he laid about him like a grim warlord so that the courtyard was filled with the sounds of cracking skulls and men's cries and groans. Then musket men ran up and trained their weapons on him. But he would not yield so they shot him in the leg. And still he would not yield so they shot him in the shoulder. His face went white as death and letting go his staff he stretched himself out on the flagstones. There was blood and spittle in his beard but he was more than half alive. Any other man would have been twice fled from the world had he sustained such injuries.

I went to get intelligence of the matter and found a kitchen girl who sobbed behind a curtain. I spoke some words of comfort to her and asked her why men at arms had attacked the Saxon. She replied that her lady, for she was to be Magdalene's maid after the wedding, *her lady had been examined*. And thereupon she wept so hard she could not speak. And when she spoke again it was to bewail her condition, *for she must be a kitchen maid all her life*. Examined? I shook her hard. Be moderate, I said. For which of us is not the servant of some higher placed personage? To which she replied that she could not bear it, to be put to the torture. Said she would surely die if they put her to the torture. Said she was only ten years old and very sickly. A pitiful creature, and I pressed her to be calm, and vowed that I would speak for her if it came to torture. The physician, she said, had pronounced her a *fallen woman*. I thought she meant herself. But it was Magdalene Wykzo she spoke of.

A fallen woman. I could scarce believe it. 'Not a virgin any longer,' sobbed the maid. And now the count was horribly enraged and had sworn to hang the miscreant before the day was out. To that end they had laid hands on the Saxon and even now they put him to question in the prison cell.

I asked her if she knew aught of the rape, that I might help her. But she denied all knowledge of it. She said again she could not bear it to be put to the torture. Again I vowed to speak for her, whereupon she threw herself at my feet and said I was her true lord and master for ever.

Returned at once to the chamber. Woke Bartholomew from his druggy sleep and told him all. Conferred next with Hudson. Bartholomew's recovery was wonderful and prodigious. He quickly took command of our discussions: said we must speak directly with the alchemist. We went to seek out his rooms but found our way barred. The soldiers were nervous. We were sharply challenged. Rough words and menacing gestures. We returned to our chamber to confer.

Came a loud knocking at the door. The captain of the guard. He was solemn of countenance and severe in utterance. His Excellence the Count von Halle, he said, had prohibited all movement out of the castle. None might come into it neither but those with special passes. We were required, he said, not to stir forth from our chamber until he came again. His Excellence deeply regretted the incommodious prohibition, etc. He gave no explanation. Nor was one needed.

We hoped the Saxon would confess. Or die swiftly. When one man is put to the torture what other man is safe? I moved we should send Hudson to Lippstadt with a message, but B. dissuaded me. Said we might have greater need yet of our *secret agent*.

About nine in the evening a silence descended on the house as though a curse had taken hold. Ten minutes passed and soldiers were marching in the passage. Their looks were grim. The Saxon had confessed. They said, 'The devil's about. The priest hastens. The prohibition is lifted.'

We ventured out. And in the great hall found a paper nailed to a beam. It was the confession of Juergen the Saxon. This pious man who read his Bible every night, the one that Luther wrote in the German, avowed that *he had seen a devil mount the maid* and swore it on that same Lutheran Bible. It was his last word and testament before he died. And none could doubt his testimony, for his word was Gospel even in his lifetime. He said it had occurred some nights before, but time had all flowed together after they tortured him, so he was not sure which day it was . . .

The girl was wont, at twilight, to sit upon cushions in her chamber. She would grow silent and still, mysterious as a fairy queen. And while the darkness wrapped her round until the kitchen maid brought the candles, it was her custom to sit thus each evening. And it was the habit of the Saxon, and indeed his duty, to stay with the maid both night and day: when she lay down on her bed he settled on the floor at her feet, and when she rose, he rose. On the day in question, while he sat in the passage and watched his charge through the partly open door of her chamber, he smelt *a strange and bitter aroma*. A shower of dust fell out the air and settled on his face. Then a great weariness seized him so that he lay back against the wall. He strove to look about him but his eyelids were weighted as with lead. He tried to call out for assistance but he had no voice. Then for a time, he knows not how long it was, he could not see, nor hear, nor move a finger, and yet he said *he was awake*. And when at last his senses cleared and he was able to open his eyes he looked into the chamber where the darkness grew thick as the night came on . . .

The maid lay on the ground and her cloak was open at her waist and her bosom all uncovered. There rode upon her and betwixt her thighs an abominable creature that was the very colour of the night and bore great wings that flapped in the air. It had a demon's face as long as a horse. And for eyes it had a gaping hole the size of a man's fist. I was seized with rage and pity. I cried out to her yet no sound came forth but a piteous squeaking. This the creature heard and drew near to me again but I could not move a finger. My terror was great. Then I fell into a pitiless black sleep. I can remember no more than this. I woke when the kitchen maid

174

shouted in my ear. I struggled to my feet and sent her away. Then I took the candles and with the Lord's Prayer on my lips I went into the chamber and found poor Magdalene all uncovered on her bed. I thought she was killed. But her limbs were warm. I straightened her gown and put a blanket on her. And I resolved never to speak of this moment for I could see nothing come of it but ill. It is for my soul's sake that I speak now. You have broken my body but my soul belongs to God. And I am but a poor Christian man who saw a devil with the maid. He mounted her and he fornicated upon her. May God take me up in His hand. May He show His mercy to her and to me. I would have died a hundred times to save poor Magdalene. For I loved her as I loved my soul. If this be a lie let me be burned in Hell through all eternity.

Rumour flew from the castle. Even as we read that damnable paper the people gathered at the lake-side and on the bridge. We went to the gatehouse to speak with the captain of the guard and there we saw the people's firebrands and heard their shouts. The captain told us not to venture forth. He said the people feared witchcraft and sorcery. They demanded her death. Her death? The fallen woman, he said. That foreigner's daughter. Suffer not a witch to live.

We weighed our advantage in this matter and for my part I found it wanting. And since it was now dangerous in that atmosphere of dread and superstition to divulge our true provenance to the count, I pressed for our immediate departure. We had passed our deadline and Bartholomew was well again. Our departure was expected and could not raise suspicion against us. But Bartholomew was fierce against this policy. Said we should *grasp the occasion to win both parties to our side*. It was not the count's wish, he said, that Magdalene should die, but neither could he save her from the people and their priests. And if they burned poor Magdalene how should the alchemist forgive his master and sometime friend? Or stay in that country any longer, where they had murdered his daughter? It was necessary, he said, and it served our ends, *to rescue the daughter from the people, and win the 'chemist from the count*. And we must contrive too, he said, to win the confidence of the count no less than the thanks of the 'chemist. I thought this policy madly ambitious. But whether his reasoning was sound I could not rightly judge. Complex contrivances, said I, will ever go awry. But he scolded me and said that I had forgot that *he* was master of strategy for that he was wiser and cleverer. I said it were best the daughter died at the hands of the people. This would bring hatred between master and servant, remove all possibility of marriage, and push the 'chemist into our arms. And later, by some other means, we might find occasion to win the count to our side. But he called me 'muddy-head' and 'sleepy Jack' and swore I was blind as a mole. 'If the daughter dies,' said he, 'the alchemist must lose the will to live.' And Hudson concurred. 'Possess the daughter,' the dwarf said, 'and you'll get the father on her.' A vile conceit.

Bartholomew had a plan. This is surely the most cunning of men: he had a preparation, he said, part herbs, part minerals. When properly mixed and prepared, and taken in right proportion, the mixture bestows the very lineaments of death. All who see the 'corpse' pronounce it dead, even learned doctors! The poison does not kill the taker but only takes off all signs of life, but *provisionally*. A second potion administered under the tongue some two hours later *entirely restores that life again*! Thereupon Bartholomew went to his trunk and drew forth from his store a small bag of grey salts. *This is the means*, he said, *by which I put her first to death that she may live hereafter*. I shuddered to hear it.

We went straight to the count and begged a confidential interview on a matter of gravest import. Our request was granted, save that the secretary, too, was present. Bartholomew addressed the count: 'My lord,' said he, 'whether she be a witch or no what man can tell? But I have a means here that will save her life.' With what alacrity that man responded! Called at once for a mastiff and commanded we furnish proof. Then Bartholomew placed some crystals on the dog's tongue and closed his maw on it . . . barely a minute passed before the dog collapsed and grew stiff. Five minutes more and his eyes had fixed on a point and gone dull as death. And the 'corpse' was cold! Neither the count, nor the secretary, nor myself could detect so much as a twitch or flicker of a heartbeat. Not by touch, sight, or listening: heart, lungs, all still as death itself. 'We must wait one hour,' Bartholomew said.

Stremel went out to speak with the captain of the guard. We stood in the eastern tower and watched the lights of the people foregathered on the shore. They were a multitude. Some had pitchforks, others had cudgels and sticks. They banged on pots and knocked at stones. 'Give up the witch!' they chanted. We saw the secretary ride out on to the bridge. A dozen well-armed soldiers escorted him. He held a shouted parley with the leaders of the mob. We understood that he promised to hand her over to them. This was soon confirmed. But they must wait until the morning, for she was sick and her father was by her side. A great shout went up and the night was filled with lewd and seditious oaths.

An hour had passed and we returned to the count's chamber. Bartholomew had been anxious. Said he feared the secretary, who might wreck the experiment in our absence. But I think it was self-doubt that shook him so. *At half past one in the morning he raised the mastiff from his death. Mirabile dictu!* I saw it for myself. The dog was raised: first his eyes grew clear and they moved a little, then his jaws quivered. Then this dog that was dead, hearing his master speak encouragement, whimpered and shook his tail. And then he struggled up from the floor! Barely three minutes passed and he was walking. Then he began to whine like a creature in torment and licked at our boots 'The hound must be watered,' Bartholomew said. 'The potion dries up the corporeal fluids.'

'Or perhaps he means to thank us,' said the count, 'for this gift of life restored.'

Henceforth I shall never count a man dead until I smell the putrefaction of his corpse. This is a terrible science. Bartholomew swears the potions will work in like manner when administered to human beings! Said he knew it for certain: *had worked it on himself!* We were amazed. 'And were it an uncertain thing,' said he, ''twere better she should die of a poison that brings no pain than suffer torture first and then be burned.' The count agreed with him, but said the affair must be secret: it offended Heaven, he declared, for it meddled with the sacred mystery of life, and it offended the State, for it robbed the people of simple justice. Whereupon he swore us solemnly to silence. This being done he brought us by a secret passage to the chamber of Magdalene. 'Let the potions be administered,' said he. So we got the confidence of the count, and thought to save the daughter's life, and hoped still to get her into our keeping.

The girl lay bound upon her bed. Her eyes were big with confusion and terror, clouding and clearing, clouding again. And yet I thought she knew us. Bartholomew spoke to her, but they were words of comfort only, having little sense. He administered the potion. Strange that she trusted him. I helped him do it: just a few granules under the tongue. And soon the girl was as 'dead' as the mastiff had been before her. Poor Magdalene lay stiff and cold upon her bed. I was affected by it for I *could not* think her living still! The count called for doctors, and for chosen witnesses from among the people at the bridgehead. 'Let all men confirm,' said he, 'that Magdalene Wykzo lies beyond men's justice now.'

13

A *picture* held us captive. And we could not get outside it, for it lay
in our language and language seemed to repeat it to us inexorably.

Wittgenstein, *Philosophical Investigations*

She was standing by the orchids; raised high on trellises their blooms
seemed to frame her broad high forehead, her apricot hair. In the glowing
light there was a glint in her eyes, blue-green and flecked with gold, and
her cheeks were suffused with red. Her lips, in a classical cupid bow, were
pale with her anger.

There was a whole section of the Subject's Documentary in which Hugo
Thayer discussed words and affixes of an imaginary language invented
solely for the purpose of celebrating this woman. He had named her
'H'lani H'nawara'. It meant 'She the Lion'; I knew it was her.

'Do you know him?' She had challenged me, looking me straight in the
eyes. She had been sipping coffee on the patio when I had found her that
morning. I had felt the need for caution and had replied that although I
did not know him in person, I had studied his posters and was writing a
book which had quite a bearing on them. She had told me then that Hugo
was in a clinic in England, following his nervous breakdown.

'Is he under any . . . compulsion? Is he confined?'

'No,' she had replied, laughing at my tone of voice. 'He is not in prison
if you mean that. Good people are taking care of him.'

'Is he free to leave, if he wishes to?'

'Only when it is finished,' she had replied.

'When what is finished? Do you know?'

'I have a message . . .'

'A message?'

'. . . for you.'

With considerable energy she had said then, 'Hugo says you must not
give up!' Her face had been full of emotion; I had felt embarrassed, and
unaccountably moved. To hide my confusion and to defer to moment of
my reply to her 'message', I had asked her then when she had last seen him
in person.

'I saw him a week ago. I had to go to Gothenberg to see Papa.'

'When will you see him again?'

'Tomorrow afternoon,' she had replied. Her voice had had the quality of warm summer rain. It was proud and sad and full of a sort of fierce loving. 'He wants you to promise,' she had said, and her tone had made it clear how disagreeable she had found it, having to extract a promise from a stranger.

'Before I promise,' I had said, 'I want you to do something for me.'

'Well,' she had said, and I had felt then how she had been mustering her energies. 'that depends on . . .' She had lilting, Nordic intonations; when she said, 'tomorrow afternoon' it sounded as if she was both astounded and aggrieved. It was utterly charming, and at times almost comic.

'I want you to tell me,' I had said, 'what you think he means.'

But she had countered with a question of her own. 'Who told you,' she had asked, 'to write a book about Hugo's posters?'

'I need to know more,' I had replied.

'Yes,' she had conceded, 'there's Bartholomew's Commission. And the painting from Lichterfelde.'

'What do you know about The Commission?'

'What do you mean?' she had said. 'What is this commission?'

'The book about Hugo . . . it's based on his diary. Didn't you know?'

She had risen from her seat and had walked swiftly down the steps and on to the cinder path. Repugnant to relate, I had followed her into the conservatory.

'Why am I writing?' I asked relentlessly. 'Do you know?'

'That is a question which you must ask yourself,' she replied. 'I'm not allowed to tell you what I know.'

'You're not being very helpful, are you?'

But she replied hotly, 'Surely you must know what you are doing!'

'Is Hugo glad about my work?'

She said emphatically, 'He wants you to finish it! As soon as you can.' She had such conviction then that for the first time since taking it up I had the idea that The Commission perhaps really *mattered*. And with that in mind, I am ashamed to tell, I felt a glad, proud moment of self-importance.

'Is it true,' I asked, 'that Hugo personally proposed it? I mean, does he really agree with the policy?'

Her face reddened and her eyes grew sharp; she stood her ground and spoke almost into my face. 'Why do you ask all these questions? Why do you have to? It is so simple! You get money from them so you must do the work! Why all this searching, searching? It doesn't help Hugo!'

179

I told her I didn't trust them. I explained that I was afraid they might be doing something that was against the interests of ordinary decent people. I told her I needed to know what I was involved in because I knew that I was personally, morally responsible for my actions, even if I didn't know what was going on. I owed it to myself to find out what I could.

'All this . . . I don't know,' she replied. 'I want Hugo to be well. That is all I want.'

'Look,' I said, and I had decided to trust her completely, 'I just can't believe that the man who named you "H'lani H'nawara" can be in cahoots with clandestine State officials. Is it possible for you to speak to him in private?'

'I usually visit him alone.' She was evidently touched to be reminded of Hugo's love-nomenclature and her attitude towards me had noticeably softened.

'Ask him if he thinks I should try and keep it from them. Will you do that, please?'

'But you must finish it!'

'Just find out if Hugo wants me to fob them off with something I wouldn't otherwise have written.'

She gave me a look of total incomprehension; and then her impatience burst out of her, 'What do they mean, all those words! Do you know, they warned me about you? They said you were a subversive person, a . . .' she searched for the word, and finding it, mispronounced it, 'a renegade. They told me you were a man who would try all the tricks to get what you wanted.'

In the heat of the moment I replied, 'Do you believe them?' But when her words had registered in my mind I was bowled over with the sheer injustice of it.

'Why not?' she replied, 'Why shouldn't I believe them?'

My face must have been a sorry picture of my inner confusion then; when she spoke again she was quieter and more sympathetic.

'You can't do anything,' she said. 'You think you are strong but you are alone. They have all the power. They can do anything. Why don't you just write it? Finish it and give it to them. Please. Then we'll be free.'

'Free?' I knew my anger and bitterness were coming through, but they had little to do with freedom, or the lack of it, and everything to do with calumny, and betrayal. 'You think we're given freedom? In exchange for something? Or that we can earn it honourably? It's up for grabs, didn't you know, every bloody day!'

She said calmly, 'It is selfish of you to put your own desires first.'

I replied, 'It's not much to ask, is it? Just find out if he wants me to withhold the writing from them.'

'They were very kind to me,' she said. 'And they helped Hugo with his business problems. They are not my enemies.'

'Who *are* they?' But I had really meant to ask her what they were up to.

She demanded, 'Why should I deceive them? Why?'

And finally I asked her, 'Are you a member of the Interested Parties?'

'You . . . you're like a dog,' she said. 'You just bark at me. What parties do you mean?'

'Harriet,' I said, 'just ask yourself one question. Wouldn't they deceive you if they thought their plans required it?'

'Don't you see,' she replied, 'they knew you would be here. They always know what is going to happen.'

And then, abruptly, for I was quite out of patience with it, 'Do what you think is right,' I said. 'And to hell with it.' I turned my back on her. I muttered, 'I'm finished with this . . .' Dark grievances rose within me. Why is it, I asked myself then, that in these situations I get so cluttered up with irrelevant emotions? As I walked off towards the door she called out after me, 'You think you are so moral. You look for bad things in people so that you can make a quarrel with them. But you won't stop the world if you stop other people. You must look for the world in yourself – that is where you must make things moral. You should remember this when you see the painting . . .'

During lunch, which was a casual affair with half a dozen picnic tables round a buffet on the lawn, I had a few quiet words with Georges Bruedelmann. I told him that one of his guests, whom I did not care to name, had offered to help me find my father if I could offer information regarding his alleged smuggling of paintings into the United States. He grinned at me in the manner of an eighteenth-century brigand and seemed not at all curious to know the author of this proposition; rather he asked me why I had decided to tell him. He seemed to think I was playing some sort of game. I told him that I didn't much care for his tone of voice; my duty to my host, I declared, far outweighed my duty to the United States Inland Revenue Service. His retort was provocative: I knew nothing, he said, and I was in no position to bargain with Burt Munker.

'So you know it was Munker, then?'

'Yes,' he replied. 'But if I give you some information of value to him perhaps you will contact Mr Munker and make a little deal?'

'Well,' I said, cagily, ignoring the insult to my pride, 'he says he can put me in touch with my father ...' I wanted to add that this was considerably more important to me than Bruedelmann's sordid quarrels with overseas tax inspectors, but I had not yet overstepped the bounds of decency.

'It is good to know one's father,' he said, and managed somehow to transcend the triteness of that remark. Then he informed me that Marilyn Moore was a personal friend of his. And he advised me to forget all about Burt Munker.

'In any case,' I persisted, 'how could a US Revenue Service inspector possibly know anything about my father?'

'I think it is certain,' said Bruedelmann, 'that Munker can help you. I know this because I too, Mr Clare, can help you to find your father. Shall we go to my study?'

Bruedelmann's study was a revelation: there were Dürer engravings, notably studies of melancholy, and a square of numbers, which I subsequently discovered was a Ficinian device for drawing down the influence of Jupiter to temper the depressive Saturnian effects of excessive study; there were Kabbalistic diagrams of the Sephirothic Tree, and more modern geometrical studies of esoteric cast; I saw several photographs of somewhat eccentric-looking types from the nineteenth and twentieth centuries, including at least two portraits of Gurdjieff; a beautiful hand-painted globe the size of a football; stones, pebbles, blocks of minerals laid out on the shelves; and painted on the ceiling in a riot of fading colours was the entire zodiac. Within its circumference the planets were circling, all in different colours and sizes and characterized by small detailed figures: the sun, for example, was represented by a king sitting on a throne, with a crown on his head and beneath his feet the golden orb itself. But there was more, much more than I could take in; and yet most notable of all, perhaps, were the four crucifixes adorning the highest points of the four walls of the room.

'This study,' I said, 'it's ... it's quite like a novel.' By which I meant to imply that the objects then present to my senses, ordered as they were in their spatial arrangements and dense in information both exoteric and hidden, quite overwhelmed me in their flow of meanings.

But Bruedelmann was not disposed to reply; instead, he unlocked a drawer in his desk and took out a tape and portable cassette recorder. 'Pkease sit down, Mr Clare,' he said. 'Let us listen together.'

Well Schorsch ... Must be forty years now. How are you?
PAUSE

I am well, thank you. Please call me Georges. You see, I am not who I was. So I have a different name now.

I can do that, uh . . . Georges, sure. I guess I'd like to get to the point soon as I can. Do you mind that?

That is a good idea, I think.

PAUSE

You remember there was this painting you showed me . . . now let me think, yeah, that was it, there was some kind of weird set-up, some kind of . . . maybe it was a . . . could have been some kind of hallucination or something. Like a whole bunch of people caught up in some kind of atmospheric disturbance. You remember that painting? You do, huh, Georges . . . I remembered it pretty well, right?

PAUSE

It depends, Mr Jackson. Different people see different things in it.

That's right . . . is that right? Tell me, did you ever get that sorted out? I mean, did you ever find out what it was all about? Some kind of code, you said. I recall.

I think it is a temporal code.

Oh? Is that a fact?

PAUSE

A temporal code, huh?

PAUSE

But I don't think I understand you rightly, Georges. A temporal code? How does that figure?

PAUSE

I believe the passage of time is the key to the mystery of the painting. And I am interested in the changes that will occur in the actual painting as the time passes. And perhaps most of all, I look at the changes which will occur in the parties who find that they have an interest in the work.

Supposing I was to tell you, Schorsch, that I haven't seen that painting of yours ever, not in any book, or any other place since that time you showed it to me. You remember that night? In the Avenue Mozart? You remember the girls, huh Schorsch? That was a good time I showed you, right?

Yes, Mr Jackson. I remember.

Remember the finger? . . . Well, let me tell you, Schorsch, right out of the blue, just a few weeks back, I saw it again, the selfsame scenario. But not on a screen, and not on a piece of canvas. How'd you react to that, Georges?

You had a vision? A dream perhaps?

A vision? To hell! No dream, Georges. I saw it. It was there, and I was there.

PAUSE

183

What do you mean, you were there, and it was there? What did you see Mr Jackson? Why do you think you saw my picture?

Not your picture, buddy. Not the goddam painting, but the fact the picture represents, the scene it is a picture of. That's what I saw.

I felt the hairs on the back of my neck stir like reeds in a slow movement of water. There was a long pause on the tape; I could hear the sound of rain beating at the windows, and the sound of someone exhaling heavily, as though smoking. I looked at Bruedelmann but he was intent upon listening, as if he too were hearing it for the first time.

There is no fact that the picture represents. It does not refer to anything at all. I must tell you, my friend, the painting is not a photograph. It is not a report. Do you imagine it is an artist's impression of something? Is that how you think about it? I can tell you, Mr Jackson, it is not like that at all.

PAUSE

OK, Georges. OK. So it's not a picture of anything. But I tell you, I saw, just beginning of last month, I saw what I saw that time in Avenue Mozart.

Georges Bruedelmann switched off the tape and strolled over to the window. The afternoon was heavy; thick yellow sunshine poured through the windows making pools of light on the carpeting. A continuous upsurge of motes misted the laden shelves of the study. I felt drowsy. Bruedelmann, who was looking away into the garden, asked me if I had recognized the voice on the tape. I replied that I had recognized his own unmistakable voice, of course, but the other voice was unknown to me. 'Is there a mirror in this room?' I asked, for I had the curious impression that he was looking straight at me.

He said portentously, 'I am the mirror, Mr Clare, but I am clouded. The air is full of dust.' He turned from the window to face me and said, 'The man on the tape, does he sound like your father? His name, if you did not pick it up, is Dennis Jackson.'

'How should he sound?' I asked, rhetorically, but I knew what he was getting at.

'Perhaps we shall know for certain,' he said, 'in just a few hours.'

He was back behind his desk, smoothing the papers that lay before him. His eyes came to rest on my face and his gaze bored into me. 'It is nearly forty years,' he said, 'since they took away my master. They gassed him and then they burned him in their oven. So many people today will say, "What does it matter? What does it matter now?" I fear there are too many people who are capable of asking such a question. There is so much work to do. And still the past is with me . . .'

184

I found his gaze exceedingly oppressive and I swivelled a little in my chair. He seemed to fall to musing. It was an aspect of himself that I had not yet seen; there was a poignancy in him then, and a terrible heaviness of spirit.

'I promised my master that I would look after this painting. In fact I honour it as his most precious possession. But when I reached New York I lost it for a time. It came back to me, however. And today it is still with me, and it haunts me like an obsession. The painting itself is a journey, and I have travelled its road for thirty years. And then out of the blue just a few weeks ago this man Jackson came back into my life and told me *he had seen what Bartholomew saw.'*

Outside, on the oval cinder drive, there were car doors slamming and the sound of a ratchety engine turning over. 'Soon we will be alone,' he said. 'Just as Mr Jackson demanded.'

'Please,' I said, 'tell me more about him.'

'Of course I was very suspicious of him. He spoke like an American but he carried the shadows of a European. I had not seen him since Christmastime, 1944. He was a hunter then, a hunter and a killer of men. In Paris he spent his time with criminals, with the most vicious gangsters of the underworld. But everyone knew he was a soldier. Not just a soldier but a demon of the war. Once, in the Avenue Mozart, he cut off a gangster's fingertip. I saw it myself. They were sitting at a table watching some girls on a private stage. There was an argument over a woman. I saw Jackson take out a knife with incredible rapidity. Like a butcher he caught the man's hand and cut off his fingertip. I remember the sound it made on the wooden table. But even that was not enough for Jackson. He put the man's fingertip in his mouth and then he swallowed it. And in the same minute he had stood up and struck the man across the face with the haft of his knife. Blood went everywhere. It went all over the table, it spattered the clothes of the onlookers, it fell on the naked bodies of the dancers. Even the man's bodyguards were too shocked to move. It was a terrible thing. One of the most terrible I have ever seen.'

'Was he deranged?'

'We were all deranged in those days. I remember he was always surrounded by women. He had a moustache which he was very proud of. He liked it when people complimented him. And always he liked to show us his good manners, his displays of the English gentleman. But he was not a real gentleman, Mr Clare. Not in any sense of that word. He was only twenty-five or twenty-six years old but he looked younger, and this was a very rare thing in those times.'

'What do you know about me,' I said, 'that makes you think I might be his son?'

'It is Jackson who knows about you. I know only what he has told me. You see, he wanted to join us. He . . .'

'Us? Who's us? I mean, who are *you*?'

'It is not important at the moment.'

'But where do *I* fit in? Why should he tell you about me if he wanted to join *you*? I insist that you tell me!'

'I know it is not easy for you,' he said. 'But at this time I have nothing more to say.'

'Well,' I said grittily, 'let's get him on the phone shall we? I'd rather like to talk to him if you don't mind.'

'Forgive me,' he said. 'I have no desire to thwart you. I must tell you that we are caught up in a dialectic, a dynamic process within time, and we must follow its laws, even as regards our utterances. I know that it is not yet time to speak more fully. I cannot tell you about the other people. Today I can speak only of him.'

Barely controlling my frustration I shouted at him, 'When am I bloody well going to meet him then?'

He replied, very softly, 'Jackson is coming here, to this very house. He will be here soon. Please remain here as my guest. Together we will await him.'

His Excellence the count, attended by his secretary, directed Bartholomew to transport the 'corpse': he was to convey it, openly displayed in the back of a wagon, some five miles distant to a small property on the southernmost border of the county. There, in strictest secrecy, Magdalene was to be 'prepared', either for the grave or for return to life. Bartholomew was to be accompanied on his errand by a full dozen of His Excellence's soldiers under the leadership of the captain of the guard. The escort was to remain at all times no less than five hundred paces distant from the cart in which the body was conveyed. Having attained the privacy of the count's outlying house Bartholomew was to await the later arrival of the count himself, in company with the alchemist. His Excellence neglected to tell his resourceful 'English' helpmeet that his escort, ever at five hundred paces, would encircle the house and keep close watch on it, letting none pass through the cordon. But so much was obvious to Bartholomew, who took the count's silence in this regard as clear proof of his host's distrust of him. He knew, too, that the soldiers would be required to stand witness at the interment, in desolate marshes on the county borders, of the sealed wooden coffin of Magdalene Wykzo.

Thus had the Count von Halle contrived to meet the challenge of a difficult situation. It was the count's intent, firstly to keep all but his secretary in ignorance of this bold contrivance, secondly to keep possession of the 'corpse', thirdly to keep close watch on Bartholomew and fourthly to prevent that individual from taking all credit for saving the life of the daughter of his friend. The difficulties, however, were compounded at the last by Henricus Wykzo's impassioned insistence that he himself should accompany his daughter in her dismal journey to her ill-starred place of rest. The count had resolved to keep the alchemist in complete ignorance of the plot until and unless his daughter was restored to life. This was a cruel decision, but I see several probable explanations for it: it may be assumed, firstly, that only the sincere grief of the alchemist would suffice to convince the people that the girl's death, although suspiciously unexpected and sudden, was nonetheless real. And secondly, it is certain, I think, that the alchemist, had he been privy to it, would have rejected outright the dangerous course of action which Bartholomew proposed, and would have demanded instead that the count's official intercession should save his daughter from the stake. But the count, of course, in the face of the hostility of his people, and ever fearful of rebellion and riot, was compelled to place politics above her life and dared not intercede on his friend's behalf. I sense, too, on the part of the count, a definite, perhaps unconscious, desire that his friend the alchemist should suffer the form if not the substance of loss of a beloved child so that both men might find in their shared circumstance a firmer, closer tie. And not least of all, I suspect the count believed that Magdalene was very likely to die of Bartholomew's bold contrivance, in which event it was better both for himself and for his friend that Henricus should know nothing of it. Probably, too, he thought that the girl's death by natural causes would increase the alchemist's dependence on himself while at the same stroke freeing himself of the politically unwise marriage promise.

But he could not, for reasons both of sentiment and policy, deny his friend's demand to accompany his daughter at dawn that morning; and yet he was loath to expose him to the blandishments of the alarmingly inventive 'Englishman'. For had he not determined to hold these men separate? Now, at three o'clock in the morning, he swayed this way and that, and fretted in his chamber. At last, after long discussion with his secretary, while the alchemist wept and cursed his fate, the count decided to permit Henricus to accompany Bartholomew in the mournful cortège. But he gave his friend a letter, and instructed him to open it *only in the event of a sudden and unexpected happiness*, and he took care to warn his friend against the smooth insinuations of the 'man from Oxford'. We may assume, as von Halle did, that the alchemist would be too distracted to ask his noble patron why it was that the Englishman sat with him in the wagon and not a soldier, or a page, or even a stable-boy whom he knew and trusted.

They placed her on straw in the back of the wagon with a simple wooden coffin by her side. It was six in the morning when they rode out of the castle and at once the people crowded round to catch a glimpse of the slender, cold body of the witch. The soldiers fought the press of bodies and cleared a narrow way with the long hafts of their pikes. In a shower of spittle and flung curses the wagon rumbled across the planks of the bridge and on to the rocky ground of the lake-side.

'Christ killer!'

'Poisoner of wells!'

'Ugly dogs! That is a Jew's nose, mark it well!'

'A Jew! Did I not tell it as it is?'

To Henricus Wykzo, who sat in the wagon as a living corpse sewed into a shroud of grief, the howls of the crowd about him, the coarse red faces stiff with rage and abomination, barely impinged upon his mind or were drowned in the din of interior demons that beset his soul, or were as nothing in the silence that marked her going. At first, in the early afternoon of that fateful day when the outraged count had told him of the doctor's report, he too had raged and had scarcely forborne to beat his slender, mute child. But soon he had matched her silence with his own and had sat brooding on this ruin of his hopes. In the dungeon where they tortured the Saxon he had hidden himself trembling behind a pillar, and when the dying man had made his confession the alchemist had fainted away and had dashed his crown on the greasy flagstones. For it was not the agony of his injuries that brought Juergen the Saxon to speak his dreadful testimony, but the stark horror of what he had seen; though he had been as a rock in the hands of his tormentors, yet he feared for his immortal soul, and when they warned him that death was imminent and begged him to make his peace with God the broken man had spoken the fateful words. With shattered fingers that ran with blood he made his mark on the confession which he had dictated to them in his last few minutes of life. And then he died, without a murmur, leaving his giant, broken corpse splayed out on bloodied straw; and the alchemist, giddy with despair and mounting rage, had torn his hair from his head and had raved, and had beaten on the walls, crying upon God. They had taken him to his chamber and bound his arms and legs with strong cloths so that he would not hurt himself. And there he had lain in the darkness, schooling himself in stoic review of his pitiful, fateful life. And later still, as though in answer to his furious sobbing cries, worse things had come: in the dead hours before dawn the soldiers lifted him bodily from his bed and took him to see his daughter. As they dragged him, uncertain of his rank and status, along the flame-lit corridors they turned deaf ears upon his frantic questions. It was not for them to inform him.

Candles had burned about the bedside where she lay, and the air in the chamber was thick with incense to hide the smell of the poison. The count was present, seated most solemnly in a great chair, and by his side stood the secretary. Bartholomew, ever true to his spying trade, stood behind a curtain, for the count had permitted him to be present.

'My dear friend . . .' said the count.

'My daughter, my Magdalene!' The old man fell to his knees at her bedside. It was as if his whole body yearned to take her up in his arms.

'Cut his bonds.' The captain of the guard obeyed. But he could not free the old man's heart which was bound with cords of stone. Shaking and moaning, Henricus took her hand, grey as tallow, and held it to his eyes. His tears, which he did not seek to quell, bathed her cold fine hand; all were affected. The count wept in memory of his son, who lay in the earth in Vienna. A young soldier snuffled. And Stremel, too, stared at the sliver of crescent moon, whose pale beams glimmered in the barely ruffled waters of the lake.

'Oh ... my poor ... love ... lovechild. Beloved. Cold ... my daughter.' His voice was like a sawblade caught in the wood. 'My gift from God. Taken away ... in my old age ... I saw eternity in her eyes. And I welcomed it. But now it is gone ... my lantern is gone out and hope is ended. I am alone. Ill-fated, abandoned. Alone in this cold world ... God's grace she was ... now taken away. And where am I to hide? Where is my comfort now? Oh my Magdalene ... But how? What cause?'

'Her heart stopped,' the secretary said, 'when the Saxon died.'

'Was it so? How true it is! He was her life-strength, her strong heart. They smashed the lantern and the light died. The light! Oh my light! The light has died ... Not death itself can comfort me!'

'Henricus, my friend, we are in haste. She must be buried this morning.'

'In unhallowed ground,' the secretary said. 'Within the hour. The people demand it.'

Henricus Wykzo could not bring himself to speak. He would go with his daughter; but oh how he hated them then, in this barbarous North. The count rose from his chair and helped the old man to his feet; led him a little to the side, and spoke to him gently, as one friend to another, and placed his arm round the little man's shoulders so that the soldiers were embarrassed and the secretary glared. The nobleman whispered in Wykzo's ear and patted his head.

'Be patient, friend. Be brave.'

And half an hour later, when the wagon was ready and the coffin had been laid on the straw, Henricus Wykzo stumbled on the stairs behind the soldier who carried her out to the yard. Then the count approached and quietly pressed a letter into his hand, and bade him be wary of the 'Englishman'.

'My good Henricus,' the count had said, 'remember your friend that loves you.'

The wagon rumbled slowly at the lake-side; all along the rutted track the people waited. Some abhorred and execrated, some only stood and stared as the white-faced foreigners passed. But the people quickly tired, for the night had been long and the drama was now at an end; as they drifted away to their separate homes the shouts became less frequent, less furious, and their distant disaffections were assuaged in the rattlings and clankings of the wagon and the heavy-hooved drumming of the horses' hooves.

'Blindly,' Henricus said, 'and full of fool's hope we stagger like drunkards in the world and think we dance. Men hate with frenzy and love with cold displeasure.'

A light summer rain began to fall; it stirred the milky surface of the lake. Wykzo began to weep.

'The air,' the alchemist gasped for his breath, 'is thick . . . with demons. How they crowd the heart. They squeeze the heart with tongs. Burning and freezing. They whisper their endless vices in our ears. They madden us with lusts for forbidden things.'

'Pray tell me, sir . . .'

'And virtue . . . is a poor girl, deaf and dumb and blind. And sold by her own father that loves her, sold to the legions of damned beings. I who was her protector. Would that I were dead and burned to ashes.'

'Did you have traffic with demons, good Doctor?'

'But the stuff of the mind . . . the soul, lives on. It is the means of hope and the end of all journeys. It is love's remembrance in the darkest of days. It is God within us . . . in her I saw my God. And am to blame that she is dead. This is a judgement. Because I killed my God.'

No doubt Bartholomew crept upon his prey, but could not yet come close to it. His thoughts tumbled, one upon the other; he slowed the horses to a dragging walk.

'No man,' said he, 'can know the future. Hope is virtue. It strengthens the soul. And we must put our faith in science.'

'I have seen,' said Henricus Wykzo, 'the form of all time. What men call time is naught but the tick of clockpieces.'

'I tell you, sir, there are many who wish you well. In England.'

'None wish me well. None.'

'In this land, it is true, there is scant love for . . . your kind, good sir. You must go where men will honour you.'

The rain had ceased and the surface of the lake was as a milky heaven fixed in eternity. It was pure white and yet translucent; and in the morning sky the clouds, becalmed, hemmed in the sun. In the back of the wagon the corpse moaned aloud.

'Ha!' The alchemist started from his misery. 'What's that?' Wildly he looked about. 'Did you hear her voice? Pray God she's not in purgatory. Or come to haunt us even as we bury her cold flesh.'

But Magdalene was silent; she was still as lake and cloud.

'A field of light,' said Wykzo, and he motioned to the burnished lake. 'It cost me my daughter.'

Bartholomew hearkened.

'Do you mean the lake, sir? Indeed it shines . . .'

'When I look into the fields of light I see the forms of all things from all points of vantage. I am at the centre of a sphere, an infinite sphere whose circumference is nowhere. All is the centre.'

'Do you speak of Nicholas Cusanus?' Bartholomew grew very excited, but dissembled his hopes. 'Good sir,' he said. 'I pray you, instruct me in this matter. What fields of light are these?'

'My fields of light which I distilled in my laboratory. They are clear yet they darkle . . . they flow like mercury and they shine like the sun . . . or grow stiff and drear. They are spiritous, they are joy, they are intelligent and welcoming, they question. They are alive.'

'Are sentient? They? Your fields of light do live?'

'Not sentient things, but the stuff of sentience itself. I think they are the substance of man's mind. The soul's substance in the world.'

'Spiritous? And say you a substance?'

'And yet 'tis not. Only a mirror to the soul. When I look upon it, it penetrates, even to the inmost man. It is a mirror of all that I am, and of all that I do, and of all that I am to become.'

Then Bartholomew said, 'How wearisome my life is. I count it as

191

nothing for I never saw a field of light. Tell me, I pray you sir, where I shall find one, for my soul's sake.'

'Here. You'll find them even in the wagon.'

'Here?'

'There, in her box of face paints. And round her neck.'

'Her neck?'

'Her necklace. All must be buried with her.'

'There are fields of light in her sweets coffer . . .?'

'Aye, in her make-up case. Where her mother kept her white lead, her sublimate of mercury, her rouge.'

'A field of light in a make-up case? This is a great mystery . . .'

'They disappear.'

'Ha?'

'My fields of light. If I do not look upon them they disappear.'

'In a golden rain?'

'Just so. Nothing would hold them. So I mixed them with the resins and the powders. They soaked them up.'

'Like a sop of bread in a stew?'

'If you will. I chanced on it.'

'Your resins, sir, your powders . . . these must be rare commodities. I mean, to hold your fields of light . . .'

'It is a spiritous thing. It is intelligent. It chose.'

'Chose?'

'Besides, I wished to hide them from his spies.'

'Do you mean the count, sir?'

'I mean them all. All of you are spies. Demons and spies and liars.'

A soft new rain was falling as the cumbersome vehicle hauled up an incline and over the ridge. The track turned sharply to the left and ran downhill towards the swirling waters of a stream. As they topped the rise Bartholomew looked back and saw the soldiers who followed them disappear from view. Magdalene's corpse was still; but her eyes had opened and shone like jewels against the pale mask of her skin. And now the rain bathed them; it washed the make-up from her eyelids and ran down her cheeks muddied with powders. Her mouth fell open and her parched tongue, stiffly protruding from the corner of her mouth, took for drink the resinous freshwater tears.

'Is it life . . .' the alchemist said, choking on his grief, 'that I am quick with pain? We are all of us dead . . . but quick with pain.'

'Her necklace has them too? Your fields of light?'

'In the resins. I made the beads.'

'Jesus.'

192

With a gathering of energy the presence of sunlight increased about them; now it lit the smooth lake with lurid fierceness. Along the stream where the wagon rumbled on stony, hard-baked furrows, willow trees and alders overhung their passing; silts and minerals darkened the swollen waters. As the wagon swayed and jolted along the road great beds of reeds, swaying and breaking the surface of the stream, brought sudden intimations of the river bed.

'We live,' Henricus cried in his madness, 'only that death might propagate upon us!'

Magdalene Wykzo uttered her choking cry and rolled from the lurching wagon. Both men turned as one. They saw how she staggered down the bank and on shaking legs had waded into the turbulent stream. Frenzied, she scooped at the grey water swirling now about her waist and sucked at it and gulped it down. On the treacherous bed of the stream her feet snagged and her long black hair was a floating blue stain marking the place where she was drowning.

'Magdalene!' Horror and exultation crowded into his voice, and calling her name again and again Henricus Wykzo ran towards the stream. His face was chalk white but his forehead and cheeks showed intense round blotches of blood. Bartholomew rushed past him, and thrashed the water as he waded in.

'My daughter! My daughter lives!' the alchemist shouted, jubilant and stricken, and it seemed to him then that the whole of his thwarted, tormented life was suddenly present in that monstrous cry.

'Our Magdalene drowns!' the Frenchman shouted as he struggled to reach her in the stream. He clutched at her hair, dragged her head clear of the sucking water; but a treacherous reed-bed caught her ballooning gown and long greasy streamers wrapped her round. Now Bartholomew, too, lost his footing. As he foundered he felt the current take him but in that instant he grasped her sinking hand and now, with all his strength, he held her and he strove. His free hand, scrabbling, found a drooping willow branch, gripped it, and lost again, and held it firm; half drowned, he hauled her to him.

The golden sun burst forth from cloud and all was dissolved in brilliance. And turning and turning as the blood burst in his head Henricus Wykzo carolled his thanks and his love . . . my God my God my God my God.

The captain of the guard, shouting to his men to stay back, stay back beyond the rise, galloped upon the scene and leapt from his horse. The body of the old man suddenly encumbered him but he threw him to the ground. Bartholomew, half drowned, and dragging the lifeless body of the girl now by the hair, now by leg or arm, squirmed up on to the bank. As he laboured he coughed, choked, spluttered. The captain looked on and mounting within him was stern, cold, immeasurable rage.

'That body,' the captain bellowed, 'belongs to the state of Rietburg.'

Bartholomew laid her on the ground, stretched her out and started to fumble at her chest.

'Stand away, hellhound!' The captain, whose repugnance was extreme, was not an inexperienced man. But something, he knew it, was monstrous in that scene — far beyond the ordinary vice of men. He drew his pistol from his belt and trained it on the Frenchman. Like a witless being Henricus Wykzo chuckled and moaned; his kicking heels scored the rain-wet ground, but he could not raise himself. Now he burbled like a babe.

And drawing deep wild breaths like heartfelt sighs Bartholomew brought his lips to hers.

'Satan!' the captain roared, and now he felt hot, raw fear in his belly. 'In the name of Jesus stand away!'

That courageous man strode forward and kicked the Frenchman with the flat of his hard boot. 'Away! I say, or I'll shoot you dead! Evil bastard. Hellhound!'

'For God's sake, captain! Have you no eyes?' Bartholomew, insensible to the blow he had taken, was forced to plead his intricate fabulation in coarse, breathless shouts. 'Look to the old man. Help Henricus! I shall explain, captain!'

'What would you do with that corpse?' Appalled, and yet relieved to hear a human voice, the soldier advanced his pistol until it touched Bartholomew's face.

'Look! Look at Wykzo there! Do you see? D'you see his eyes? Look at his face! Do you see, captain? 'Tis the daughter that lives in his flesh!'

And Henricus Wykzo, as though in confirmation of what Bartholomew had said, lay with grey face and clouded eyes that stared at heaven. Then his head lolled and it was as if he looked at his daughter with an obscure, irrational love.

'Can't speak, can't hear,' Bartholomew shouted. 'She knows her father though.'

'What's this? Her father? ... Herself?' Half disposed to believe, the soldier fell into bewilderment.

'I seek,' Bartholomew gasped, 'the spirit of the father ... in the flesh of the child.' And he pumped at her chest and brought his lips to her mouth, but despair rose in his chest; for he could feel no breath in her, and her eyes were closed.

John Pike wrote of that critical moment that the captain nearly shot

Bartholomew dead. But once that impulse had passed the soldier knew he had lost the initiative. Now he squatted on his haunches and with eyes of glass peered between his leather boot-tops, gazed uncomprehending at Bartholomew, who sucked at the air and pressed his lips to hers.

'Godless magic,' the captain muttered. With the hammer of his pistol he scratched his beard. 'Demons ... witches ... I'm a soldier; I'm not afraid.'

Up on the rise, from three hundred yards away, the mounted soldiers of the escort peered at the scene: bodies on the ground, but their captain sat near by; and now a vapour from the drying ground rose all about them, and the hard sunlight of the morn set things to sparkle; one of their number struck up a song.

Magdalene groaned, coughed up water and blood; and the captain of the guard was up and running, but stopped himself some way down the road and turning, levelled his pistol, but knew not at what he aimed. His horse, sensing his master's dread, cantered after him. Magdalene's eyes had opened wide. And Bartholomew, who stared into her upturned face, was filled with pride, and then with love.

'Captain,' he yelled in his jubilance, 'see her eyes! She's sane, she's rational, she's intelligent!' Magdalene's eyes were serene indeed, and shining, and filled with a sweet spirit. He rubbed her hands in his and kissed them. He gave a hoarse joyous shout.

And in reply the captain, from thirty paces distant, shouted in a strained thin voice, 'Horrible! Hellish practice!'

'Captain! We must find shelter! We must be private! Have you forgot your master's commands? Help us, man. Quick now! Quick! From the eyes of the soldiers ...'

'I?' Now he was astounded. 'I'll not help *you*. Damnable wizard!' But to see the witch, to see her live again, it shook him so — he could not speak his outrage.

'Hold off your judgements, sir. You have misconstrued. Be quick now. Your master depends on it! I pray you, let yourself be guided.'

It was perhaps this sudden restoration of a semblance of the normal that steadied the soldier's nerve; and he knew what it meant that his master depended on him, for he was a soldier through and through. And if he must carry out the orders of the magician, or wizard, or whatever he was, then it was as good as done. And if he must handle the living flesh of a dead witch ... aye, aye, that too.

'What would you have me do?'

'Go to your men and tell them ... tell them to search the stream.'

'The stream? To search it?'

195

'Yes, yes . . . the stream . . . for a ring that is lost.'

'A ring?'

'A gift from your master, to Wykzo, his servant. And you must take the alchemist straight to the castle. Take him without delay, and bring the doctors to him.'

'No, no, good sir! I stay with you.'

'Then go instruct your men. Be quick captain! These are matters they should not witness. Did not the count forbid it? But first, here! I pray you, assist me.'

They laid Henricus in the wagon, and placed his daughter next to him. She was passive, and seemed to understand that she should not move. Then the captain, his face set grimly against his own doubts, rode up the hill and ordered his men to search the stream for the count's lost ring. 'Shall we search the wind for a fart of his?' said one of them.

'Stupid sons of dogs!' Their leader's face was strained, and full of rage. 'Search it, d'you hear! Search it proper!' This convinced them. They spurred their horses to the water-side; stiffly they climbed down and waded into the stream; they patted the water pointlessly, staring at their captain. He rode away. Then they fell to cursing him, at first splenetically, viciously, and then with playful abandon.

As the captain galloped up the road behind him Bartholomew planned his course of action. He whipped up the horses and doubled their speed. The captain drew alongside and grasped the reins of the team.

'Slow down, Englishman!'

'Speed up, captain!'

In the back of the wagon the alchemist lay, like an idiot child, in the arms of his daughter. She kissed him and stroked his brow and made soft sounds to him and clucked her tongue, and all the while, from the old man's hideously open mouth, there rolled down his chin into his sparse grey beard a thin and constant stream of spittle.

It did not greatly tax Bartholomew's powers, as they sat round a fire in a hovel some few miles further up the road, to convince the captain of the need to keep silent about what he had seen. The captain saw, but could not understand, that the girl who was dead was now restored to life; it filled him with unspeakable revulsion. And it was plain to him, too, that Wykzo was sick unto death. What should he make of it? He was a trained man, and loyal. He was not disposed to lie to his master, but 'the magician' soon persuaded him.

The magician persuaded that soldierly man that no one would believe his story, not least the count, unless he brought the girl back to Rietburg and surrendered her to the crowd. But this would give the lie to the doctors, and terrify the people, and enrage them too, for many would think the count had duped them. Thus he impressed upon that man, if he told the truth he could not fail to bring dishonour upon his master, and would himself fall from favour. When the soldier countered, resolutely, that the girl's unchristian and sudden return to life proved that formerly she was truly dead, and this being so must prove her truly a witch . . . since only a witch could be restored to life after concourse with a demon had caused her death . . . Bartholomew brought him to look into her face; and there he found such sweetness and virtue as he could not believe the devil was able to summon.

'Can this be a witch?' Bartholomew pressed him.

''Tis a very sweet countenance,' the soldier allowed.

'Have you no daughter, captain? No niece?'

'She is beautiful,' he said.

And Bartholomew contrived for him the following story to carry to the castle: Henricus Wykzo, as they rode along, had desired to bathe her body in the stream before they committed her to the ground. As they went into the water the alchemist cried out to God and begged him take his own simple life and restore that life to his daughter, for he wanted his life no longer. And God heard his prayer and granted it, for the old man fell to the ground even as the girl began to live again.

'She moved,' Bartholomew said, and his face shone with wonder and piety. 'Even as I held her in my arms, she moved.'

And the miracle had so astonished him that he slipped in the water so that he and the girl had nearly drowned. And now, most convincingly, he took out a small Bible and swore upon it, by his soul, that Magdalene was alive in the stream.

'May God now strike me dead if this is a lie!' he said. 'You are witness, captain, a privileged man, for you have seen here not witchcraft or wizardry, but a miracle of providence and grace.'

The captain, in the face of these protestations and pious oaths, was finally persuaded, at least to hold his tongue; Bartholomew swore he would hide the girl away and she would never again be seen in that region. And he begged the soldier to transport poor Wykzo to the castle where doctors might tend him.

'And what am I to tell my master?' the captain asked, doubting again.

'Tell him we went into the stream to bathe the girl. And Henricus slipped and was nearly drowned . . . and now he is quite out of his mind.'

'And what of the girl?'

'The girl? What of the girl, good captain? Was she not dead when she left the castle?'

'Aye, aye. She was dead then,' said the soldier, sourly.

'Of course she was dead! She was a corpse until her father prayed and God vouched safe a miracle. Why think captain, *if poor Magdalene had not been dead how could she not have drowned?* Did I not tell you her hair caught in the reeds? She was a long time under water.'

'Aye, aye, so you said.'

'Tell your master I have taken her to burial in unhallowed ground. Tell him none in this country shall ever see her again. And tonight, by sunset, I'll be there again at Rietburg castle.'

It is hardly to be supposed that the seasoned military man could wholly trust his new-found confidant of that hour of inconceivable trouble. Yet he saw plain enough that the tale had much to recommend it and was likely to cause the least trouble for everyone. He reasoned that even if the alchemist recovered from his sad condition he would remember nothing of what had happened and would not contradict his own account, which Bartholomew had provided. Perhaps what swayed him most was desperate reluctance to report this foul, discreditable resurrection; his Christian reason and all his worldly beliefs recoiled from its contemplation. He resolved to say strictly what Bartholomew had advised.

'And what shall I say to the other Englishman?' he asked, as he mounted his horse, with the idiot, listless alchemist slung like booty across the saddle.

'Him? Why, good captain,' Bartholomew declared, 'tell him the same. Tell him what you will.'

14

I am the poison-dripping dragon, who is everywhere and can be
cheaply had . . . But if you do not have exact knowledge of me, you
will destroy your five senses with my fire . . . I contain the light of
nature; I am dark and light; I come forth from heaven and earth . . . I
am the carbuncle of the sun, the most noble purified earth, through
which you may change copper, iron, tin, and lead into gold.

'Aurelia occulta', *Theatrum Chemicum* IV

The Salamander was making for the château, and it was my part to wait
for him. Bruedelmann showed no inclination to pass the time of day with
me, nor I, indeed, with him; as the shadows were lengthening on the
lawns of his beautiful château gardens he ushered me, somewhat clinically
I thought, into the library. There, between rows of medieval tomes, I
settled down to read of the aftermath of the illusionistic yet nightmarish
Lippstadt Mission.

I read for some hours; then shortly before midnight Georges Bruedelmann returned and questioned me as to how much I had read.

'Actually,' I said, 'I think I'll turn in.'

'Absolutely not,' was Bruedelmann's reply. 'You must not sleep
tonight.'

'Why ever not?'

'Jackson,' he said, 'is expected in the hour.'

'Is he so close?'

Then Bruedelmann said, 'Put oil in your lamp, oh wise virgin,' and I
laughed long and loud.

'It is best,' he said, when I had quieted, 'to view Bartholomew's
painting only after a vigil. The opportunities are greatly enriched by lack
of sleep.'

So I went to my room and took a bath; for half an hour I soaked in the
tub, clearing my mind of all manner of dark conceptions. Afterwards, at
half past one in the morning, I went back to the library and took up again
John Pike's account. But I could scarcely concentrate, for the imminent
arrival of the man who might be my father had put me in a state of
adolescent excitement; and something like fear of the painting which had

sent poor Hugo Thayer mad preyed on me as I sat there, slumped across the beautiful polished table, with the box of A4 sheets and the snapshot photograph that Munker had given me lying there before me.

I read; and I looked a hundred times at the snapshot. Was this man my father? Ever since I had learned that I was an adopted child I had yearned to meet him and to be with him. I had imagined him in countless different ways, but I had always returned to a secret inner picture of him; and although this sense of him, deep within myself, had remained ever abstract, indefinable, lacking any concrete or physical features, I felt, obscurely, as I looked at Munker's snapshot, that the man it portrayed was alien to me, would remain for me always an imposter only; and if it was subsequently proven that he and I were father and son in blood, what could it mean to me but that the indifferent world had contingently intervened, and that a false blood, a blood that was not mine, coursed in my veins? And in that perverse conception I found a relief of sorts; for no matter how it all turned out, I told myself, whether Dennis Jackson was my father or not, something more beautiful would be preserved. But if you had asked me then which option I preferred, a known and living man, albeit brutish and with blood on his hands, or a still unknown perhaps never knowable and more perfect being who was no more to be found in the world, I could not have given you answer. My thoughts were as a dark flood, and I did not know where I was, and I did not know who it was that was lost.

While the soldiers of the count searched in the swirling waters of the stream, and cursed, and played, and brawled among themselves, the captain, with poor Henricus slung across the saddle, rode back to the castle at Rietburg. And even as he rode, Bartholomew and Magdalene went south with all speed to Frankfurt. And in that city Bartholomew found employment with a merchant, who welcomed his copious information and secretarial skills. The potion that Bartholomew had employed in the deception that saved her life he continued to prescribe for Magdalene, albeit in very small doses, and in the course of time her vision cleared and she became less prone to the distraction that used to fall upon her. And yet, in spite of all Bartholomew's efforts to liberate his Magdalene from her vocal silence, she remained obdurately dumb; then they made for themselves a language of signs, which they amplified by drawing on paper, or on the ground, or even on the sheets of their bed of love.

She was a dreaming tree, Magdalene said. *And Bartholomew was but half a man . . .*

*

We may suppose she expressed herself without constraint, but what she meant by these things, and whether Bartholomew understood her meaning, who is to say? And by this same undependable means she told him of 'the little swarthy man' that her father had created, or had sought to create by Kabbalistic methods in his laboratory at Rietburg.

And herein may be found, or so I believed for a time, the fundamental enigma of Bartholomew's story: there had been much written in the ancient treatises of arcane practices by means of which those initiates of the art could draw down spirits from the spheres above and imprison them in man-made effigies of pagan gods. And there was a tradition in Jewish Kabbala of a form of magic based on the sacred letters of the Hebrew alphabet. This 'gematria', as it was called, enabled the practitioner to create, by skilful arrangement of permutated letters and signs, a living creature in the form of a man, who would expound mysteries to his master and serve him for a time before dissolving into nothingness. This little man was called a 'golem', and in the alchemical texts of the Middle Ages he took the Latin name *homunculus*. It was believed, too, that some practitioners had got the skill, by means of the sacred names of God, to make an image and bring it then to life.

Was it of a golem that the alchemist's daughter 'spoke' when she 'told' Bartholomew of her father's researches? The problem of meaning in Magdalene's communications is compounded by the historical tradition of enigmatic writing, for it was the custom amongst adepts and magicians to obscure their truths from the vulgar mind by steganographic and meta-phoric means: where herbs and minerals and living organs were intended there was talk instead of toads and dragons, and all manner of things like trees, and kings and Indians; and steganographic glyphs abounded, so that a diagram or figure might bind and transmit elemental, celestial, angelic or diabolic forces.

She said she was a dreaming tree and Bartholomew was but half a man. What did he make of these things, her sometime abuser and providential husband? Were they chimerical envisionings, which she shared with her husband as best she could? Did he take them for nonsense, her obsessions, or did she draw him into her world so that he found the means to share with her these phantasms of her mind? Again and again she would signal to her ill-faced, ardent husband these notions of a small dark, man, and of a sacred fire, and of a dragon; and she reminded him urgently that she, Magdalene, was a dreaming tree and that he, Bar-tholomew, was but half a man.

In March, 1583 Bartholomew sent a letter to his former master in London. He begged a meeting with one of Walsingham's agents and proposed the venue of La Rochelle, a port on the coast of the Gulf of Gascony and, since the 1560s, a fortified free Huguenot town. And later, when that meeting took place amongst the taverns on the waterfront, and John Pike saw again his accomplice of old, Bartholomew was no longer with Magdalene and had been travelling alone for a year. It is unclear whether he had any intention of returning to her; and when John Pike asked him what had become of the alchemist's daughter the Frenchman admitted to him that he and she had lived together as man and wife far to the south of Mark-Rietenburg, and she lived there still. Pike, whose interest in Magdalene was undiminished, pressed his former colleague for further information; whereupon Bartholomew grew surly, but told him that Magdalene had changed her name and was safely in the service of a woman who loved her. Her benefactress had the run of her prosperous merchant husband and was mistress of her household. She had made her husband call Magdalene 'daughter' and they had adopted her as their lost love-child.

Since parting from Magdalene the Frenchman had returned, alone, some twenty-five years on, to his birthplace in Garogne, and there had revisited the crumbling hovel where his grandmother had raised him. Thence, led perhaps by instinct, or by a simple desire to find a place for himself in the life of the demesne, he had gone to the gates of the manor-house and begged an audience with the seigneur. At first he had been denied admittance, but eventually, for who could withstand his blandishments, he was brought before that dignitary and saw at once how similar to his own were the seigneur's facial and physical characteristics. And he recalled then the sinewy stableman who had visited him when he was a child, with whom he had eaten rabbit pot supper, and who had extracted from him a terrible promise of revenge. As he stood in audience with his disquieted, superordinate look-alike, it was clear to him at last who it was had been his true father in this world; but he wisely kept his silence.

When asked to state his business Bartholomew requested to be taken into the household as a skilled herbalistic physician. The seigneur demanded documentary proof of his studies, and Bartholomew, of course, had none. He replied, however, that he could furnish such letters of commendation if he were given time to do so. But the seigneur, who was no mean judge of men, noted his visitor's demeanour and sensed the danger in his presence. Bartholomew's humility was ill-contrived, for the supplicant, it seemed to him, made small effort to conceal a more palpable self-confidence unseemly in a low-born man; nor is it improbable that the seigneur was himself intelligent, for was he not a blood relation of Bartholomew himself – if only by fact of his father's *droit de seigneur*. He may have marvelled, cynically perhaps, at the obvious similarities in their facial characteristics. He curtly refused Bartholomew's request and had him escorted from the grounds.

But Bartholomew would not go from the gates and shouted in a loud calm voice that he was a son of the same blood and as good as the seigneur. There were violent consequences: the seigneur's servants seized Bartholomew and soundly thrashed him as he lay upon the ground. This experience had a salutary and quieting effect upon his reason, however, and he was content thereafter to leave the region of his home, never to return.

About that time he began to acquire a notoriety as a mountebank and agitator of the people: he would speak at length both to the men and the women he met in villages on his travels, asking them probing questions about their lives and fealties, and awakening in them not only a burning sense of the injustices they suffered but also a giddying, momentous insight into the fathomless spiritual resources possessed even of simple folk, such as themselves, who could not read or write and knew no Latin or Greek. And since he used all manner of tricks, by means of chemicals and potions and powders, to impress the credulous villagers, he quickly won a following of malcontents and despairing, reluctant outlaws. It was said of him that he had a way to read the secrets of a soul, and could foretell the future of a man by rubbing a certain substance into his hand; or by raising his own hand and placing his palm upon that person's face he was able to know all his secrets, even to his deepest innermost desires. And all the while, though he lived a wandering life, he continued to perform his experiments. He had visions, and would hold his circle of followers spellbound as he recounted to them in detail what he had seen: how he had ascended through the spheres, and had travelled in 'the fields of light', and had seen the forms of a future time and knew the destinies of the soul. And if we are to credit Master John Pike's account of it, it was about that time that he conceived the idea of putting his secret knowledge into an image.

It is to be remembered that Bartholomew was a master of memory systems and had studied the writings of Trithemius on the art of codes and secret writings; and this, I suppose, is why John Pike chose to interpret Bartholomew's Commission as an image which encoded esoteric knowledge, for he declares in his account that Bartholomew employed an artist to fix an image on a canvas. The reader must decide for himself if Pike's account bears scrutiny. For my part, Pike's story of a deliberately commissioned work raises important questions to which it cannot, I think, provide adequate answer. For why should a wanderer, virtually a vagabond, encumber himself so, with a painting three feet long and two feet wide? In this my short account of the last few months of Bartholomew's ill-starred life I find I am prey to certain dark intimations; and I hope that my readers too will find their suspicions awakened by the apparent facts of Bartholomew's demise. For myself, I am inclined to believe that the erstwhile masters of the now self-styled Bartholomew de Gaillac had formed some clandestine agreement with high-placed contacts in the Huguenot stronghold; perhaps a nefarious deal was struck, for Bartholomew was a proven renegade, disloyal, treacherous, and all too autonomous for the time in which he lived. The remarkable swiftness of his passage from arrest on the waterfront to his probable death at the stake suggests foul play to me, as much as it savours of injustice.

In June, 1583, John Pike arrived at La Rochelle. He was carrying a copy of Bartholomew's letter to his former master, Sir Francis Walsingham:

Sir, [Bartholomew had written] *and sometime father, how they have represented to you my removal from your service and the abandonment of your cause, I know not. But by the thanks I owe you for preserving my life I give you my word it was an act of love towards another and not an act of hate against yourself. I had a wife, and if she had borne a male child his name had been Francis in honour of yourself. But she could not conceive, and besides, we have parted.*

I have lately travelled to the village of my childhood and there discovered that I am the bastard son of a noble lord of that region, who died when I was a lay-brother in the monastery at Montauban. I met his son, my brother in blood, and I saw that I bear the same thickness in the nose and the same crooked ears that he has. So I name myself henceforth by my rightful title: I am Bartholomew de Gaillac.

That dear person whom I call my wife taught me how to open the gates to other worlds. And since my life is now directed to that end I am become a hunted man. Soldiers search for me, and I am pronounced a heretic and wizard, a strewer of discontent. And for that I dance when I convey my truths, alike to men and to womenfolk, I am called demon, and incubus, and adulterer. I tell you these things only to inform you of my developments; but I have news for you which has a sharp savour, and cannot but interest you, for all men know you are a friend of voyagers and New World explorers.

I was lately in Bordeaux; there I met a little Indian from the New World. He cleaned the boots of travellers at the inn where I stayed. He had lost the use of his right hand, for the tendons had been cruelly severed, and he had a round hole in his tongue from a hot iron. When first I saw him I felt he was my brother whom I had lost. I spoke to him in French but he understood me not, then I spoke to him in Latin and he understood me somewhat better. I could not say how old he was, but I thought he was like me in his soul and with him I felt the keenest sense of kinship of the spirit; he is my true brother in

God, I know it. He understood me best when I used the Italian tongue, which I learned in Paris. But I was hard put to make any sense of what he said to me for he was maimed and spoke a very crude Spanish. I gave him money but he returned it to me, and by touching means conveyed his thanks; I understood he would rather talk with me. He took my hand and placed it upon his head, and next, by difficult means, he conveyed to me his history. It was the most affecting I have ever heard. But it is no matter for this letter, sir. It is enough to tell you that he brought me news of a certain tree, which exists in that part of the New World which explorers call Amazonia, after the female warriors they saw there. The tree of which I speak has wondrous properties.

If ever you once did trust me, sir, or did ascribe to me judgement and wisdom, or a degree of science beyond ordinary knowing, remember that time. For this little Indian brings news of a tree, a leaf of which bestows upon that high-born man who holds it in possession strange and momentous advantage. I swear this by the memory of Magdalene. And I swear it by the kindness you once did show me. Send a man to speak with me upon this matter. I have in mind a journey to Amazonia, and seek in this your great protection. The advantage in it shall redound very greatly to your credit, sir, and greatly empower the State you serve, in the arts of both peace and war.

My little brother and I must go to Zaragoza. We shall return, God willing, in three months' time. Send a man to meet with me, three months from this day, in the port at La Rochelle. He will find me amongst the taverns on the waterfront.

From a servant who loved his master but grew out of service into the one true mastery of the self, I am, sir, that I am,

Bartholomew de Gaillac

The letter was dated March 16th, 1583 and had been posted in Bordeaux. Bartholomew could not have known that when his letter reached its destination his erstwhile friend and patron, Sir Francis Walsingham himself, was at the time abroad upon some dubious errand for his shrewish, ungenerous Queen; for Elizabeth was notoriously ungrateful in her dealings with this man, whose fanatical commitment to Protestantism had repeatedly saved her from Catholic plots against her life. For the period of Walsingham's absence from London a lesser man was performing his duties, and this person, I suspect, probably determined to make an example of the renegade spy who had presumed to put his own interests before those of his masters. The official in question, a sometime dealer in land and trader in wool, despatched John Pike to meet Bartholomew at La Rochelle, and directed him to bring the miscreant back to England. If other, more clandestine arrangements were made, it was probably unbeknownst to John Pike. I think it not unlikely, however, that the masters in London wanted more information about the tree in the Amazon, for Walsingham was indeed a patron of adventurers, and had subscribed to Fenton's voyage, and had corresponded with Lane who explored Virginia, and had taken Richard Hakluyt into his pay.

205

At La Rochelle John Pike sat among the taverns on the waterfront, drank wine, and comported himself in conspicuous manner. He felt a light touch on his shoulder. It was Bartholomew.

'Well, Pike. Still a spy?'

'Aye, Frenchie. And a free man. No thanks to you.'

'You accuse me false.'

'What's false to you? Or true? You were ever a Catholic and a casuist.'

'And you? A fishy piece on master's plate. Not eaten yet? Pike grows cold.'

'How would it be if I killed you? Now?'

'With my last breath I would forgive you. Will you forgive me?'

'Forgive? I owe you a life, Bartholomew. You saved me on the Muenster road. I do forgive you, but the masters are more passionate than I. And more wronged, I warrant.'

'I am Bartholomew de Gaillac. I am my own master. And God's errant servant.'

'Be that as it may. Whoever you be, they'll have none of you neither, unless I meet your Indian man, your little brother.'

'To business then.'

Sitting with Pike in the tavern on the waterfront Bartholomew recounted to his former comrade the catastrophic history of the little Indian: whose family, friends, and tribal life had been annihilated by the vengeful conquistadores; whose spiritual journey, in servitude to a hard and avaricious master, had brought him to the Spain of the Old World, and to a household in Zaragoza where he had found again the sacred chalcedony artefact of his tribe — only to lose it a second time to the same inveterate enemy. And Bartholomew, true to his avowed intentions, had succeeded, by his own account, in stealing it back for his new-found Indian friend. I think if anything marks him out — this strange, troubled man who could find no surface in his life, no coherence in his world, this ruined renegade — if anything proves that his life was not wasted, it must be this, this above everything. Which is to assume of course that the little Indian existed in actual fact and was not either a conducive lie spun to delude and manipulate the English state, or an unreal entity of Bartholomew's own fevered and delusive ontology.

'And what is Walsingham's answer? Will he help us?'

'I must see him first. Your Indian and his artefact.'

'You may not see him, Pike.'

'May not see him?'

'He will not show himself. Not to you, I know it.'

'Then I must see his piece, or the master will spurn the project.'

'I'll draw it for you only. You may show him the form of it, but you may not see the thing itself.'

''Tis like an "S", set in a spheroid figure? And what's this here, these transverse lines that fan out thus and so?'

'Tell the master he must seek in the Kabbalist *Conclusions* of Pico of Mirandola: the seventh and the fourteenth. It is Tetragrammaton, the ineffable name of God, but with an "S" set in it; it makes the name of God audible, it incarnates the ineffable, 'tis the Word made flesh: IESU. And tell him to read *De verbo mirifico* of Johannes Reuchlin.'

'Have you gone mad, Bartholomew? This is a savage object from the Amazon! How can it be that the Hebrew name of God is writ thereon?'

'Not *written*, but coded. It is a found thing. It was in the earth.'

'But Indians are savage men! They are like dogs and horses. They have no souls until they become Christians by conversion.'

'All men are equal, John. God is in everyone, man, woman, child, all the world over. In every human being, and in equal proportion.'

And then, as they sat at table in the tavern, Bartholomew and Pike were suddenly arrested. A half dozen men at arms took Bartholomew into their charge. John Pike, however, when they had learned his name and his provenance, they pushed aside. They then put irons on Bartholomew and threw him into the back of a cart. And they informed John Pike that he might visit the miscreant in the prison-house.

'In the prison-house? Upon what charge is he arrested?'

'Tomorrow. You may come tomorrow.'

'Ah, John Pike! Have you betrayed me? Did I not save your life on the Muenster road?'

Pike ran beside the cart and called out to his former comrade. 'This is none of my doing. I swear it on my mother's grave . . .' For his pains he took a cudgel blow to the head.

On the next day Pike visited the prison-house, and after they had asked his name, and checked a record, they gave him access to the prisoner. Bartholomew had been tortured.

'Why have they done this to you?'

But Bartholomew had his wits about him still and was suspicious of the Englishman.

'Why have they let you come? How are you sure of your safety?'

'I swear to you, Bartholomew, I know nothing of any plot against you.'

'Come close, Pike. I can scarcely see.'

Pike knelt on the straw and brought his face close to the chained, prostrate magician. Bartholomew took a small piece of wax from his ear and rubbed it on his palm. With trembling hand he held his palm to Pike's wide brow.

'Now I see your soul, John.'

The Englishman trembled.

'Bartholomew, my mind is clouding over. What are you doing to me? My head is burning.'

'These are the fields of light, John. They are the ground of truth, and we are its measure and its source. Truth flows through us, as in a river.'

'A field of light! Even before my eyes I see it! 'Tis a field of light!'

'The fields of light prove all forms spiritual in nature. I have seen the form of time, and the form of all being. They say I am a wizard, and a heretic. They'll burn me, I know this, John. Even tomorrow.'

'What do you see, Bartholomew?'

'I see that you know nothing. You understand nothing. It is the master, the master has betrayed me.'

'What shall I do? How can I help you?'

'You must fetch me some of my grey salts.'

'The same that killed Magdalene?'

'And when I am dead in the eyes of my gaolers you shall claim my body.'

'Where shall I find them, the salts?'

'Wait, they'll follow you there. Be cautious. I'll draw it here. Look, in the dust . . . There, too, you'll find the painting.'

'What is this place?'

'A barn. And near the barn . . . the cave. There, seek for yourself. If you fail me, John . . . study the painting. Go with the little Indian.'

'A painting, you say? I'll go to it, straight.'

'A painting that is no painting. In a jar in the cave. A roll of canvas only. It is my testimony. Study the painting and you will see what I have seen. You will have powers then, even as I. Make study of this painting and you will live for ever.'

'Think not of death, Bartholomew. I'll bring the salts. We'll have you free of this prison . . .'

'You must put them in the water butt, in the yard.'

'In the water butt, just so.'

'They torture me with water. Do you see? I shall be free of them soon . . . Be sure to claim my body. They must not bury me.'

'They shall not bury you, or first they must bury me. You shall live again, Bartholomew, as Magdalene lived again . . . But tell me, I beg of you – where is poor Magdalen? I long to see her.'

'Oh you shall, John, I know. But not in this poor world.'

'Ah Bartholomew . . . have you killed her?'

'Pray for me, John. It was a great sin.'

'Killed then? You have killed poor Magdalen'?

'That demon, John . . .'

'Aye, aye, the demon . . .'

'The demon at Rietburg castle . . . it was but half a man.'

'The creature that raped her then?'

'I was that demon, John. I raped poor Magdalen'.'

John Pike left the prison and followed the directions which Bartholomew had scratched in the dust of his cell. He relates that he found the roll of canvas; it was stowed in an earthenware jar which was hidden under brushwood in the cave. According to his account he then scoured the cave for the salts which Bartholomew so desperately needed, but he could find nothing. He searched for the sacred object, and for some trace of the little Indian, but of them, too, there was nothing to be seen. Then he brought the roll of canvas to the mouth of the cave, which was a hole concealed in the hillside, and examined it. It was Bartholomew's Commission; and, of course, he could make no sense of it. He rolled it up again and scrambled out of the cave where he fell into the hands of waiting Huguenot soldiers.

The soldiers escorted him directly to the waterfront and put him on a boat with two soldiers to guard him until it sailed that night for London. Pike concludes his account with a short discussion: he briefly entertains the possible theory that Bartholomew's little Indian had already removed the grey salts from the cave in order to put Bartholomew's plan into effect; in which case, he argues, it is not improbable that Bartholomew and the little Indian together escaped from La Rochelle, may perhaps have travelled to the New World. Alternatively, he proposes, Bartholomew's little Indian was but a figment of Bartholomew's drug-induced madness; as was his sacred object also. He closes his account with a brief valediction to his erstwhile comrade.

The roll of canvas had passed into Huguenot hands. In 1685, at the time of the revocation of the Edict of Nantes, Huguenot refugees brought it to England. Two hundred years later it became the property of the uncle of Georges Bruedelmann's master. And now it was kept in the Normandy château, in the underground chamber below the library where I sat. And like Hugo Thayer before me, I was soon to view it.

The great bronze Helios boomed: once, twice, great rods of sound rang in the silent corridors. Starting up I clutched at a sheaf of papers, my hand flew to my tie, I felt sweat on my palms. My heart beat savagely.

Five minutes passed; then Bruedelmann came into the library.

'Is it Jackson?' I asked.

'My dear Mr Clare,' he replied. 'You must remain calm. You must not expect too much. I will bring you something to restore your self-command.'

'I'd rather . . .' I called out after him, but he had gone. I felt terrible; I was pale and tense and trembling and my hands were freezing cold. And moments later, as I followed him along the panelled corridor, I was saying to myself *how could it fail to be an anti-climax?*

Dennis Jackson was standing in the darkened window bay of Bruedelmann's study. It was light enough now to make out the shadowy forms of trees in the garden and there were occasional muted bursts of birdsong to be heard. He turned to look at me, showing a face devoid of all emotion; I took a step towards him and politely held out my hand.

'Well now,' he said. 'Well, now.'

Physically there was about him a manifest retrenchment suggesting a more youthful version, now lost for ever, of great ferocity and power. His skin was dark, a combination of sun and the failure of cells to reproduce the pristine complexion of youth, and there was mottling around his eyes and across the bridge of his long, fleshy nose. His eyes were bleary, and hooded with heavy lids. His hair was silver, tawny and wavy, and brushed straight back from his head and clear above his large, heavy-lobed ears. Here and there, gleaming with oil, patches of scalp showed through. His face was lined and his neck was thick with leathery folds of skin.

In that moment of contact my bowels seemed to turn to water. His hand was hot and dry, and physically very strong; it was the handshake of a man who cares for no one.

'Good-day to you Mr Jackson,' I said.

He grinned at me. 'My manners aren't as good as yours,' he said. His voice was coldly mellifluous. His accent was impossible to identify; but it wasn't English, nor recognizably American. He sat down heavily on a cabriolet chair, squared his back and casually stretched out his legs in front of him. He wore heavy-soled, patent leather chukka boots with elastic sides; he rested his heels on the carpet. I watched him, unblinking, as in a dream; he pulled out a cigarette case from the pocket of his rumpled safari jacket and with fingers that seemed as bony and as merciless as talons he selected a cigarette and lit it, ignoring me completely. I found a chair and sat.

'Georges here says you know something about me already,' he said.

'Very little,' I replied.

'I guess you'll want to know more.' He drew on his cigarette and looked away over my shoulder.

'That's a strange thing to say,' I ventured.

'Not,' he said, and now he coughed in a strained way, 'not if it turns out,' he coughed again, 'we're . . .'

'Consanguineous?' I said.

'Shit.' He exhaled heavily. 'You know, I never heard that word in forty years. Con san guineous. Yup. Maybe I never heard it at all.'

'The resemblance,' said Bruedelmann, 'is there to behold.'

'Doesn't everybody look like somebody,' said Jackson, languidly flexing his toes; his shoe leather creaked rhythmically.

'Some resemblances, however,' Bruedelmann continued, 'are curiously non-physical. But it is the face that carries the sign.'

Jackson seemed to focus his mind on the garden.

'Yeah,' he said. 'Who knows.' His tone was crushingly inconsequential.

'Perhaps then it's not so important,' I said. And now I felt as if a stone lay on my chest.

'You bet your boots but it's important,' said Jackson and his spirit came at me like fire. I knew in that moment he was a man of extraordinary energy; a Salamander.

'It is, of course, most important,' said Bruedelmann, gently. His calm deep voice, so cultured, took on a precious, fastidious quality against the rough, indifferent silences of the Salamander, who now examined his finger-nails.

'Mr Jackson,' I said, 'I feel I must say this . . . to clear the air . . .'

'Sure,' he said. 'Say it.'

'If you are indeed my father, then you have wronged me. Wronged me beyond words. And if you are not my father, then you are a stranger who is obliged to deal with a man for whom your presence is necessarily a bitter disappointment. And even if you tell me that you are not my father, then I am caught in your presence between hope and despair.'

'Sure,' said Jackson.

For a moment nobody said anything at all.

'I can see you're a writer,' he said. And now I could hear it clearly, the American twang in his voice. 'I get what you say. I respect you for it.'

'Well?' I said, and my heartbeat was going up again, 'Are you . . . that person?'

He looked at Georges Bruedelmann, who smiled, as always. Like a large predatory bird rearranging its feathers Jackson shrugged his heavy shoulders.

211

'Maybe,' he said.

I blurted out, 'Is that good enough for you?' I had asked the question of both of them. Suddenly I felt unbearably weary.

'Not at all,' said Bruedelmann, briskly. 'It is of the essence that we find out for certain.'

'We're trying to find your mother,' said Jackson.

'Is she still alive?'

I felt a distant stirring of emotion, a wing-beat.

'Nope. That is, if I'm your old man she's dead.'

I sat quite still with my eyes closed. This was the intolerable dynamic: if he is my father, then my mother is dead. Only if my mother is dead can this man be my father. And that, I suppose, was the beginning of my new life, because even as I sat there I wished with all my heart that my mother was still alive.

'How can you find out for certain?' I asked.

'We can talk to people,' he replied.

'And when will you know?'

'We thought we'd know a while back.'

'What's the delay?'

'Internal confusions.' His face took on a very sour expression. I noticed vaguely that Georges Bruedelmann had got up and was quietly leaving the room.

'You know,' said Jackson, 'it's too bad you think you've got something on me.'

'Got something on you?' I found myself echoing his words in a thin, mournful voice. 'It depends, I suppose . . . I mean, I don't know if I want anything from you.'

'Anycase, we don't know for sure.' He finished it abruptly.

Each of us looked at the other; he coolly, with apparent indifference and yet acutely, I with a thrill of dread and fascination.

'How old are you, if you don't mind . . .?'

'Sixty-three,' he replied, and as he spoke he let wind escape from his mouth. '′cuse me.'

'You know,' he said, between draws and exhalations, 'I don't hold with any kind of guilt.' He gave me a sharp look. 'But I guess you do, huh?' His contempt was palpable.

'Is that something that shows in my face?'

'More in your tone of voice. I get the idea you're a young man who easily feels guilt. And you look for it in others. Too bad.'

Somewhat awry in my emotions I said, 'Surely it's something to do with being civilized.'

'Shit.' He said it quietly; there was a sort of generalized regret in it.

'It's part of the process of culturing the emotions,' I said.

'Oh sure.' He seemed to agree with me. 'But what is it you get when you culture your emotions? Nobody gets to be any better by it. Not so much as an inch. Maybe more efficient, more devious – is all.'

And now I sensed his fathomless anger. He was enraged, but it lay far off in some distant part of his being; I had the clear perception that it was always there, always with him.

'I don't want to piss you off,' he said, 'but I want to tell you this. I was in the war. I did special operations in Korea, some political stuff in 'Nam. I just came back from Nicaragua. I've been to parties with presidents of corporations and presidents of republics. There's so much bullshit it makes you blind. I've seen priests who fuck with little boys and girls. I've seen the morals brigades with blood on their fingers, robbing and raping peasants. Soldiers who cried like babies after a kill. They say there's good and there's bad . . .' He got up and walked to the window bay. There was something feline in his gait; his shoes creaked. 'Shit.' This time he said it like a curse. His hands started to twitch. 'They talk about good and bad. But you won't slide a knife-blade into the difference. Not in this bastard world.'

He stood in the window bay and stared into the garden. His back spoke to me of his experience; of his animal intelligence; of his violence. In the gloom I peered at titles of books on magic.

'Fuck it,' he muttered to himself. 'Fuck it.'

'Munker said . . .' I began. He swung round and glared. I trembled. 'Is he a friend of yours?'

'Munker,' he said, spitting tiny shreds of tobacco on to the carpet. 'Munker is meat. I'll fuck Munker.'

I was afraid of him then. I was frightened, too, for my beliefs. And still I was aware of the need in myself to hear his words, the words of the father who had broken his long silence; to take them into my soul, each one for what it was, to be laid down like sacred stones.

'England,' he spoke up with a fierce menacing rhythm, 'what a corruptor of souls. And all mixed up with its notions of privilege and its great tradition of contempt for the powerless and the poor. Corrupt heart, bones, bowels. Corrupt, perfidious Albion. Not just one person now and then, but everywhere. All the god damn time. Don't think you're going to be any better.'

I felt my heart thudding in my chest and I read book titles. His anger came in waves. The hair on my head stirred in the current of his energy.

'Tell me,' he called out to me, more in challenge than in question, 'd'you feel I'm your old man? I get no signal from you at all. You could be anybody!' He laughed abruptly. 'Hell, I could be anybody!' He came back to his cabriolet chair and sat heavily. 'Are you anybody or aren't you?'

I said sulkily, 'Everybody is anybody.'

'And no one is nobody, huh?' He laughed again. 'Well, we need somebody now, to clear up this business of the painting. I don't think just anybody is going to do here. Is it you? Is it me? If you're my son I reckon we could be in the end phase already.'

'Is that all it is to you?'

'Christ,' he said. 'There it is again. Jesus I hate that tone.'

'All right then,' I said, and showed a little spirit at last. 'Tell me if the only interest you have in me is this painting thing. That's what I'd like you to tell me.'

'Now that's a whole lot better,' he said. 'Now you sound a whole lot more like my kind of guy.'

'Where do your roots lie? I mean, are you English, or . . . or . . .?'

'Oh, that thing again.' He lit another cigarette. With a curved brown fingernail he picked skin off his nose. 'When I have to, I can draw on the English past I had. But you know, that country, England . . . It would've turned me into a slave. You know how it is, the stiff lip, aping your superiors. Taking their crap, taking their heroes. Did you ever study the Victorians? Jesus! Weren't they a horde of holy shit-minded bastards. It's what made this country what it is, you know that? Nineteenth-century England — it's where the devil lives.'

'I don't know much about it.'

'You don't know what it means to live like that? Beating the shit out of your fellow slaves. Fucking your children . . . You know what it means? You stamp your spirit and your imagination. You keep your place in the shit pecking order. Pretty soon you learn to despise yourself. Pretty soon there's your whole life ruined, when you've maybe only just started. I turned my back on it just as soon as I could. Some people say I betrayed. That's bullshit. There's only one thing anybody ever betrayed, or could betray, you know what that is?'

'No.'

'The little bit of humanity we've all got some place. Buried inside. The only ones who got betrayed, you know who they were?'

'No.'

'All the young men. And the women who got raped, robbed of their loved ones, got bombed in the war zones.' Imperceptibly his voice had

214

changed; the emotion that came from him was scalding. A tear prickled in my eye. 'All the young men of all the wars that ever were. Sold out. Cancel-led.'

I said hesitantly, 'People say it's all changed. Since the war.' He was looking out through the curtains, but I felt he was very aware of me, aware of my every move.

'They do,' he said, 'Yep.'

'Did you ... did you find something better? When you turned your back on it?'

'Hell no! It's just the same shit. Different forms, maybe.'

'Don't you have any loyalties?' I asked. 'No fealties at all?'

'You know,' he said, 'I don't want to get you rattled,' he laughed dryly, 'but it's plain to me you just don't know where you're at. Who are you anyway? How are you playing it? It seems to me you just don't know.'

'That's hardly to be wondered at!' I hotly exclaimed. 'I don't know who my parents are! How could I know where I'm at?'

'That shit, that's just history you're talking about. Mum and dad my ass! You don't get to know who you are by working on the past. You find yourself *out there*. Out there! Tomorrow! And the shape you're going to show is just what you planned today. The past, my ass. The past will sink you. It'll eat you up. Foisting bastards on our children, that's history for you. That's family! Get out there and be what you like. Where are your instincts anyway?'

He paused, and his energies seemed to subside. The birds had embarked on a dawn chorus and it was growing light outside. Jackson's face was livid and his eyes were bloodshot, but his concentration was intense. It was like being in the room with an artist at work. When he spoke again he was calm, and if he was at all regretful it was a quiet regret, and based on an unshakeable self-regard.

'I never saw my old man after I was sixteen. And my old lady – I turned my back on her when I was seven years old. Me too ... you know it happened to me too.'

'What did?'

'I was without my own family just like you. Living with strangers. You want to try and be like me, Mark, or is it Robert? There's a streak of it somewhere in you. I can tell.'

'A streak of what?'

'Raw spirit, I guess. Fight, I s'pose.'

I said, 'No one believes anymore in Social Darwinism.'

'Maybe no one believes in the devil either. But he's there.' He stared at me with bleary, hooded eyes. His gaze was frightening. His spirit was like fire in a field of corn. 'Now what *was* that I read there? In that Subject's Documentary. Hugo Thayer. That's the name, right?'

'Yes, that's right.'

'The guy's a head case, a nut. And then maybe he's not. I can see rightaway you don't hold much with the world, hey? Neither does he, right? But he said some things in that diary. You know all the shit in this shit fuck world. It's what we make. We make it, I tell you. This guy Thayer says that things up there are like things down here. Up there, out there, over there, in there — hell, who knows where? But the difference is, what's making things up there is pure spirit. And what's making things down here is bad meat. But it's words that make it, whatever it is, both ways. So you'll find they look the same, things up there and things down here. But what's down here . . . well, you can bet your dollar it's going to be the shit version. Take those poor guys who danced in heaven. They weren't really dancing. They were forced, starved, beaten into movement. But up there, the real thing, the realm of the spirit . . . providence, now that's what I call dancing. That's the real thing, Robert. Yup, that's where all things are made free, made in beauty. Don't make shit for me, OK?'

Georges Bruedelmann came back into the room. It was time, he said, to view the painting that Bartholomew had commissioned.

'What about Mr Jackson?' I said. 'Isn't he coming too?'

'All in good time,' said Bruedelmann.

'It will not surprise you to know,' he was saying as he led the way, 'that I am suspected by various governments of attempting to corrupt the young. There have been one or two trifling scandals, it is true, but my intentions have always been honourable. It is believed that I have an overall plan of evil, that I possess a key . . .'

'A key?' I had the feeling that he was leading me in circles along the corridors.

'The key to a herbal preparation of a hallucinogenic nature. It is said to be encoded in Bartholomew's painting. What nonsense it is, don't you think so? Who could believe such a thing? Their true interest in me is of course something quite different. Do *you* know anything about it, Mr Clare?'

'No, I don't. Really, I don't.'

'It is true in a certain sense that a key exists but not in the sense that my enemies understand. As to the existence of a herbal mixture . . . well, you must judge for yourself, now that you have read Bartholomew's story.'

'Do you mean that tree that Bartholomew talked about? The one in the Amazon? He called it *citadel . . .*'

'He also called it *Heaventree*. I very much like this name, Mr Clare. And if it were true that such a tree existed, how could I not dedicate my life and all its energies to discovering that tree and finding the key to the preparation of its leaves? Is it not ironic, Mr Clare, that a mischievous misrepresentation of my life's work is actually so closely related to its moral truth?'

'But, I . . . why don't you just tell them so and be done with it?'

Now we approached a narrow winding staircase and my apprehension mounted alarmingly, for it was four in the morning and Bartholomew's painting had sent poor Hugo mad.

'Ah, Mr Clare . . . Powerful people in powerful institutions are very like dogs. They have the mind of the pack. What did poor Henricus the alchemist know of chemical means to wage war? What did he wish to know of such things? But Count von Halle believed to the point of obsession that a man who dabbles in mystery cannot fail to be the possessor of magical powers. And inevitably he wanted to put those powers to political and military use. He did not hope or plan by their means to enhance life, to enrich human existence. He pursued only dominance. It is a type of thinking which characterizes my enemies.'

'Is that what you are . . .? A sort of Henricus figure?'

'There are parallels, of course. But you know, I am simply a man who dwells alertly in the mystery of things. To some degree, it is true, I manipulate what materials come into my hands. But I do this in response to the most subtle inner promptings and not for reasons of wealth or power.'

'I get the feeling,' I said, cautiously finding my way down the stairs, 'that you don't really want them to leave you in peace.'

'Did I not tell you before? This painting is my life.'

It hung in an underground chamber, in a carefully controlled environment, and was at first sight no more threatening or occult than any normally-to-be-encountered work in a gallery of modern art; it was not a bit Gothic, being in fact very modern, and yet, if occult art exists, this work exemplifies it. The painting is roughly three feet by two feet in size and is set in a nondescript yellowish frame about two inches deep all round. Its overall hue is predominantly greyish, but closer inspection reveals a just discernible range of colours, as though in a complex woven fabric. It is not representational, for nothing, so to speak, is depicted in it; but nor is it strictly-speaking abstract. It reminded me strongly of something between a Wassily Kandinsky and a Jackson Pollock.

217

And yet, although I hesitate to write these words, *the painting addresses the viewer*. It is charged with an energy, *a presence*, and I felt I had encountered in it *a familiar, expectant stranger*. I felt *accused* by it, too. My immediate reaction was to think it a trick of Bruedelmann's, a sort of ventrilocution by art, but in a language of the sixth sense. I looked sharply at my host, who was sitting across the room from me on a high metal stool. Whatever you see, Mr Clare, he seemed to say to me then, is nothing to do with me . . .; and I felt it intensify about me, uncannily, that intimate, alien otherness that streamed from the painting.

I have since given much thought to this work and am now able to report that within my limited experience of it the psychological effects of the painting are threefold, and work upon the viewer in stages: at first one is struck by the rightness, the justness, the irresistible accuracy of the work so that one is brought to say straight off, 'this painting has really got it'; but this effect soon disappears and one finds instead, as one stands before it, a growing sense of *resonant personal intimacy with the work*. It is as if the work spoke directly and profoundly to one's private inner self. And only lastly, if at all, one becomes aware that the painting is not presenting or re-presenting an aspect of otherness to the viewer, but is *reflecting*, faithfully expressing only what the viewer is, and knows, and thinks, all through the levels of that person's being. And although I did not know it at the time, the texture of the work was subtly changing even as I looked at it. Only with hindsight, and after Bruedelmann had made his confessions, and I had read through his copious files of other viewers' impressions, did this truth emerge for me.

It is, I suppose, a common purpose in all the arts to work on the viewer in this fashion, and the reader may object that such a work cannot be termed 'occult'; but Bartholomew's painting seems to work these effects not purely, as it were, psychologically, but *ontologically, in the real thing itself*, so that in subjecting the thing to sustained examination one finds not that the work, itself remaining fixed and unchanging, merely stimulates in the viewer a gamut of changes of reflexive thought and perceptions: rather *the painting itself reflects those changes as they occur*, and conveys too a heightened impression of how the nature of those changes faithfully portrays the self that they expose. The work, with its subtle texture of colours, does not play upon our perceptions as with non-occult art; or even stimulate us to see it in subtly different ways; or even to 'see' subtle changes in its contents. Bartholomew's Commission seems to reverse this normal process, for even as I looked at it *I felt I was being looked at, and what looked at me was changing its mind*. And this was a process that was wholly abstract.

There was, additionally, a more crudely immediate occult feature to the work. Delicately and precisely painted in was a portrait of Hugo Thayer; I was certain of it — it was almost as though he had been painted from the very same photograph that had been sent to me after my 'chat' with the computer. But Hugo's tiny portrait was only one of four such faces in the work. They were each about an inch in diameter, and clustered about the centre of the work, and seemed to be looking at each other, or to the centre, like introverted cardinal points; two were male, and two were female.

'I found H. T. in Paris,' said my host.

'But I don't understand,' I said. 'What are they all doing in this painting? I mean, they've been *added*, haven't they?'

'I was hoping,' he said, in a very dry tone, 'that *you* might be able to tell *me* rather more about that.'

'Well of course I can't,' I said. It was patently absurd.

In fact the faces in the painting were many more than four; everywhere I looked across the surface of the canvas I seemed to see faces and yet more faces, but only the four tiny portraits had distinct physical attributes. There were no eyes, or ears, or mouths to the other faces; and yet there were discontinuous sets of sentient presences, each acutely personal, each evoking in every case an irresistible impression of a knowable being. It was as if the painting were a patchwork of presences: kindred, existent, sentient view-points, intending, disposing, desiring, all clustering together like little islands — an archipelago of abstract persons. And the horrible idea seized me that the normal faces of our everyday lives, exemplified there by Hugo Thayer's tiny portrait, were only degenerate, downgraded approximations to the more exact typology of those other more intense, more abstract existences.

I said stupidly, 'There are all these weird face . . . face-things . . .'

'Ah!' said Bruedelmann, 'is that what you see? Be so kind as to describe them to me.'

'Not possible,' I said without hesitation. 'You'll just have to study them yourself.'

'Please,' he said, 'show me where they are.'

And as I pointed them out to him — I think I must have shown him a dozen or so straight off — I realized, to my amazement, that Bruedelmann could not see them.

'What else do you see, Mr Clare?'

'Just the faces,' I said. 'And I can't even see those really, not in the same way that I can see these four portraits here.'

'Perhaps you would move around a little, sir.' He waved his arm and I found myself moving about the room.

'Look here,' I said, annoyed at the ease with which he manipulated me, 'what the hell's going on . . .?'

'Everybody,' he said, calmly, 'sees something different in this work. It is occult art. Some people see more than one work in it. It helps if they move about, or spend some time in contemplation of it. In the broadest sense, it depends on their point of view.' And even as he said it I seemed to see in the work a quite different scene. But it was no sooner present to my consciousness than it was gone again.

'Ah me,' he said. 'That is a look I know too well. You have glimpsed something in the painting but it frustrates your mind. Can you make it stay? Can you say what it is you saw?'

'I think, I think I saw . . . it was a sort of tree. But it was . . . it was moving.'

'A moving tree. Did it have branches? And leaves?'

'No,' I said. 'No, it was more . . . more abstract than that.'

'Well,' he said, 'that is something for you to think about. Of course, it is perfectly possible to develop your awareness so that what you saw will no longer resist your conscious mind.'

'I'd like to do that,' I said.

'So that you could study it more carefully, and find out its secret?'

'Something like that, yes.'

'It is a mistake,' he said.

'A mistake?'

'Please,' he said, and he waved his arm again. 'Please continue to move about. Keep looking, Mr Clare.'

But soon enough I saw that I had exhausted my possibilities; for quarter of an hour I had wandered slowly about the room, staring all the while at Bartholomew's painting, but nothing new had emerged for me. Interestingly, I could not in the same moment see both the flickering, vivid, abstract faces and that other thing, *the moving 'tree'*; each seemed to exclude the other. And yet I was able to entertain both conceptions at one and the same time; and this, it seems to me, suggests that both were somehow 'out there', in the painting itself.

'What do *you* see?' I asked of my host, who was carefully examining the bottom right hand corner of the work.

'Many things,' he said. 'Many many things.'

'Well, perhaps you'd tell me how you think it works . . .'

'We do not know how it works,' he replied. 'It is occult.'

'But I mean . . . are the different things that people see in the painting *actually there in the work?* Are they actually rendered in the brushstrokes? Or are they private aspects of the viewers' own minds?'

'That is a distinction,' he replied coolly, 'that is not so real nowadays.'

'Well, what do *you* think?' I asked.

'What do I think? I promise you, I do not know what I think. That is why I like to look at it.'

I puzzled over that one for a moment and then I gave it up. 'What about Mr Jackson?' I said.

'Please remain here,' said Bruedelmann. 'I shall fetch Mr Jackson now. I shall be fascinated to discover what he will see today.'

Three minutes passed and then the two men returned: the huge, bald Austrian with the youthful, suntanned leathery skin, and the no less leathery, lined, diminished but formidable American Englishman, now smoking a black cheroot and puffing smoke about him.

'You know,' Jackson said, 'first time I looked at this painting I was taken with it. It just seemed to be so right. So damned accurate. No flim-flam. Now I look at it and the damn thing speaks to me. Like a friend. Or maybe it's just the old enemy talking.'

He threw his cheroot to the floor and ground it to shreds beneath his heel.

'But you must please tell me,' said Bruedelmann, eyeing the mess on the beautiful parquet flooring, 'what it is you see in the painting.'

The Salamander turned his aggressive, bleary gaze on the art-occultist.

'But you must move about in front of it,' Bruedelmann said. 'And you too, Mr Clare.'

Bruedelmann was plainly amused to see us then, shuffling about before a work of occult art while we searched for a common point of view. I encountered again the manifold of formless accurate faces, and once only, for a timeless instant, I saw again that other thing. And at just about the same time Jackson came to a sudden halt and let out a long, low whistle. From the corner of my eye I saw that his face was suffused with blood and his eyes shone.

'That's it, Schorsch! It's the Disko all right!'

'What can you see?' I asked, almost as excited as he was.

'I can see the dancers,' he said, and he gave me a look of malevolent inquiry.

'You mean you can see people dancing?' I was astonished, and, I think, delighted.

'Hell no!' But now he looked at me with a more temperate expression and said, 'You don't see it?'

221

'No,' I replied, with evident disappointment. 'But do you see it clearly? The thing you see, the dancers?'

'Nope. It's . . . it's like, smoky.'

'Through a glass, darkly,' I said.

'Now there's a thing,' the Salamander said. 'Through a glass darkly? Yes indeed. But some things have gotten clearer. You know, there's a worm that eats the mind. But it nibbles only on the weak stuff. The strong lines of you remain when everything else is gone. And then you come to a deeper understanding of the needs you never knew you had. Those are the secrets of the citadel.'

'You see the secrets of the citadel, Mr Jackson?' Georges Bruedelmann was intensely interested. 'You see that in the painting? Is that what you are saying, sir?'

'I don't think he means what you mean, Georges,' I interpolated.

'Hell,' said Jackson, turning his energy upon me so that I blushed and chilled, 'what in hell do you know about it?'

With bated breath I asked him then, almost in a whisper, 'What are they? Your secrets of the citadel?'

He shook his head as though half remembering a long forgotten joke. He shook his head more vigorously.

'Oh . . .' he said at last, 'something to do with love, I guess.'

And Georges Bruedelmann, more excited, more thrilled than I had ever seen him or ever imagined that he could be, had rushed upon us and was wringing Jackson's hand with extraordinary sincerity and vigour. 'My dear sir,' he was saying, and in his excitement his accent was clearly Germanic, 'I'm really so very grateful to you! I must thank you, sir. Now more than ever I am convinced that my poor master was there. Yes, my poor master was there, at Ludwigslust! He was an experimental subject.'

Jackson said he wanted to sleep and needed a bed. Bruedelmann offered to take him to his room. We all trooped up the narrow winding stair, and as we went I said to Bruedelmann:

'It's so amazingly modern! Surely it's not from the sixteenth century? I mean, it could have been painted yesterday.'

'Today,' said Jackson, heavily, from the top of the stairwell. 'It could have been painted five minutes ago.' His voice was sombre, and very tired.

'We have documentary evidence,' Bruedelmann informed us. 'For a time it was in the possession of a certain Huguenot family in La Rochelle. In 1685 the Edict of Nantes was revoked and the painting came to London with its family of refugees. About one hundred years afterwards a certain Parisian, a descendant of that family, came to England to claim it. He brought it back to Paris where it stayed in his house until 1861. That is when my master's uncle bought it, along with several other works of art from that bankrupt household.'

The château garden was richly blooming. I followed the winding path where broom and laburnum hung from trellises, past white viburnums of ravishing scents, pale lilac blossoms, climbing buddleia; and here and there amidst foliage and flower the pouring sunlight threw upon the path a glowing amber parquetry of patterns.

It was later that same day; and following some hours of sleep I had gone out into the grounds in order to contemplate the questions I should put to Dennis Jackson. I assumed that his tolerance of questions would be minimal, and that he would probably be disposed to be secretive. Since everybody I had so far talked to about Hugo Thayer and about my role in The Commission had been taciturn to a fault, I thought I could hardly be blamed for developing a little necessitous cunning.

In the depths of the garden there is a curious well-like structure where cooling odours of water and stone commingle with the scents of exotic flowers. It is a garden folly, situated at the centre of an expanse of ground about two thirds the size of a cricket pitch. It is sparingly roofed with trellis-work abounding with flowering plants and trailing vines. From a distance it appears to be an ornamental pond of triste Romantic character, for the water seems to rest on one level alone; as you come closer however, you discover not an ornamental pond but a well of three different and separate levels. The entire structure is about forty metres in diameter and its different levels take the form of three concentric bands of water; the outer level, virtually flush with the terrain, is narrower and shallower than the second, which, in turn, is shallower and narrower than the dark deep centre of the well. A natural stream, flowing below ground through much of the château garden, continuously feeds the outermost band of the well, from whence, by peaceful degrees and stages, it falls into the well's deep centre where there sprawls, a little below the water-line, a statue of a drowning man. A low-slung narrow catwalk in wrought iron, with a waist-high railing of intricate design, spans the well and leads to a circular viewing platform at the centre. It is much like the crow's nest on the mast of a sea-going vessel of bygone times, and stands about three and a half metres above the water-level, supported by a thick black pillar of iron.

Georges Bruedelmann was standing in this point of vantage, his arms crossed on the waist-high railing, his tall, bulky body absurdly crammed into that lofty stanchion. I called out to him and he beckoned to me to join him.

Making my way cautiously along the catwalk I felt the drowsy heat of the sun trap and the thickening of the air about me. 'Looking for anything in particular?' I asked him, as I reached the centre platform.

'I am looking,' he said, 'for right vision.'

'Ah.'

'Things are not as they appear. Much that is fair-seeming is rotten. It is important too, at all times, to have right understanding of people's motives and their points of view. Otherwise I shall fail. Ah, did you see?' He pointed into the dark water beneath us where a slender silvery form was undulating slowly amidst dark green fronds.

'I'd hate to fall in there,' I said.

'The water is deep, but it contains the statue. The reptiles are not harmful. It would be unpleasant, but not injurious, Mr Clare.'

I leaned on the railing and looked about.

'You know, walking along the path in there,' and I pointed to the dense foliage beyond and about us, 'you'd never think there was such an open expanse at its centre. But there's really no view at all from here. It's like a vista that never was.'

'Predilections for vistas,' he replied, 'as Monsieur Rousseau tells us, have their roots in the tendency of most men to feel at home only where they are not at the moment. This well is a call to the present, a celebration of the intricacies of place, and it is a reminder to us of the flow of time.'

He proceeded to describe to me in considerable detail the dimensions of the well's construction, which had been calculated according to the principles of the Golden Mean. And he expounded the imperspicuous relevance of Fibonacci's mathematical studies of the distribution of seeds in a sunflower head, and talked of snails' shells, and conches, and the distribution of leaves about a stem, the logarithmic spiral ... That unlooked for and extended lecture was a Bruedelmann meditation, of course, but I did not know it then, and besides, I had more pressing pre-occupations.

'Mr Jackson,' I said, 'is not a man to encourage love in a son ...'

This, my urbane bid for some straight talking, elicited from Georges Bruedelmann a ponderous quotation from Johann Wolfgang von Goethe.

'"While life is carrying us away we believe we are acting out our own impulses and choosing our actions and our pleasures. However, on closer inspection there are only the plans and the tendencies of the epoch, which we are compelled to fulfil."'

'I think I know what's coming,' I said.

'Quite so. "If the youth of the son coincides with a period of transformation, he will have nothing in common with his father."' He looked up, turned about and abruptly left the viewing platform.

'I take it that he . . . that he . . .' But Bruedelmann's large figure, striding ahead of me along that narrow catwalk, so reduced the visual cues I needed for my balance, that I gave up the attempt to express a difficult emotion . . . until I reached the land, and then I said, all in a rush, 'I take it he's half disposed to like me?'

'He is very interested to meet you,' Georges Bruedelmann replied. This artful linguistic evasion was typical of Bruedelmann, who has conspicuous difficulty with English only when it serves him.

'Oh come on,' I said, bluff as could be, 'do be a bit more forthcoming.'

'Nice garden,' I said, as we strolled towards the house.

'Is it not wonderful?' he replied. 'Gardens cannot fail to provoke a chastening contemplation in a cultured and sensible man. They show how the force of nature may be influenced by man according to his intellectual and aesthetic understanding. In the correspondence of idea between man and garden on the one hand and God and man on the other there is a resonance both edifying and inspirational.'

'Yes,' I said. 'How long is Mr Jackson staying? I mean, he hasn't gone away yet, has he?'

'Soon, Mr Clare. Perhaps tomorrow.'

'Look here, though,' I said, taking up his ideas, 'those plants may be beautifully arranged about the place, like words in a poem, if you like, yes, plant genes on the one hand, man's letters and words of language on the other . . . but you know, the fact is, those plants are all in ferocious competition, bitter rivals for minerals, water, air. And personally,' I finished with a flourish, 'I don't find that particularly edifying.'

'We must be as artists, Mr Clare, illumined by our spiritual natures. We must make efforts to order and dispose these primitive forces in new and more beautiful arrangements. Out of those lower-order patterns we must learn to make patterns of a higher order; out of the gross, inordinate impulses of nature, out of wasteland, jungle, *Ur-world* – let us cultivate and refine life's energies in ever more beautiful harmonies. It is our spiritual destiny, Mr Clare, to make anthropic beauty of great forces.'

225

'That's all very well,' I replied, doggedly, 'but I'm not so sure that human spiritual behaviour is any great shakes, if I may put it that way.'

'How very interesting that you should make the observation,' said Bruedelmann, and he gave me a hypnotic stare. 'You see, much of my work has to do with the problems of communication which exist between differing religious sytems. By means of our work we hope to reconcile all religious types. For we are as gardeners in this world, and from the green fuse of life we shall cultivate a spreading tree of love.'

It was clear that my host was in expansive mood; is it Jackson, I wondered, who has affected him like this? And suddenly my head was ringing with questions.

'All our perceptions, Mr Clare, are elements in the larger pattern of life. They may remain throughout our lives at the same primitive level or we may elevate them into higher forms. Our phenomenologies are as the gardens in our heads.'

I blurted, 'How did Munker know that I would be here this weekend?' Bruedelmann stopped short and showed me an utterly expressionless countenance. 'And how did Munker know that I might be related to Jackson? Did you tell him? And how could *you* possibly have known?'

Bruedelmann fetched a deep breath.

'My dear Mr Clare,' he said, 'remember what Doktor Wykzo said, I beg of you.'

'Eh?'

'If the cosmos is an infinite sphere whose centre is everywhere and whose circumference is nowhere, then you may console yourself with the sure knowledge that just because you seem to find yourself at the centre it does not mean that you are not in fact at the margins.'

But I was not so easily shaken off.

'Why,' I rejoined, 'is Hugo Thayer in Bartholomew's painting?'

We stopped in the shade of a gingko tree. Its leaves, vivid yet ghostly green, cast shimmering spangles on the cinder.

'I put him there,' said Bruedelmann, with equanimity. 'I painted him into Bartholomew's Commission two full years before I ever met him, before I ever knew that he existed.'

And then he told me the story of how he had taken himself off to America after amassing a small fortune in black market deals in post-war Berlin. But before leaving Europe he had returned to Austria to retrieve some paintings he had hidden there when he had fled Vienna in 1944. In order to smuggle them into America he had concealed them in the walls of a coffin, for whose real but deceased occupant he had obtained, by means of a little money, official documentation to the effect that the deceased was his uncle. But Bruedelmann contracted scarlet fever on the boat and on arrival in New York was quarantined. When he was discharged from hospital he discovered that his 'uncle' had been committed to the ground.

He employed some local villains to dig up the coffin in the dead of night, and so retrieved the precious canvases, among which was Bartholomew's Commission. He took them back to his lodgings for safe keeping. Shortly thereafter he was burgled and all his goods and possessions were taken from him. Penniless, he was obliged to live on the streets for a time. By chance he met a Jesuit priest who had been trained at the seminary in Gloggnitz, in Lower Austria, where Bruedelmann himself had first gone to school. His fellow Austrian sheltered and supported him, and in the course of a few months taught his youthful compatriot a more cultivated English and introduced him to the study of the intellectual history of Europe. Nor was Bruedelmann slow to find his feet, but quickly established himself as a picture restorer. About that time, his already well trained eye became virtually infallible in the detection of forgeries, and he found himself able to charge high fees to establish the genuineness of paintings which had found their way illegally into the United States as a result of the upheavals occasioned by the war. Such works were seldom laid before the eyes of more respectable art experts, many of whom were government consultants and vigilant employees.

'Did they take the Book of Bartholomew too?'

'Fortunately I had it with me at the time of the robbery. I was reading it in a library. It was much warmer there and quieter than in my lodgings. But a year and half later I was reunited with Bartholomew's Commission. You see, I was invited to value a painting for a gangland boss who lived in a mansion on Long Island. His son was to marry the daughter of a wealthy Ivy League family and it was his intention to give the painting to the bride's father. But first he wished to assure himself that it was worth a lot of money. When I arrived at the house I was taken to meet a very conceited man in a dinner jacket. He spoke only broken English and had a strong Italian accent. His mind was very dark. It was obvious at once that this was a person who had the habit always to put himself first. He believed, with the most passionate conviction, that he was right, always right about everything, and he considered that all other human beings were mere tools *zu Handen*, to hand in the gratification of his will. He took me into a room that contained nothing but an enormous billiards table. And there, on the wall, was the painting that Bartholomew commissioned.

'You may well imagine, I felt such joy to see it again; and also great sorrow to find it in such company. The monster demanded that I should value Bartholomew's Commission . . . I told him it was a reproduction of a work which had enjoyed great popularity in the early seventeenth century. I added, politely, that the painting was considered a trifle, much like certain Victorian works, which were originally executed as advertisements but enjoyed for a time a certain vogue in the market-place far beyond their true value. He looked at me with hatred and asked me how much money it was worth. I was very foolish then, but you must remember I was young, and I found it so difficult to contain my ill-feeling towards this man. I told him the painting was worth twenty-five dollars. He swore viciously in Italian. He started to shout at me in English. "Fucking art. Fucking experts." He was very red in the face and I was afraid he might attack me physically . . .

'Suddenly he pulled on a bell-rope . . . three seconds later a man ran in with a gun in his hand. Now I was very frightened. "Shoot it fucking shit thing," said the man in the dinner jacket. His servant at once fired the gun. I saw a puff of plaster come through the canvas of Bartholomew's painting. This was my master's most loved possession. You can imagine how I felt then. "Again! Again! Fucking shit thing!" the gangster screamed at his lackey. And the man obeyed. Before my eyes he fired four bullets into Bartholomew's Commission. I felt sick in the presence of such violence, such baseness, such vulgarity. "Wait sir!" I shouted. "Please wait! I will pay you thirty dollars for it, this very moment." In truth I would have paid him everything I had and all that I could borrow too but he would have killed me for it, I am sure, if I had so revealed my artifice. He told me that I had insulted his honour; that I was lucky to be alive. He looked at me with murder in his face and demanded from me one hundred dollars. And all the while he grasped and shook his testicles. With trembling hands I wrote the cheque for the painting. But when I took it down from the wall, reeking of cordite and shattered pigment, I felt my master's presence reach out to me. I was full of hot tears, Mr Clare, tears of joy and sorrow. But I hid my feelings of course, as I hurried from that evil palace.

'I repaired the holes in the canvas and then I had to decide how to fill in the gaps in the picture. It was impossible, as you can imagine, to restore what had been destroyed purely by studying the surrounding elements in the work. And I hesitated to tamper with this painting. My master had believed it to be occult, a magical painting. For years he used to meditate upon it. So I waited, and thought about it, and I thought about my master too, and of his Kabbalistic ideas. And after a time I started to dream of a face. And soon I began to see it even when I was awake. Eventually I took a pen and drew it. I drew it many times until I was sure I had captured it, and then I painted it on to the canvas where one of the bullet holes had been. *Just two or three days later I met for the first time in my life the person whose face I had painted on to the canvas.* I showed him the painting and in the next days his whole life changed. He said it himself. He was a wealthy man and urged me to accept a donation of ten thousand dollars so that I could continue to research the secrets of Bartholomew's painting. He said it was certainly a form of magic, and I believed him. Since then I have followed the same procedure at least a dozen times. It never fails to provoke transformations. I am at the stage where I can detect certain lawful but subtle regularities between types of experience in the life of the pictured persons and their position and orientation in the picture.'

'I've heard,' I said, with a set to my jaw, 'that Hugo Thayer is very ill.'

But Bruedelmann calmly replied, 'Hugo was exhausted when I met him. Harriet helped him very much but he still felt grief and despair. I showed him the painting and he overcame these feelings.'

'I also heard,' I said, 'that he's gone a bit mad.'

'Yes,' he said, 'but it is a necessary madness.' And now he had a faint smile on his tanned, smooth face.

'By the sounds of it,' I said, controlling my feeling of outrage, 'it was pretty bad luck for Hugo that he happened to bump into you.'

'Bump into me, Mr Clare? Hugo Thayer "bumped into me" in Paris, where he was sent by my enemies to deceive and betray me.'

I became aware that Bruedelmann was studying me expectantly. It was clear that he wanted me to divulge what I knew; but I felt no pressure from him, only a quiet, hopeful expectancy.

'Hugo was very interested in words,' said Bruedelmann. Again he seemed to be waiting for me to proffer revelations. 'He was very interested in Logos. He felt that it was possible to gain illumination by creating the right kind of connections between words and non-verbal phenomena. He believed in a condition of transparency in which the external flux of phenomena and the inner experiences of human beings can be wholly harmonized. In that moment all mind will be at one with itself. He thought of it as a window, through which he might reach out to the world of external things and direct them according to his own moral conscience.'

'Like riding the tiger,' I said, a little too glibly.

'Riding the tiger?' he echoed. 'Perhaps. Hugo called it being at one with the dragon. However, he is now following a different line of thought . . .'

'Oh?' My ears had pricked up pretty sharply. 'What line of thought?'

'I am afraid,' he said, weightily, 'that since the onset of his illness Hugo has turned his back on the world and has taken refuge in a form of gnosis.'

Jackson didn't surface again until late that afternoon. In the presence of Georges Bruedelmann he told me about his absurd accident on Lueneberg Heath in July 1944: of his meeting with Erna and the hours they spent together under the parachute awning in their sandy trench: he described the corpse on the kitchen table ten months later, and the baby boy in his cot on the window-sill, where the morning sunlight played over him. And he told me that he himself was the person funding the monthly considera-tion of Dutch guilders which I was receiving for my work on The Commission.

'*You!*' I was astounded. 'You are the Interested Parties?'

But he insisted that the Interested Parties were in British security, and in no sense at all were they friends of his. 'I'm just the guy who foots the bill,' he said. I pressed him to explain but he laughed and shook his head. And when I asked him about the dancers he had seen in the painting he told me that I was out of line, and blew grey–blue smoke on to the carpet.

Sitting with them then I was aware that they were jointly pursuing a shared and secret project, but it was impossible to draw it out of them. 'Ludwigslust', if I hadn't misheard the word, I took to be the name of a society of the arcane. It was evident that Jackson knew quite a bit about The Commission; he was aware, of course, that I was receiving a monthly consideration, paid for by himself, and he indicated that he knew some-thing of my commissioned task to produce a text on the Subject's Documentary. He also confirmed what I had learned from the machine, to the effect that The Commission had come about in response to a proposal made by Hugo Thayer himself. To judge by the freedom with which he spoke of these things in front of Georges Bruedelmann it was evident, too, that Bruedelmann was now similarly informed. That, at least, made things so much easier for me. I hadn't had to break the terms of The Commission, but I no longer needed to lie to Georges Bruedelmann.

However, I still didn't know why The Commission had come about; I couldn't for the life of me see any reason why Hugo Thayer should have come up with the proposal in the first place, and certainly it seemed to me outlandish, to say the least, that British security officials had deemed the proposal worth putting into effect. And as my thoughts turned to Burt Munker, I said to Dennis Jackson, 'If you as a private citizen are paying all this money for The Commission, then you must either own a share in it, whatever it is, or you are fronting for a different organization.'

To which he replied, after a moment's thought,

'Too right I'm trying to get a piece of it, but not of The Commission. They let me in because they figure I owe them something. That's why I'm the guy who's paying for you to write.'

This suggested to me two things: firstly, that Jackson was involved with Bruedelmann for reasons of personal profit, whereas Bruedelmann's involvement with Jackson was more occult, and presumably non-mercenary; and secondly, that the Interested Parties were merely making use of Jackson while pursuing their own peculiar objectives, which, I deemed, quite rightly as it turned out, had more to do with my own particular task.

Only much later would I discover that The Commission had come into being as a result of a timely but disparate coincidence of Hugo Thayer's and Dennis Jackson's separate interests and concerns. For each was working independently of the other and following quite different sets of motives; and although these two quite different men were each a necessary condition of The Commission's existence, it was only jointly that they became sufficient to make it real. The only relation between Jackson and Thayer, I was destined to discover, was purely *logical*.

At about nine o'clock that night Jackson left the château. Together we walked down the steps at the front of the house and on to the cinder drive. And I saw then what I hadn't registered before: that his teeth were perfect, as were his fingernails, and his hands and fingers were sinewy. I had wondered earlier if his body might be soft and sagging . . . but now I knew that it didn't matter, for he was still a hard man and very formidable. It came through in his gaze, which was calm and intent, and in the way he held his head, as though he was about to attack you. And I saw quite clearly how wary Georges Bruedelmann had been of him, even though it was evident that the Salamander was nowhere near as sharp in his impressions, nor as deep in his insights, nor as imaginative or visionary as the Austrian. Jackson motioned carelessly to the mouldering satyr which now wore a Mitzvah cap of delicate white bird droppings, and he winked at me broadly with a heavily hooded eye.

'If you ever get it published,' he said, 'put me in it. You might even put my name in the title, if you think you owe me. Pay your debts, Robert Mark. Always.'

'I can't put "Jackson" in the title,' I protested.
'How about Salamander then?'
'Too hackneyed,' I said, and I thought myself rather brave.

PART IV

and the beings of fire grew sane;
they raised the children in the dead forests
they wrought a gift from the fire of themselves
it was a tree of fire with a dragon coiled
round and solid like the earth

then Earth made a boy-child and a girl-child
the girl-child with the water of herself
the boy-child with the tail of the dragon;
she taught her children to be one
and they brought forth this Word . . .

we are a fruit-bearing tree
may our tree bear fruit
we celebrate the Cross that formed in the Void
which is the Tree of Man – the Tree of Love
with roots in Heaven and with branches in Earth

we quench the dragon's thirst that all may flourish
we make the dew that is the quenching of its thirst
we fill ourselves with the dew of the dragon
we bathe ourselves with the water of the woman
we become the light of the World

From *Fragments of Lost Cosmologies: An Anthology of Myths
Collected in the Amazon Basin* by Hernando S. Gordon.

15

The concrete koan is a dance.

Hugo Thayer

In that characteristic ugly-speak of the racist bigot, Pearson had called me a 'nig-nog'; and certainly he was not the first to have deemed me Indian by blood — in itself a false belief to which I personally had no objection whatsoever. Now that I had read The Book of Bartholomew, however, and had seen Bartholomew's Commission, I was strongly reminded of Pearson's remark — and Hugo's poster, too, and Sarah's comments on my appearance, clustered together in my mind. There was, it seemed, a patterning to behold; but I could not yet grasp its rhythms, nor apprehend its geometry of adventitious repetitions. And yet it was not that I lacked a point of view, so much as that I seemed to sleep as I wandered in its ambit.

Images, images: large and small, fixed and still, celluloid and resinous. I was building up quite a library, I thought to myself, quite a catalogue of filmic entities. As I plugged in the video and slid the tape into the machine it struck me that if I was, in any sense at all, a similar little Indian — and had not Bruedelmann suggested in his cryptic note to me in Paris that I shared with that person a certain curious feature? — then I was fortunate indeed to know how to read photographs and films, and make sense of paintings, because it gave me, no doubt, a far better chance than he had had to find his way back to whatever he believed he had started from. And it was certainly true that my own desire to find my way back to my origins was unremittingly strong, and yet invariably frustrated by other people's projects. When I had asked Dennis Jackson to give me the address in Westergellersen of the mother and daughter who had saved his life, he had refused me that information on the grounds that until my lineage was confirmed it would be wrong to make too much of them . . .

The Interested Parties had shown true to their promise; on my return to Canterbury I had found awaiting me at the Post Office a videotape of Hugo Thayer — talking to Robert Mark Clare.

The Subject of the Subject's Documentary looked artful and knowing on film; his face was secretive and his gaze, which was alert and intelligent, did not seem to rest on any object for more than a few fractions of a second. He had a markedly oval head and somewhat gaunt features. His hair, which was a pale mouse colour, flopped down on his forehead without concealing his receding hairline. He looked about forty but I knew him to be ten years younger. He was seated on a sofa in a neat, drab sitting room, his right leg placed over his left and his arms folded.

Off camera a voice said, 'Come on old son, sweeten up the physog.' Then the camera zoomed in and gave a close-up of his face. The Subject looked worn and depleted, like a man at the beginning of a convalescence, but unmistakably, too, there was about him an air of wit and wiliness, and of suppressed exasperation. 'I feel,' he said in a hard, fine, studied voice, 'like an exhibit in the house of the damned.'

'Don't you believe it, mate,' said the voice off camera. 'You look just lovely.'

'Mark!' said the Subject of the Subject's Documentary, 'I'm Hugo Thayer.' He gave a smile to the camera, but it was wry, quick, ironic; when he spoke again his voice was intensely dramatic and warm. 'How close I feel to you, Rob Mark Clare! They tell me you're anxious about things. Well, that's just as it should be. I'm going to try and put your mind at rest and I'm going to try to share with you some of the awesome, breath-taking secret of our joint undertaking.' He leaned forward and stared, conspirator-like, close into the camera. 'Listen,' he said, intently, 'I'll tell you a story: there was a baby, and for the first month of the baby's life the radio was playing a certain song in the room where the baby lay in his cot. The baby wept and screamed. And when the baby was a man, whenever he heard that same song played he was troubled by a secret grief and a sense of a world-pervading anguish. The song was sung by the forces' sweetheart and it promised a time coming when the soldier would return from the war zone to learn about loving from the woman he had left behind. And because the song was deeply associated with the Second World War the man studied history at Oxford. You see, he thought the song was speaking to him of that time and he thought that the grief he felt in response to it was the grief of millions of people who had suffered because of the war. And because he wanted to make sense of it, to master it and be free of its power, he studied history!

'It was Georges Bruedelmann who told me this story. I said to him, "Georges, *I studied history at Oxford. Tell me the name of the song.*" And then he sang it to me, beautifully, in a rich baritone . . . My hair stood on end and tears came into my eyes! "It's me, you're talking about!" I shouted. "It's me, that baby!" You see, Rob Clare, the man reads minds! But that's only half of it: Georges convinced me that the song *for me* relates not so much to the war and the horror of that time, but far more to the feelings I had as a new-born baby arrived in this world. And I realized suddenly that I had attributed those feelings to the song . . . but the song, you know, the song was a timely expression of what was happening all around me. You see, there *was* a war still going on — a war of the sexes, between mother and father, and their war was a family expression of the greater war which had ruined their adolescence . . . and I myself was a still more tiny version of that war and my feelings then were my response to the world that was a place of such war. And it was all the *same war*, don't you see? The Second World War itself was an expression of something on a larger scale still, and my parents were the expression of the Second World War, and I was an expression of them . . . and then it turned round, do you see, because the ruined children they carried in themselves found their expression in me — I was father and mother to the children in my parent's head, and they themselves were father and mother to the reality of their time; each of us was a war zone — and it was simply an expression of the pattern, and the pattern found expression everywhere, at every level, in every person. And that little song . . . it was as if Nature had artfully presented to me, in a perfectly resonant key, JUST HOW IT WAS GOING TO BE FOR ME. That's gnosis, Rob Clare. And that's why I'm here.' Hugo Thayer sat back and wiped his brow.

'And then do you know what he said? He said my posters project was my chosen means for solving this puzzle of war and a ruined world. But I haven't solved it, I said to him. It's just the opposite — look, I've lost my wife because of it. My posters, he said, were *my method of pleading for higher consciousness*. And everybody I spoke to, and tried to sell them to, assisted me to reach it. He convinced me that my posters are gnostic devices! And I saw suddenly that I had known it all along, but I didn't know that I knew it because the archons in my head couldn't permit it! And Georges Bruedelmann, God bless his soul, helped me to see it.'

'Steady on, old chum.' It was a different voice, cultured, self-confident, authoritative.

'And that's what's going on here, Rob Mark. I'm talking about the self and the cosmos, about the individual and the State, I'm talking about gnosis, and about art. You must read the Gnostic Gospels, Rob Clare, just as soon as you can. Will you do that for me? The people who are looking after me, the ones who asked you to write about my life, you know that they represent the State. And just as the State insists that we identify with it but keeps secret from us how base, how unjust, how corrupt it can be in practice and in principle, so too, according to the gnostics, the forces of materialism, the lure of sexuality, of money, of power – our own socially constructed selves – all keep us in a state of forgetfulness . . . But if we can awake from this half-sleep of ignorance we'll be empowered by the fathomless, eternal, miraculous nature of Mind. We'll be one with God, just as we always were before we got separated . . . And just as the secret agents of a state are difficult to spot, easy to forget about, and bent on keeping us in a condition of forgetfulness, so too do the forces of repression in our own heads keep us from illumination. The original gnostics believed that these forces were demons, called archons, and they guarded the spheres that wrap us round like layers on an onion. And when we seem to be beginning to awake they close us round more tightly. This is why we need art, d'you see? *Art allows us to smuggle realizations past the archons both inside and outside our heads so that we begin to see without appearing to, so that we may awaken even as we seem to continue to sleep!* They're desperate, don't you see? . . . Desperate to keep us in the dark . . . It's their brief, their *cause célèbre*. They have to, d'you see, because our ignorance just is the very source of their being. They feed on our sleep, they grow fat on our forgetfulness. And yet . . . and yet the archons too are fallen creatures. They too want reunion with God, to live purely, in pure joy again, at one with all-being in eternal life . . .'

'Fuck me, Hugo. What a load of old cobblers!'

'That's enough of that now Hugo, if you please.'

'Sophia called out to him, "Adam! Live! Rise up upon the earth!" And Adam rose up from creaturely darkness and opened his eyes. And when he saw Eve before him he said "You shall be called the Mother of the Living, because you are the one who gave me life." You see, Rob Mark, the Gnostics believed that Eve was a spiritual principal in humanity. She raises up poor Adam from his base material condition. She is Hahwah, she is Hokhmah, she is the Mystical Silence, the Holy Spirit, she is Wisdom. But of course Judaism, Islam, Christianity got rid of all the female symbolism in their belief systems. And look what they made of the world! But in the Gnostic Gospels God is dyadic – many of the symbols used to describe God are of the female sex! When Valentinian Gnostics congregated together they all enjoyed equal access to the mysteries and equal participation in the rites. They all had equal claim to knowledge! There was no sexism, no virulent patriarchy, no dogma – it was up to you to find your own relationship with God. *You made it up*, you see . . . YOU MAKE IT UP WITH GOD. Remember the phrasal verbs? It's the creation of the Matropater, the mother-father, the mother of All.'

238

Hugo Thayer had leaped to his feet, staggered a little, and now he stretched out his arms and began to dance.

'I say Hugo, steady on . . .'

To the Universe belongs the dancer. Amen.

'Jesus! Has he got clearance for this?'

'Has he hell!'

He who does not dance does not know what happens. Amen.
Now if you follow my dance, see yourself in Me
who am speaking . . .

'I think he knows. You want me to stop the tape?'

'Christ, it's obvious isn't it? He's just dancing. He knows nothing, I tell you. How could he?'

You who dance, consider what I do,
for yours is this Passion of Man which I am to suffer.

'It's going to be vetted anyway, right?'

'No it's not. It goes out just as it is. That's the condition.'

For you could by no means have understood what you suffer'
unless to you as Logos I had been sent by the Father . . .
learn how to suffer and you shall be able not to suffer.

'Don' it give you the creeps!'

'In the Garden of Gethsemane,' Hugo Thayer continued, his arms still outstretched but his dance ended, 'according to the Acts of John in the Gnostic Gospels, Jesus made his disciples dance with him, and as he danced he taught them the song I have just been singing. And did you hear what these guys were saying just then? What is it they're afraid that I know about? *What is it that I know and speak that they can't be sure that I say?* It's gnosis, Rob Clare! Gnosis . . .'

His face was illumined with intense exhilaration as he sank back on to the sofa. And now a look of such intense sweet yearning came over him that I was touched to see it; he seemed to be on the verge of tears.

'Don't you see, Rob Clare? Our truths are actually incorporated into our very bodies! Our bodies are the only possible ground of truth for us. And if we want truth in our lives the only thing we can do is arrange ourselves in space in certain ways, according to certain rhythms. All we can hope for, you see, is coherence. And the closer we get to it the more powerful become our thoughts.'

He closed his eyes, and his fingers came up to his forehead; and there the fingertips seemed to graze, like mites grown to prodigous proportion. 'The demi-urge keeps us in darkness, Mark, far from the true source of being. All roads are blocked; each sphere is guarded by an archon — a principle of ignorance. The first of the many, I found, was the fundamental illusion of reality: the idea that things exist in space, have upper and lower parts, have insides and outsides, come before some things and come after others. I decoded the phrasal verb and I found that there *is* no up and there *is* no down, no in, no out, no before or after. There are only patterns, patterns in the air, patterns which our fathers made, which we must now unmake, d'you see? The point is to make the world to rights – just like the song she sang when I was a tiny babe!'

I stopped the tape for a moment while I jotted down in my notebook: *H. T. has gnostic delusions (look up in library); also some symptoms of religious paranoia (does he think he's Jesus?); has the idea, through his phrasal verb posters, that the things from which phrasal verbs derive their literal, concrete meanings, i.e. dimensions – height/depth/breadth, interior/exterior/surround, temporal and spatial sequence, etc. don't really exist. According to H. T., believing in these non-existent things contributes to our spiritual incarceration in the materialist world!!!*

'Jesus told his disciples, according to the Gospel of Thomas, that when you make the two one, and when you make the inside like the outside and the outside like the inside, and the above like the below, and when you make the male and the female one and the same ... then you will enter the Kingdom of Heaven. And we can do it in the world, we can make heaven here on earth if we can change the patterns of things. That's what we've got to do, you see ... male and female polarities, up and down, inside and outside ...'

'What is it about film?' he was saying. 'Remember Blake's bounding line? I learned it off by heart when I was a kid; *the great and golden rule of art, as well as of life, is this: that the more distinct, sharp and wiry the bounding line, the more perfect the work of art, and the less keen and sharp, the greater is the evidence of weak imagination, plagiarizing, and bungling.'*
Now he was staring, confiding, *sotto voce*; he was awake, alert and paranoid. 'A few months ago I suddenly became aware of this film, Rob Clare. A film over my eyes, a film that wrapped my whole body round and clung to it. I became aware that underneath its blinding stifling surface I moved without definition. I was a formless shifting lump – no bounding line, no vitality! And there was a film over my words, too ... my voice was muffled. And when I breathed in you could see the horror in my eyes. This was the film of Hugo Thayer and I was trying to be it. But how could I be it, for what was there to be? Hugo Thayer is a fiction, Rob Clare. Hugo doesn't exist!'

'Don't you think you should change the subject now, Hugo? There's a good chap, hhmn?'

'You see, Rob, I sit here and I ponder, and I'm starting to get somewhere at last. And I really want to impress upon you that your writing is actually helping me along. It's a vital part of the process! Please, please don't stop again. I don't think we've got a lot of time. Don't go worrying yourself about the whys and wherefores. It's an experiment. We're all involved in it together. Of course our motives differ enormously, and because we all have different stories to tell we all see it in quite different ways. But you see, we're all pursuing our own several projects *in a sort of unity*. It's a manifold, a folded intricate thing ... It's beautiful ... bizarre, and just as it should be. When we meet I'll tell you more ... Goodbye, Rob Mark, until we meet one day ... But not as in a glass, darkly, but face to face. And then we'll know each other, even as we are known.'

He was exhausted; for a minute he sat still and said nothing at all. When he spoke again he was hoarse and whispering.

'Ordinary human experience is a spiritual death. Don't take resurrection too literally. You can rise from the dead right now. But gnosis is required. The dance is a concrete koan; the concrete koan is a dance.'

He seemed to go to sleep where he sat. The camera zoomed in on his face and the tape ended.

And so I had discovered that Hugo Thayer, although in questionable mental health, nevertheless had an amicable arrangement with his supervisors, and far from protesting at his lot was at pains to allay my suspicions; additionally, he positively wanted me to continue my work on his diary. Accordingly, resignedly, I took up the latest batch of papers from the Subject's Documentary and started working again. But it was with a certain squeamishness that I did so, for I was privy to the private writings of a stranger I had now seen on film; and he had come across as bizarre, complex, profound, and probably unhinged — but he had had about him a quality of sterling goodness, and a vibrant kindliness that made me feel mean by comparison.

16

Lonely one, you are going the way to yourself. And your way leads past your self and your seven devils ... You must consume yourself in your own flame; how could you wish to become new unless you had first become ashes.

Nietzsche, *Also Sprach Zarathustra*

February 12th, 1982
You want some fish and chips, Yougo?

Asleep on his black foam mattress in the squat on the Isle of Dogs, in greatcoat and winter shoes, with four hundred sets of unsold posters stacked around him amongst the litter of the squat, Hugo Thayer thanked them, no, and was surprised at the precision and clarity of his voice. Then dizzyingly, in a rush, his mind filled with pictures; he thought of the time when he and his wife had gone to Portugal together. All day long she had lain naked on the wide sand beach between the pounding waves and the piled grey scree. In the afternoon he had run half a mile along the sand; naked, hot, profusely sweating, his body was bathed in golden light. Afterwards he had swum out over the rocks, peering into the green chambers of the deep. In the warm salt embrace he had swirled and rippled.

> *What does it matter if she doesn't love me any more? She is inert in the sun. She sleeps. And I am swimming in this living element, living this salt seas moment's magic. If she doesn't love me any more, what does it matter? Don't I still love her?*

With smarting eyes he duck-dived down, down into the cool gloomy caverns of the sea. When his lungs seemed about to burst and his ears could no longer stand the pressure he looked upward, to where the light was blue. It was a silver blue curtain, the surface; it awaited him as he rose.

In January, 1982 his marriage had broken down, and Hugo Thayer, self-employed publisher and teacher of the English Language, had moved to the squat on the Isle of Dogs, where he stayed for nearly a month. He feels very grateful to his erstwhile host and benefactor, the emigré physicist from Prague who had invited him in. Once at winter's midnight, fearing the bailiffs on his own account, Ivan the physicist hurriedly moved Hugo's entire stock of posters into an adjacent flat. When Hugo returned next evening after a two-day selling trip among the Brighton language schools, he hired a van and took his entire stock to Folkestone, where he had access to a house. From there he travelled to most of the language schools on the south coast of England. Having slashed his prices and knowing now the rudiments of salesmanship he was able to sell his product with a modicum of success. But he soon exhausted the home market and decided to go to Paris. In May, 1982, just ten months before I cashed my first bank draft and thereby signalled my commitment to undertake The Commission, Hugo Thayer borrowed fifty pounds from a friend and, thus capitalized, began his export drive.

In Paris he threw himself into his task; by Saturday evening of the same week he had cheques in his briefcase to the value of five hundred pounds. During his short trip he had made contact, through a friend of his wife, with Karina J., a Swedish au pair girl living in the west of Paris. Although he is convinced that this person felt hostile towards him she nevertheless found him somewhere to stay for his five nights in Paris, and introduced him to the proprietress of an apartment block in Auteuil. Somewhere in his diary he declares himself extremely fortunate with regard to his women friends, who support him in his practical everyday concerns, or console and comfort him emotionally, or cause wisdom to awaken within him. In the event, the proprietress of the apartment block promised him an attic room for the entire month of June, should he wish to return to Paris; and Karina J.'s friend Harriet, a Swedish girl from Gothenburg, fell in love with him.

May 15th, 1982

Bought some beers and went to visit Karina. A tiny room on the roof of an apartment block in Auteuil. A tall fresh-faced young Swedish bloke called Mats, a shy, solemn English girl, and a round-faced Icelandic girl with plump arms, ample buttocks and carnal smile. And Karina. And one other Swedish girl ... an unnatural shade of peach yellow hair, eyes greyish-green, a listening look, an explosive calmness, intelligent, quick. I saw tiny flushes appear in her cheeks when I turned up. We talked about literature. Mats said he wanted to be a writer. What an occupation. I was trying to figure out why they were all so nervy, particularly the English

243

girl and writerly Mats. They told me a fellow called Ernst was in town, on his way to London to be with my wife. This was the German guy Fiona met when skiing. I suppose they thought I was the incarnation of beastliness. Not just a businessman, but an estranged husband, and of a woman they had all met and liked. Seems they all shared a chalet in the French Alps last Christmas.

Harriet asked me if I was all right in my little room. Yes thanks. She looked pained. I asked her how long she planned to stay in Paris. A fortnight longer than everyone else. I said I hoped she wouldn't be lonely. She laughed sweetly. 'I'm never lonely,' she said. What loneliness does that bespeak? I got up, shook her hand and left. As I walked away I turned and waved to them. They were all staring. Was it the emotions I could not allow myself to express that played on them then, thrilling them and flooding them with dread? In the lift, through the iron mesh from across the roof, I faced them all for the last time. I saw that Harriet was the energy source that would light them in a tableau for my memory. The rest of them barely existed. Then the black walls were all around me and the lift was descending. It was even darker in the basement and I had to grope my way along the wall. A little staircase led up to the street. Harriet, I hope I see you again.

Hugo returned to England and deposited his hard-earned, desperately needed cheques. His bank charged him heavily for negotiating each cheque and later returned them to him complaining that they had not been honoured. Thunderstruck, he made aggressive inquiry and learned that French currency controls required each cheque to carry a 'justification' to prove that it was not a fraudulent instrument of illegal currency exportation. He saw that he would have to take all the cheques back to Paris. Before he returned to Paris, however, he collected his mail from his rented business address. A Mr Stansfield, the young receptionist told him, had rung him two or three times about an application form. What application form? he wondered. When he opened his letters he found one from an association named Oxbridge Graduate Solidarity. It informed him that the association was funded by wealthy Oxbridge graduates who had made their fortunes after graduating from colleges in Cambridge and Oxford. The purpose of the fund was to assist recent Oxbridge graduate entrepreneurs. Although Hugo fell squarely into this category he knew also that his business skills were so wanting and his performance so poor in terms of initiative and good business practice that it was highly improbable that he would qualify for assistance. No one backs a loser, he said to himself, tossing the communication into the basket. In the last week of May he returned to Paris.

June 1st, 1982

Am installed in the attic room in Auteuil. Rent is 400 francs. The landlady is washed-out bourgeoisie, willowy, slatternly, sexual. 35 years old with come-on eyes. Thanks be to God. The Algerian guy down the corridor watches football with his door open. Had a beer with him. Poor devil. We watched the Algerians play Germany. His room stank of socks, couscous, pickles, stale sperm, despair. Left as quickly as I could. Down the corridor the other way three young Lebanese are sharing a room the size of a broom cupboard. 'Come in, come in!' So I went in for a chat. Two blokes and a girl. She's very pretty. Coppery-coloured hair swept back but worn long and wavy. Eyes the colour of almonds, very bright and clear. What a beautiful person. Such languid, haremesque sexuality. They watched me watching her, their faces shy and arrogant. Pure *joie de vivre*. I crept back to my room and lay on the bed. Too late to read – the light's too dim. Lonely as hell. What to do but play with the member. Disconsolate man at the end of his own elbow. This is Thayer's Paris.

June 3rd

Heard the troilists making love in the night. Pictured the arrangements. Instrumental Arabian music, long and repetitive. Felt unbelievably desolate. Then, from the Algerian's room on the other side came a pure animal cry of suffering. And from the troilists a polyphonic wailing – I took it for ecstasy. Then it came again, that horrible cry of suffering. It said: *loneliness, frustration, heartsickness, homesickness, rage, despair. I am desolate, godless, stranded in a strange land.* Twenty minutes more I burned and froze in the shadow of ecstasy. At last it ended. On both sides of me calm descended – the stained wings of a pigeon. I lay awake all night. Fiona my love; Fiona my life.

June 10th

Last night I had visitors! Harriet and Karina, on the way to the opera. Wish I was a Swedish au pair girl. They sat on my narrow bed and watched me fix coffee for them on the single ring camping gaz. Only one cup, so they shared. They offered me a sip. Guardedly. Harriet watched me, as though she expects something of me. Don't think she fancies me though. Bloody hot under the roof – had no shirt on. They got up to leave and Karina told me there was a big party that night at Fiona's flat in Battersea. I felt a sharp pain in my heart. Asked her how she knew about the party. She said she'd just rung Ernst at the flat. I felt an enormous weight crushing my vital organs. My head swam, the world opened its ravines. I stared down into the Void.

'Oh,' I said. 'She'll have finished her exams then.'

'Yes,' she said. 'That's why Ernst was going to London.'

Harriet turned pale as death and took her friend away.

Alone again I sat on my bed and tried to control my emotions. The clock ticked next to me. The sky was like slate; it deepened and thickened and turned to distant stars. But I couldn't escape my anguish. And the business situation was completely hopeless. No matter how it all went I knew at the end, if I ever reached the end, after a fantastic effort had been made I would still be £7,000 in debt. And I would have expended my life-force. Already I was nearly spent. I never slept for more than a few moments, and this was no sleep but a torment of dreams that threw me like straw into the hurricane of emotions. Grief took my appetite. All day long I worked under pressure of money, cooped and cramped in airless phone boxes, bursting with distress. And the nights were extreme theatre where exiguous moments of sleep wrought images precisely expressing what my conscious mind could barely comprehend: by turns she deceived me, betrayed me, sold me into slavery, danced with another as I wept.

In that little room, well beyond midnight, with the temperature in the nineties, the night like a sack about my head and a stone upon my heart, my mind still lingering in that bright parade of my barely-ended life with the wife I had lost, whom I pictured in her partying ... embracing her lover, laughing, giggling, lubricating ... the horror of my life was suddenly viewable and precisely ordered. It was as if there was a great weight that had found its form at last, and now it was poised above me, ready to crash down on me but for a slender strut of self-resolve which was only the last reserve of my spirit. It was poised for an instant ... and then I broke. The thing crashed down and beneath its weight I was hurled into an abyss. And like my brother in the cell beside me I cried out:

HELP ME! PLEASE HELP ME GOD!

Where was time then, as I lay there like a stricken thing with the taste in my mouth of a slab of scummed stone licked by innumerable tongues? Time was not. But I know I heard a voice. It spoke to me directly. It wasn't in the room. It didn't come through the wall or in at the open window. It came from within me, somewhere unimaginably deep and yet inside myself. The voice said:

I AM WITH YOU. I AM ALWAYS WITH YOU. I WILL WALK WITH YOU ALWAYS.

And suddenly everything had changed. Whereas it had been hot and suffocating in the room now it was cool and fresh, even somehow fragrant. I knew I had come forth from my prison. Another, who loved me, who was invulnerable and all-powerful, loved me, and held my hand.

June 11th

Went to see Harriet early evening. Wine, cheese, and baguette in a bag. Found her at the bus stop on her way to have dinner with a friend. 'Come tomorrow and visit me,' she said. I went home, drank the wine then went for a walk. When I got back about half past eleven I found a note under my door. It was from Harriet. She said *I was eating her mind.* She said she was waiting for me. Did she mean now, tonight? Couldn't believe my luck. For the first time in months I went to bed with a feeling of hope.

June 12th
Got home from work to find another little note. A key in the envelope. *This is the key to my room. My room is your room. Please come and see me soon.* Went round there at once. It has begun!

Hugo and Harriet spent two weeks together, living in Harriet's room in the rue Victorien-Sardou in the 16th arrondissement. Hugo remembers that her shoes were blue, and her bed had blue sheets and a pale blue coverlet, and the walls were papered in blue, and her limbs were cool and straight. At the end of June Harriet returned to Gothenburg and Hugo returned to Folkestone. But she would come back to him soon.

In the arms of Harriet in Paris, Hugo had forgotten Oxbridge Graduate Solidarity, but their interest in him was undiminished. On his return from Paris in July, 1982, he attended an O.G.S. drinks party in Knightsbridge. A Mr Stansfield, who was very keen to hear about him, buttonholed him there: grants of up to £2,000 were available; four hundred applications had been received, including twenty or so which were very promising; the application procedure was likely to include three separate interviews and could prove very time-consuming. Hugo Thayer, in the face of this battery of obstacles, wearily informed Mr Stansfield that he actually had no intention of applying, whereupon Stansfield expressed surprise that Hugo should have come to the party. Hugo, eyeing the champagne, indicated that he wasn't in principle against submitting his application. Stansfield at once ushered him into a little office where he loaded him up with forms. Hugo showed signs of peevishness; Stansfield pointed out to him certain short cuts in the form-filling; Hugo decided to leave; Stansfield asked him if he planned to return to Folkestone or would he be remaining in London; Hugo, objecting to Stansfield's tendency to stare at him fixedly, coldly requested of that person some proof of his identity, whereupon Stansfield produced an O.G.S. liaison officer's credentials; Hugo gave Stansfield his Folkestone number, drank five glasses of champagne, then left the building. Next afternoon he received a phone call from Mr Stansfield who asked him if he would mind putting his case to a colleague of Mr Stansfield who was in a position to offer Hugo the sort of assistance which had presumably motivated his application. Hugo should know that it was all remarkably 'old boy', and it was a bonus that Hugo happened to be a Keble man. Scenting at last a true opportunity, Hugo arranged to meet Stansfield and colleague the following lunchtime.

Stansfield's colleague, Mr Charlie Monson, scrutinized Hugo very carefully and with evident satisfaction. He asked Hugo a number of searching questions, including several on the subject of his finances, and wanted to know about his immediate plans. Hugo said he had arranged to spend the next six weeks in Lippstadt.

'You're joking,' said Monson.

'I wasn't aware that I was,' said Hugo.

'No, do go on,' said Monson.

'I'll be teaching English to managers at Hella,' said Hugo.

'Hella or *Halle*?' said Monson, whose face had taken on a most curious expression.

'Hella,' said Hugo. 'And then I'll be going back to Paris.'

'In August, old chap?' said Monson.

'End of August,' said Hugo. 'For the rentrée.'

'Of course.'

Mr Monson told Hugo that he was in a position to influence the award process if Hugo was willing to do a little work for him in Paris, and possibly also in West Berlin.

'Work?' said Hugo. 'I mean,' he added hastily, 'what kind of work?'

'All sorts of run of the mill little things,' said Monson, smoothly. 'But it would be of direct value to your country and would be entirely legal and wholly in the cause of democratic freedoms.'

Hugo was incredulous and suspicious by turns.

'How could I possibly . . . I mean, what have you . . . what have I got to offer you?'

'Actually, old chap,' said Mr Monson, 'it's your physiognomy.'

'My what?' said Hugo.

'Your face,' said Mr Stansfield.

'You see, Mr Thayer, there's a chap in Paris whom we need to know rather more about. He's one of these types who go in for cults, you know the sort of thing.'

'I'm not sure I do,' said Hugo.

'Magic, spiritualism, that sort of thing.'

'I see.'

'The truth is, we need to win this chappie's confidence. And you're in a position to help us. Rather a lot, I'd say.'

'It's something we'd very much like you to do,' said Mr Stansfield.

They hinted, in a tight-lipped fashion, that the person in question was implicated in matters relating to recreational drugs. Winning his confidence was imperative if the welfare of countless young people was to be assured.

'Of course, we wouldn't be seeking your co-operation gratis.'

*

Once they had started to talk money Hugo quickly overcame his own doubts. He extracted from Messrs Monson and Stansfield a promise that he would be paid £2,000 for the odd bit of work that might extend over a year. Half of this sum he was to receive in advance; but before that could happen, they said, he would have to put in an appearance at one of their offices in London. They emphatically requested him to observe the utmost discretion. Hugo declared himself ready to start at once. He would be required, they told him, to join a cult, or at least to make himself known to it, and to allow himself to appear to fall under its influence. They bought him another drink, clapped him on the shoulder, paid the bill and departed. Wide-eyed and exhilarated Hugo Thayer slurped his whisky and thought about two thousand pounds; he also thought about his estranged wife, Fiona, and about Harriet, his new girl-friend.

The Interested Parties could hardly have been surprised that their man should later suffer a nervous breakdown. They must have known about his marital estrangement, and about his enervating financial difficulties brought on by the posters project; and they must have been aware too that his tutors at Oxford had considered him impressionable and unstable. In this context of febrile, emotional arousal Hugo's ensuing exposure to Bruedelmann's occult teachings and to the work which Bartholomew had purportedly commissioned could well suffice, in their view, to push Mr Thayer into nervous collapse. And this, I am certain of it now, was something which Hugo most brilliantly exploited. For it is certainly the case that Hugo Thayer proposed The Commission; to what end he did this, and by what means he was able to lend credibility to his suggestion will soon be revealed. Hugo calls himself 'Gnostic Phrasal Verb Man'; it is an appellation, I find, which he richly deserves.

Two days after his firm acceptance of the offer he attended an induction; they asked him to put on a sixteenth-century costume, and then they photographed him systematically from a variety of different angles and through a range of different lighting conditions. In addition, they gave him a text to read.

'Shall I just read it out?'

'Or you might declaim it. Whatever you feel like, old boy.'

Hugo Thayer paced about in doublet and hose and recited from a text. He now believes that the text in question was the main body of the letter that Bartholomew wrote to Henricus Wykzo at the Count von Halle's request. At odd moments he had 'the funniest sensation'. He had 'a sense of everything melting away', and 'a feeling of sickening familiarity'. It shook him 'to the roots'.

Next he was subjected to a cursory medical examination followed by a short interview with a psychologist. It was clearly inadequate in view of what happened to him six months later. I suppose they dispensed with a true examination of his health just becasue they knew he was unfit but could not do without him. Ultimately, of course, this was to work to Hugo's advantage. Immediately afterwards he was given a cheque for £1,000 and a Paris phone number. They thanked him for coming and deposited him in the Strand.

Five days later he went to Lippstadt to fulfil his teaching obligations.

On returning to Paris in September he moved into a room in the countess's house and rang his Paris contact to ask for instructions. He was directed to go to the Louvre the following Sunday morning between ten and eleven. If he saw no pedlars on the steps of the main entrance in the Place du Carrousel he was to go away and come back later.

On his first visit to the Louvre at the directed time he met a man selling postcards. This individual looked at Hugo very intently, and seemed to intimate, without speaking, that he and Hugo had much in common. Hugo had the curious idea that he was 'dangling his face in the river, like a piece of cheese on the end of a line'. He asked the man if they knew each other, but the man just shook his head and went on selling his postcards to the groups of tourists around him. Hugo went into the museum, where he spent a couple of hours looking at paintings. It appears that he was followed; he left the Louvre by a different entrance and went to a bar in Châtelet, where the same man who had been selling postcards appeared out of nowhere and asked him in English if he could sit down with him. Then from his batch of postcards he selected one and passed it to Hugo Thayer. 'Please look at the picture,' he said, without any preamble whatsoever. It was an air-brush portrait of Hugo Thayer, exactly as he appeared in Bartholomew's commissioned painting. On the back of the postcard *Bruedelmann Publications* was printed; the address was the art gallery in the Marais. This, then, was the route by which Hugo Thayer came to spy on Georges Bruedelmann, who welcomed him with open arms and took him, in the course of time, into his deepest confidence.

When they recruited Hugo, Messrs Stansfield and Monson were clearly aware that Hugo Thayer, or his look-alike, appeared in Bartholomew's Commission; no doubt they thought that the bearer of Hugo Thayer's face would serve their purposes very well. I find it both incredible and yet not in the least surprising that they did not pause to question how such a thing might have come about; having no reason, I suppose, to suspect a conspiracy they probably neglected to entertain the thesis that Georges Bruedelmann's 'magic' might be a little more potent than mere run of the mill deceit and manipulation. I have the impression, too, that even when the coincidences began to pile up rather too thickly, the Interested Parties continued to overlook all evidential indications of the numinous. In their defence it should be said, of course, that their true interest in Georges Bruedelmann was founded not a whit on his occult activities with paint and brush but on their recent discovery that the Austrian had lately become a subject of great interest to the Americans; and they had inferred, quite rightly, some important connection with Disko 39.

In November of 1982 Georges Bruedelmann went to Berlin for three months in order to supervise some restoration work at Dahlem Gallery of Art. Hugo Thayer was only too pleased to accompany him there since Harriet was herself about to leave for Berlin, where she had arranged to follow a language course. Furthermore, Hugo hoped to sell his posters to West Berlin schools.

26th November, 1982, Berlin

Got off the 11 Bus at Hildburghauser Strasse. In wintry light in crumpled coat wanting to be in Bermuda. Walked down Stanzer Zeile, crunching snow underfoot, lugging the posters past silent solid domiciles secure inside their sacred wooden fences.

Comes a dog running, all along the inside fence. Thinks I'm Who? Stares at me. Can't figure it out. Why run to greet him? This isn't My Human. Dogpuzzle. Dogthink. Dog gone. Where else and when else am I such — the degenerate version of an expected stimulus? This is what fate is: dogs in wait, to bite or lick who passes.

But I'm all right. When Harriet saw me on that rooftop a voice in her heart said, 'You are the One. I have waited and waited. And now you have come.' She is H'lani H'nawara, She the Lion, a gift from God.

Would you like to drink a cup of coffee?

May I stay with you a little while? Here in your blue room, in your blue bed?

The First Kiss said: eons and vistas the World is, and each of us crouched in an ingle. But you may be sure of this: we are One Here Now. This Kiss Is. Come out from your ingle and breathe.

And next day in the tunnels of the Metro, carting the posters, I saw the Peruvian buskers. Falls of light, booming. Not like this morning in Clay

251

Allee when the tanks went past. The soldiers were fat-faced, heavy larvae, sullen and powerful. In their metal shells they were pale and soft-bellied. They threw up a black exhaust that darkened the avenue.

Buoyant in love we walked round the lake at Grunewald. In the late November light we found echoes of forgotten words, and traces of forgotten magical things. You were the colour of peaches and golden larches, and the spirit within you was a flame, shaped like a birch leaf, lit with your love.

You said, birch leaves are heart-shaped. Yes, but only conventionally. The real shape of the heart is more like a box or a ball. But have you noticed, you said, the shape of a birch tree with all its leaves gone is just the shape of a single leaf when the green has gone and the pattern of the leaf is visible? The skein of the leaf, I said. In the death of a single leaf the whole winter birch is mirrored ... I bet you haven't noticed, I said, in November, when its leaves are golden and reflected in the stillness of the lake, the birch tree is just like ...

Like what? you said.

Like you my love.

Like time, you said, which is a white lake. And we are all reflected in it.

And back we went to that vile little box we live in. A converted gents' hairdresser's. Big basin. Very small water heater. One narrow bed. And tarting up the wall a filthy crappy picture of a beach in the Canaries slabbed with pork-bodied girl with hair all blue from second-rate developing. And flimsy plastic panelling got up like wood to create the illusion of a wall around the basin. And to dine at: a small black plastic coffee table before a sofa of blue nylon, eighteen inches high. How hateful it all is — these economic artefacts, contemptuously fashioned, contemptuously sold.

I lay on the too short bed with feet banging the toe-board. And in the sprayed-on grain of the plastic wood I saw a Munchian madonna ... she was worn down to a spindle of suffering. And while the radio played ludicrous crooner-music, pitched at terror level by sentimental men in woodlore boots and green felt hats, I heard inside my head the owl-like tremolo of twin recorders catch the sound of hope. An image came to me: in the gardens of St John's the graduates were playing a galliard. And my love and I were dancing towards evening, in distant radiant England, upon a summer's green.

There's something funny happening to me. I keep hearing things. Sometimes traces of voices, sometimes musical sounds, sometimes a murmuring, like muted colloquies in a garden. And images emerge that have no bearing on my memories.

Something alien has entered my head.

*

252

The snow comes slanting and lays softly. The fir tree trembles, waves its prong-like branches. On the radio they're playing rock from the sixties and seventies. I feel wobbly. I feel moved. Here's a German version of 'Leader of the Pack' . . . *hi Baby, ich bin der Boss der Bande* . . . and the guitars are bellowing, heavy-horned steers. Somewhere up the road a baby's crying. How it carries, even through the muffling whiteness.

B. and I were in the art gallery at Dahlem. We had stopped to look at a seventeenth-century French work, can't remember the name. 'That's nice,' I said. 'What's nice?' says he. 'Nice face,' I said, 'nice colours, nice clothes, pretty sky . . .' He actually started shouting! An attendant approached us at top speed without appearing to move his feet.

'The brushstrokes,' he was shouting . . . 'Keep your voice down, Georges, for God's sake!'

'The brushstrokes,' he says, now he's just very loud, '– it is imperative to study the brushstrokes! These are the vectors of the painting, they are the grain of things, they contain the determinants and they are distributed right through the world!'

'But what about the fact that the brushstrokes render faces, and the faces have bodies attached, and the bodies wear clothes?'

'It's just a coincidence,' he shouted.

What was he trying to do? Embarrass me? He often makes a scene, pretending to be very angry, or very sad or something, always in a public place, and he always goes at it full belt. I'm sure it's one of his techniques . . . 'It's just coincidence,' he bellowed, 'or rather,' and suddenly he whispered strictest confidence, 'it's the marvellous workmanship of God.'

I know he's softening me up for the big day when he shows me THE PAINTING.

When we were leaving the art gallery in the main hall I saw a kid come in pulling a little toy dog on wheels. Up comes one of the custodians with hands clasped behind his back. He had a heavy jocularity – it was oppressive and squeamish at the same time. 'The dog will have to stay outside,' says he. I thought he thought he was joking. But was he? Did I?

My God, now I feel so wretched again. These mood changes, where do they come from?

Landlady at the door. Listen. Are you there? Can I come in? No, go away.

She's burst in. No time, I say. I've got to give a demonstration at the Goethe Schule. Got to catch the 17 bus. You must, she says. What's this must? The must-of-your-own-good. She's thrust into my hands a camel-haired kidney warmer. What's this? Must he? Musty? She's tugged it away and has thrust it under my nose. Musty warmer. Must he warm her? Me, I'm just sitting there. Now she's plucked it away and smooths her cheek with it. Lovely, she says. Look where I sewed it for you! If Harriet wasn't looking after you I'd spoil you like mad!

How lucky he was with his women. Did he play victim? Was he, despite himself, sneakily, courageous and burning-eyed — the son who holds off from the mother? It was a form of coquetry — grotesque because sterile. There was not even the possibility that the implied promise could be fulfilled. He knew he was arid sand inviting the wasteful pouring of waters. She sat down beside him carrying the gift of the kidney warmer and asked him for a kiss, a friendly little kiss of thanks. He demurred with intricate mutterings. He twitched his fingers. She flinched. She left. A cold sadness come to haunt him.

How clearly I recall today reading those pages from the Subject's Documentary in the first few weeks of The Commission two years ago! At the time I felt like a man who hears a piece of music on a tape, but the recording is so bad it is almost impossible to identify; and occasionally, the snap of fingers of an unknown listener gives anarchic punctuation to the sound. It seems arhythmic, unco-ordinated, clumsy. Yet the listener dreams; and in that flow of self and sound he is entire and wholly alive. Who is the finger-snapping listener on the tape? What is the music that he hears?

It was in Berlin, at the beginning of February, 1983, just seven weeks before The Commission began, that Georges Bruedelmann showed Hugo Thayer the painting which Bartholomew commissioned. It had a devastating effect on Hugo, who proceeded to have a nervous breakdown. Within a few days the Interested Parties had brought him back from Berlin and had installed him in a private clinic. Soon afterwards Hugo proposed to his employers the idea of The Commission. It must have seemed to the Interested Parties that he was seriously deluded, and nothing whatever would have come of it, I conclude, if the Salamander had not chosen that time to submit to his former masters his strange request for a deal.

17

Now when Pistis Sophia saw him moving about in the depth of the waters she said to him, 'Child, pass through to here,' whose equivalent is 'yalda baoth'.

On the Origin of the World from the Nag Hammadi Library

Soon after my weekend at Bruedelmann's Normandy château Sarah and I struck up a very congenial friendship. I had found her one afternoon, sitting alone in a tea-room by the cathedral gate. She was eating a huge cream cake.

'The next stage'll probably be alcohol.'

'Oh,' she expostulated, 'I was with a friend, you know. But he's gone off in a huff. Since you mention it, though, I'd like a Florentine next.'

'You're very stagy today, Sarah,' I said.

'I'm in another play.'

The angry, fluorescent orange stripes had almost disappeared from her hair; she looked a bit tired, though, which I put down to her studying habits, and her hands trembled slightly, which I put down to excess of dramatic emotion. Her eyes reminded me painfully of Lucia, whom I asked after and learned nothing of. Sarah wasn't interested in talking about her sister.

'How's Nolton?'

'Herman's fine,' she said.

'Did you know,' I said, 'that he's an expert *martial* artist?'

'What a silly idea,' she said. 'He does T'ai Chi. It's just like yoga. He's not the type that learns how to kick people's heads in and calls it spiritual practice.'

'Well, you can keep him,' I replied, with heartfelt sincerity.

'He asked after you, actually.'

'When?'

'Recently.'

'What did he want to know?'

'If I'd seen anything of you.'

'What else did he say?'

'Nothing! Why?'

A week or so later I rang Nolton and he insisted that we meet; our venue was a quiet pub down the road. He put his stick on the table, which disturbed me greatly. As I selectively recounted the events of my weekend at Bruedelmann's château it became clear that whatever he knew about Burt Munker he had no intention of sharing with me, but he was quite disposed to talk about Marilyn Moore; he reeled off facts about her almost as if he was reading a record card.

'Born 1940, in Brazil,' he said. 'Father: citizen of United States, Swedish extraction, white, middle class, Ivy League. Mother: indigenous Brazilian. They call her the Amazon. It's quite a good joke.'

'Joke?' I didn't relish the prospect of a joke with Mr Nolton.

'She's a very soldierly person, you would say. Explosives, hand to hand combat, small arms expertise.' He gave a dry, macabre laugh. 'They used to call her "No-way-up".'

'"No-way-up"?'

'No way up the Amazon. Unless you were very brave, or mad.'

I told him about my conversation with Harriet, mainly in order to give the impression that I was faithfully recounting everything that had happened to me during the weekend in Normandy. And because I knew he was expecting it and I hoped thereby to minimize what it would be necessary to reveal, I talked about my meeting with Jackson; he asked me about Jackson's interest in Bruedelmann's work, and I answered simply that I thought it had to do with the painting that Bartholomew had commissioned.

'He's a renegade, that one,' he said. 'I knew him in the war.'

Next we talked about the Book of Bartholomew. Nolton seemed to know all about it, and informed me that there had been two copies originally, one of which had been stored in a library in St James. The library in question was strictly private and contained historical books and documents which 'certain civil servants' were encouraged to browse in. The other original copy had been kept in the house of a wealthy Oxfordshire knight, Sir Herbert Kittlesleigh of Noke, and had been presumed destroyed. I told him that, far from being destroyed, it was now in Bruedelmann's possession. I also mentioned the additional writings (reports, critiques, analyses etc.), which had been pasted into Bruedelmann's copy; these had been stolen, Nolton declared, from that same library in St James.

'Stolen? Who would have stolen them?'

'Well, it's pure surmisal so I won't name any names.'

'Is it so easy then,' I said, 'to nick books from your library?'

'That depends,' he replied, 'on who you are and whether or not you have access.'

'Dennis Jackson,' I said, 'thinks he may be my father.'

'He's not very sure of it then?' He rolled his stick to and fro on the table top, producing a menacing, dry rattle. 'What is your feeling in the matter?'

'I think,' I said carefully, perhaps framing the thought for the first time, 'I think he is not my father.'

He asked for my impressions of Bartholomew's Commission. I told him truthfully that I had never encountered an object so manifestly imbued with occult qualities. And now for the first time I felt the need, obscurely, to confirm the reality of Hugo Thayer's madness and more particularly to locate its cause in the painting.

'It doesn't surprise me in the least,' I said, 'that Hugo Thayer went round the twist. Anybody who was a bit overstretched might flip out after viewing it.' I felt like adding, 'better not go near it yourself, Herman,' but that would have been crass, and hateful. I did not tell Nolton that Jackson and I had viewed the painting together, and I refrained from asking him anything about the 'Disko' that Jackson had mentioned. And, as if to complete this my family of new allegiances, I gave Nolton no indication whatever of the increasingly cordial relations which existed between Bruedelmann and myself on the one hand, and between Jackson and Bruedelmann on the other.

Instead I asked for more information about Hugo Thayer. I hoped that Nolton might advance my prospects of an early meeting with him.

'What is it you wish to know?' he asked, with a thin smile.

'Just two things really,' I said. 'I want to know why Hugo proposed that I should write a novel about him, and I want to know why the Interested Parties agreed to it.'

'A novel? Is that how you see it? I hope you will understand that you have been commissioned to do rather more than that.'

'Like what, for example?'

'Well,' he said, slyly, and he put a long thin finger into his ear, 'gad about, I suppose, much as you are doing now. Find things out, root out intricacies, all that.' He removed his finger from his ear and nibbled on it.

'To what end?'

'I'm not at all sure that anybody is all that sure about ends.'

'So you were in the war then,' I said, and I had been surprised to hear it. His lank slovenly hair and his degenerate demeanour belied that he had ever been trained in the habits of military discipline.

'Yes, Mr Clare, I was in the war. I'm even prepared to talk about it.'

'Everything,' I said pompously, 'seems to contribute.'

'Oh indeed, yes,' he said. 'I couldn't agree more. I passed most of the war as an intelligence officer in Berlin.'

'Berlin?'

'Yes,' he said, 'I was in the SS.'

'The *German SS*?'

He nodded. It rocked me back.

'But I worked,' he added, 'for London.'

'You were a . . . a double agent?'

'Amor vincit omnia, Mr Clare.'

'What?'

'Yes, it does seem rather unlikely. Would you like another drink?'

And then he told me about his recruitment, as a schoolboy, into British Military Intelligence operations, and about his time as a military science liaison officer during the years of the war. He had a great deal to say about the Nazi Party, and about certain of its most prominent officials; and he told me about his parents, particularly about his mother, and about the day in the birch forest in Poland.

Nolton's mother had been a golden-haired belle from Pevensey Bay on the south coast of England. In 1912 she had accompanied her father on a business trip to Berlin and she had never left Germany again. In July 1914 she had married Adalbert Noltke, and their son Hermann had been born three years later. Adalbert Noltke had joined the National Socialist Party when Hermann was still a small boy and had risen quickly to a position of power and influence in its ranks. He had raised his son as a dedicated child of the Nazi vision.

Hermann Noltke had learned English at his mother's breast. At the earliest opportunity, he had joined the Party. Perhaps, however, he had intuited, obscurely, even as a boy, his mother's horror of all that her husband stood for. She had wept to see Communists, socialists and anarchists gunned down in the streets by the Freikorps. But she had feared, too, to be separated from her son, and while still a young woman she had become silent and grave. Her exile of the spirit had become ever more complete when her husband, in order to protect his prospects and those of his son, compelled her to deny all connection with England. Adalbert Noltke succeeded in having his family records altered and all official trace of her lineage disappeared.

But she had not been forgotten in England, and when her son was sent to Brighton in his seventeenth year as a member of a visiting school party, she had reminded him, in secret, of his Eastbourne family connections. And she had spelled out to him her loathing of National Socialism and had begged him to turn his face from that path. The boy was terribly confused; in his heart, in his bones, he had always known of the gulf of ideology that separated his mother and his father. His love was all for his mother, but his hunger for glory and acknowledgement was all directed to the Fatherland, and to his father's vision of the world.

Amor vincit omnia, she had said, the beautiful young woman he had met during his schoolboy stay in England. She had claimed to be his mother's youngest sister, and he had been completely overwhelmed; she had given him an address and had begged him to write to her secretly, and at her solemn bidding he had sworn never to speak of her to anyone, not even to his mother. It was only a matter of time before he took a secret vow to serve his mother's cause all his days; thereafter he embarked upon his double life. In 1937, when his alien contacts told him that war was inevitable and asked him to help them, for his mother's sake, he transferred his allegiances to the enemy in England and from that day forth, as a fully-fledged traitor, he worked with intensified zeal to rise through the ranks of the Party. Inevitably he had joined the SS, where he had sworn terrible oaths of loyalty and had participated fully in the behaviours that were expected of him. In 1942 Hermann Noltke became a captain; in 1943 he became a military science liaison and security officer.

'It is a curious fact,' he was saying of his mother, 'that after I joined the SS I could not tell her any more how much I loved her. And I loved her so much. Even now, after all these years, I have a trench of darkness in my head. It splits my mind into two parts.'

It was in June, 1941, however, that the paradox of Hermann Noltke's divided life achieved its terrible consummation.

His SS training had brought him, as a member of an Einsatzkommando unit, to Poland; to a natural clearing in a birch forest where birds sang sweetly and the early morning sunlight softened all lines and fluffed up the texture of all colours. The smell of earth rose to the nostrils and the air was balmy. Against a backdrop of slender silvery trees sixty-one people huddled naked. A light wind caressed the long hair of the women, who had had all hairpins and clasps removed so that their tresses, abandoned, fell on to naked shoulders. Some covered their breasts with their hair, modestly hid their genitals with their hands. Others hugged their naked children, or clasped in their embrace their naked fathers, their husbands, their siblings. The children stared at the men in grey uniforms

259

and the men in black uniforms, who intently carried out their preparations. It was in the eyes of the children most of all that you saw it; they looked with wide, round eyes at the men with the heavy guns and yearned to please them. And the unnameable horror of it was mirrored in their gaze not as something real yet incomprehensible, but as a dream of the inconceivable shielded from itself by sober childhood.

Shovels were handed out to the men and boys and they were told to dig. Like sleepwalkers they plied their naked heels to the shoulders of the spades and dug up the summery earth. None of them seemed to think of running away. Was it because they were among their families? When the shallow trench was completed they stood like people in a church, awaiting a sombre epiphany.

A deathly pale young soldier set up the heavy machine-gun. A sergeant stood by him directing his work. The brass cartridges, long and thick as full-grown fingers, wound out of the ammunition boxes in ungainly glinting folds, gleamed in the breech of the machine-gun. There was a smell of earth, and gun oil, and human wind.

Nolton paced up and down. His boots hurt him, his cap oppressed him, his leather belt seemed to dig into his sides. He noticed that he was barely breathing. He thought he could feel every fibre of his tunic through his white undershirt. When he heard the commanding officer give the order he forced himself to turn to watch. He opened his eyes and saw that he had turned away instead. He swung back trembling and saw them, the massed naked Jews at the lip of their trench, waiting for death. They were silent and unreal, like mental images, but solid, and fixed, and very close. Children clung to the legs of their mothers. Fathers hugged their dear ones. Some pointed to the sky with quiet looks on their faces. The little children stared up to see.

Despite all his efforts then, Nolton had a sense of his mother; stealing upon him in that forest glade his childhood had come back to him. He remembered his own uplifted gaze; his mother's looks caressing him; her hands which were love's embodiment on his flesh. Something she used to sing to him when he was very small was borne to him suddenly, out of the distance of earliest memories, borne upon that summery breeze.

The commandant gave the order. The sergeant nudged the gunner.

> Baby baby bunting,
> Daddy's gone a hunting . . .

Nolton felt a vigorous tugging at his thigh. He glanced down and saw that the young soldier who was manning the heavy gun had snatched his Luger pistol out of his holster. He saw with grave slowness how the white-faced soldier, his mind intently concentrated on the act, raised the barrel to his own head and squeezed the trigger. His brains shot across the clearing in a sudden gory rain. A terrible moan went up from the huddling people. The commandant shouted curses at his young officer.

Gone to fetch a rabbit skin
To wrap poor baby bunting in . . .

'I sat on the regulation stool and pulled the trigger. You see, it was my punishment. I had to take his place, that young soldier who killed himself. As I pulled the trigger I saw a half-dozen of the women rush forward. "Save our little ones." But the heavy rounds just tossed them aside. I hear the sound in my dreams. I cannot go near a butcher's shop. I cannot bear to see people dancing. Everywhere I go I have to be careful of what I see. These emotions come up. Terrible emotions.'

He spoke as though he was watching it all unfold before him. I felt a current around him, something dark and black. He filled me with dread and pity.

For half a minute the machine-gun clattered and boomed. Then stopped. The air was thick with cordite and the smell of human excrement. The fatigue party went forward and tossed the bodies into the grave.

'I hope you will never see what I have seen, Clare. The light going out in a child's eyes. Some of them were still alive. I know it. When you kill like that you are with them; you are with each one of them. Some of them were still alive and I see their faces in my dreams. I write long letters to them. You see, I've learned the language. But the vileness goes so deep. Everything I write is infected. There's a demon inside me. I know it.'

His voice shook and quivered, then steadied. He had dropped his precise, clipped English accents; his voice was German, speaking English.

'You are a young man still, Clare. For God's sake be careful . . . what you have in your mind will one day be made real. It will one day be manifest outside you, like your private stage, and you will find yourself compelled to act out the part you have made for yourself. You should pray to God that you will never be placed in such a position . . . where you must yourself commit evil so that finally less evil will be done. Because even if your reasons are honourable – and what man can be sure of that – even then you will be infected. It will take up its place in your heart and in your soul. It will feed on your strength. It is the single event of my life. Everything else is preparation or aftermath . . . I could not bring myself to . . . I never spoke to her again. In 1944 she was killed in an English air-raid. That's when I came home. "Home."'

I had to get away from that terrifying presence. I stood up to leave but he caught hold of my wrist with that preternatural energy of his and pulled me down to within an inch of his face.

'That day,' he said, 'something else had taken over. I swear it. I see their faces all the time. That is why I wear these glasses. I want to be blind inside.'

'Let me go, please.'

'Listen to me, Clare. When you next meet Jackson I want you to say to him from me, say to him: "Don't think I can't see you." Have you got that?' And now he shook me as though I was a child.

'Let bloody go of me, will you?' I shouted at him, and flicked my wrist round and upwards, breaking his grip. In the same instant he pushed me and I sprawled to the floor. The publican, who had been watching us ever more nervously, moved out from behind the bar; half a dozen drinkers stared. But Nolton sat unmoving in his chair, rolling his stick to and fro across the table.

'I'll tell him,' I said, quietly, picking myself up from the floor. He said, with needle-sharp precision of voice, 'He will understand. Oh yes he will. You see, I owe him something from the war years. I want him to know that I have not forgotten.'

And then, as though once was not enough, he repeated it, but now his tone was inhuman; it seemed to come from somewhere outside of him.

'Tell him, tell him you met a man . . . and this man says to him, "Don't think I can't see you."' His voice became a sort of dry sob. 'Have you got that, Mr Clare?'

'Don't think I can't see you,' I said. 'Don't think I can't see you.' I walked from the room.

But he followed me out to the car park; he was laughing, a dreadful, lacerating sound.

'Picture it for yourself, Mr Clare. You're a writer are you not? Picture at Nuremberg the wicked Captain Noltke . . . They said I did what had to be done. But I was Banquo at the feast, do you understand? I am the loneliest man in the world.'

That same evening Bruedelmann called me; he said that conclusive evidence proved that Dennis Jackson was not my father.

'Then who is?' I called down the phone. 'Who is my father?'

But Bruedelmann didn't know. I put the phone down and staggered to a chair. I told myself I would never wish to have such a father; but now that he had been removed from consideration I felt the loss as a profound depression. I went up to my bed and lay down. And as I lay there it came to me that Nolton, who was Noltke, had tried to kill Erna. If Jackson had been my father I might never have been born. I lay like a man in fever . . . and realized at last that the phone was ringing. It continued insistently to ring long after I had decided not to answer it. But at last I yielded.

'Mark! I just *knew* you were in.' It was Vicky. 'Come to Germany, Mark!'

'Germany?'

'Don't you remember? We're supposed to be going to visit Herta Geschwisterheim. You've got to come with me, Mark. She's expecting you.'

'Vicky! Things are happening to me so fast now. It's like a carnival!'

'I know, Mark, I know!' She sounded very excited. 'Don't you see? I've told her about you!'

I was haunted that night by Nolton's story. *Herman has a grave tenderness towards horrid vile things*, Sarah had said when we had talked about the letters they wrote together; I wondered if she knew that they were communications with Nolton's murdered dead. He dictated them to her, and with the ornamental pen she wrote them down, long-hand, on the yellow parchment paper. 'The pen is like marble,' she had said. 'It's bluish-red, and the nib is 22 carat gold. So is the filament thing. All the bits inside, and the holder round the top of the cap, all solid gold.' She had picked up a knife from the table and tested its weight. 'It's so beautifully balanced. It's a dream to write with. You don't notice the weight at all. But the slightest touch on the page gives a lovely flowing line. It's perfect!' And of the yellow parchment paper on which she wrote down what he said she had commented freely, 'It's almost like skin!' I had replied that it was probably vellum. 'Used to be made from sheep.' Now I understand that her innocence and her courage might be a means of grace in Nolton's life, and that she took the stewing poisons from him through the ornamental pen. Beautiful Sarah. Handmaiden of grace . . . In my dream, sheep were being herded into a pen by mystical types in peaked hats and long black boots with bright red laces. I realized that the bleating of the sheep was actually a call for paper and pen and at once the pen had turned into an inky pit, and then it was an ink-pot filled with bluish-red broth. I found myself holding a clipboard on which I was ticking off names with Nolton's stick. I noticed that something was shining on my chest; it was a pendant, of intricate design, in a black mineral, like coal but highly polished, and it seemed to radiate a brightness that was somehow invisible but immediate. Harriet walked by; she was holding a brightly burning candle, which made me afraid for her loose white muslin dress, and she was singing a beautiful and poignant song which made my heart light and heavy though I couldn't actually hear it or make out any sound at all. In her wake came Nolton waving the ornamental pen like a baton or a swagger stick and tapping his feet to the rhythm like a hovering, leaden-footed puppet; and after him came Georges Bruedelmann holding a tarot death card. On the back of his hanging Byzantine gown was a life-size portrait of Hugo Thayer peering through a film. I felt there was a sombre intelligence overlooking us, observing us all in our carnival. 'Has my father come?' I asked. 'Has my father turned up?' And Bruedelmann whispered to me, 'Mark this well: Papa's in the pen; feather's in the inky pit.'

When Vicky picked me up at Dover she was driving a three-year-old Rolls Royce of a beautiful dark blue and was chauffeuring her father, a highly successful inventor who has made two fortunes from the invention of ingenious gadgets. Wilfred Straightwood, for such is his name, is a very amiable engineer; he identifies strongly with John Dee, the Elizabethan mathematician and mage, and true to that conception he has been working for years on what he terms a manual of moral self-improvement exercises for Westerners. He likes to think of his daughter as a witch, and this I take to be a projection of his own close identification with Renaissance philosophers. He was very congenial company indeed, a tall, straight-boned individual with a twinkle in his eye and a great deal of brusque but kindly wit about him.

He talked compellingly and knowledgeably about the Theory of Natural Selection, and insisted that it was necessary for us all to somehow trick our genes, for only thus might we transcend the drives of our lower natures. Thomas Huxley, he informed me, had predicted that biology would some day arrive at an understanding of the aesthetic faculty, by which he meant an as yet not wholly developed desire in people for a society of self-restraint; in place of thrusting aside, as he puts it, or treading down all competitors, it requires that the individual shall not merely respect but shall actively help his fellows. The whole thing can be summed up in the vision of a society in which it is not the survival of the fittest that is paramount, but 'the fitting of as many as possible to survive'. He talked too of gnosis, which was a word which I was destined to hear more and more often in the months to come.

He considers that his life is nearly over and he feels obliged, nay driven, to leave behind for his grandchildren a gift which should endure, *something above the material*. Hence his book, which he plans to call 'The North-West Passage'. I greatly enjoyed meeting him and I hope I shall meet him again.

We dropped him off at The Hague, where he was attending a

conference, whence we motored on in stately fashion, crossing the border into North Germany.

We drove into Bergen in the early afternoon; at the end of a winding narrow track that led between birch trees right and left into the very heart, it seemed, of the woods around the village, we came to a cottage in a shining clearing among the trees. I was amazed at the stillness. Nobody came out to greet us, nor did Vicky knock at the gnarled, weather-beaten wooden door. Instead she closed her eyes and started to speak, or perhaps she was singing. I felt self-righteously alienated as Vicky chanted, slowly and clearly and with remarkable emotion, to the listening trees and the quiet eaves:

> borne into being yes but ever in the Mother
> a channel I am, for all that was or can be
> and all that is, is of my living body
> but endlessly dispersed, yes,
> and mirrored upon mirroring eternity
>
> I am woven and I weave, I am wave upon wave
> wave never breaking wave ever breaking
> and always on some distant shore
> which is here, and now, and everywhere
> and is past, present, and future

'What are you *doing*, Vicky?'

'Shshh,' she told me, and then she repeated her little song. I was aghast.

And when she was done she said to me, 'You don't have to do it, Mark. But if you want her to think of you as a friend you *must*. She insists on it.'

'What *are* these words?'

'Well, what do they *sound* like, stupid? It's a translation. There's one for every European language.'

'What'll she do to me if I don't say it?'

'Well for a start,' she said, 'she won't put you in her cage and fatten you up for me. But worse than that, Mark, she'll *ignore* you.'

I hadn't made the journey for the purpose of being ignored so I repeated each line as Vicky spoke it for me. We did it three times in all; once for practice, the second time she thought me insincere, and she was only half satisfied with the third rendition.

'Oh that'll do I suppose,' she muttered. 'Why are you so un-cooperative?'

*

Herta Geschwisterheim, anthropologist, art-occultist, psychotherapist, faith-healer, herbalist, homoeopath and experimental ecologist, wears wood and bone and cotton and wool and leather; there are rings on all her fingers, embossed with ordinary minerals. Her eyes are cool and grey and full of understanding. Chronologically she is about fifty years old, but her complexion is as fresh as a child's and utterly without wrinkles. Her hair is as Vicky had described it: so red it is almost black, and reaching to her waist. Her lips are forbidding, and she has a diminutive snub nose. Although she is barely five feet tall and slenderly built, so that she has the figure of a prematurely developed girl-child, she is unnervingly prepossessing. I was reminded of Nolton in the dojo; it is as though she were a whole crowd of people all at the same time, all crowded into the same spot, all of one mind and yet each characteristically individuated and possessed of something distinct, specific and important to impart. And I was reminded, irresistibly, of Bartholomew's painting. When Vicky introduced me to her I found that I was unable to return her gaze. It was obvious that she was wholly free of any malice, or unkind intention, and yet her moral firmness was inexorable. At moments she was a stern, priestly teacher; at times she was the Queen of Foxes: dry, remote, unaccountable.

She engaged not a jot in the normal courtesies, and her manner with me was unbendingly severe. For the first ten minutes of our acquaintance she stood as firm and fixed as a tree before me, and spoke directly into my face. And as she lectured me I felt I was rooting into the ground.

She said, among the many strange things: that she would not grow old if she kept her brain active, and to this end she barely sleeps; that men think 'penilinearly', which is a thought-habit which leads to bloodshed all over the world; that so long as she felt she was needed she had no use for sleep; that if I could not love and be loved in turn I was already in a sleep of death. If one loves without partiality, however, and without cause, then one is whole, and not only in communion with all things, both animate and inanimate, but also *of* them too, in *just* the sense that the lily is of the field. She had much to say about the corpus callosum, which functions as a minimal bridge across the two separate hemispheres of the human brain; but it is a bridge that serves more to highlight the gap than to overcome it. She grinned at me then in a way that alarmed me and told me that *it is necessary, if one wishes to be a witch, to find means to unite these separate modes of the self.* Such people are healers, and acquire powers; but people who live out the paradox of two almost separate realms of experience remain but half-beings all their lives.

She stopped quite suddenly and asked Vicky, not me, why it was I was so depressed. I interjected, saying that I was fine, thank you, but Vicky said:

'He's just learned that the man he thought was his father isn't related to him at all.'

Herta Geschwisterheim looked into my face; she scrutinized its contents as though she were peering into an ill-lit cupboard. There was so much spirit in her gaze, and a sort of powerful living intelligence which had nothing to do with rationality or the processes of logic and mathematics.

'Why do you look for your father?' she asked me, and her voice crackled with energy. 'You'd do better to ask yourself who is that woman at your side.'

Instinctively I turned to right and left, but there was no woman to be seen.

'Don't you know her?' the witch continued. 'Her name is Eva.'

I confess that I giggled then, much like a schoolgirl, and this made Vicky laugh too; but I could tell from the sound that she was very nervous indeed.

'You must learn to look for your mothers,' Herta said, as though I had more than one mother, or even one at all. 'Then you will find your fathers too, but among your docile brothers, all of them strong . . . and holding no terror for you.'

The problem of rightly understanding her was compounded by her broad dialect German, which she pronounced with a strong Middle European accent. But I was not so bold, in that situation, to tell her to speak more clearly, or more slowly, or to repeat what she had said. I stood there and listened hard, and reflected carefully, and with great speed, and was in large part uncomprehending.

She reached out and touched my face with her hard hand. It was a caress and also a confirmation of power; but her power was not like anything I'd met with before. It was more like the power of a tree, or perhaps a number of trees grouped together in the forest.

'Tell me about your father,' she said. At once I felt deeply moved. It was unthinkable to refuse. I started to talk about a man I had never known, a man who lay at the base of my being, an imperative of blood. I mumbled about a man who had died perhaps at the end of the war in Europe; who may have been a Jew, an Englishman, a Celt, a Pole, a Frenchman, a Serb, a German. Or a Russian, I murmured.

'How was he, this man?' she asked me.

I found myself talking of his character, but I did not need to extemporize an image as one had long ago formed in my mind. It was defined and unmistakable, yet abstract, like one of the faces in Bartholomew's painting.

'He is gentle and kind,' I said, but she interrupted me at once.

'Not kind, not gentle.' Her words were like bony fingers drumming on my head.

'And he is full of love,' I said.

'Not love, but lust. Fire maddened him. He was lewd and rapacious. And he hated himself.'

'Who are you talking about?' I yelled at her.

'Speak to me of your mother,' the witch said.

After a while I became aware of the silence in the room. I raised my head. I was under the impression that I had been sleeping, but the witch had not moved. Vicky, pale and awed, was fixedly staring at us. Herta Geschwisterheim's smooth brown face showed no trace of time, was as blank as a wall, and yet I felt a current of energy from her; it was pushing at me, full of intending, full of meaning. I could feel the hairs on my arms stirring under the influence of her gaze, and I was mesmerized.

'I'm going to have to wake you up,' she said, and there was in her voice then a quality of energy that filled me with gladness, with relief, even as it caused me to shudder with apprehension. As she walked away across the room I studied her pale green cotton dress. Her bare feet, which flopped down flatly on the darkly stained floorboards, made no sound. From a cupboard she took a little bottle and poured a dram into a glass.

'Drink it all,' she said. 'Then you will remember your mother.'

I had it in mind to refuse, but she placed the glass in my hand, and my resistance slipped away.

Even before my first tentative sips had reached to my stomach I suddenly realized, for the first time in my conscious life, that I did not remember her, not in the least sense did I remember my mother. I could not even imagine her, and her complete absence from my mind was only oblivion, and was not real. *But to live without God and without the Mother . . . he knew he was arid as sand, inviting the wasteful pouring of waters.* Where had I read those words? I felt as if I had barely survived a long-forgotten war in which half my being had been shot away; I saw quite clearly, shockingly, where once there had been a central ground of being now there was nothing. It was a feeling that was blinding in its intensity, and as quickly gone. I think I groaned aloud then, and gulped down the liquid she had given me. It was oily, and slightly bitter. It had a sharpness to it that rose quickly to the brain, like fumes.

And within moments passing I felt the change come into my limbs; my arms and legs and chest seemed to awaken from a long sleep so that I

268

became horribly aware of the bones, the sinews, the muscle, the blood in the veins; and I had awoken only to find myself carrying an enormous burden. I staggered to a chair and flopped down. My head swam and I thought I was going to faint.

The next thing I felt was the passing away of that heaviness, and I was left with an exhilarating feeling of insubstantiality. I had risen to my feet and now I was moving around the room . . . It was wonderful! Everywhere in my body I was getting feedback, feedback! It came from the floor, where my feet just touched the boards; it came from the walls, and from the ceiling as my gaze went round and round the room. A stupendous exuberance mounted within me: I felt I was an ocean; my currents pulled and surged, whirled across thousands of miles, were immeasurable quantities of water tonnage responding to my slightest whim. And now, now I seemed to hear . . . the stirrings of a sound . . . from far off it came . . . growing, gathering, ordering itself. At first I thought it was the sound of the sea that I had become, for it was murmuring, and rhythmical . . . now it grew percussive . . . maddeningly joyful . . . and as it broke upon me in a rushing wave, a phantasmal deluge of sound, it lifted me, it took me straight up into itself, and I knew it for the most glorious music I had ever heard. It took me, and moved me, and it was how I was; and moving with it I was the music that I was . . . and I was DANCING! . . . dancing! . . . And my eyes were searchlights; and from the centre of me, booming in the light-filled tunnels, the waves of joy came surging, surging; my voice rang out, filling the room with laughing . . .

I heard friendly voices about me; they seemed to be ushering me away . . . 'Go now,' they seemed to say, 'there's no need to fear, go now, it's time.' They were voices I seemed to know, but I could not put faces to them, or say what persons were speaking to me so; but I knew that I loved them in an ancient, timeless, graceful way; and I felt summed up, stripped down and delivered up as though on the very pinnacle of my being, and given up to the light with a sense of joy.

And I was moving now in the clear eternity; but I sensed I had begun to descend . . . I was descending into something that was like a whirlpool, winding down into absolute blackness. As I neared its centre I was flooded with dread . . . I passed through a turbulence that was first dark blue, then blue—red, then red and blue and black . . . and I saw at the heart of it, awaiting me, an immense and terrifying fall. And now I was plummeting in absolute dark.

It went on and on, and I gave myself up to it; there could be no violent end to it, for the falling itself had become as a substantial thing. I plummeted, and I gave myself up to it, and it seemed to dream my life forth . . .

... I heard calls of encouragement all around me; I felt how I was propelled out through caverns of red fire and black blood and the din in my head. I glimpsed how she carried me, through the snow-filled woods, mournful as a chapel. I saw myself on the plane, flying over Holland, my lips to a bottle on Lena's lap; and then it all seemed to go very quickly. I saw my school-days: the imposing buildings against the changing, familiar skyline of the seasons; the blue-tinged frost on the autumn rugby field, the glistering swathes of red and yellow leaves; the smell of gun oil in the Nissen hut; the fights I had with Wolff and Larcombe. And then I was making love for the first time and sobbing with the joy of it. But it all seemed to grow cumbrous then, and I wearied of my life at the university ... I awoke to find myself in my little house in Friar's Walk. I was awake again. My normal self, surely.

And found instead that I was falling still in the spiralling, lightless oblivion; and I began to feel new things, emotions that scorched me, that rubbed my heart raw in my chest, that burned my eyes and pounded in my vitals. I felt her scalding fingers, and the sonorous bellow of my mother, and I was flooded with memories: memories, emotions, intuitions, memories flowed through me, but they were hers, not mine ... a wide swathe of deep, slow water, for my mother flowed through me ... and in the depths of her I saw a child with grim, harsh face fighting the waters with his eyes closed, tiny feet frenziedly kicking. 'Isn't he drowning?' I asked. And a voice in my ear, surely the very voice of love, never so gently said to me, 'He is being born in this moment. See he is born into his nature. This is the life he will live.'

And then I awoke for real; I was in my kitchen in Canterbury, making tea and singing a silly song about Lucy's 'titties'. And suddenly I had an overwhelming sense of *déjà vu*; and then a wave of nausea came over me as I understood that I had done this already, but somehow I hadn't done it enough, and so I was doing it again, or perhaps I was somehow still doing it for the first time, but it had infinitesimally shaded into a repetition. And the crushing futility of what I was doing made my stomach heave. But it had passed away in a second and I was standing there, frozen with horror, teapot and tea-bags in my hands. What was it I had seen? What was it I had just that instant forgotten?

'I'm still sleeping,' I bellowed.

And it was this that woke me: I was lying on the couch where Vicky had sat. Through the window I could make her out moving among the sunflowers in the garden. They dwarfed her and their great golden heads showered light on her hair as she passed. And the sound I had taken for a drone of bees I now understood was Herta's voice. The two of them came to the window and looked in on me; it triggered in me an unbearable sense of shame so that I looked about for somewhere to hide, but mercifully they understood and turned back into the garden. Her back, and the black-red hair that hung down in tiny waves, shone with intensity.

My first impulse was to slip away to the car. I knew it was entirely irrational behaviour; I knew I had to stay longer, or find a suitable excuse to get away for a while. And it is fortunate, to say the least, that I had one to hand: while map-reading for Vicky as we had driven through Westphalia I had noticed, with something of a shock to the system, that Herta's cottage near Bergen was actually on Lueneburg Heath. And when I had next searched for the tiny village of Westergellersen I had found it to be barely sixty kilometres from where I now lay, exhausted on a couch.

It was just a mile or two from Westergellersen that the Salamander had landed that night in 1944. And since my meeting with him at Bruedelmann's château Jackson had found cause to let me have the old woman's address; in fact I had it with me, in my wallet. And I was possessed now of a burning desire to visit that place, even though I was quite aware that the cause of this desire lay in my present embarrassment. For how could I make sense of it otherwise? Jackson was not my father, and Erna was dead. I had no call to be visiting there. This, at least, is what I told myself as I lay there on the couch. It was most ironic, and astonishingly apt; I had every reason to go to Westergellersen, and yet I could not see it. And so I was compelled, by my own way of doing things, to invent a pretext for going there. How right had been Georges Bruedelmann when he had taken me to task for my layers upon layers of delusion!

The two women came in from the garden and I said at once, 'I'm thinking . . .' but I spoke only to Vicky, and with halting voice, and I kept my gaze averted, 'I mean, I intend to visit an old woman who lives in a village near here. Right away.'

But Herta, that witch, insisted on questioning me.

'Have you found your mother now?' she asked.

'No,' I muttered. 'But I want to go there anyway.'

'Then she must be your grandmother,' said the witch, with staggering conviction.

'She can't be my grandmother,' I said angrily. 'If he's not my father then she's not my grandmother!' There was a rage building up inside me. But the woman clapped her hands and laughed aloud.

271

'You hear that, Vicky! Do you understand now what I've been telling you? Just listen to this foolish man!' All the while she had been wagging her long bony finger at me; now she turned to me and said, 'What do we care if he's not your father? We don't care a fig about your father! But don't you see, you duffer, she can still be your mother's mother!'

I stared at Vicky accusingly; but she shrugged her shoulders and looked away.

I asked Vicky to lend me the car, but she was very worried about the after-effects of the stuff I had drunk. I swore that I was all right, but she was sceptical, refusing to entrust the Rolls to me. Herta stepped in and offered me the use of her car.

'That's perfect!' said Vicky, quite shamelessly. 'Herta's got a lovely little beetle. It's a joy to drive, Mark . . .'

Somewhere in my memory a warning had sounded; and when we all three trooped out to the garage and Herta showed me her Volkswagen Beetle a shiver went up and down my spine. I knew I was going nowhere in Herta's vehicle.

I said to her, 'Haven't we met before?'

She looked at me dispassionately, and as though from far away.

'Cars like this are numberless,' she said. 'You find them everywhere.'

'Countless as the stars?' I said, suddenly remembering. And even as I spoke my flesh was creeping at the impossibility of the connection.

She said, 'I'll give you a cup of speedwell and lily. Then you'll be all right.'

'Actually,' I said abruptly, swinging my body away from her, 'I don't think I'll borrow your car.'

And now I remembered all too well the scratch of a wing on the roof of a car, and a sense of impending doom. But hadn't I only dreamt that encounter in snow-cloaked, night-filled, frozen valleys? My flesh crawled.

'What's happening suddenly?' Vicky was scared. She shouted, 'What's wrong with you both?' She stared at us, looking from one to the other, her face pale as death.

'I must have your car, Vicky!' I thundered.

'All right,' she said, shocked at the violence of my speech. 'Take it.'

As I drove across the heathland in a stately blue Rolls-Royce my thoughts were on Marilyn Moore. I had seen her just a few days earlier, in a hotel in London, to which she had invited me, peremptorily and clandestinely, to discuss the Salamander. Our meeting, which was very brief, had been entirely devoid of that romantic quality which had made our first encounter, in the wardrobe room at Bruedelmann's château, so magically memorable. It was obvious that she didn't want to see me and had agreed to meet me solely for the sake of Dennis Jackson. She had been waiting for me in the coffee lounge of the Wayfarer's Hotel.

'I have just twenty minutes,' she said, and looked pointedly at her watch.

'How's Dennis Jackson?'

'Dennis's got problems,' she curtly replied.

She poured herself another coffee. 'You want a coffee?'

'No thanks. What sort of problems?'

'Put it this way,' she said, and her mouth grew tight, 'he just loves to make enemies. They gave Munker a free hand.'

'Burt Munker? I thought he was some sort of tax investigator.'

'Sure,' she said briskly. 'He can do that too. This is unofficial, you understand? The last thing Dennis wants is you open your mouth at the wrong moment, OK?'

I nodded vigorously.

'Dennis said,' and she laughed in her throat. 'He said he was going to put Munker's dick in a baguette . . .'

'You've seen him recently?'

'. . . and feed it to the clochards. He isn't exactly *discreet*. Yeah, I saw him Tuesday.'

'Tuesday this week?'

'I have something for you,' she said. She looked intently round the lounge; then she took an envelope from her bag and passed it to me.

'Just put it away, will you.'

I hastily stowed it in the inside pocket of my jacket.

'Can you tell me what he's supposed to have done?'

'You said *supposed*? There isn't any *supposed*. He did it. He did that and more. The short answer is I can't. Most definitely negative.'

I felt the edge of envelope pressing against my chest.

'Don't you think I should open it? In case I need to consult you?'

'He's the best there ever was,' she replied. 'No way. My involvement stays minimal. Keep it right there. In your pocket.'

'Is the old woman's address in here, do you know?'

'I have to tell you the guy's name. Ernst Schwirrer. Got that?'

'Who's he? Ernst Schwirrer, yes I can remember that.'

She looked hard at me, then she pulled out a tatty little notebook with a leather cover and flicked through the pages. She appeared to calculate something in her head and then she jotted down a number on a small piece of paper. I picked it up and shoved it in my pocket.

'Is that how you're going to lose it?' She was acerbic. 'This old guy'll tell you all about the Disko. Lives in Berlin. Dennis says you have to go see him. Got that?'

She was unrelentingly offensive.

'I won't lose the number,' I said. 'I won't forget the name.' I'll try to forget, too, I told myself, that I ever met you. And yet I yielded to a nostalgic impulse and said, 'Why were you so ... pleasant, that time we met in Georges Bruedelmann's house? Remember, I was trying on that costume? You wore the ...'

'I was doing a favour for Munker,' she cut across me.

'Is Dennis Jackson a good friend of yours then?'

I felt sorry that Jackson was in danger, and I felt sad that Marilyn Moore had turned out to be such an incredibly hardbitten character. She looked at me then like someone judging a distance.

'Once,' she said, quietly, 'way back. We were lovers. He saved my life in Vietnam. He was one hundred per cent. The best operator you ever saw. I guess he knows just everything about character. But if you're asking me if I loved him or something, I guess nobody ever loved a guy like that.'

I said, 'Someone did, once. It was during the war.'

'You mean the Second World War?'

'That one,' I said.

'I know about it,' she said. 'Maybe that's where this comes from ...' She reached up and with short, thick, powerful fingers took something from her hair. She passed it to me across the table. My gaze rested on her wavy, pale blonde hair and I seemed to recall a beauty that was no longer visible to me.

'Will you look at it?' she said, and now there was a touch of amusement in her voice. Then her mouth tightened. 'We've got seven minutes.'

It was a chalcedony hair-clasp. Its colours were pale pink and yellow and it was polished almost to pure translucency, and it was formed in the shape of an 'S'. Attached to one end of the 'S' was a slender clasp fashioned of the same material, but with a slight ribbing to its edge so that it looked like a gnarled piece of wood, or a twisted tree creeper. At the other end of the 'S' was a narrow, ribbed cross-piece on a hinge.

'Doesn't it fall out?' I said. 'The clasp seems loose, and it's so smooth.'

'That fits over there,' she said, pointing an opaquely lacquered fingernail at the cross-piece. 'It just slides over the middle of the "S", right here, and it locks in at the bottom there. It's one hundred and fifty per cent. You can't get it off unless you undo the clasp.'

I held it to the light and saw into its fiery pale transparency.

'Dennis said it's petrified wood. I can't really wear it too well. When my hair is this wavy.'

'Yes, it's very nice,' I murmured. 'What's it supposed to be?'

'What d'you mean?'

'Well,' I said, 'isn't it supposed to represent something?'

'I never asked him,' she said. 'It's just a hair-clasp that Dennis gave me. The only time he ever said he loved me. He said I reminded him of somebody. But he isn't a guy who talks about the past.' She gave me a cool stare. 'Maybe you can tell me,' she said, 'who I reminded him of.'

'I . . . I haven't the faintest idea,' I stammered. 'I suppose it could have been Erna.'

'Erna?'

'A German girl,' I mumbled.

'Oh yeah,' she said. 'When he fell into the trap, right?'

I nodded. I was acutely aware that I should keep my remarks to myself.

'Can you pass a message to him? From me?'

'Sure, go ahead.'

'Tell him I met a man in Canterbury, and he asked me to say to the Salamander, "Don't think I can't see you." Have you got that?'

'I'll tell him,' she said.

'And tell him . . . tell him to look out for his name in the title of the book.'

'What's the name of the guy in Canterbury?'

'Well, I know him as Nolton, but he's also Hermann Noltke. Noltke says "Don't think I can't see you." '

'Which name?'

'Come again?'

'You said Dennis should look for his name in the title. Which name for Chrissake?'

'I don't follow,' I said; in fact I had had the sudden idea that she might tell me something very much to my advantage.

'You tell me,' she said.

'Salamander.'

She looked at me coldly, and yet provocatively. 'Dennis,' she said, and she drew heavily on a newly lit king-size cigarette, 'thinks you may be a faggot. I guess you're not a faggot, right?'

'No,' I said. 'I'm not actually a faggot, I think.'

'Gimme the hair-clasp,' she said.

275

I placed the hair-clasp in her tense open palm. 'S' for Salamander,' I muttered.

In his letter to me, conveyed by Marilyn Moore, Dennis Jackson had written:

Too bad Robert we're not consanguineous (took me five minutes to look it up). I would have been OK about you as a son with a bit of time. I heard what you did to that guy who came to your house and hassled you. Attaboy. Well, the old lady in Westergellersen sure pulled the wool over my eyes. I'm not your old man and Erna wasn't your old lady either. But I haven't any hard feelings. She really begged me to get you to visit her. I promised. Will you do that for me? Could be interesting for you.

Those bastards in Brit. Int. ran me ragged with the same story. I reckon the real reason they lured me over here was to sniff out a mole. Either that or something to do with the Disko. But I can't figure it out. Maybe I've got so I can't think any more. There's more moles in Brit. Int. than in any other intelligence network in the world. Or maybe the West Germans. I know for sure they've got a mole but there's nothing I can do about it. He's too smart for all of them. Slimy bastards. Nobody's got any balls any more, 'cepting the Prime Minister!

Now I'm in deep trouble again and I'm taking off. I've decided to sell out completely. I can't tell you what's going on for your own sake. But I can put you on to the Disko.

I've pulled the plug on the payments for The Commission so you probably won't get any more money. As I see it that puts you in a position of injured party. It's a clear-cut case of breach of contract. Should give you some leverage. If I read you right you'd be happier getting to write the whole story than keep your mouth shut and get paid for it. I reckon you'll be able to write your book and publish and they won't want to touch you. I'd like that a lot. They say you're a good writer. That's good. Only two things can get things done in this world and that's guns and words. Maybe they'll let you publish. I'll keep an eye out anyhow. I guess you should wait, though, maybe two, three years before you try.

The Disko: go see Ernst Schwirrer. He's in the American Sector in West Berlin. Lives right across from Uncle Tom's Cabin. This guy was one of the original researchers. You should know that the thing has been developed in the States. They've taken it a whole lot further than the Germans. And now the Europeans are trying to buy their way back in. You don't know how typical that is, Robert. I know, Schwirrer's old and ready to talk. Mention my name and he'll tell you all about the original research. All this stuff needs to come out. It's got to come out just as the smoke comes up from the underworld. So get your notebook out and be useful Robert!

You know what I told you about Erna? D'you think it was real? Her emotions? I know it was the stuff that did it to us, but does that make it not real in your book? One thing I decided just a short while back — if it wasn't real then I'm damn well going to make it real for myself. Because if I ever should've loved anyone I should've loved Erna. Potion or no potion. You make it real just if you decide to do it. Get above the conditions of the thing. Lift clear of the determining factors. Make it a matter of will. Ha! That's what they told me in the army, can you believe it! So I love Erna. Now. Now dammit, and for the rest of my whole life.

S.

PS Keep this letter and hide it somewhere SAFE. It's going to be evidence one of these days. And if I get stopped maybe somebody is going to carry the can for it some day.

The mill-stream at Westergellersen was a peaceful, almost unmoving stretch of water where three or four ducks quacked loud alarums and shook their tails as I passed, and a weeping willow trailed slender tips of branches among the lily pads. I followed the stream round the back of the old mill house until it disappeared into the concrete foundations of the building. A little way along I found a blue door in the wall; wisteria grew along the wall and around the dark blue door frame, but the flowers had long since bloomed and disappeared. I pulled an iron bell-pull and heard a tinkling inside.

It had occurred to me that I should at least have telephoned beforehand; but Jackson had not given me a phone number and, anyway, I didn't think I would mind very much if no one was in. After all, I had no clear or precise reason for being there. I suppose I had the half formed idea, however, that someone in the house might know something about the provenance of the little boy who had been lying on the sunlit window-sill while Erna lay awaiting burial. But I was aware that probably no one could be certain, nearly forty years on, that I myself was once that baby boy. After all, Lena was long dead, and my folks in Portugal, my adoptive parents, didn't know where exactly she had brought me from. And yet as I stood there at the door it didn't seem to matter at all . . .

A slender old woman: she was slightly stooped and her hair was silvery. She wore a pair of spectacles with thick lenses that made her eyes seem enormous. She stood quite still and stared at me.

Mr Jackson sent me, I told her in German. 'Ich bin Herr Clare, aus England.'

'Ja! Sie sind Herr Clare! Kommen Sie bitte herein.'

I wiped my feet conscientiously and went in; the cottage interior was spotless, and perfectly ordered. There were photographs all along a mantelpiece over a blocked-in fireplace, and everywhere I looked I saw a crucifix or some other representation of Christ. In the corner an ornate grandfather clock, decorated with forget-me-nots, speedwell and scarlet pimpernel, ticked with solemn propriety. In the serene atmosphere of that cottage I felt instantly at home, and at peace with myself. I sat down on a small sofa and watched the old woman go slowly upstairs. I tried to imagine what this room had been like in 1945 when Jackson had visited the cottage and had found a baby on the window-sill, a baby presumably that wasn't going to be me, and Erna lying in death on the kitchen table. I hoped I might get a peek at the kitchen ... How detached I was then; merely a voyeuristic writer, and so keen to see.

Voices sounded upstairs, then the old woman came slowly down to me and offered me some tea and cakes. I said I did not wish to trouble her, but she answered with spirit that it was nonsense not to have tea and cakes. She had a wry quality, almost as though she would have winked at me if she had felt able to control her eyelids. For my part, I felt unexpectedly cheerful.

'Let me help you!' I said eagerly, as she went towards a room which I took to be the kitchen.

'No,' she said. 'You look at those photographs,' and she indicated the row of black and white snapshots in their little wooden frames on the mantelpiece. But a firm voice sounded from the top of the stairs:

'No no, Mr Clare! You must wait.'

I sat down again and waited.

There was a heavy footstep on the stairs; a second old woman came into view. Out of politeness I stood up and went to help her. She was a solid, bulky figure, her feet enclosed in small black shoes. She wore grey stockings, which gave her plump old legs a quiet dignity, and a dark blue dress of fine material. Around her neck and over her shoulders was draped a woollen shawl of dark green and black, patterned with floral motifs in yellow and pale blue. Her hair was cut short, and was white, and lay flat on her head. With one firm hand she grasped the banister while the determined fingers of her other hand clutched the knob of a stick, on which she leant her considerable weight. Confidently, yet with great care, she made her way down the stairs.

'May I help you, madam?' I asked, solicitously.

She had been looking intently at her feet, but now she took up a firm position and relaxed her grip on the banister. Her head came up and she fixed her gaze on me; her eyes were deep blue, her face square and heavily lined. I noticed that she was wearing a little make-up around the eyes. She, too, was disposed to stare.

'Ach du grosser Gott,' she muttered. 'Da ist mein Eva.' Then her head went down on to her chest and she seemed to go to sleep where she stood. I took a step or two towards her and discreetly looked up into her face. There were tears running down her cheeks now lightly stained with her mascara.

'Let me help you,' I said, very gently, 'just a little bit.'

'Ja, ja,' she said, 'that's lovely. You can help me just a little bit.'

She had used the personal form, not 'Sie', but 'du'. It was very unusual given her generation and the difference in our ages. I offered her my arm, and as we descended, step by step, she said to me between determinedly taken breaths, 'When I am an old woman, I shall go to bed in the kitchen. And there I shall die, among my pots and pans.'

'You'd be warmer in the sitting room,' I said.

'No I wouldn't,' she replied stoutly. 'There's a stove in the kitchen. And that's where the children were born.'

'Omschka,' said Liselotte, as we reached the bottom of the stairs, 'where shall we sit?'

'In the kitchen, of course. You see, Lotte! Didn't I tell you? He's come back!'

A farmhouse table took up fully three-quarters of the length of the kitchen; a half-dozen chairs were ranged about it. In the corner, by the stove, there stood a sturdy, antique rocking-chair. All along the wall a variety of pots and pans hung from pins, and there was a motley set of kitchen knives, some of which were very old. The floor was of bare planks stained a deep velvety earth colour. And there was an all-pervading smell of the hearth, and a sense of human lives; and more than anything else, there was a smell of kindness, of simple compassion, a smell of love.

'Will you please, Liselotte,' said the plump old lady, who had settled herself in the rocking-chair by the stove, 'please bring us the photographs now.' Then she turned to me and said,

'Wir sind Familie, kleiner Mann.'

I waited for her to say something else. She had said that we were family. Had Jackson not had the decency to disabuse her? I supposed the old woman must be Erna's mother.

'I was born in 1897,' she said. 'That was the old world. When were you born?'

'In 1945,' I said.

'Yes,' she said, 'you were a March child. Right in the middle of the month. It was very cold. Yes, and the snow was very bad.' She had the habit of moving her head about as she talked, as though she was swimming, sluggishly, and wished to keep the water from coming into her mouth.

'Mr Jackson . . .'

'Der Unmensch,' she gave a vehement chuckle. 'Der Drache!'

'Mr Jackson,' I continued, 'used to think that Erna was my mother.'

'My daughter,' she said, nodding. 'That was Erna. She caught him in her trap when he fell out of the sky! What a surprise for him that was!' She was chuckling again. She had called him the monster, the dragon. I found her chuckling highly infectious.

Liselotte spread a pile of photographs across the surface of the table.

The woman in the rocking-chair said, 'It belongs to you now. Alles,' she waved her bulky arm in a generous sweep of the building, 'everything will belong to you.'

'Madam . . .'

'Madam!' she mocked me joyously. 'Omschka bin Ich!'

'Omschka,' I said, 'Dennis Jackson is not my father.' Even as I spoke I heard the strangeness of it, that I should be telling *her* this fact.

'Ja, das ist richtig,' she said, slowly, as if I had begun a complex explanation and she wanted to be sure to follow everything. 'Jackson is not your father, and Erna is not your mother either.'

Thank God for that, I thought. At least I'm not going to be the bearer of bad news.

'Look at the photographs,' she said, pointing a fat wrinkled finger at the fading images spread out on the table.

'You were born in March,' she said. 'But you were a child of victory. We wanted you to be a child of victory.'

'Who *are* you?' I said.

But she did not immediately reply to my question. Instead she plucked up from the pile of snapshots one particular portrait of herself and her daughter. In the photograph Omschka was sitting with her hands clasped in her lap, a magnificent matriarch; and standing at her left side with both her hands resting on her mother's capable shoulder stood Erna. I felt a thrill pass through me. I recognized at once a clear resemblance between Erna and Marilyn Moore.

'That's . . . she's . . .' I stopped myself. The old woman's eyes, I noticed, had grown moist.

'But of course,' said Omschka. 'Of course. That's my daughter. My Erna.'

I was suddenly overcome with bewilderment. Was the old woman senile? I felt an acute pain in my heart. And what *was* it about that photograph? I had the distinct impression that something was missing from the portrait.

'This picture,' I muttered. 'There's something wrong with it.'

Indeed, there was a palpable absence that seemed to press upon me as I looked at it. Omschka appeared to be sitting right up against a wall. It blanked off her right side completely. As I stared at the photograph, puzzling over these things, Omschka took a wallet or something from somewhere and removed from it a narrow strip of celluloid. With trembling fingers she placed it on the table, and pushed it up against the portrait. The two parts fitted together; a single, uniform image sprang into being. I gasped; my breath ached in my chest, tears shot into my eyes.

'I'm your grandmama,' she said, and her hand reached out and grasped my own. 'You are Eva's boy. Eva and Erna were twins.'

Twins.

'Zwillinge!' said Liselotte, and in her lined and feathery face there was a kind of wild joy.

'Ja, Zwillinge!' said Omschka. And the two of them laughed aloud, with the tears running down their cheeks.

I stared at my mother's photograph. Her right hand hung by her side, near her curving hip, and her left hand, long and slender, lay on the shoulder of her mother.

Mother. Mutter. I felt that something was trying to break inside me. Intently, absurdly, I joined the two portions of the photograph as precisely as it was humanly possible to do. I wanted to see all of her. My whole mother.

'Why did you cut her off?' I asked hoarsely.

'The dragon,' said Omschka, her voice thick with emotion. 'Der Unmensch.' She dabbed at her eyes with a tiny lace handkerchief. 'When the dragon came everything was cut in half. But now we can be together. Everything will be all right again.'

And Liselotte chimed in sweetly, 'Now we can put things together again.'

'Twins,' said Omschka. 'Your mother was Eva. She was born first. And five minutes after came Erna. For two whole years I hardly knew which was which. There she is. That's Eva. My Eva.'

'Is she . . . is she . . .?'

Omschka went stone-faced and looked at the table. Liselotte took my hand and held it between her own light, frail hands. I got up from the table and went to the window. Just below me, in the quiet mill-stream, I saw small dappled fish basking, and on the other side of the building the towering, deep-russet crests of a beech tree noiselessly stirred.

'It was pneumonia,' said Omschka at last. 'She walked back from Ludwigslust. It was the beginning of March. But she was caught in the snows and had to lie down in the woods.' The tremor in the old woman's voice was like swift, light wavelets on a deep water. 'My poor Eva.' She put her handkerchief over her eyes and sat very still.

'But . . . but Jackson thought I was his son! Why did he think that? Who was the woman who lay on the table? Wasn't it Erna?'

And then, even before she answered, I saw it clearly; my mind reaching back, as through a narrowing tunnel, to an image that I had created only at the prompting of the Salamander.

'It was Eva . . .' Omschka's voice was almost inaudible. 'It was your dear mother.' Liselotte uttered a shrill little coo of concern for her friend. 'But that fool,' said Omschka, growing firmer by the moment, 'he thought it was Erna lying there.'

'He told me that you'd said I was his son!' How harsh I was then. Even today I can hear it still, that unremitting fierceness.

'No. It's not true. I didn't lie to him. He wanted to believe it was Erna. He wanted to believe that you were his son!' And now, in her voice a note of pure distress was unmistakable. I came back to the table and sat down.

'Omschka,' said Liselotte anxiously, 'you mustn't over-excite yourself. Make shorter sentences.' With a hand that trembled with emotion she poured more tea for us. I couldn't hold the question any longer.

'Is my father alive? Omschka?'

She closed her eyes.

'We don't know,' she said. 'Nobody knows what happened.'

I asked her why she had never contacted me before. She said that no one knew where they had taken me. Jackson had promised her that Lena would supply all the details on her return from England; but Lena had never come back to Westergellersen. Omschka sent dozens of letters to various government departments in England, and for months pestered the authorities of the British occupying forces in her own region in Germany; but she received no help, and no relief. Rules had been broken; important men had been compromised; there was no official record of such a child. She was reminded, persistently, that hundreds of thousands had gone missing during the war years. She must be patient and live in hope. And when she dared to attempt to trace the man whose life she had saved on

Lueneburg Heath the veil of silence became impenetrable; all her subsequent requests for information had been curtly refused. She waited nearly forty years, but in March of 1983 Dennis Jackson came back to the little cottage by the mill-stream. Omschka said she had recognized him immediately. He interrogated her about Erna and about the little boy that he had arranged for Lena to take back to England. He wanted proof from her that I was his son. Of course she could not give him proof, but neither did she reveal to him her secret. The first time he had stood in her kitchen she had seen a way for Eva's little boy to grow up a child of victory, and so she had encouraged him to believe that I was his child by Erna; but when he returned thirty-eight years later she knew at once that he would not help her to trace her grandson unless he continued to believe in the deception. So she had continued to let him think that Erna was mother of his son; and he, confirmed in his original belief, had promised to send me to her. Later, by some means or other, he had found out for certain that I was not his son, and yet he had kept his promise to her. 'Always pay your debts, Robert.'

Omschka held my hand tightly and said,

'I knew I hadn't lost you for ever. I felt it in my heart. I knew I would touch you again when I was old.'

She asked me why I had so little interest in my mother. Why did I not want to know about Eva? The words found their way at last.

'I always thought,' I said, 'that she abandoned me. In that military vehicle. I . . . I am ashamed.'

Her face registered the heavy shock of a lifelong injustice committed against her first-born daughter. I winced at the sight of it.

'You have no generosity,' she said at last. 'You are unkind. Eva was a wonderful woman! Eva never abandoned anyone. How could she abandon her own little child? No woman was ever more faithful, more loyal, more brave.'

I knew I would have to sort this out for myself, later, when I was alone, when I might confront everything in myself that had grown in response to a false and ungenerous assumption. I knew it was something that would shake me to the foundations, and I could not bear to think about it then. I told myself I wanted to keep my mind clear until The Commission was completed. Omschka no doubt sensed my evasiveness. What a wise woman she was. As I drove away her words were ringing in my ears:

'She went to see your father. And you were in her belly. She walked all the way to Ludwigslust. But when she was coming back through the woods she was forced to give birth prematurely. You were born in the snow, Robert. In the woods on Lueneburg Heath.

18

And from matter the ruler made for himself an abode, and he called it heaven.

On the Origin of the World from the Nag Hammadi Library

Half-way back to Bergen I felt so charged up that I stopped the car outside a local bar and rang Georges Bruedelmann. I hoped he might be able to contact Jackson and pass on my thanks to him for I was now twice indebted to the Salamander. Bruedelmann wanted to know what my plans were . . .

'You are going to Berlin? I beg of you, Mr Clare, please come first to Paris. Come to my hotel. I shall most gladly cover your expenses . . .'

As I drove away I belatedly understood that the locals had been disappointed not to recognize me . . .

Bruedelmann had politely requested me, since I was going to Berlin, to return the Lichterfelder Watteau to its rightful owner on Lichterfelder Ring. Accordingly I reserved a couchette on the Paris train, and Vicky brought me to Hannover Central Station. As we were saying our goodbyes I thanked her again for the good that she had brought into my life. She said with great excitement, 'Herta's going to initiate me. Tonight!'

The somewhat cynical thought came to me that Vicky was destined to live out her father's fantasies. At the time this struck me as very ironic; and I thought to myself, with a certain grim satisfaction, 'at least that isn't going to happen to me'. How wrong I was, and how much greater was the irony that gripped me then.

Bruedelmann's master, who taught him the art of picture restoration in pre-war Vienna, and whom Bruedelmann believed to have been a subject in the research camp at Ludwigslust, had himself been trained by his uncle, a certain Monsieur Leon Braques, a Sephardic Jew and Kabbalist who could trace his descent back to fourteenth-century Valladolid; it was Leon Braques who had acquired Bartholomew's commissioned painting in the

1860s in Paris. But not all that man's fortunes were favourable; in the immediate aftermath of the Franco-Prussian War of 1870 — disastrous for the French nation — he had fallen foul of the authorities on a charge of selling the national heritage, in the form of original Watteau oil paintings, to the barbarous generals of the invading Prussian war machine. In order to prove his innocence of this charge Monsieur Braques submitted a plea of fraud, and set about forging a Watteau oil *from memory* while awaiting trial in his prison cell. So promising was his progress with this work, and so rich the potential in his story, that certain left-wing intellectuals took up his cause and encouraged him to publish in Charivari a satirical cartoon depicting the duping of a Prussian militarist wolf — resembling not a little a capitalist French war chief — by a clever French cockerel sporting the colours and insignia of the First International. However, the forces of anti-Semitism were so prevalent in Paris at the time that the ploy was turned upon its instigators, for it was argued by an influential clique that the French cockerel thus depicted was neither French, nor witty, nor brave, but being manifestly Semitic — it was, after all, supposed to represent Leon Braques — was merely squalid, self-seeking and pusil-lanimous. The scandal was such that Monsier Braques never came to trial; instead, he was given seven days to leave France in perpetuity and was permitted to carry with him into exile only as much of his property as he could fit into two horse-drawn wagons. The probable alternative, he was advised, was an indefinite sojourn on Devil's Island. The Lichterfelder Fête Galante, which I had first set eyes on in Bruedelmann's gallery in the Marais quarter in Paris, was believed to be the very painting which had brought about Braques's downfall. But as to its true provenance and status, I think even Bruedelmann himself remained unsure.

'May I ask you,' said Georges Bruedelmann, in a private room at his Hôtel Vienne, 'where in Berlin you are planning to go?'

'Uncle Tom's Cabin.' But I did not intend to go into detail. 'Tell me, Georges,' I asked him in turn, 'why do you think the Salamander came back to Europe?'

'He came because he remembered Bartholomew's Commission from the time when I showed it to him in Paris. And recently, in the United States, he saw something important, something very secret which reminded him of it. But he needed to negotiate free passage with the British and with their friends in Europe. There were two conditions, Mr Clare: he had to put up money for your work, as you know, and I believe that he was also required to identify somebody who works in British Intelligence and is thought to be a . . . how do you say?'

'A mole?'

'Quite so.'

'You know,' I said, confidingly, 'this is a time of great revelation for me.'

He replied, in a curiously prophetic manner, 'My dear sir, I can tell you with absolute certainty that you will have more revelations. Perhaps more and more . . . And in return, may I ask you please to be more generous in your dealings with myself? May I ask you please to let me know what you discover in Berlin? I am particularly interested in the project Disko 39. It was a psychological research project and it was carried out during the war. I am certain that my dear master was one of its victims. It is so very important to me to know about this.'

'Don't worry,' I said, 'I won't hold out on you.' I was instantly sorry, however, for I felt I had made a promise I might not be able to keep.

'Here is the Lichterfelder Fête Galante, and here are the documents you will need. You will have no difficulties at Charles de Gaulle, nor at Tegel. It is all as it should be. You are merely the carrier.'

'There's not a coffin in this painting, is there?' I shook the bulky rectangular parcel. 'Or a corpse full of dope?' In fact a worrying thought had occurred to me: if Bruedelmann wished to see the painting returned to its rightful owners why did he not perform that act himself?

'Why me?' I said. 'Why not return it yourself?'

'Don't you think,' he asked rhetorically, and savoured the enigma of which he delivered himself, 'that you are a more rightful representative than myself?'

'Representative of what?'

'Of Hugo Thayer, perhaps.'

'Eh?'

'It is because Hugo knows the rightful owner and used to teach English to him in Berlin that the Lichterfelder Watteau is to be returned.'

'Why now, all of a sudden?' I persisted. 'What's the hurry?'

'You must fly with the dragon,' he said cryptically.

'You mean Jackson?'

He said simply, 'You must learn to trust me, Mr Clare. There is no greed in my heart, no lust for power. I have faith, hope and charity.'

The taxi had arrived for me, but I was not quite ready yet to go.

'I remember you once told me the painting was yours,' I stubbornly remarked. 'And now you seem to be admitting that it is rightfully somebody else's.'

But Bruedelmann remained as cool, as imperturbably suave as ever.

'It is my property,' he said. 'I bought it in good faith in uncertain times, and it cost me very much to acquire it. Today I give it back to the family from which it was stolen by a monstrous and criminal government.'

As I was going out of the door Georges Bruedelmann thrust an envelope into my hand.

'What's this?' I was instantly suspicious.

'I have so much money,' he said. 'Please. It is for your expenses.'

In the taxi I inspected the contents of the envelope: it contained one thousand pounds in three different European currencies.

As I approached, airborne, the fortified zone and barrier which still, at that time, divided East from West Germany, I had a map of West Berlin upon my knees. I discovered that Lichterfelder Ring was situated in the southernmost part of the city just a hundred metres from the Berlin Wall. I stared at the patterns before my eyes: the pattern of fields and glinting waterways laid out for my inspection thousands of metres below; the criss-cross pattern of streets and transport lines that was West Berlin on my lap. I became aware of a curious sense of detachment; but of course, once I had landed, the map would take on an import, a directedness, an urgency of meaning which for the moment it did not possess. As long as I remained detached, uncommitted to any need to follow a certain direction, to find a way through and across terrain, the map on my knees and the patchwork layout of smooth shining fields below were free of the constraints of the cardinal points of the compass, and were somehow reversible, too, in space and time. It was only when I was in among the given things, orienting myself, desiring the attainment of my objectives, that maps and terrain would become enclosed arenas of hope and passion, of gratification and disgruntlement, of frustration and pain. I thought of Bartholomew's little Indian, who would have needed a map to find his way home; but of course, no map existed to lead him then. He would have been compelled, by his own choosing, to make his own; it was to be his life's work that would be mapped about him.

I had no sooner got off the plane than I found myself prey to a deep-seated and ominous feeling of tension. As I wandered in the well-lit tunnels of the Berlin underground system I had the clearest impression of myself as a detective . . .

Partly, of course, it was my mother on my mind. I felt guilty for the wrong I had done her; and I was experiencing the first glimmerings of insight into the form which that wrong had taken in all the

phenomena of my life. I became aware that I was a detective of sorts just
became a detective presupposes a crime; no wonder, then, that I was
fascinated at the time by maps and patterns, for I would need both maps
and patterns in order to make sense of my life, in order to revisit the
scenes of the crime.

In the bright, modern, yellow underground train a young German
woman sat opposite me. Her voice was husky but elegant, and her nose
was small. She had high, prominent cheek bones and thick, fluffy, curly
hair that was fair and short and trimmed at the back like an adolescent
boy's. Her eyes were full of wit and good humour, yet touched with
malice. She held in her gloved hand a blue woollen cord which was
attached to her small son, who was about five years old. 'Come over here,
my little man,' she said, and she pulled on the cord so that the boy was
jerked towards her. 'Come,' she said, and as she tugged again the child
swung round, and stamped his foot in play, and was hauled in like a
muscular fish. A woman friend, sitting with the mother, laughed coarsely.
Deftly the mother unbuttoned her small son's leather jacket and pulled it
half-way down his back. Now he was trapped and he started to wriggle;
but it was evident he loved this game they played together. The cord ran
between his two mittens, joining the one to the other; but it had slipped
from around the top of his back and was now entangled round his waist.
Quickly she wound in the slack. The cord that dangled from his wrist
went snaking up inside his sleeve; he watched it gleefully. Now she took
the slack and placed it about his neck so that the cord ran all the way
from his left wrist, up his left arm, across the back of his shoulders and
down the right arm to the right wrist. 'OK,' she said, 'OK,' and she
pretended to release him. He stared at her and his face was joyous and
cunning. He stamped his feet and made to whirl about. He gave a sheer
burst of childlike laughter. He knew she had cheated him. Even now she
had hold of the cord and jerked him back, like a dog on a lead. Her coarse
friend laughed loudly. Now, as though he were a flattened pillow, she
roughly plumped him up at the shoulders. 'Now my little man, now.'
Then she held him, fully hers, with his head between her open palms.
'Does it itch up there?' she asked, and with her strong fingers she tugged
at the thick woollen hat on his head. 'Hum,' he said, as if to say, 'I
wouldn't tell *you*!' She pulled him in then, fiercely, and kissed him full on
the lips so that his little boy's nostrils were squashed up against her own
foxy nose. Then she pushed him away and they laughed for joy, each
looking directly into the other's eyes.

Watching them helplessly, entranced by the ironies in which they bathed by choice, I found myself thinking of Bartholomew de Gaillac, and of John Pike, and of all the spies I had read of or imagined. Spies, like actors, themselves life's consummate players and often its tragic victims, contrived to play with the facts of their lives, but in deadly earnest: the former deliberately, intending to dupe, manipulate and deceive; the latter in order to teach and delight, in the high play of art. Spies must be actors, and actors must be spies . . . but if Bruedelmann was right to say that *the falsities by which we live, and on which we ground our experience, are fated to be reversed and inverted in the events of our days* . . . then actors would find in the phenomena of their lives resonant echoes both farcical and tragic; and spies, most schooled in deceit and monstrously duplicitous, might live, perversely and unbeknownst to themselves, demonic-saintly lives.

I watched them at play, and my heart seemed to ache in my chest. She played at having complete control over her son, and he consented to it, gleefully; but what would it amount to in years to come? What was its future form? I wondered. Perhaps it was a pattern in their lives, one which they would experience again and again, through all the range of emotions. I wanted to sketch it out on a scrap of my notebook, the dynamic of their relationship, and pass it to them even then: 'Here,' I would say, 'this is the map of it, this is the terrain; the rest is all emotion still to come.'

Lothar Reh, the rightful owner of the Lichterfelder Fête Galante, was a student of Hugo Thayer when Hugo and Harriet were in Berlin. He is a man of less than average height, grey-haired and about seventy years of age. He is mild in manner, gentle and courteous, and touched with melancholy. I had the distinct impression that he had put on a suit specifically for the occasion of my visit. He led me into the living room and introduced me, with soft, quiet, almost womanish gestures, to his Prussian wife. She at once departed to fetch us a bottle of wine.

'I am a friend of Hugo Thayer,' I had told him on the telephone. 'May I drop in?' And now I placed the thickly wrapped painting on the sofa and said, squarely, 'Hugo wanted me to return this to you. It's a painting.'

'Painting? What painting can this be? Hugo has no painting of mine.' He was taken aback, and not a little concerned.

'Perhaps it's best,' I said, taking up the package, 'if I just unwrap it.'

As I removed Bruedelmann's expert packing I could feel Lothar Reh's anxiety mounting. His wife came back with a bottle of wine and he muttered to her in consternation. They were afraid I was a confidence trickster who had come to sell them something.

'There!' I steadied the unwrapped canvas on the buoyant cushions in their well-cleaned dark grey covers.

'My God!' he said in German, turning to his wife. 'It's not possible! Clara, this is Grandpa's Watteau!' He plucked up the painting and almost hugged it. 'My God,' he said, 'where did you find such a thing?' I started to say something but it was apparent that he wasn't listening. 'I never knew my grandfather,' he said, 'but my dear father told me all about him. He was a famous military man, you know. He was one of the generals in the Franco-Prussian War. This was his favourite painting. But tell me please, where did you get it from?'

'It was acquired,' I said, choosing my words with great care, 'by an Austrian gentleman who now lives in France and insists on remaining anonymous. He acquired the painting in 1947 from a former official of the Nazi Party, who was responsible for cataloguing works of art which came into the possession of the Party . . .'

'Those gangsters! They stole it from us!' His head had come up and his face showed a spirited, pale anger. 'The damned Third Reich! It's true, they stole it from us! From my family! And they took my father and my mother, and my sister, and everything we possessed. I was in a concentration camp for the last year of the war. My mother, dear mother, God rest her, was a Jew.'

'I'm afraid I must tell you,' I said . . . and then stopped, horrified at myself.

He said in faltering tones, 'You want to tell me that it is a forgery? But I know it already. We have always known it . . . but it doesn't stop love.'

'Are you absolutely sure it's a forgery?' I asked.

He said, with great excitement, 'But it was painted here! Yes, in this very house!'

'This very house?'

'Yes, here in this house, in Lichterfelde. The painter . . . oh but I can't remember . . .'

'Leon Braques?'

'Braques, yes! Leon Braques was a friend of the family. He stayed here for a whole summer, in 1867, I think. *He* painted it. From start to finish.'

'Did you tell Hugo that?' I inquired.

'No,' he said, with a puzzled look on his face. 'No. But once I described the painting to him. In great detail, in fact. It was part of our English lesson you see. He asked me to describe the colours, the forms, and the psychological effects of my favourite painting.'

'Ah,' I said. 'He must have recognized it from your description.'

'Do you think so? Otherwise, how would he know . . .? Unless . . . well, you know Hugo Thayer is a very unusual man. He has the gift.' He looked at me inquiringly.

'I'm sorry,' I said. 'I'm not with you. What gift did you mean?'

'The Lichterfelder Shining,' he replied. Then a shadow crossed his face, and his voice lost its conviction. 'But I don't understand,' he muttered, 'how did Hugo get to see it?'

'Oh it's nothing,' I said, with slight impatience. 'I assure you. Hugo just happened to meet the man who acquired it from the official. I think he must have persuaded the man to let you have it back.'

'It used to hang on the wall half-way up the stairs. As a boy I must have looked at it a thousand times.'

'You said something about the "shining"?'

'Yes, yes. Here in Lichterfelde there is a tradition of second sight. People have had visions. Ever since this part of the city became inhabited. Hugo had them too. He used to tell me his dreams. Did you know, he lived just a few houses along the road?'

'What sort of visions?'

'He saw things from the war, and even earlier. He used to hear things and see things that were not there any longer. You know, it was strange, he came here to talk English with me but *he saw into my life.*'

'Do you mean he's *psychic?*'

'Hugo is psychic, yes. When he made an example, to illustrate a point of grammar or a new word, he always used an example *from my own life.* At first I didn't notice it, but after a time it . . . it hit me. I asked him about it. It was perfectly innocent, I am sure. *He did not even know that he was doing it.* Yes, I am sure he had the shining. You know it is quite famous around here. Lichterfelde . . . that's what it means, you see.'

'Fields of light,' I said, as in a dream.

'That's it,' he said. 'The fields of light.' Then he added, with a slightly crazy smile. 'And don't forget that we are living on the Ring.'

'The Lichterfelder Ring?'

'Yes. You know that Hugo lived in this same street? He was at number 39.'

He saw me to the door.

'Please tell Hugo,' he said, 'that he has brought great joy to us. You see, Grandpa's Watteau is the only thing in the entire world that is left to me of those days when our family was together. And my memory is so bad now. You see, they were all killed. The Party took everything.'

'I promise I'll tell him.'

I shook his hand and he gave me a small, embarrassed hug.

'Hugo has made an old man very happy. He will understand, I know it. I love this painting for the same reason that my father and my grandfather loved it. We love it for what it means to us. What is real, what is false, who can say? But love must be. It is what makes a life worth living.'

On my way to the bus stop I walked into Lilienthal Park, which Hugo Thayer had written of in his diary. It is pleasingly landscaped with small hills, and contains two stretches of water; there is an ugly, rectangular ornamental pond densely populated with oversize gold fish, and a quiet, more natural lake surrounded by gloomy beech and willow trees. A tarmac cycle-way winds through the landscape and is lined with small, fragrant pines.

In the Subject's Documentary Hugo tells how he and Harriet came into Lilienthal Park during the last night of their stay in Berlin and threw two of his shoes into the lake. One was a heavy brogue, the other a black saloon shoe. He seemed to set great store by the act, and I now pondered what deeper significance it might have had for him. I looked carefully all round the edge of the lake. There were twigs, and submerged branches, and a sodden pot pourri of leaves, but no brogues, and no saloon shoes. Strictly speaking, it was an act of vandalism they had committed, although I did not doubt that leather shoes would soon disintegrate, or at least supply nourishment to underwater creatures. I pictured cheerful tadpoles in his brogue.

I got up aimlessly and wandered along the tarmac cycle-way and on to the grass. As I walked, a bicycle came into view; it was ridden by a large, energetic fat woman puffing and blowing her cheeks. And in the basket attached to the handlebars before her, in a state of wide-eyed enchantment, there sat an infant boy. To this day I am convinced that I heard that child say 'das Leben, das Leben!' with a note of ecstasy, as they passed. Life, oh life! Again I felt a now familiar hollowness shudder within me. Omschka had given me some photographs of Eva, my mother, but I had tucked them away in my wallet and I knew I would not look at them properly until I felt the time was appropriate. The tension within me mounted, and I recalled the proximity of the Berlin Wall. Like a sleepwalker I went towards it. As I emerged from the park at the corner of Schuette-Lanz and Lichterfelder Ring I met another mother with her child. The child was screaming so furiously that it could barely walk straight, and all the while the mother guided the raging infant with calm, long fingers. As they went along she was saying to him sweetly, 'Toll! Ja toll!' Lovely, great, fantastic!

I walked down a quiet, leafy street that was lined on both sides with graceful silver birches, and came to a metal sign. It informed me with all but apocalyptic solemnity that I was leaving the American Sector *now*. Several feet beyond the sign and barely visible through a tangle of gnarled and spindly trees was the wall: a monstrous, sepulchral grey edifice with a drum-like, concrete crest. I listened hard; on the other side of the thing was a barking of dogs. Nothing else. Suddenly I remembered the dream I had had that day in spring when they had delivered the word processing facility. I had dreamed that I had awoken to find myself dead behind a wall. Had it been a premonition? How could I have awoken; how could I have been dead behind that wall? I walked back up the road and felt a chill creep over my body despite the balmy weather of that summer afternoon. *We had to cut everything in half when the Salamander came*, Omschka had said to me. Where was he now? I wondered; Dennis Jackson — fire-being, war-god, father of mine that was not my own.

As I walked into Steglitz library, I saw, in the main hallway, a poster that shook me to the core. It was A1 size, a muted yellow in colour, and it depicted in black and white snapshot portraits a score of men and women, their faces all arranged in orderly rows. Under each face there was a sad little text describing where the person had been found, and how old they were thought to be, and in some cases there was even some indication of possible family. Their common fate was that they had all been separated from parents and loved ones during the last great European war, and had been found as little children wandering among the ruins of houses, or lurking shocked in bomb craters amidst the rubble.

WER BIN ICH? asked the poster in shrieking capitals. WHO AM I? And the twenty or so faces stared out at me, and beside each one of them, in a small insert set against their adult faces, was a war child; ragged of dress, a staring face, a makeshift little person.

I had never before seen one of these posters, nor had I even heard of their existence; no wonder then that for a moment I felt as if I were in a magical city full of long-forgotten echoes, where I was forcibly confronted with all that lay deepest in my being. I must have stood there for quite some time, staring at the poster. Perhaps I was reminded, too, of Hugo Thayer's poster in the bookshop window; or of his performance on the video, where he had talked about his interest in the war; or of his diary writings, in which he persistently questioned himself . . . *who am I, what am I doing?* And I thought, too, about the abstract faces I had seen in Bartholomew's Commission. Posters and faces: they seemed to plague me now. I began to murmur to myself the names displayed on the poster, the pitifully concise descriptions of where the children had been found; and I thought, too, of Bartholomew's little Indian, from whom everything but life had been taken away. I gawped; and jostling me a burly drunk shuffled past, muttering, 'The music . . . it would not stop. We could not stop the music. Like a dance in hell it was.'

In the twenty-minute taxi ride to Ernst Schwrirrer's house in Dahlem/ Zehlendorf I was preoccupied with the idea that the abstract faces I had seen in Bartholomew's Commission might constitute a deliberate part of his code. In his induction interview he had declared that he could encode information in a flower – had he been speaking not literally but meta-phorically? It struck me that each such face might represent a thinker, either of Bartholomew's own time or from antiquity, and might refer to that thinker's beliefs. Perhaps, then, the spatial arrangement of the faces about the plane of the canvas might reflect a similar arrangement of petals in a flower-head, or perhaps, more probably, the arrangement of flowers in a vase – suggesting a discourse, a sort of synthesis of the sets of ideas which the faces respectively represented. In which case, to cite but one possible example, two faces directly opposing each other might be thought of as the two sets of ideas being placed in contradiction. Alternatively, there might be a proper sequence to be followed, ir-respective of position on the canvas; and if this were so, well, there it was again . . . a map would be the key to the encoded information; or perhaps, as Bartholomew had himself proposed, it might be conveyed by a set of steps, a dance in short . . . Of course it was a fantastical conception, and I did not seriously entertain it. Nonetheless it had the merit of establishing a link between the possible true mystery of the painting on the one hand, and Bruedelmann's work with faces on the other.

It was a ground-floor flat in a huge house set in the grounds of a walled garden among towering Wellingtonia trees. Professor Schwirrer's house-keeper let me in. She spoke German with an American accent but she insisted, with a curious coyness, that she was German by blood. It was clear that their relationship was a long-term matter of the heart. He looked at her as he talked, and he had the manner of a husband who shares his confidences out of long habit. For her part she had an easy way with him that was nonetheless tender. Professor Schwirrer was very forthcoming; and when I ventured to ask him if I might tape the interview he expressed his unreserved approval. Most of life's misunderstandings, he told me, are caused by a failure to keep proper records.

'It was one of Himmler's initiatives, you see,' said my host, who was an old man in his eighties with a cracked and faded voice. His mind however was clear, and his speech was lucid. His face was very lined and his hands, which he occasionally moved a little in the air in front of him as he talked, were big and bleached almost white. His appearance had astonished me; he wore a wig that was itself a study in dishevelment, and reminded me of nothing so much as the chevelure of a seventies rock star. I understood that he was actually bald and wore this improbable hair-piece because it was both airy and warm. Compounding the effect of his unexpectedly zany appearance were the dark glasses he wore despite the mildness of the evening light; and yet, for all that, every light bulb in the spacious study-cum-bedroom where we sat was burning brightly as though it were night. He had his chair by the open French window, where it was rather cool, and yet he wore a thick pullover, a woollen scarf, and a pair of moon-boots. His housekeeper had forewarned me of his eccentric appearance and had explained that Professor Schwirrer felt the cold terribly, particularly in his feet, and his eyes could not tolerate light; yet he craved fresh air, and he needed a lot of light about him for it kept his spirits up. While we were talking he frequently fiddled about with the controls of a hearing aid, which he had placed on his lap. It looked just like a Walkman.

'But he cooked it up with Goebbels. They wanted a special way to show the Fuehrer that he was right about the Jews. They thought it could be an important instrument of propaganda. In the Russian campaign the Fuehrer saw that he could not win the war against the Slavs. He dreamed of an alliance with the British and the Americans. Hitler, you see, believed in the Protocols of Zion. He thought the Bolshevist Jewry wanted to achieve world domination. The team at Ludwigslust was very good, but it failed to produce a result for his birthday in 1940. Nevertheless, the chief scientist of the project was presented to the Fuehrer and he received considerable encouragement. I was a mathematical psychologist when I was instructed to work on this project. Of course I have forgotten the real name. But you see, after we saw its power we called it Disko Neun und Dreissig.'

Disko 39.

'What happened to the research station when the war ended?'

'Well, you know, the original location of the camp is now in the People's Republic. I suppose it is a building used for science researches.'

'Do you have any photographs?'

'It was forbidden to possess photographs, even after we were liberated. The Americans took everything away for examination. What is it you want to see?'

'Well . . . anything that will help me understand what it was you were doing there.'

'When you young people go to your discos, I have seen them myself, the beautiful young children dancing under the changing lights . . . I think always of the Disko 39. We showed the way. In the experimental chambers at Ludwigslust we created it!'

'What did you do to the subjects in the experiments?'

'It is difficult to remember details. Over forty years ago it all happened. I have lived a new life since then. I have studied and made researches in many other areas of my discipline. But I remember the results very well.'

'Could you perhaps give me an idea of what was in the experimental chambers?'

'We wished to create in experimentally controlled conditions the logical form of the average phenomenology.'

'I'm sorry?'

'That is to say, we wished to replicate the contemporary human phenomenology in its historical matrix. The attributes of the experimentally-induced mentality should reproduce in their logical form the prevailing historical forces. That is to say, in the somatic, the societal and the egoic domain.'

'I don't understand, Herr Schwirrer.'

'I am Professor Schwirrer. I held two professorships.'

'Excuse me, Professor.'

'You see, it is not easy to talk about these things. You must imagine the typical consciousness of an average person in the context of twentieth-century Germany. That consciousness will be a matrix of forces with some inertia in the system. It will derive from the historical and social forces operating upon the individual and in addition from the inner psychic promptings. There will be a continuing process of adjustment in pursuit of a psychic equilibrium. The consciousness of the individual will be a product of the drives from within, which are outward in direction, and the drives from outside which press inward upon the individual, consequently inducing changes in his beliefs and in his hopes and desires. We wished to study this process experimentally. In order to do so it was necessary to create an operational environment.'

'Operational, Professor?'

'We mean an environment which is exactly specifiable in all its aspects and exactly reproducible. A scientific experimental field. Do you understand me?'

'Yes, I see. Thank you.'

'We wanted to know how the experimental subject would respond to different types of environmental stimulation. So we needed first of all a measure of his basic psychological type. When we placed him in the experimental chamber we could read the electrical signals coming from the organism and we could also measure changes as he encountered new aspects of his environment. We discovered that where an aspect of the environment is ambiguous or unknown, the organism makes an intense effort to make it known, to give it meaning, ja, and this process is recognizable on the scan as a peak of electrical energy. Also we discovered that when subjects made choices of any kind . . .'

'Choices?'

'When they chose one form of activity in preference to another. They *chose.*'

'Right.'

'When they made choices we saw the same electrical effects on the scan.'

'Choosing and making sense of the environment showed as the same thing on the scan?'

'Ja. They were operationally identical. The experimental chambers contained stimuli which ranged from the known to the unfamiliar, including such things as, for example, yes, taps with or without water, water that was hot or cold, some heating and cooling elements which were adjustable by the subject, and some food mediators, sometimes simple, sometimes complex in form . . .'

'Food mediators?'

'Food dispensers.'

'Ah.'

'The foods contained in these devices were also subject to the same experimental variation. Sometimes it looked good to eat but it gave you a shock, or made you sick. Do you understand?'

'Yes. I understand, Professor.'

'We also exposed the subject to phenomena and artefacts which were unknown to him. Some of these artefacts were designed to show encouraging and rewarding characteristics once the subject had learned to master them. And some of them had the opposite effect.'

'What do you mean "rewarding"? And what would be the opposite effect?'

'For example, an object might prove to be a small radio transmitter capable of playing music quietly to the subject, or it might emit a sudden intense electric shock.'

'I see . . . What did you hope to discover?'

'At first, as I told you, we wished to establish a fundamental behavioural difference between the Semitic and the non-Semitic racial type. We looked for a difference at the level of gross behaviour. We wanted to give people a means to identify the Semitic racial type. We later hoped to identify the physiological aetiology.'

'By doing autopsies.'

'Autopsies? Yes, but not always when the subjects were dead.'

'Don't tell him any more Ernst,' the woman shouted suddenly. 'He doesn't respect you!'

He ignored her and continued, his pale, shadowy monologue.

'We hoped also that the difference or differences would be manifest at some level of higher psychic functioning. I mean art, or in the religious orientation.'

'And what did you discover?'

'We found that there was nothing to differentiate the phenotypes.'

'Phenotypes?'

'The people in our different experimental groups.'

'You mean the subjects?'

'Yes, yes. I mean the subjects.'

Abruptly he stopped speaking. I actually prayed then that they would not throw me out. I held my breath and waited.

'You see, it was very disappointing for us. There was really no difference whatsoever between Jews and the others. It seemed as if all men were the same in the sight of God. We became very anxious about it. Then we decided to concentrate on the data, that is to say, the electrical recordings, mainly. We applied many different tools of analysis. Eventually we interpreted the signals in terms of musical frequencies. That was my own idea. I said we should order the electrical signals as musical entities. We modelled the data on musical keys and time signatures. We found that individual subjects had generated the most remarkable musical compositions. This we called the Eigenmusikswesen.'

'How would you translate that, Professor?'

'Oh, it is not difficult. Something like own-music-being. Something like that.'

'Did you get a music off every subject?'

'No, we didn't. And the effect was not always so striking. Some people had little passages of the Musikswesen, and some people had only fragments, or just a basic phrase which was always repeated. Some people produced only noise. Their phenomenology was a frightful chaos. They had a sort of hell in the head.'

'Was there any broad difference in this respect between the Semitic and the non-Semitic types?'

'Well, you know, there was a slight tendency for the Semitic phenotype to show less variation in the intensity of the effect. That is to say, the

Jewish subjects were more likely to get a good experimental result. But in general this tendency was not significant in statistical terms. We thought it was probably an experimental artefact. It was negligible, you understand. It was associated, I think, only with a sub-set of the experimental population.'

'You did not draw attention to it?'

'It would have destroyed our careers.'

'But if you could have shown that the quality of the Eigenmusikswesen was a proof of the inferiority of the phenotype . . .'

'Exactly. We would have published it. In the Reich, you see, we were all like rats in a maze.'

'Was there any particular type of subject who predictably generated a good Eigenmusikswesen?'

'There were few psychological tests available at the time. So we created our own. We discovered that there were at least three different factors in our tests that helped us to predict a good result.'

'What were they?'

'Well you know, it depends how you interpret these factors. At the time we called them by different names. They were different concepts then. But I know now what they were in fact.'

'Could you please tell me, Professor Schwirrer.'

'People who had high positive affectivity. People who were able to suspend disbelief. People who were able to forgive. A person who showed evidence of all three of these qualities invariably produced a clear experimental effect.'

'Faith, hope and charity?'

'Ja, ja. Something like that. I too have had this thought.'

'And these people invariably produced a beautiful Eigenmusikswesen?'

'Not always, but generally, yes. A beautiful effect. I remember there was a time when we particularly processed subjects of mystical orientation. I mean, for example, they called themselves Kabbalists in the case of the Jewish subjects. We sent out a special priority requisition order. They came to us in very large numbers, from all the new German territories. Yes, I remember we had a rich sample. We had one or two particularly good subjects from Vienna, and from Prague. They produced some very good results. But you know, there was one man in particular who was not a mystic in any sense as I remember it. We called him the Original Dancer. He produced a very striking result because he endured. Yes, he endured. He was a Jew, from America I think. But I cannot remember his name. And this is a pity. I suppose, now, he must be dead.'

'How did you think this might be of value to the Fuehrer?'

'We were told by the authorities that such a finding would have important implications in the thousand-year Reich. They had their own scientific advisers, you see. There was a think-tank. They were very interested in our findings. We were permitted to continue with our research right up to the last days of the war. Schaffer had some very influential contacts, I remember.'

'Schaffer?'

'Schaffer was one of the leaders of our team of scientists. A very important man.'

'Ah. Yes? . . . You were going to say . . .?'

'That's right, I must tell you that we had a problem. It was a very big problem for all of us.'

'Yes?'

'We discovered firstly, if you played the Eigenmusik to the subject he would dance. Ja, he danced. I tell you, that was a strange and moving thing. Even in the case of the Semitic phenotype! We put a number of the subjects together in one communal chamber and each had his music played to him exclusively, by means of headphones. Then they all began to dance in the experimental chamber. We had the impression that they generated a sort of field.'

'A field?'

'Yes, it was an energy field. We began to investigate it at the end of the war.'

'What sort of field?'

'We didn't finish our investigations. We were liberated.'

'I would very much like to know more about this field, Professor.'

'It was an electromagnetic effect.'

'Like a . . . a sort of light?'

'Yes, you could say that, I think.'

'It was a sort of field of light?'

'Yes. A field of light. It was uncanny. I remember there was a destabilization effect.'

'Destabilization?'

'Of structures. Things appeared to lose their solidity. The dancers seemed able to change things around them.'

'In what way, Professor?'

'Well, you know it was not just people dancing. We had the feeling that they had generated a certain power amongst themselves. A power to change the nature of the phenomena around them.'

'Was it *physical*?'

'They had a power to alter reality. But I prefer not to make this distinction between the physical and the non-physical. I say it was a field of electromagnetic forces. Also, it was beautiful to look at. We had to put them in a chamber that was lined with lead. At first we thought it was an artefact of the experimental psychosis.'

'Psychosis? You mean they were mad?'

'Perhaps not really mad, you know. But our experiments, you see, had intensified their choosing behaviour. They were very highly aroused when they chose things.'

'I don't quite understand. Why were they aroused, Professor?'

'You see, we had energized the subjects. They had food and water only when they were in the experimental chamber. They were filled with energy because their choices really mattered.'

'You said there was a problem.'

'Yes, it was a big problem. You see, we had to play the music to the dancers in order to study the effect. But we discovered that after five or six hearings of the Eigenmusikswesen the experimental subject became completely useless to us.'

'Useless in what sense?'

'After five or six hearings of his Eigenmusikswesen the effect was extinguished in the subject. The subject entered into a cataleptic condition. The subject was awake. Sometimes the subject was alert. But he was out of reach of our manipulations and we were unable to bring him back. He had no more desires, no more beliefs. You see, he was *useless.* The person had completely disappeared and we were left with a purely physical resource. We applied all available technologies to this problem. In the last four months of the war we processed 800 dancers. Yes, we called them dancers. In April, 1945 we were liberated.'

'You were liberated by the American army?'

'No, no. In fact they were English soldiers, I remember. They wore the uniforms of the Waffen-SS. And Jackson was their leader. We went across the Elbe and then the Americans collected us. It was very strange to go from Ludwigslust to Dallas.'

The interview, seemingly, had ended. As I got up to leave, one of the books on his bookshelf caught my eye. It was an old hardback study of English phrasal verbs.

'Are you interested in phrasal verbs, Professor?'

'Once I made a study of them,' he replied. 'We made some use of them,' he added, 'in our research.'

'At Ludwigslust?'

'Before we discovered the Eigenmusikswesen we recorded the behaviours of the subjects by means of phrasal verbs.'

'But, but don't you have phrasal verbs in German?'

'The English phrasal verbs were found to be more flexible.' He was obviously very tired now, and his voice was faint. 'And also the layers of meaning . . .'

'Yes?'

'In English it is easier to distinguish and categorize the semantic structures. The different layers of meaning are more perspicuously manageable and consistent.'

Professor Schwirrer had fallen asleep.

19

... what meaning would our whole being possess if it were not this,
that in us the will to truth becomes conscious of itself as a *problem?*

Nietzsche, *On the Genealogy of Morals*

Professor Schwirrer had said of the subjects in the experimental chamber
at Ludwigslust that choosing and making sense of the environment were
operationally identical phenomena. That is to say that the chosen methods
of measurement, namely skin conductance of electrical charge and electrical
patterns of brain activity, showed the selfsame recorded pattern whether the
subject was actually making a choice, or simply determining for himself the
nature and meaning of elements of his environment. Anything we think or do,
provided we feel either that it is deliberately thought or done, or that it serves
our purposes and does not manifestly get us into trouble, we tend to say we
have chosen to think or do. Most of the behaviour of any human being falls
under this description; *making sense of the environment*, however, is closely
related to the search for meaning in one's life, may even be the meaning of life
itself. As I travelled back to Paris it seemed to me that the dancers at
Ludwigslust had physically encoded the very meaning of life ... and if
Jackson had seen 'the Disko' in Bartholomew's Commission, whatever he
meant by it, who was to say but that the painting itself might hold a similar
secret? I tried it, experimentally, as a possible proposition; I said to myself as
the plane flew over France:

Bartholomew's Commission encodes the meaning of life.

If I may be permitted the understatement, this would explain the
interest shown in Bartholomew's Commission by the Interested Parties,
and by whatever intelligence organism Burt Munker represented; after all,
any state or big business corporation which possessed that secret would
be enormously empowered by it. For wouldn't we all become as browsing
cattle, milked of recalcitrant energies? It was an apocalyptic vision, and I
could not bear to entertain it. It cannot be, I told myself, for it would be
the ultimate form of ideology. And I convinced myself that I was making
a fundamental error of interpretation; or it was a trick of science. I
reminded myself that the experimental chamber at Ludwigslust was
hardly the world.

But Hugo Thayer's gnosis came to haunt me. Hadn't he danced on the videotape? Hadn't he proposed that I should write a novel about him after he had been exposed to Bartholomew's Commission? Hadn't Nolton talked about 'novel' methods of investigation and experiment? What was a novel, after all, but a study in the meaning of life? And hadn't Bartholomew suggested, in his induction interview, that an entire painting, a densely informative image, could be encoded in a dance? It was unnerving, to say the least; and of course, I was overtired.

However, there was one aspect of the idea which pleased me very much: only in the case of those experimental subjects who had faith, hope and charity was there generated a music, and hence a dance, of great beauty and power. It seemed to me a confirmation of what I have always hoped and believed: that only by virtue of the habits of moral intelligence could the meaning of life be physically conjured before our eyes; for only the best of men and women could encode life's meaning in a dance.

At the Hôtel Vienne, where I had arranged to meet Georges Bruedelmann, the young man with the air-ace moustaches handed me a letter:

Dear Mr Clare,
You must come at once to Normandy. Something of great importance to you personally has occurred. It is essential that you should come to Normandy. I await your earliest arrival.

Georges Bruedelmann himself opened the great front door of the château. He looked at me very gravely. This ill-concorded with his appearance, however, for he wore a cheerful little beret and a dark blue smock that was flecked with grey, red, green and yellow paint stains. He led me directly to his study.

'Doing a spot of decorating?' I said as I strolled along beside him.

'You shall see,' he replied.

'D'you think I could have a cup of tea?'

'My assistants,' he said solemnly, 'are at present with the local police. I'm afraid you must make it for yourself.'

'Has someone committed a crime?' I asked.

'Most certainly,' came the sobering reply.

In his study he unlocked a cupboard and fiddled about at the controls of some sort of console.

'Please,' said Bruedelmann, motioning to a television screen which I had never noticed before. 'Let us watch a little film together.'

*

Black and white images appeared on the screen; a costumed figure was groping its way to a door in a darkened room. In the corridor, which was also dark, the figure fumbled along, knocking askew the pictures on the wall. A male voice was muttering. Then the lights came on and I saw what I had already divined: it was me.

'What's going on?'

'But surely you remember,' said Bruedelmann, smoothly. 'After our dinner party the lights failed. But François was able to restore them.'

It was indeed true; the lights had failed just as I had started to undress in my room.

'But . . .'

'Please,' said Bruedelmann . . .

Prowling along a corridor was Dennis Jackson. It was night. The cameras followed him to the top of the winding staircase, and then another sighted him, creeping down the narrow spiral stairway to the chamber where Bartholomew's Commission hung. He went to the painting and carefully examined the wall and plaster around it. He cautiously lifted the frame and shone a pencil beam of light underneath it. With his spare hand he reached in through the narrow gap and fiddled about for a moment. With a grunt of satisfaction he lifted the painting off the wall.

I stole a look at Bruedelmann. I had never seen him look so serious.

'Is he . . .?'

Bruedelmann nodded with unquestionable conviction. It was so typical, so characteristic of Dennis Jackson, the man who had sold all those people at the end of the war. It was perfectly self-evident that Jackson was stealing Bartholomew's Commission.

Horrified by what I had seen, and needing to break the silence, I asked when it had happened.

'Last night,' said Bruedelmann. He was impassive, but I could sense that he was devastated.

'It *was* Bartholomew's painting, I suppose . . .'

'Yes.'

'I'm really very sorry, Georges. The man's a lunatic.'

Bruedelmann exhaled heavily.

'It was to be expected,' he said. 'But, you know, I was so sure that he had changed.'

I sat and looked at my thumbs. In a curious way I felt guilty; but I was also repelled by the revelation that Bruedelmann recorded on film all happenings, night and day, in probably every room in his house.

'Do not blame yourself,' said Bruedelmann. 'It was the Disko that brought him back.'

305

In the underground chamber, which was now the scene of Jackson's recent crime, there was a smell of beeswax in the air. An easel had been set up at one end of the chamber and at the opposite end stood a tall, adjustable stool with long steel legs. There was a canvas on the easel, with a cloth draped over it. Where Bartholomew's Commission had hung there was now a blank space, paler and cleaner than the surrounding plaster. A few wires stuck out of the wall.

'Please,' said Bruedelmann, directing me to sit on the adjustable stool. 'I have been working on a painting.' He went to the easel and pushed the drape aside, revealing several pieces of tape on the back of the canvas. From where I sat they looked like sticking plasters. 'Would you please sit for me a while?'

'Are you doing a portrait of me?' I asked.

'In fact,' he said, taking up a brush, 'it is necessary only to add a few finishing touches.'

I looked around the room. Next to the easel stood a work-bench, littered with tubes of paint and small jars of chemicals. A palette showed evidence of work in progress. The mounds of paint were like a fragmentary landscape in many colours. On the other side of Bruedelmann stood a decorator's table, and laid out upon it were a chip-fryer, a few pots of large crystals, and an iron. As he painted he talked, and his voice had a dreamlike softness so that I grew calm and meditative under its influence.

'When Dennis Jackson first came to see me I taped our conversation. And I asked him to tell me more about the phenomenon which he had seen. If it was true that he had recently seen something which he had only seen once before, in Bartholomew's Commission in fact, then I thought I had a right to know more about the phenomenon in question. But you know, in the beginning he was not amenable. Jackson is a man who tries to get more than he pays for. I told him that I had nothing to say to him, either about the painting or about my own researches if he could not prove to me his bona fides. Eventually he talked about the camp at Ludwigslust and described his role in its liberation. Then we bargained. You see I wanted to know more about the project Disko 39; I had good reasons of my own. He made a promise to bring me more information, and he kept his word. The Americans are continuing to research the Eigenmusikswesen and have taken it far beyond the stage that was reached at Ludwigslust. But they are very jealous of their secrets. Do you know any of their secrets, Mr Clare?'

'I'll tell you what Schwirrer told me. But that's all I know.'

But it was clear to me after a minute or two that Bruedelmann knew just as much as I did, if not more.

'Please don't move,' he said.

'How long will this take, Georges?' I was querulous. 'I'm very tired now, you know.'

'Only a few more minutes, or so. Please be patient.'

'Do you think, Mr Clare, that Jackson has stolen the painting on behalf of the Americans?'

'It's possible, I suppose, yes. But he sent me a letter a couple of weeks ago, through ... a mutual friend. And the letter suggests that he's freelance at the moment.'

'He is, I think you say ... a wild card,' said Bruedelmann. 'But who can say who else is in the pack?'

I nodded, and said, as an afterthought, 'In his letter he gave the impression that there are people after him. Probably the British.'

'And now we may include the French police,' said Bruedelmann.

'Georges,' I said, winsomely, 'what did Jackson tell you about the American developments?'

'He said he had seen them dancing.'

'Who?'

'Some new experimental subjects. They were students, and they were paid to take part in the experiment.'

'That's one better than the Germans,' I said.

'And that is what brought him to Normandy. Forty years ago he saw the dancing in Bartholomew's Commission. And last year, in Texas, he saw it again.'

'Strange, isn't it ... I mean, what do *you* make of it?'

'I understand,' he said, 'that people who experience this dancing see visions. They report that their minds are subject to a wonderful change. They say their perceptions are altered. That material things merge and dissolve.'

'The fields of light,' I said. 'Schwirrer talked about it. And did you know about the Lichterfelder Shining? Hugo Thayer is psychic.'

'The Lichterfelder Shining? Please tell me more, Mr Clare.'

I told him then about my meeting with Lothar Reh; I told him that according to Herr Reh, Leon Braques had painted the Lichterfelder Watteau in Reh's own family home, shortly before the outbreak of the Franco-Prussian War. I told him too about the Lichterfelder Shining, and as I was doing so, it struck me that if Hugo Thayer had the shining then perhaps Leon Braques had had it too. A great change came over Georges Bruedelmann. He laid down his palette and his brushes, closed his eyes and seemed to go into a trance. His voice came to me, deep and still, 'You must tell me more, sir.'

He was very compelling, and I searched my mind for every last detail of my talk with Lothar Reh. When I had finished I waited, in complete silence, for Bruedelmann to pass comment.

'That is most extraordinary,' he said. 'I must visit Herr Reh. I am very grateful to you, Mr Clare. This information is precious to me.'

'Do you believe,' I asked him, now that he was painting again and time was heavy on my hands, 'that your master's uncle sold the "Watteau" to Reh's grandfather?'

He stepped back a pace and squinnied at the painting. 'I think it is unlikely, Mr Clare.' He took up a fresh brush and mixed some paint on the palette. 'It was a gift; a gift of prophecy, I think.'

'Well it's a hell of a coincidence,' I rejoined, 'that Hugo Thayer taught English to Lothar Reh, and all the rest of it . . .'

'Voila! Now it is finished,' said Georges Bruedelmann, wiping his hands on his smock. 'Please come and see.'

I got down from the stool and crossed the room to view my portrait.

It was a half-completed copy of Bartholomew's Commission; and it contained now not four but five conventional, diminutive portraits. And I, I was lodged in the north-west — in the picture at last.

'Do you find it a good likeness?' he asked.

'I don't understand,' I mumbled. In fact, I was flabbergasted. 'Is it me?'

'But of course,' he said, smiling broadly. 'I am very content with it.'

My sense of outrage at last overcame the calmness into which he had lulled me, and I thundered at him. 'How dare you! It's a bloody liberty! I don't want to be in the painting! Not even in the copy!'

In fact it was an exceedingly good likeness of myself, and a very promising partial copy of Bartholomew's original painting; but it lacked all trace of that presence which had been so remarkable in the original work. I saw here something of the material body of the thing, but the spirit had fled from it. It was like a map which had ceased to interest anybody at all. How could it be, I wondered, that an accurate copy of a painting was so utterly different from the original? It was a typical Bruedelmann puzzle.

'I'll thank you,' I said fiercely, 'to bloody well unpaint me right out of the bloody thing. Right now if you don't mind!'

He took up a paintbrush and said, very smoothly, 'Very well. If you wish I shall remove you immediately. But I must tell you, Mr Clare, that you are also in the original. I can paint you out of the copy just as fast as you like. But you must first find Jackson if you want to be removed from the original painting.

308

I had wandered off across the room and was now slumped down on the beautiful parquet floor. 'Oh my God,' I said. 'What a bloody circus. It's really obscene, what you're doing.'

But Bruedelmann had taken advantage of my irresolution to lay aside his brush and start out on his explanation. Once he'd uttered the first two sentences I was captive to his persuasions.

'When we look at the world,' he was saying, 'so much of the time our perceptions are fragmentary and our understanding of things comes to us, like photons, in discontinuous packets of sense. It is a nonsense to expect clarity. Things come sharply into focus only in part, and perhaps for a moment only, and then the confusion returns. We cannot see how things hang together, we cannot even be sure that the separate parts remain the same from moment to moment . . . and this is perhaps the most important communication in the Cubist movement in art. At best we can explore connections which we glimpse by virtue of unremitting attention. These are the fruits of truly conscious living.'

He talked for a long while; and now I am sure that he was able to summon it at will, a tone of virtual entrancement . . .

'Bartholomew's Commission is truly occult. Perhaps the developing science of the next century will explain the nature of its power, for it has a power, I assure you. I have seen proof of it many times. It has the power to clarify, and to reveal. It draws things together, it enhances effort, it nurtures illuminations. I must tell you, Mr Clare, that our mutual friend, the Salamander, asked me to paint you into it; he believed in its power. It is not so important that we cannot be sure of his motives; it is enough that good shall flow from it.'

'Well,' I said, with heavy-handed irony, 'that'll no doubt console me if I have a breakdown like Hugo Thayer.'

'Hugo had such energy. His breakdown was the last expression of his wrong-headedness. It was the beginning of his health.'

'Why,' I asked him, and I was desperately keen to know, 'did Jackson want you to paint me into the picture? What did he think would happen?'

'He expected, and I expected too, that the connections which exist between you and him, and between myself and both of you, would become sharply manifest, and real.'

'But he and I are not . . . consanguineous,' I said. It was a word which would remind me for ever of Dennis Jackson. He had stamped it with his signature.

'But you have found your mother,' Bruedelmann countered. 'Just as

309

Hugo Thayer has found himself. And I am sure that you will discover new things about your father too.'

'But it's . . . it's almost criminal to take such liberties with people,' I protested. 'You can't just stick people in a magic circle without even bothering to ask their permission . . .'

'We could not tell you,' he replied. 'It would have distorted the effects. You see, you are far too self-conscious, Mr Clare. And you must remember this: if the painting is not occult then all that I do is to paint portraits on an existing canvas. And if it is in fact occult, then you may be sure that it works always to the true advantage of the person in question. I have told you before: the painting reveals. It reveals, and ultimately it promotes the good.'

He asked me, ironically, if I would prefer him to devote his energies to learning languages. Was this a reference to Nolton? How much did he know of my life in Canterbury? He protested, too, that he did not himself invent this 'alchemy of destiny', for it had already existed. Since, however, he had been chosen to carry it further he had made of it a principal reason for living.

'When I was still a young man I chanced upon a mystery. I poured into it my energy and my belief. As the years passed it grew more potent and more real for me. Now it is a tree which has put forth many branches. And it has made many people very happy. I have no family of my own, no children of my own to occupy my attentions. I and my fellow researchers – good men and women of all ages – live together in the light and shadow of this tree.'

He talked about Bartholomew and John Pike in the prison house at La Rochelle; had I forgotten, he asked me, that Bartholomew had promised John Pike that he would find the means to live for ever if he looked into the painting? Bruedelmann declared that the painting was for him a portal on the immortal plane, a means to acquire immortality-in-being. 'But Bartholomew had powerful enemies, just as I do. I am harassed by state-employed individuals who have no understanding of my work. They do not know what they are looking for, they do not know what to believe. I must tell you, my friend, it is not a question of a drug. Such an idea is stuff and nonsense. And you know, of course, that Hugo Thayer was employed to spy on me.'

'And so you exacted your revenge?'

'You are unkind, Mr Clare. I saw his rich potential, and when I thought he was ready to see it, I showed him the painting. I considered it my duty. You must remember that I painted him into it long before I ever met him, or even knew that he existed.'

'But why? Why?'

'It was the painting itself,' said Bruedelmann, at his most mysterious, 'that prompted me to do it. It was a vision which came from my own meditations upon it.'

'And how do you explain it to yourself?'

'You ask me to explain to you everything I believe about human lives and destinies; you ask me to show you our spiritual origins, our spiritual destinies, our spiritual ends; you ask me to instruct you on the spiritual laws which rule our very existences. I must refuse you, Mr Clare. But I will tell you now that my master, who meditated upon this painting every day for thirty years, who was a Kabbalist, a spiritualist, a necromancer, died in the camp at Ludwigslust.'

'I don't get it,' I muttered. 'I really don't. And why was it your duty to show Hugo Thayer the painting? What are you up to? What's the point?'

By then, of course, my belligerence, I think, was more the product of frustration than outrage. And I was excited, too, by the claims he made for the occult powers of Bartholomew's Commission.

'I am an alchemist of the modern day,' said Bruedelmann. 'And the materials which I work with are the minds of men and women; people like yourself, like Harriet, like Hugo Thayer. I have submitted to the painting, and to what it enjoins me to do. I precipitate moral value in the minds of Europeans. It is a procedure that will use up all the remaining years of my life.'

'Well,' I said, and I wasn't sure then whether to be glad or sorry, 'now that it's been stolen, I suppose it's all over for you . . .'

'But wasn't it stolen from me once before? And didn't it come back in to my life? I am quite content to lose it for a time.'

'Hocus-pocus,' I said, dreamily. 'That's what the machine said. It blamed the new physics . . .'

'Hocus-pocus?' came Bruedelmann's comic echo. 'You find Bartholomew's painting so enigmatic, but you refuse to believe that it could be what I know it to be. It is enough, however, if I present the enigma, if I give it body; the rest is up to all of you. We are awaking to the challenge of a world that is filled with the mysteries of ancients and sages. In the face of it our metaphysical structures are dissolving into silence. Who knows what is going to happen? Who knows what has happened to Hugo Thayer? How has he changed? I do not know, it is too early to say. But I am filled with vigilance, filled with expectation. Believe me, my friend, since I have been working with the painting I have had no disappointments. I look for illumination, for signs of the life of the spirit and its laws. I am a researcher into hidden things, a scientist of the realm of the psychic. It is alchemy, Mr Clare — our historical materials are the thoughts of the Greeks, the cosmogonic insights of the gnostics, the spiritual revelations of Christ, the European traditions of Kabbala and magic ... Today we are able to add to this treasure-store the latest discoveries of modern physics. How could I do other than I do?'

His conviction was passionate, his sincerity beyond question. I had a headache coming on, and a dizziness shook me. I rested my head on my chest and fell into a sort of reverie.

'Do you think,' he asked me then, 'that you would know the things you have only recently learned if Jackson had not believed in Bartholomew's Commission? If Hugo Thayer had not been affected by it? If Bartholomew's life had not been such as it was?'

'Look,' I said, with a great weariness upon me, 'I can't afford to believe in it. I have to be sensible about things.'

'"I have to be sensible about things?"' The Bruedelmann echo wholly undermined what I had said, but I was not yet ready to yield.

'Come on,' I said. 'Once you start believing in these things, where do you draw the line?'

'But didn't you once write a book on occult matters?'

'Yes, but it was basically sceptical.' And even as I spoke I felt my certainties to be perverse and burdensome; and I wanted to shed my conviction — I wanted to float and flow.

'We cannot be sceptical about death, Mr Clare. It is death I have addressed all these years. And how should I understand death if I cannot make sense of life? I like to think that each of us, each individual being, is an inestimably precious part — a portion of a timeless psychic stuff; we enrich a composition that we cannot perceive or comprehend. I look for connections, for intimations, and I find them everywhere. And what awaits me, I wonder, in the Project Disko 39? Will there be messages for me personally, communications from my master? Am I going to learn something new about Bartholomew's Indian? There is a wave coming, Mr Clare. Shall we be carried with the wave, or shall we be drowned?

He told me that he and his assistants had made a film of Lothar Reh's Watteau.

'A film?' I said, awaking with a start from my reverie. 'How can you make a film of a painting?'

'We recreated the visual information which the painting conveys.'

'But surely the painting captures a timeless moment? As soon as you put it into time you will distort it.'

312

'We did not allow this consideration to inhibit us, and our time was not wasted. Now we need only the dialogue.'

'Dialogue?'

'Would you like to write a dialogue for us?'

'I wouldn't know where to begin,' I said. 'The mind boggles.'

I watched him clearing up at his work-bench. He put such thought into each orderly movement. How was it possible, I wondered, to commit oneself wholly to what one is doing in the moment while holding a conversation at the same time?

'You know, we filmed it in Belsen,' he said. 'It cost me a very large sum of money to organize. It is the product of three years' work . . . It may interest you to know that we were able to find the identical background of trees. It was as though M. Watteau had painted it himself, just a few months ago.'

'But it isn't a Watteau! It was painted by Leon Braques, on Lichterfelder Ring.'

'Quite so, and that is no less remarkable, don't you think so?'

'It's the weirdest thing I've ever heard. Were the actors all dressed up?'

'Exactly as in the painting. We had to have the costumes made for us. Some of the costumes were worn by my guests when you came to our weekend gathering.'

'In Belsen . . . And you keep talking about *we*, for God's sake.'

'Myself and my fellow researchers, Mr Clare. It is our intention to show this film to schoolchildren and to the general public all over Europe. We are also exploring the laws which produced both the painting and the film . . . I think we can say that the man who painted it had a prophetic vision of Belsen — a fact which teachers and critics, we hope, will make clear to its audiences. As to the question of taste . . . this film is not an attack, not an affront. Nor is it in any sense a morbid revisitation of a catastrophic failure of the human spirit. It is not the point of our film to make racist statements or to stir up hateful memories. We wish only to remind all governments and societies of our modern world that where the prosperity and well-being of a few privileged individuals are set above the human well-being of the mass of ordinary people, then we are still on the road to the death camps.'

'I find it unbelievable,' I said, 'that the trees are exactly the same. It's horrible.'

He replied, calmly, 'Man is a tree. Our roots are our branches. They are in heaven and they are in earth. We are rooted in air and nourished by light just as much as we are rooted in earth and nourished by matter. The tree is the supreme symbol of our humanity. That is why Christ was

313

crucified. We may turn the tree of man upside down and there will be no difference whatsoever in the picture. In the spiritual realm there is no up and there is no down. There is only a cross, a mingling. Trees are the context and concrete image of our being.'

'Well,' I said, after a few moments' thought, 'I wouldn't mind having a look at your film.'

'We welcome you to do so, whenever you are ready.'

'But look here ... you seem to be saying that the Lichterfelder "Watteau" is as much an occult work of art as Bartholomew's Commission ... I mean, how many more of these things have you got?'

'Not so,' he replied. 'Bartholomew's Commission is very special indeed. It is the jewel of my collection. But of course, since I am a collector of occult art, you may be sure I have other such works. Certainly the Lichterfelder Fête Galante is a product of a psychic clairvoyance.'

'Well,' I said, for I found the thought of his collection quite overwhelming, even nauseating, 'I must go home. I've really had enough.'

'You will find your room prepared for you.'

'No thanks,' I said. 'I'll go back to Canterbury.'

'As you wish.'

He accompanied me to the great front door. I planned to walk into the village and there organize a taxi for myself; Bruedelmann did not try to persuade me to stay.

'You know,' I said, 'I don't wish to imply that you are anything special, Georges ... but people who set themselves up as teachers outside the system often come to a sticky end.'

He laughed loudly and long. 'I am in no danger,' he said. 'I have little influence. I have little skill. You see, it would be easy for them to discredit me. For this reason I am safe, and my work may modestly continue.'

'What are you going to do, now that you've lost the Bartholomew Commission?'

'I shall use all my powers,' he said, 'to get it back. But please, Mr Clare, do not be in any doubt at all ... Jackson has taken away the painting which Bartholomew commissioned. I would like you to be sure *to include this fact in your writings.'*

A troupe of models on a catwalk: the music was their cue, and as they pranced and strode to the changing beat it was artfully bodied forth. The music took concrete form in their bodies, endowing the models with a quality of mind at play which they would otherwise have lacked. It was as if they had given their bodies to the music and in return the music had breathed its soul into their flesh. On the brief flight to London I sat idly watching the images flicker on the screen; and I started to think about the secret nature of music and its concrete form, the dance.

The dancer rides the tiger in a dream, for he so identifies his movements with the music which he hears that he breaks free of its power; even as he bodies forth its message he plays it down, and makes cool drama of its inexorable logic. It is as if he had himself created its pulse and its rhythms so that he might give form, albeit abstract, to his own abstract being. No cause for wonder, then, that when we see a dancer who is ungainly and inept in his movements we are pained to laughter by it, for we see there embodied before our very eyes the misery and slavery of human existence. But what is it that so enslaves us? What is it that sustains the logic?

I dozed; and found that I had a recurring vision of a man dancing in a horribly contrived and alien environment. Nolton had killed all those people in the forest near Lodz, and had seen in their last seconds of life a sort of ungainly dance; the man in the library at Steglitz had talked about the music that would not stop, a music to which they all had danced, whether they wanted to or not. And in Hugo Thayer's Poster 5 there was an image of a man dancing, and the text which described his behaviour was composed entirely of phrasal verbs; the text itself had a song-like pattern, was a dance of words. And now I felt the burden of all the pain I was coming to know from my safe, cool distance: the pain of my mother, who gave birth to me alone in a snow-filled wood on Lueneburg Heath; the pain of the violently killed; the pain of the mass murderer; the sorrow of Hugo Thayer when he had lost his wife; the pain of the dancers in heaven; the pain that Jackson felt when he lost his Erna; the pain of the little Indian when the Christians cut his tendon and burned a hole in his tongue; the pain of those who cried out from the war poster WER BIN ICH? — who cast their question even into my face, I who asked the same of them.

Below, on the glassy black of ocean, here and there were odd twinkling lights. I felt so tired, so overcharged with emotions that I wept cool tears of deep regret. And hiding my face from the passengers beside me I asked myself and them, in solemn silence with inner voice, WHO ARE WE? AND WHERE ARE WE GOING? AND WHAT ARE WE GOING THERE FOR?

And later, when I was calmer, more optimistic, I thought of all the dances I had seen . . . moments of wonder came to mind, as when, on occasion, on the dance-floor of a discothèque I had seen all the dancers suddenly merge in a oneness of coherent movement; and even though each dancer danced his separate dance and remained individuated on the dance-floor, there emerged in that wondrous instant, from that flux of disparate elements, a unified field that was motionless and timeless, and indescribably beautiful. And yet nobody was actually going anywhere, and nothing had actually happened. It was as though the physical movements which constituted the dance itself had been transcended; and where, but a moment before, the drama of the Newtonian arena had seemed to be all that was there to behold, now an intense abstract stillness had supervened. It was a field, numinously charged with moral sense, and imbued with a meaning which could not be spoken or depicted. The movements of the dancers had ceased to be vectors in a four-dimensional frame and were now pure signs, fixed for ever in a pattern which ravished the mind.

I imagined the dancers at Ludwigslust, and I pictured the pages of Schwirrer's records, full of English phrasal verbs; what was it that Hugo Thayer was at pains to impart? Could he have had knowledge of the Disko project prior to producing his posters? And if this was so, then how had it been communicated to him? Or was it that Hugo Thayer and Ernst Schwirrer, each separately and in his own individual way, had chanced to touch upon the same, perhaps essential, yet still hidden truth?

All my life I have exercised strategy, at all times I have been at pains to hold in mind the probable and improbable eventualities of my life. I have sought to minimize danger, to outflank its lurking presences. Logic, intuition and cunning have been my constant, everyday resources. That night, however, as I flew towards England, I found that I had reached a point where it was no longer possible for me to think in that way. I had the sense of a decisive encounter with the indefinable, the ineluctable, the irremediable darkness of tomorrow; and with it there seemed to flow out of me all resistance, all policy, all tactic. I felt willowy and calm. I, who had always been so leery, how could I be sure now that all would be well?

Awaiting me, on my return, was a package of papers from the Subject's Documentary, a note from the College of Further Education, and a postcard from Lucia.

Lucia's handwriting is expansive yet coy, large and bold and yet full of predictable complexities. She said she was planning to marry a film-maker in San Francisco. I studied the postcard: a tall, self-satisfied, suntanned man in silky yellow shorts and brightly coloured socks disported himself on dazzling chrome roller skates. Reading the printed text I discovered that the postcard was personalized: the hedonistic skater was Lucia's husband-to-be. His protectors of golden leather on elbow and knee displayed his initials in racy silver lettering. I chucked it in the bin.

I opened the package from the Interested Parties and skimmed:

How could it be done? To have this life in the darkness of fate, a wave of consciousness moving forward, ever onward in the chambers of sense?

They were like creatures from different planets, Hugo Thayer of the Subject's Documentary and the man on the postcard. It was obvious what Lucia was saying to me. I fished the thing out of the bin and stuffed it in the drawer. I went upstairs to bed and slept for five hours through the broad summer daylight.

It did not surprise me that I received no monthly payment for July. And my own input to The Commission became half-hearted; I wrote perfunctory sentences on to the screen and thought about my mother, who was dead, and about my father, of whom I knew nothing except that he had come to Germany in the late nineteen-twenties from America, and had subsequently spent many years in German prisons for his political activities. This information I had received from my grandmother, Omschka.

I was still very keen to hear from Hugo Thayer, who would at least explain to me, I trusted, why he had proposed The Commission and why indeed it had been taken up. Of course I was heavily disinclined now to labour at writing a dramatic narrative around the contents of his diary, for it was akin to writing a false history of the man down the road. And it seemed perverse to look within when what was outside me was now partially unveiled. But I soldiered on, remembering my promise . . .

On August 10th the screen cleared and the few hundred words displayed upon it disappeared for ever. I didn't really believe the machine had broken down; I waited, half expectantly, for a message, but none was forthcoming. I tried, foolishly, to type one on to the screen. Eventually, I switched off and went away. Half an hour later I received a phone call from Mr T. E. Visse, the Secretary to the Interested Parties. Speaking with a marked Dutch accent he informed me that he would be in England during the next few days and he requested a meeting with me. He directed me sternly not to tamper with the word processor.

I told myself that my bank balance was healthier now than it had ever been; and yet for the remainder of that day I could think only of Visse's tone of voice, particularly when I had complained about the machine: it had been conclusive, disdainful, and valedictory. I found myself wanting to write long, explanatory sentences on to its accommodating screen.

I mooned about. Might not Mr Visse permit me to keep the word processing machine, I wondered, by way of compensation for premature termination of the contract? A long letter came from Bruedelmann. He talked long and hard about the double helix of words. I could hardly bring myself to read it and pinned it up on my modest notice-board for later consideration; he said he would be away for a time, but that we would meet again etc. . . . I felt restless, over-excited, and disenchanted . . . How had it been, I wondered, at the brink, when the urge to dance had ceased; was it the shedding of a great weight, a moment of supreme buoyancy in that ocean of sound . . . or a catastrophic descent into nothingness?

Visse was not as I had expected; he was young, slim and well tanned, the sort of man you might expect to find graduating from a leading business school a year or two after giving up his law career. He wore a quiet, expensive suit and an unremarkable, expensive haircut. He was about forty, with very smooth skin and large rectangular spectacles with frames of dark horn. His fingernails were exquisitely manicured and he spoke precious English with a cultured Dutch accent.

'I'll make some tea,' I said.

'Yes, thank you.' He sat himself down on the sofa and folded his hands in his lap.

'Would you like to hear some music?'

'A little Chopin if you please.'

I asked him what was going to be done to repair the word processor. He informed me that it was to be removed; The Commission was concluded; there would be no more payments.

'But surely that's in breach of the original agreement!'

'There are certain clauses in the agreement which, you will find, cast uncertainty upon that assumption. You will be apprised of these facts in the event of taking legal advice.'

'If the contract is so open to question what's to stop me writing everything I know and sending it off to a publisher?'

'Only a cautionary tale, Mr Clare, which may colour your final resolve.'

'Colour my final resolve' . . . Where did the bloke learn to speak like this?

'Cautionary tale?' I queried.

Mr Visse told me a parable, or perhaps it was a true story: about a hitherto unknown writer who had succeeded in having his book published by a major publishing house. He claimed that he was not himself the originator of the work but only the instrument of its appearance in manuscript form. He declared that the book was a commissioned work and that he had received the material contained in its pages in a series of packages sent to him through the post. He told his publishers and his interviewers that it was in accordance with the terms of the commission he had undertaken that he had incorporated such material into the work. Neither in the work itself, nor in the preface, did he explain why the commission had come about. Nor did he identify the commissioning parties. His publishers understood this talk of a commission to be a ploy on his part, an elaborate gimmick by means of which he might draw attention to his work. Critics were of the opinion that it was an aesthetic device designed to overcome the technical problem of the all-knowing narrator. It had happened quite recently, Mr Visse told me, in the city of New York.

'As you can imagine, Mr Clare, he was the talk of the town.'

'Well, I'd say good for him,' I replied, somewhat bullish.

'Not entirely so, I fear,' said Visse . . .

In short, the writer in question was visited one night by professional criminals who threatened to torture him if he did not sign a certain legal document. It was a declaration to the effect that in encouraging people to believe that the commissioning parties did not really exist he acknowledged that he had attempted to cheat the existent parties who had actually commissioned him. He signed. And in addition he signed a public statement expressing his repentance of the deceit he had practised. Thirdly, he signed the book over to its 'rightful owners' — his tormentors. On the following day these criminals visited the publishers and reached an out of court settlement with them: it was a sum of three hundred thousand dollars.

'Well,' I said heavily. 'What exactly are you driving at?'

'Driving?' he said, humourlessly, although it was obvious he was acquainted with the turn of phrase. 'I do not doubt,' he said, 'that you will wish to protect yourself from similar coercion and abuse.'

'Yes please,' I said.

'It is very simple,' he said.

'I'm agog.'

'You must not write it, Mr Clare. More particularly, if you should write it, and that would be very foolish, I think, you must not attempt to have it published.'

''Fraid no can do, ol' pal.'

'I beg your pardon?'

'I'll say I made it all up.'

'That would be a lie, Mr Clare. Did you not say yourself that it is a grave, solemn, moral activity to write?'

'I'll figure something out,' I muttered.

He stood up and straightened his jacket. He pushed his horn-rims to his nose.

'I have much to do,' he said. 'I wish you good day.'

He walked briskly out of the room and down the hall. He pulled open the front door and said over his shoulder, 'Perhaps it will interest you to hear that heaven is now a particle accelerator. Quite secret, of course.'

That was the last I ever heard from Mr T. E. Visse, and the very last word I received from the Interested Parties, unless you count Nolton among them.

20

Properly speaking, a mystery is an obviously absurd dogma which
nevertheless conceals within itself a sublime truth.

Schopenhauer, *Parerga and Paralipomena*

In September I went back to work at the College of Further Education
and the weeks sped past. The clocks went back; Taurus and Orion filled
our evenings. But I had not been entirely idle since the day they had
taken away the word processor, for I had been organizing my thoughts,
structuring the events I had read of or heard of in the months of The
Commission; and I had not yet given up the idea that sooner or later
there would be revealed to me whatever it was I still needed to know.
Unconsciously, of course, I was depending on Bartholomew's Commission;
for had not Bruedelmann painted me into it? And I felt in my bones that
Hugo Thayer and I must sooner or later meet.

'Have you found out about that hair-clasp?' Sarah asked me one afternoon.

'The one she got from the Salamander? Actually, no.'

'Well, let's find out about it, shall we?'

My friendship with Sarah had blossomed. She had become a regular
visitor to my little house in Friar's Walk, and I cherished her company. I
had talked to her about my mother, and about the mantrap on Lueneburg
Heath, and I must have mentioned, too, the woman with the hair-clasp,
Marilyn Moore, whom I had first met at Bruedelmann's Normandy
château.

Without more ado we rang Omschka in Westergellersen; when I asked
her about the hair-clasp she was curiously evasive and wanted to talk
instead about some exercise books of my mother's. But when it became
clear that I had rung for the purpose she admitted that she had given the
hair-clasp to the Salamander when he had asked for a memento of Erna.
Then she was silent for about twenty seconds.

'Omschka,' I called several times down the phone, 'Omschka, are you
all right?'

'Ja, ja,' she said at last. But I could hear that she had become very emotional.

'Omschka, is this too painful for you? Shall we stop?'

'No, no, Robert,' she said. *'Die Spange gehoerte nicht der Erna. Es war Eva's Spange.'*

It went through me like a jolt.

'What is it?' Sarah asked.

I said, 'The hair-clasp was not Erna's. It belonged to my mother.'

It made sense, of course; for it had been Eva, not Erna, who lay in death on the kitchen table when the Salamander returned to Westergellersen. Omschka sounded deeply distressed, and ashamed. I tried to console her, but she cut through my efforts with a further revelation:

'It was Michael,' she said. 'It was your father. He gave it to Eva. When they got married. Yes . . . it was a love token.'

Poor Eva. Poor Omschka. The Salamander had taken the clasp from my mother's hair and had pocketed it. And Omschka had turned her face to the wall, It was her war face, a face of stone.

'Omschka,' I said, 'dear Omschka . . . You had to do it. I know you did it for me . . .' And suddenly I was overwhelmed with sadness; for I had handled the hair-clasp myself, just a few weeks before, a hair-clasp that my mother had worn through eight long years of separation from her husband. It was of petrified wood, I remembered, and it was thoroughly imbued with the spirit of the woman who had borne me. The remembered hair-clasp locked into something within me and a shudder of sorrow went through my body. Omschka was crying; and so was I.

At last, towards the end of November, I had a phone call I had been waiting for.

'Hello? Robert Mark Clare here.'

'Hello Robert,' said a fine, studied voice. My first thought was that everybody was calling me Robert these days. And then I recognized the voice.

'Who goes there?' I said, gleeful and challenging.

'Yous go there,' the voice said. 'Hugo's Thayer.'

'You're well then,' I said, amazed and delighted to speak to him at last.

'Yes.'

'Look, I'd very much like us to meet, if at all possible. There are some questions I need to ask you. Is that going to be possible?'

'We'll meet in December,' said Hugo Thayer. 'Have a word with Harriet now.'

Harriet came on to the line and invited me to attend a Swedish celebration due to take place in about three weeks' time.

'You mean a sort of Christmas party?' I asked, somewhat anxious to know what I was letting myself in for.

'Well,' she said, and I recognized at once the lilt in her voice, 'it's not really a party. But we can all have coffee and Swedish biscuits. It's a religious festival really, but you don't have to be religious.'

'And Hugo will be there?' I asked.

'Yes,' she said, liltingly. 'And Georges Bruedelmann too.'

'Has it got a name, this festival?'

'We call it Lucia,' she said. 'Santa Lucia.'

On a cold December afternoon I stood waiting on the pavement outside the Swedish Church Hall just off Marylebone Road. Harriet and Georges Bruedelmann turned up in an old black London cab. They looked so well and so much at ease with each other that I felt a pang of strangeness. Harriet, whose beautiful apricot-coloured hair was glorious in the clear winter light, came straight up to me and gave me a kiss and a hug. She was wearing a luminous royal blue woollen cloak with a flamboyant burgundy scarf; her gloves were bright yellow.

'You must not look so suspicious,' she told me, her voice full of music. 'We are all very happy now.'

'But . . .? Where's Hugo?'

Harriet and Bruedelmann exchanged a look that seemed to say much to each of them and little or nothing to me.

'My dear Mr Clare,' said Bruedelmann, smiling broadly and extending his enormous hand. 'You look so pale, so very English!'

This was a bit much, I thought, considering that half my students at the C.F.E. think I'm Pakistani.

'And you look exceedingly fanciful,' I said, 'in your half-hitched Persian carpet,' In fact the cloak he was wearing looked like nothing so much as a beautifully woven, expensive Persian rug.

'It is my poncho,' said Bruedelmann. 'I'm going to Peru.'

'Hugo is coming, I presume?'

'He had to be with his father,' said Harriet. 'He asked me to say sorry . . .'

'I'm sorry too,' I said, remembering my last meeting with Harriet. 'I'm afraid I wouldn't have come if I had known.'

'And so am I sorry,' said Harriet. 'I'm sorry that I was angry with you. But I was suffering then for Hugo.'

I demurred, shuffled my feet, looked to the side.

'But it's all right,' said Harriet, taking my arm in hers, 'I can tell you everything that Hugo wants you to know. I'm a gnostic, too,' she

323

said, gaily. 'It's a very democratic system,' she added, 'it's for women too!'

We walked the hundred yards to the church, where the festival was due to take place. As far as I could tell it was an ordinary Catholic church but it was filled to overflowing with Scandinavian women and their beautiful, joyous children. A young, rather stern-faced priest walked up to the altar rail and gave a short speech of welcome in Swedish. I soon realized that the whole service was to be conducted in that language.

'Is this a Christian hymn?' I asked Harriet.

'Of course,' she said. 'Sweden is a Christian country.' I felt a bit stupid. She hadn't quite got the point.

The hymn came to an end and the congregation fell silent. The lights dimmed and there was an expectant hush. All around me were breathless children, their eyes glittering with excitement. With one mind they turned their heads and looked behind them; I, too, turned to look, and in that moment I heard the singing begin, very quietly at first, right at the back of the church. And then there emerged from the darkness at the bottom of the aisle, as though to give body to the beauty of their song, a slow, rapt, solemn procession of little girls, walking in pairs, the smallest at the front of the procession, all clad in long white cotton dresses, with glitter in their hair and glitter round their waists, and each, in her trembling hand, held a slender, flickering candle. At their head walked Santa Lucia, her dress of white satin swishing on the floor, and long-sleeved like a Victorian nightgown, but ornamented with subtle lacework, and with frills about the bodice; in her silvery-golden hair she had a wreath of blueberry sprays crowned with four white candles, swaying and casting light as she went. The red sash at her waist trailed down to the floor, and she held her hands in prayer. As they swayed and swished down the aisle they trilled the following exquisite song, in Swedish:

> Passing with heavy tread
> round homesteads sleeping
> dark night surrounding us
> deep are its shadows
>
> still our hearth quickens
> and candles are glowing
> Santa Lucia, Santa Lucia

In the wake of the half-dozen pairs of attendant girls the little boys appeared; they too were clad in nightgowns but on their heads they wore wizard hats with golden stars, and each held in his hand not a candle but

324

a thin white stick with a golden star at its end. These were the *stjaerngossarna*. And behind them, right at the very back of the wondrous procession, were tiny tots, dressed up as gnomes, in red costumes with little bobble hats. These diminutive creatures, called *tomtar*, arranged themselves around Lucia at the front of the church, and there, a feast for us to gaze upon, they sang the remaining stanzas of Santa Lucia's song:

> hushed in our vigils
> we hear a rustling
> as though from swishing wings
> stealing about us
>
> look there the threshold!
> her white gown and candles!
> Santa Lucia, Santa Lucia
>
> soon night will lighten
> and flee from our valleys
> these joyful tidings
> she sings them to us
>
> bright day is dawning
> sunrise and skies of rose
> Santa Lucia, Santa Lucia

It was enchanting. After the Lucia song had ended the miraculous choir sang 'Silent Night', and then a song about the little boy who looks after the horses. In the middle of the freezing, black, winter night he sees the star of Jesus . . .

All too quickly the cycle of songs was completed; the Lucia song began again and the procession of children, calmer now, and sweetly sad, filed past us in the aisle, wending their way back where they had come from. And as the last of them passed out of sight their song died softly about us. We strained our memories to hold back its soaring sweetness, but it had passed on, leaving us staring, wide-eyed and chastened, in the gloom of the silent church.

As we shuffled out of the building we saw proud parents photographing their exquisitely costumed children. And thronged with loving admirers stood Santa Lucia herself, perhaps fourteen or fifteen years old; she was radiant Child-Queen of Light, and her eyes were brilliant with happiness.

Traditionally, after the service has ended, the congregated people gather again in a hall or in a large house and eat cakes and biscuits specially made for the occasion. Coffee is also served. We walked back to the Swedish Church Hall where Harriet provided us each with a plate on which lay a *pepparkaka* (a thin gingerbread biscuit), and a *lussekatt* (a yellow currant bun, shaped like an S and flavoured with saffron). There was a sales point too, where expensive Swedish foods and tinned national delicacies were displayed, and an excited crowd jostled the tables. Harriet steered us into a reading room which was constructed almost entirely of wood. We ate our sweetmeats and drank our coffee while Harriet translated the Lucia song for us.

'I wanted to ask Hugo about Bartholomew's Commission,' I said, making no effort to conceal my disappointment, 'and about Lothar Reh. And most of all I was hoping that he would tell me why he proposed The Commission.' I gave expression to a mild gesture of disgruntlement and looked glum.

'Hugo himself,' said Harriet, 'will tell you why he proposed The Commission. But everything else I can tell you.'

'You mean you *know*?'

'Yes,' she replied, '*I know*.'

'I should tell you, Mr Clare,' said Bruedelmann, 'that much of Hugo's thinking he shares with Harriet. Indeed, much of it derives, I think, from her.'

'We are in love,' she said, dramatically. 'It is an illumination — like Santa Lucia's candles. What do you want to know?'

'Well, for a start,' I said, rather perversely addressing my question to Bruedelmann, 'what's the news of Bartholomew's painting?'

'It's not a painting,' said Harriet. 'It is like a woman's make-up,' she said 'or perhaps it's just like paint on a wall.'

'What?' I confess I felt rather put out by her unnerving assurance. I was annoyed, too, that Hugo and Harriet had failed to warn me of his absence. 'I'm talking about Bartholomew's Commission,' I explained.

'It wasn't commissioned,' said Harriet, who was clearly enjoying herself. 'It just *happened*.'

This, I thought peevishly, is what happens when people delegate.

'Do you remember the Lippstadt Mission?' she asked me.

'Yes.'

'And you remember the little man?'

'Hudson the midget.'

'And you remember that he came back one night and talked about the fields of light which poor Doctor Wykzo created in his laboratory?'

'Of course.'

'Please, Mr Clare,' said Bruedelmann, heavy with *bonhomie*.

'We talked about it,' said Harriet, 'and we realized that Doctor Wykzo had discovered what alchemists called the Prima Materia, what Eliphas Levi called the Universal Magical Agent. But it was a substance which could not be stored or contained. In fact, it was a substance that had to become *something* in order to remain in the world. Do you understand?'

'I'm happy to take your word on it,' I said, amicably enough.

She continued in her lilting voice, 'Doctor Wykzo turned it into paint. He also turned it into cosmetics for his daughter. He wanted to keep it in the world and so he stored it in the resins, because they soaked it up. Also he needed to hide it. Isn't that right?'

'Yes, I suppose so.'

'Well,' she said confidingly, leaning forward in her chair so that I caught a whiff of perfume and found her eyes gazing into mine most disconcertingly, 'you know, in those days there was hardly any difference between paint for pictures and paint for faces. That is why he hid it in Magdalene's make-up.'

'An interesting image,' I conceded.

'Yes it is. Hugo says it is . . . *sublimely appropriate to art, more particularly to occult art. What Wykzo had produced in his alchemical labours was* PURE BEING.'

I was stunned.

'But you know,' said Bruedelmann, taking up the thread, 'he had obviously departed from received religious practice and was full of guilt. When his daughter suffered her tragedy he blamed himself. That is why he intended to bury the make-up case with Magdalene, in the marshes.'

It was obvious that Georges Bruedelmann was very attached to Harriet, who seemed to bathe in his regard.

'But why do you say the painting wasn't commissioned?' I asked her.

'Bartholomew experimented with the resins,' she replied. 'And one day he rubbed them on a canvas, just as if he wanted to make a painting with them. Then, when he carefully examined his "art" . . . well, you've seen the "painting", haven't you?'

'You mean the painting is just a canvas that Bartholomew smeared with the resins that had been imbued with the fields of light?'

'We think so,' said Harriet. 'And the more he studied it the more he became enlightened by what he saw.'

'So it was more a device for spiritual practice than a painting?'

'Like Hugo's concrete koan, do you remember?'

'Yes, yes . . . it's in the Subject's Documentary.' Now I was becoming quite excited. 'Or like Hugo's idea of the ontological window?' But now I had lost the thread.

'When Being is one with itself in the material things of this world,' said Harriet, who had pulled out a little notebook and was reading aloud from it, 'then it's possible to change everything. It's like a window through which we can reach out, or reach in, to grasp the noumenon, the *Dingan sich* accessible at last, and directly compliant to our will.'

Georges Bruedelmann gave a happy laugh and clapped her on the shoulder.

'So whereas we normally look at a painting with a view to understanding what it's about,' I struggled to keep it all clear in my mind, and spoke slowly and groped for words, '... in the case of Bartholomew's ... uhm ... canvas, there is nothing being referred to, there's nothing *else* for us to see, or notice, or understand. There's not even an image, really. What we're seeing is the thing itself.'

'And the thing itself,' said Harriet, reading again from her notebook, 'the thing itself is hidden in the paint, deep in the mire of the material world. The thing itself,' she said with a flourish, 'THE THING ITSELF IS YOU.'

'And that,' said Bruedelmann, 'is occult art.'

'Is that what you think, too?' I asked Georges Bruedelmann.

'It is not a question of agreement,' he said. 'We must all make of it what we will. But I must tell you that Harriet and Hugo together enjoy much insight into these matters. They are endowed with a spiritual talent.'

'Because we are in love,' said Harriet, 'and our love is real.'

Thinking then of Dennis Jackson I asked Bruedelmann if he had managed to get the thing back.

'I shall get it back very soon,' he said.

'So you've been in contact with Jackson, then?'

'It is better,' said Bruedelmann, 'that you do not ask me this question.'

'OK,' I said, mildly. 'But tell me, Harriet, did you ever meet Dennis Jackson?'

She replied with a degree of heat, 'Dennis Jackson is a dinosaur.'

'I would never have met my grandmother,' I said, 'or found out who my mother was if Jackson hadn't turned up.'

'Without Dennis Jackson,' said Bruedelmann, 'The Commission could not have come about.'

'And people like Jackson,' I said, 'saved Europe from fascism.'

Poor Harriet, she could not have expected such a chorus of replies.

'Besides,' said Bruedelmann, concluding, 'are we not all of us dinosaurs, ridden into town by schoolchildren?'

*

328

'Harriet,' I said, 'is Hugo avoiding me?'

'No, he is not avoiding you,' she sweetly replied.

'Well, what are his plans for the coming months? I suppose he's dropped his posters business, has he?'

'Oh yes,' she replied. 'He is going to walk to Scotland.'

'In the winter?' I said, smiling to myself.

'Oh no,' she said, 'he must in any case wait for the spring.' Her smile was very engaging.

'And what's your opinion of that?'

She laughed. 'Well,' she said, 'he's very *spiritual* at the moment . . .'

'You mean . . .?'

'Yes,' she said. 'So he doesn't do very much good for me now.'

We all laughed, but Harriet, surprisingly, blushed deep scarlet.

'And I am going to Iquitos,' said Bruedelmann. 'Tomorrow.'

'To look for the little Indian?' I said.

'Hugo says that you are the little Indian, Mr Clare,' said Harriet.

'I'm not Indian.'

'But I think you must agree,' said Bruedelmann, 'that it's something to think about?'

I gave him a polite smile.

'Well, what *are* you going to do in the Amazon Basin, Georges?'

'I shall travel down river,' he replied. 'And I shall take the canvas with me. I shall paint in men of power: politicians, cruel land barons, secret policemen.'

'So it's over there already is it, the painting?' I asked slyly.

Bruedelmann gave me a big smile; and it was precisely at that moment that I first suspected that Bruedelmann and Dennis Jackson were working together. With all my heart I wish them well.

'Don't go getting yourself killed,' I said. 'The powers that be are less patient over there.'

'Heh heh, you know death is my friend,' he replied. 'I am not so easy to kill, Mr Clare. I have my resources.'

Harriet clapped her hands together and leaned across to me and whispered, 'Didn't you already know,' she paused for breath, 'Georges has powers.'

'Why did they part?' I asked. 'I mean Bartholomew and Magdalene.'

'Because,' said Bruedelmann, looking very grim, 'in the resins with which they experimented they saw the terrible secret of their own relationship. As Magdalene grew more conscious and clear-headed she recognized in Bartholomew, who was her man and husband, not her saviour but a demon rapist.'

329

'Oh that's horrible!' said Harriet.

I said, to nobody in particular, 'I suppose that's what she meant when she said that he was only half a man.'

But nobody said a word.

'Maybe,' I said, in a moment of inspiration, 'maybe the pigments on the canvas are imbued with a true union of their separate identities . . .'

'That,' said Harriet, 'is gnosis!'

But she would not explain herself further save to say, cryptically, 'You must read the Book of Philip, in the Gnostic Gospels. It's about the union of male and female. It's one of the new patterns, for the new world.'

The conversation pattered on for quite some time. I felt happy and entirely at home with them. We had become a convivial party. 'I am so glad,' said Georges Bruedelmann, 'that we have had this happy meeting together. You are all very dear to me. And there is something that each one of you can do for me. It will not cost you very much, I hope. Please be so kind and wish me well.'

In a rather absurd, self-conscious little ceremony we wished him well. He asked us to remember that wishing him well was both a ritualistic act of the moment and *a continuous benefaction by thought*. We nodded sagely, although I felt a bit foolish, even though I sincerely wished him well.

Georges Bruedelmann took a hip flask from his pocket and poured a little brandy into our cups.

'Let us have a toast,' he said.

'To the Heaventree,' said Harriet, 'which is rooted in the human heart.'

'To the Salamander,' I said.

'To the good in ourselves,' said Bruedelmann, 'and to our own dear planet.'

21

The philosophers have only interpreted the world in various ways; the point, however, is to change it

Karl Marx's tombstone

Ten days before Christmas I met Nolton in the high street in Canterbury. He had just emerged from the video shop across the street and was carrying a large, blood-red plastic bag advertising its wares. My first inclination was to disappear into the crowd but even as I had the thought I felt his attention upon me, insistently beckoning. In the dense current of harried shoppers he stood perfectly still, waiting for me to cross the road to him. I strolled over, and as I greeted him he gave the bag a sudden shake; the man's solitary, haunted, eccentric world instantly wound me round.

'Mr Clare,' he said, in that needle-point voice of his, 'there are one or two things I shall have to discuss with you.'

We walked slowly along the street.

'Writing all right?'

'No,' I said, curtly.

'Not a happy man?' he asked, in uncommonly wry tones. 'Not a lot of it about,' he observed, as though savouring the idiom. 'Especially at Christmas.'

'Nothing,' I complained,' is really concluded.'

'Concluded?' Deftly, with his stick, he swept a piece of litter from under his feet.

'Well is it?' I said.

'I didn't imagine you would think it was over,' said Nolton.

We walked a few paces more and then he said, 'Now, what is it I am to say to you . . .?'

'Nice videos?' I had the urge to match his tone, which was studiedly inconsequential. It occurred to me that the man probably didn't give a damn about anything any more. And to my surprise and satisfaction I realized that I was no longer afraid of him.

'Tawdry pestilential entertainers,' he said. 'What would people do at

Christmas without the Second World War? If you turn on the telly on Christmas Day you will see so much slaughter of man by man. Execrable planet.'

'I don't imagine,' I said, 'you've got Mary Poppins in the bag.'

'Kindly see for yourself,' he said and held open his red plastic bag. It contained half a dozen children's films. *Chitty-chitty Bang-bang, Bedknobs and Broomsticks*. That kind of thing. 'Never mind, old chap,' he said.

'Well,' I asked, somewhat too sharply, 'what have you got to tell me?'

'Jackson is alive and kicking,' he said.

'Great!'

'They nearly got him in Manaus.'

'Who did?'

'The Americans are after him too, you know.'

'Manaus?' I repeated, thinking of Georges Bruedelmann and his trip to Peru.

'It wouldn't surprise me at all,' said Nolton, slyly, 'if Jackson and your old friend Mr B. are hand in glove, as they say.'

'Really?'

'But Jackson got clean away, of course. Left no tracks at all. That woman helped him, you understand.'

I said, rather proudly, 'Of course she helped him. She used to be in love with him.'

'I think probably she is in love with him still,' Nolton replied. 'She made a great effort to rehabilitate him with the security people in Europe. And in the United States, too, I believe. The man's a renegade. An outsider. An entrepreneur. He's got a lot to thank her for. That woman has bags of influence.'

'Why did you bring him over here in the first place?'

'That's something you will never know, Mr Clare.' There was a very hard edge to his tone. 'Not if you know what's good for you.'

'Something to do with a mole, was it?' I persisted. ' "Don't think I can't see you"?'

'Don't even think about it, Mr Clare.'

' "You won't be a mole, then"?'

'And neither will you, now, will you old chap?'

'And the other thing?' I inquired.

He stopped walking; we stood together on the street corner and little flocks of snow came flying suddenly out of nowhere.

'Two things actually,' he replied. 'But they are closely related.'

'Oh good-oh.'

'Your book,' he said. 'This little matter of your scrivening . . .'

'Yes?'

'Wouldn't you like to know what it's all about?' 'I mean your book, of course.'

'All right,' I said, and I found myself disposed to beg, 'I'm all ears.'

'Good-oh,' he said. He paused to collect his thoughts. He started walking again, and then thought better of it.

'The trouble with us,' he said, 'is that we have no money. Our best scientists frequently decamp and set up in America. As you know, we were cheated of the original research findings.' He stared at me through his small green lenses. 'You do know what I'm talking about, don't you?'

'Yes,' I said, cautiously. 'You're talking about the Disko.'

'As I say, we were cheated from the beginning. But we knew it was important work and we knew that the Americans had started to look at it again. We were actually very keen but they shut us out. Quite understandably, of course. Then we heard that Bruedelmann was asking questions about it and so we put Thayer on his back. As you probably know by now Mr Thayer cracked up in Berlin and when he came home he was babbling about the need for a writer. He even specified particular conditions. Utter nonsense, of course, and we closed his file. Then Jackson turned up and it became obvious that he was keen to work with Bruedelmann. He was also anxious to trace his "son". In both cases it was the painting which was the catalyst.'

'I know most of this already,' I said. 'What I really want to know is why Hugo Thayer proposed The Commission, and more particularly, why you decided to take it up. After all, as you said just now, you had closed his file, right?'

'We took him up on it because of the coincidence of Jackson's appearance on the scene and his willingness to foot the bill. And of course, there was one further little coincidence: we looked very carefully into Jackson's past and discovered that his putative son, your good self Mr Clare, was a writer resident in Canterbury.'

'Yes, I can see the effect it might have had on the decision-makers. But there must have been some cooked-up rationalizations; I mean, Hugo's babblings, Jackson's cash and my assumed blood relation to the Salamander were surely not in themselves enough. I mean, the Interested Parties would have looked silly on paper, wouldn't they, if they had given those considerations as their reasons for something as fantastical as The Commission.'

'Quite right, Mr Clare. We surmised that Jackson's interest in Bartholomew's painting had some connection with the Disko research. That's why we stepped up our surveillance. We desperately needed a bargaining tool *vis-à-vis* the Americans. And since virtually all the information relating to the original research findings was closed to us we concluded that we would have to draw on our cultural strengths — I mean our historical, cultural and intellectual European traditions. We asked ourselves this very pertinent question: what is it that makes us favourably and profitably different from the Americans *in their view of us*? We concluded that our historical European mind was the essential differentiating factor between them and us, a factor which they highly esteemed. And since the continuing research related very much to magic, mind, and language, and since the Americans use English as their working language, we thought we might try our luck with The Commission. Since Jackson was going to foot the bill for it we really had nothing to lose. But of course, we dressed it up in some very fine terms. As you see, Mr Clare, we lacked the political and economic leverage to compel the Americans to share with us, but we had the great cultural heritage, enshrined in our thought and language, and it was the secrets of language that lay at the heart of their research. All we hoped to achieve by it was a seat at the negotiating table.'

'Hocus-pocus,' I said, 'became the order of the day.'

'That is correct.'

'But let me get this straight,' I said. 'You knew that the continuing research was getting into the realms of the psychical, the mystical . . .'

'Yes indeed.'

'And so you decided to create a project, namely The Commission, which could not fail to yield negotiable information if what the Americans were doing had a real basis in fact. Am I right?'

'And you, Mr Clare, have done us more than proud. Just imagine, your father was in Heaven . . .'

'What?' My hair stood on end. 'What?'

'Oh! You didn't know?'

'Please, Nolton, please tell me about it!'

'Oh I'd like to, Mr Clare, I really would. But I think it will be subject to how amenable you prove to be.'

'Don't do this to me, Nolton.' I felt like tearing my hair. My pulse rate had jumped and I felt a wave of energy shoot up my spine. 'Please, please tell me what you know!'

'Your father was in Heaven, Mr Clare. That is all I shall tell you . . . until such time as we have a written commitment from you.'

I could have wept blood. I wanted to beat him to death. I bit my nails instead and raged inside. Was the man a sadist? Was he enjoying my agony? With Nolton it is impossible to tell.

'There are facts emerging,' he continued, 'which have given us more than the simple bargaining tool we had hoped for. You are an asset to us, Mr Clare, one which the Americans lack, and which they are very keen to acquire. It is certain that they will contact you. But it is of the utmost importance to us that you should keep silent. Mum's the word, now.'

'You said my father was in Heaven,' I was furiously herding my sluggish thoughts, 'which I take to mean that he was an experimental subject. If you know it, then the Americans must know it too, from the archives that Jackson brought out of the camp . . .'

'That is where you fall into error, Mr Clare. The Americans know nothing about your father, except that he was an experimental subject at Ludwigslust. Do not allow yourself to be persuaded otherwise; they will deceive you, and you will find too that you will have incurred our very great displeasure. It will be treachery, Mr Clare, a betrayal of your European heritage. It will be a very great cost to bear, believe me, I know.'

It must be said that this speech had a chastening effect on me. I didn't want to end up like Nolton; and I do feel a terrific loyalty to the European ideal.

'What hope do I have then?' I asked, pitifully. The snow blew into my eyes.

'Good-oh,' said Nolton. 'I welcome this note of co-operation. And I may tell you that there is quite a controversy raging about your book. If you will content yourself to wait a little while I feel there is every chance that you will be permitted to write it, subject, of course, to our editing.'

'Couldn't we get out of this bloody snow?' I said, and I felt miserable as sin.

'Not at all,' he murmured, 'I like the snow.'

'And what about the information you possess about . . . my father? Will you give me that too?'

'Oh I expect so, Mr Clare. Why ever not, after all?'

'How are they developing it, the Americans? I mean the Eigen-musikswesen.'

'Thought transmission, negative entropy, and such like. It seems that you might have an aptitude for . . . well, you may be a rather good channel.'

'A channel?'

'They've put it out to a syndicate. There's a substantial portfolio of spin-off projects. They're very interested in death, did you know?'

'Who isn't?'

'It depends on what the dancers dream up, you see. I suppose you might say it could change the world.'

'So it's the experimental psychosis that interests them,' I said, knowingly.

'Oh, there's a great deal more to it now. Lots of developments. Fields of energy and all that.'

'Fields of light?'

'Oh indeed yes.'

'Predictable, really,' I retorted.

'But I must come to the point,' he said, and even in the light, flurrying sleet about us I could detect at once that his mood had changed. 'Listen to me, Clare. You must not come to any agreement with them. None whatsoever. If there's going to be a deal, you will permit ourselves to strike it. Is that understood, now? We want no more Salamanders, do we now?'

We stood there, deeply absorbed, in the wind tunnel of the high street amidst thronging tourists and sudden tiny whorls of snow. I felt utterly trapped, encumbered, outflanked, under their ban; and my heart yearned to be with my father, perhaps in memory only, but with him, in Heaven, or wherever else he had gone. And if ever I felt that life was not worth the candle, it was then, as I stood there with Nolton, who was the loneliest man in the world.

22

Truth ... is in the sensible object as in a mirror; in the reason, through inference and discussion; in the intellect, through premise and conclusion; in the mind, in absolute living form.

Giordano Bruno, *De l'infinito universo e mondi*

Three shopping days before Christmas I received a small package from Hugo Thayer with a short note apologizing for his failure to meet with me. He said that he would be away in Africa for an indefinite period visiting his father, who was *withdrawing from the world*. He had enclosed a tape for me, *to be getting on with*, as he put it.

Hugo Thayer's tape contained his own interpretation of gnosis, and some additional biographical material which I have used to supplement my account of his involvement in The Commission. I learned from the tape that when Hugo had proposed The Commission to the Interested Parties he had actually stipulated that the commissioned writer should meet a number of highly specific requirements, which were as follows: the writer should be ignorant of his own mother; he should be drawn to words, not as mere instruments but as creative levers upon the world; he should be a person haunted by problems of personal, social, historical and spiritual identity. He says that he 'saw' in Bartholomew's Commission a pattern of elements to which he could give expression only by means of his understanding of certain gnostic myths, which he had gleaned from reading the Gnostic Gospels and other commentaries on the codices discovered in Egypt at Nag Hammadi in 1945. He says that he was deeply troubled to find himself on the side of Georges Bruedelmann's enemies; after seeing Bartholomew's Commission, which he considered a truly occult and spiritual work, he understood that his employers were at pains to take possession of something to which they had no title, something which should and must be freely available to everyone. He chose the myth of gnosis, he explains, because it reflected his own situation *vis-à-vis* the Interested Parties, and he emphatically declares that the Interested Parties are archons.

Hugo:

In proposing The Commission I was giving expression to something which I had not thought out, which I barely understood . . . I was a channel. I can't say I believed what I was saying, I mean, gnosis to me then was a compulsion, not a religious belief system that I had committed myself to . . . it was a sort of metaphor which had taken possession of me. Now, you can say either that it was a poetic form of madness on my part, given my nervous breakdown and the oppressive sense I had of needing to smuggle information out to the world, past the Interested Parties . . . a concrete poem of personal strategy in the world . . . or you can say that it was Anthropos, the archetypal principle of humanity in me, and in everybody else, that was directing my will. In which case you'd have to say that I was a man who had become an instrument of a spiritual force. The fact that Jackson turned up at the same time and they knew that he had some involvement in Disko 39 and linked it to Bartholomew's Commission, is either a pure coincidence, a million to one chance that swung things my way, or it was a timely, independent confirmation of a new-wave Anthropic phenomenon. At the moment I can't be sure what I believe, but I can't pretend that there isn't something personally momentous about it all. You remember my experience in Paris? I think it was Anthropos, Jesus-in-man, who spoke to me. But you know, my vicissitudes over the last couple of years had brought me to a spiritual awareness which I wasn't really ready for. I'm still in the dark even now. Too much mud yet in the spirit. I'll have to find a spiritual teacher to help me on my way.

. . . Irenaeus, who was one of the great critics of the second-century gnostics, complained in his book Adversus haereses *that the gnostics created enormous fictions. It seemed that every gnostic he came across had a different story to tell about his own personal relationship with Christ. But then, you see, original creative invention is the hallmark of anyone who becomes spiritually alive. If gnosis has truth in it and I have indeed participated somehow in that truth, then it seems to me now that a writer, a fiction-making creative user of words, if he was in the appropriate psychological condition, would be enabled to make a fiction of me that might express what I myself was unable to say. And this is important, you see, because truths have to come to light. After all, we're all one. And it takes just one of us to light up the world. And because you were looking for me, you were helping me along my road. That's just how it is. The gnostics tell us that truth is only available to us in fictions and images. And truth, the truth about everything, is incorporated into our very bodies. That's why the concrete koan is a dance.*

. . . and that's where the phrasal verbs come in, you see? Dance is the form of flux, and phrasal verbs give expression to that flux like nothing else in the English language. Phrasal verbs are layered, having both simple, concrete, dynamic meanings, and abstract, static, moral meanings too. And between the

two layers, or fields, there is a sort of flickering. Call it the cast of words, if you like, or irony-in-life. So there are two worlds present in these words: one is noisy, dynamic, dimensioned; the other is still, eternal, and dimensionless. And because I have only half awoken from a spiritual death and I am not yet ready to be at one with the higher world, where there is no up and there is no down, no in, no out . . . because I'm only half-way there I am compelled to live it, like a paradox, and that is why I dance.

. . . I live a contradiction . . . between the dimensioned world and eternal space; between motion and stillness; that's why I dance. In the dance, what is is not, and what moves is still. I am the Gnostic Phrasal Verb Man and I Dance.

It's really important for me personally that you write about all that you've experienced through The Commission. I see two problems which you are likely to encounter, but I want to say right away that these are not problems at all, it's just your way of seeing the world: first — you'll find that the Interested Parties will probably refuse to let you publish. But I tell you, you needn't worry about the Interested Parties. Tell them that you have seen them for what they are: tell them that you know them to be archons. Then they'll let you pass. Second — you'll be worried that people won't believe you if you write it and try to publish; you'll say to yourself . . . but people will think I made it up! But that's just perfect, don't you see? Because if people believe that you have made it up, and they very probably will, then you'll get less hassle from the Interested Parties. From their point of view you'll have turned them into a fiction. And nobody believes a fiction, now do they? And if some people are disposed to believe that this is not a fiction, that we all exist — you, me, Jackson, Georges Bruedelmann, the Interested Parties, Bartholomew de Gaillac, the dancers of Disko 39 — then the effects of that belief, the belief that this is really how things are, will be quite wonderful, I promise you. Gnosis awakens the supreme spiritual archetype in our humanity. In each of us the principle of perfect love and charity will be nourished. The more people who experience this gnosis, just by believing it, the better it will be for the world and for the whole of humanity. And finally, of course, if people believe you've made it all up then you'll be presenting at the very least a suggestive case for gnosis, just because gnosis, like nothing else, has original creative invention as its hallmark! Remember that God is, even if we have to make it up . . .

The day before Christmas Eve I had a phone call from Vicky Straightwood, who I had not heard from since our trip to Germany.

'Mark,' she said, 'I'm coming to work on you.'

'To work on me?'

'Don't you want me to? There's something I want to try out on you. It's something to do with sexuality. Oh do say yes, for heaven's sake.'

'For *heaven's* sake, Vicky?'

She assured me that it was precisely because I was *a heavenly subject* that she wanted to test her new skills on my person. Then she reminded me of the erotic pleasures of our last meeting, when we had spent the night together in a guest-house on Lueneburg Heath . . .

My pulse rate quickened. 'I'm yours, Vicky.'

And thinking about the conversation afterwards I had been struck by the resonances; it was almost as though Vicky knew all about The Commission. When I put the question to her she retorted that she no longer needed to be told things about the people she knew; she said she could feel *the real facts* of their lives like bumps on a surface. Must be a bit like reading braille, I had suggested. *And a fat lot you know about it* was her reply. Vicky grows more exacting with every trip to Bergen.

She arrived at Friar's Walk that same evening. She was thinner, but she was glowing with health. She seemed to be entirely in the moment and had a shine on her, reminding me not a little of Herta Geschwisterheim. She told me that she had been following a programme of mind-exercises, devised to induce . . . well, let's wait and see.

We went upstairs together and into my little bedroom, and the first thing she wanted me to do was to push the wardrobe out into the hall. I protested, but Vicky was determined to have space for her 'witchery', as she called it, so I obliged — but not without great difficulty and considerable expenditure of energy. She rolled up the carpet and swept the floorboards; then she lit a solitary candle and turned the lights off. Next she told me to take my clothes off, which interested me not a little. I had to lie face down on my bed while she straddled me, in her knickers, and proceeded to give me a massage. It was one of Herta Geschwisterheim's herbal creams, and she rubbed it deep into the skin of my back, lower back, buttocks, and around my perineum, which had me a bit nervous, actually, for the stuff was diaphoretic and hot to the skin. Then she turned me over, and taking scant interest in my tumescent condition she started in on my chest. The stuff released a deep vibrant warmth in me, even to my bones; her clever fingers plied, rolled, nubbed, nipped wads of flesh for fully half an hour, and all the while she seemed to be saying something to herself, or concentrating on some inner point within. And soon, as though I had smoked a powerful drug, I could feel my own brainwaves running in rippling bands from forehead to nape. And my desire, my lust for her grew so intense I was amazed that I could want her so much, so urgently, anyhow.

340

And when at last she deigned to acknowledge my passion it was only to bring my desire to pitch; then calm and deliberate and resolute she slipped away from me and went to stand in the centre of the room where she stripped off her pullover and her blouse. Her breasts, like small hunting horns, curved to narrow conical points and blossomed there in pale pink nipples. Against the pale gold of her naked skin a gleaming dull silver amulet graced her throat and reminded me intently of our first night of love. Desire tugged me from my prone position on the bed and I went to her, but she fended me off with a quick, almost cunning laugh; her eyes were bright, sparkling, empowered; her small, white, sharp, regular teeth flashed in the flickering light of the candle. With a swift, deft movement she stepped out of her knickers and tossed them to the side; and stood there in her long socks, naked and splendid, a tuft of dark brown hair like a shock of rich pelt neatly exuberant between her thighs.

I started to say something but she placed her finger on her lips and sent me a look that was full of warning. Then she turned and faced, in turn, each cardinal point of the compass and made some kind of obeisance, all the while muttering something that I could not properly hear. Then she closed her eyes, lifted her hands into the air and like Shiva, raised a leg and started to dance. I was greatly impressed by her balance, for she kept her eyes shut throughout; then she started to hum . . . and now I felt a change of energy in the room. It was as if the walls were no longer there, or as though we had grown small so that they seemed suddenly far away. There was a thickening, and yet a quickening in the air, as though a strong wind were blowing, but it seemed to be blowing in circles, and we were ourselves its centre. Then the candle flame flickered and went out and I felt the chill caress of fear.

She began to sing: strange words, that could have been Greek, or Sanskrit or anything. In the darkened room her voice had a quality of weather in open country. And then in the tenebrous murk about her I saw something forming; a shape seemed to fill out and billow about her, a flowing winged thing and I smelt mud and fur and faeces. And suddenly I wanted urgently to be out of there, but I could not have left the room even if I had determined to because I found that I was semi-paralysed, sprawled on my bed; then she called out to me, abruptly. 'What do you want to see Mark?' Um, Oh my God, I thought. Cripes . . .

'Hurry up now,' she called, and there was no brooking her tone.

'I want to see myself,' I shouted, half delirious with the madness that was suddenly upon us, 'as I really am!'

'No!' she shouted, with a terrible gravity. 'Not allowed!'

'Show me,' I shouted, almost at random, 'show me Dennis Jackson!'

In fact, in my first request, I see it now, I had wanted to make things easier for Vicky; for I had assumed, with shameful yet characteristic smugness, that she was merely putting on some kind of magic show that could never be anything but rudimentary, uncertain, a crude amalgamation of auto-suggestiveness and psychological archetype, heightened, I am sure, by the incredible current of my unfulfilled sexual desire. But my alternative request, I suspect, was born out of bloody-mindedness, was to have been my revenge upon her for scaring me so; I didn't for a moment imagine that she could pull it off. Besides, I was sure that she had never even met Dennis Jackson, though I had spoken of him to her.

In the murk of shadows about her body a light had appeared and I saw a man with a round helmet peering and squinting; I felt I was in him, and he in me, and he bent down to peer into the green gloom and it was all around me, the dark green fronds, the heavy glistening leaves, the smell of tree and leaf mould in a brooding, vegetative darkness of the soul. He leaned forward and his eyes were glaring, his face running with sweat, his spirit oppressed by the virulence, the ubiquitous, sprawling, tireless vegetation. And staring so in the blank, raucous forest he pulled at his helmet and wiped his brow on the mouldering sleeve of his doublet, caught an insect crawling in the hairline and crushed it. And he cursed them, his companionable, renegade adventurers whose deaths had left him solitary in this wilderness with only a lame and starving horse to whip and cajole across endless, incoherent wastes of forest. He smelt of fever and of dysentery; his hands were flayed from the undergrowth; his leather doublet was rotting off; his hose so ragged that his pale skin, plucked like turkey, shone through with a dull menace; his boots, proof once of manliness and standing, now were sprung and his bruised and bloodied toes peeped through. And how he dreaded it, the gloomy-bright unreal green; things were so close and yet seemed so far away: was it an eyeball he saw, so near to his own, returning his gaze from the coarse, green confusion?

And then I was there myself, in the undergrowth, a small naked child-man, hunkered down, stock-still, staring in fear and wonderment; and I was not alone, for a girl was with me, brown-skinned, small, her eyes of bright brown velvet filled with passionate curiosity. We saw how one slow hand went to the pocket of his doublet while his other hand loosed from the mildewed scabbard at his side a hacked and dented sword. He crouched down and his face smiled; he proffered a small round sweet thing. His face was twisted with untruth, with self-hate, with disgust towards the world. 'Come hither little Indian,' he said to me, 'come hither to me now.'

And I spoke to him: a small swift sound, like pattering rain. He cocked his head and seemed to listen. 'Oh aye, 'tis true, aye, aye.' He thrust the sweet in among the leaves and I took it and put it to my mouth. It was sweet like nothing I had ever known. I broke it in two and gave some to her, who was by me. Then the man broke through the leaves and took us by the hand. When he saw the girl-child, naked and brown and young, he was glad; a cruel smile covered his spirit and his root hardened.

And even as I recognized the face of the Spanish conquistador the vision was banished by something stronger, more immediate, more vivid and external; now I was truly afraid, for whereas in the case of the former vision I had half known that it was myself that dreamed it forth, and as such it was mine to sustain, contain, or banish . . . the aftermath was real, irresistible, menacing. It was Jackson: but now he wore a combat jacket, and a pale green sweatshirt underneath. His face was grizzled with grey—white beard and he was grunting and sweating somewhere in the forest, and it was obvious that he was drugged, or drunk, and he was intoning something, like a curse like a prayer . . . 'I see in that painting . . . things. I see I want to go to you and take you in my arms and hug you like my son, my mother, my brother, myself, like life itself, and say to you like a leaf falling, like a blade of green grass waving in God's sunlight *I love you and we are one* . . . And I see all the corpses, all the dead I did for like bits of myself there, and I did for them with knife, gun, voltage, flame. And I guess I loved them, all of them, like I love you now . . . and I eat my friggin' tears but they keep coming, that's the world for you, son . . . And I want it to be a green time again, once and for all, such as I never saw, never in my blasted, cursed, hate-filled life. And I know it ain't going to do any good just to die for it. No, never again to die for it, kill or be killed. But something's going to be done . . . and you're part of it, son, little friggin' Indian . . . And I'm sending you a piece of that canvas, to treasure, and to make good what's done . . . Georges is gone. Bruedelmann's gone. I'm on my own right now. On my own again in the heart of it. I'm sending a piece of the painting, son. Maybe, Bruedelmann . . . maybe they killed him . . . I eat my tears when I think of how it's been.'

'Salamander!' I shouted to the apparition. 'Can't you see me there? Jackson?'

I knew it was an illusion. I ran into its ambit and I felt a charge, a multitude of electromagnetic responses in my body as I walked right through him. I heard a terrible groan come from Vicky and she slumped to the floor.

I found the light switch and flicked the lights on. Vicky was lying very still, stretched out on the floorboards. I half lifted her, half dragged her to the bed, and with one final effort heaved her up on to it; I too felt completely drained of energy. Flopping down next to her I heard her breathing: faint, but regular. I pulled the covers up over us and fell into a dreamless sleep.

Later she woke me, digging her fingers into my ribs.

'Vicky,' I said, and I was instantly awake, 'that was terrifying. Did Herta show you how to do that?'

She nodded triumphantly. 'Was it really good?'

'Didn't you see it then?'

'No,' she said, 'it came through me. I was the channel.'

'It was absolutely . . . phenomenal! Dennis Jackson was there, talking his heart out. Somewhere in the rain-forest.'

'Was it really as if it was actually happening for you?' She was very serious.

'Well, I mean, well obviously Vicky, he wasn't *really* there, now was he?'

'Then nothing is ever *really there*, Mark.'

'Oh come on, Vicky . . . after all, it was a fantastic vision . . .'

'Listen to me,' she said, '*I know*. Nothing is really there in the way you like to think. It's all just a question of degree. Some things give you more to experience, not just something to see or hear but something to smell, to touch, to find in your way: like a rock, a horse, a person. Whatever. Nothing is really outside us Mark, and for that matter nothing is really inside us either.'

'OK, Vicky,' I said. 'I respect what you're telling me. I particularly respect you. But I do suppose, correctly I think, that *you* are *really* there, don't I? Aren't you?'

She reached down and touched me.

'Where's this thing rooted?' she asked. 'Is it here? Is it there?'

And then we made love; but she was very problematical. She kept stopping me and insisting that I wasn't doing it right. 'What?' 'You're not thinking about me, or about it, in the right way!' 'Well how am I . . .?' 'For a start don't even think. Or if you have to think, think like *this* . . .!' 'Eh?' 'Now you're feeling it as it should be . . .' 'Jesus, what did you do then?' 'You must merge, merge with me, be one with me . . . and when you've got it right we'll do another experiment.' 'Another experiment, Vicky?' 'It'll blow your mind. Just wait and see.'

23

. . . and we made Mr Secretarie (Walsingham) privie of the North West passage, and all charts and rutters agreed uppone in general.

Jan 24, 1583. Private Diary of John Dee

At four o'clock in the morning on Christmas Day of the year of The Commission I had a telephone call from Hugo Thayer. There was such a marked time-lag between his actual speaking and its transmission to my ears that it sounded as though he were addressing me from another planet — as though he were speaking through a narrow tube, a channel, infinitely precious, spanning an enormous distance. And that of course is precisely how it was.

'Wake up Rob Clare!' the lunatic shouted. 'Wake up from the dead! It's Who Goes There!'

'Hugo!' I yelled back, panic-stricken and yet still asleep so that I felt as though I was backwards tumbling in night-black space, 'Have you gone bonkers again? Are you round the twist?'

'Listen,' he shouted, 'listen to me! It's just come to me, at last! Bartholomew's little Indian was a gnostic voyager, d'you see? And spies, spies are all around us. And do you know what it is about spies, Rob Clare?'

'Tell me about spies,' I yelled down the phone. 'Put me in the picture!'

'Spies,' he shouted a second later, 'are the fallen version of the gnostic spirit in all of us, seeking its passage outward and upward to God. Did you know that Blake was a gnostic?'

'Blake?' I was really befuddled. 'Yes,' I mumbled, half-asleep, 'yes I suppose Blake escaped . . .'

And the lagging roar came distantly, 'William, you Wally! Not George!'

Of course, of course; he meant William Blake, the English poet and visionary. And I had been thinking of the notorious spy George Blake, who escaped from a British prison in the sixties. And now he was yelling to me, booming down the phone, 'Gates and passwords. Shadowy figures creeping past the watchtowers. Finding ways in, finding ways out,

345

smuggling precious insights. Yes, spies are the gnostics of the material world.

> *I give you the end of a golden string*
> *Only wind it into a ball,*
> *It will lead you in at Heaven's gate,*
> *Built in Jerusalem's wall.*

'You see, Rob Clare? Even Yeats thought that Blake had made it all up! But he hadn't, you know. William Blake was an eighteenth-century English gnostic.'

EPILOGUE

'Existence is a synthesis of the infinite and the finite.' But, says
Kierkegaard, this synthesis is the very opposite of a true identity and
out of this fact despair is born. 'Despair is the expression of the
relation of separation in this synthesis.' What's to be done, then?
Why, you must "put on your red shoes and dance," say I. For the
dance is the union of opposites in the One.'

Hugo Thayer, *The Subject's Documentary*

And so to the last and most remarkable of this my litany of illuminations.

If Nolton was to be believed, the Americans had said that my father
was in Heaven, and they had referred thereby not to that place which
Jesus intended, but to the fallen version — that camp at Ludwigslust where
Jews were starved and beaten, terrorized, tormented and shot; and Nolton
had forewarned me, insisting that the Americans had no significant
information to impart to me.

As Nolton had predicted, I heard from the Americans in February of
the following year. We met in a luxurious hotel suite in London. They
were three persons; a female in her fifties with a calm kind face, and a man
in his middle to late twenties were clearly the scientists; the third person,
who looked about sixty, had the self-confidence of a self-made man and a
slack but not wholly forgotten military bearing. He was very amicable.
The woman, whose manner was quiet, winsome, and thoroughly professional, did not introduce him to me, sufficing merely to indicate him to
me delicately, with a deferential inclination of the head and a quick,
intelligent, sideways glance at me that was both proud and apologetic. She
seemed to imply that he was there purely to observe; and certainly he sat quite
still, and was relaxed and silent until eventually I addressed him myself. The
other man, the youthful scientist, was balding, over-energetic and machine-
oriented. He wore big square-framed glasses like a console windscreen.
During our talks he twice got up and went to play a video machine.

'Science, Mr Clare,' she was saying, 'is the only way we're ever going
to find out about our human destiny. Who we are, what we are and what
the future holds for us. Only science can supply the answers. We know
you're sympathetic to this kind of approach.'

347

'Are you friends of Mr Munker?'

'Munker?'

'Do you know Dennis Jackson?'

'Sure,' said the younger man. 'We heard of Jackson. The Princeton logician, right? Works on mental states.'

'No, not that one.'

'Is that a problem?'

'No,' I said, 'it's no problem.'

'In the observational field,' said the woman, 'the dancers dance to their music. But we've discovered that in the closed system of the experimental chamber, which is very tightly controlled, we have something truly novel happening. We have an input of energy which is accounted for: I refer to the music which we transmit to each individual subject, the lighting and heating of the chamber, and the physical condition of each of the dancers. When we're dealing with people we calculate energy in terms of mass, Mr Clare. I'm sure you know that already. But we're finding an additional, secondary input of energy which is functionally related to the observed system.'

'What?'

'There is energy being *created* in the chamber. This is a decrease in entropy in a closed system, Mr Clare. Now a –'

'Sure! A decrease in entropy you never find in a closed system. Never.'

'We are forced to conclude that there is an energy input which we haven't been able to isolate or identify. The only possible channel of this energy input has got to be –'

'The mind,' her colleague cut in. His face gleamed with energy.

'That is to say, the mental experiences of the dancers are energizing the environment in a way that works like a step-up transformer. We are getting a whole lot more energy out than we put in. And the cause of it must be their thoughts, their beliefs. That is to say, their mental lives.'

'We sure want to run some tests on you, buddy.'

'We have in mind some psychophysical scaling. Nothing out of the normal range. I understand you have a degree in psychology, Mr Clare.'

'That's right, yes.'

'It seems that we are talking about a field of energy. It's something that appears to be non-localized and is capable of operating outside the normal constraints of time and space. We think you will probably have some enhanced sensitivity to this field because . . . Well, as I understand you to be aware, you were . . .'

'Yes,' I said, dully. 'My father was in Heaven.'

'Oh, there's more to it, as I'm sure . . . you see, Mr Clare, you were actually conceived there, isn't that right?'

'I was conceived in Heaven?'

'Oh! . . . you mean you didn't know?'

'Look,' I said, 'I have been instructed that your information as regards my parentage and origins may not be accurate.'

'Oh. Well, I don't rightly know . . .' She looked inquiringly at the older man, who gave a slight nod. 'That's right, Mr Clare,' she said, with more conviction. 'We can tell you with absolute assurance that you were conceived in Heaven.'

'This is really incredible!' the younger man interpolated. 'You know you're unique about that?'

'We'd like to run some tests on you, Mr Clare.'

'We're talking big bucks, here, pal.'

'In fact I can tell you that we're authorized to offer you initially 50,000 dollars.'

'50,000 dollars!'

I was staggered. But in true comic tradition I think they believed I was inclined to bargain.

'Just to get the whole thing off the ground. Sure! There'll be more!'

'Well, I . . . I should think I would be interested, certainly, but I must tell you that there are complications.'

'Let me tell you about the dancers! You want to have *big being*? Big being like a rock star? These guys have got some energy you wouldn't believe! These guys, they're like rock stars right in the middle of a mega-concert! They got charisma, they're impactful! You wouldn't believe. These people are stars, really.'

'You may like to know, Mr Clare, that our subjects show enhanced positive affect and score very highly on social orientation tests. Indeed they are beings of a very highly developed moral awareness.'

'Man, you got to see this!'

'It seems that they have an enhanced capacity for . . . well, I guess it's *agape*. Wouldn't you like to be part of it, Mr Clare?'

'You got to join us, you know that? We're the future of mankind.'

'I'd like to, I really would . . . I think. But you'll have to square it . . .'

'Square it?'

'You'll have to come to some sort of arrangement, I mean an agreement with . . .'

'An agent? Sure, we'll talk to the agent.'

'Agent? I . . .'

'You got an agent or something? A manager?'

'No, no. I mean with the security people over here. The British Security people. They've got the last say.'

349

'Hey, you don't have to worry about that! They'll come round. Once we show them you joined us. Sure.'

'No I ... there's a lot that hangs on it. You see, I've made a commitment, really.'

'Hey! I don't believe this! This isn't happening! You're saying you're gonna put your own national and patriotic considerations before this great leap forward for mankind? Did I understand you right?'

'It's a question of honour too,' I said.

'Honour, Mr Clare?'

'Sheeese. Over here's like middle ages! Gimme California.'

'You stole it in the first place. From the Germans. It's a German development.'

'Hey! The States just *is* Europe! *And* the whole world. But not for fifty years yet. You come over to the States you'll be working with Europeans all the time.'

'But I believe,' I said, 'I believe in the Europeans.'

'The Europeans, they'll never get it together, pal. I got to tell you that.'

'Perhaps that's only because our best people go over to you.'

'So it stands to reason! We're the future of mankind!'

'No,' I said, 'No. I'm sorry. I'm not convinced that you *are* the future of mankind. I can't help you, I'm afraid. Not at the moment.'

They looked at me in their different ways; the young male scientist was thrusting in his insistence, provocatively self-assertive, combative in his silence. She was weary, and I thought a little alienated. The older man smoothed his jacket and studied the wall.

I said, conclusively, 'I'll wait for the Europeans.'

The young male scientist jumped up from the table and flicked back the lapels of his very expensive blazer. 'You'll wait for ever, pal,' he said. 'G'bye.' His body was stiff with controlled infantile fury. 'G'bye pal,' he repeated, and stomped from the table. He jammed coins into a video machine and started playing something that made his face suddenly radiate skewed beams of blue and red. He stabbed at buttons and swivelled the mouse control like one possessed. His face became cool and hateful, and now and then a shadow seemed to pass over it. In the lurid glow of the animation his mouth twisted with curses.

'Mr Clare, would you just tell me one thing . . .'

'For God's sake,' I said. 'Who is that bloke?'

'He's a world-leading artificial intelligence expert. They thought you'd like him. But I guess he thinks you're holding up his career.'

'They thought I'd like him? My God . . .'

'Would you please tell me,' she said, 'I have to ask you this: did you have any strange experiences in April, 1983?'

I was instantly alert. 'What kind of experiences?'

She saw the intense interest in my face and warmed to her theme.

'Well, it was a phase of the experimentation that we were forced to abandon, but we want to start it up again. Actually, it was my particular field. *Really it was my baby.*'

'Well, as a matter of fact I did have some quite strange experiences, yes.'

'Oh you did?' She was delighted. 'Oh would you, could you please tell me about them . . .?'

I told her about my funny turns: the experiences in Paris, when I first met Bruedelmann; my dream encounter with the woman in the Volkswagen on the lonely wintry road.

'Oh my!' she said, 'this is just so exciting! This is just the most wonderful news . . .'

'But why? . . . Surely you'll tell me!'

'Oh I'm so sorry, Mr Clare. I really can't do that. But I'm going to do everything I can to get you involved in the research. We really do need you! Please don't think too badly of me, I don't wish to tantalize . . .'

The older man cleared his throat, and smiled.

'There's just one possibility,' I said, and I turned to face him where he sat, as it were enwrapped in a cloud of unimpeachable credibility . . . He looked at me with cold eyes and a polite degree of interest. 'I suppose you have a file on me,' I said.

His mouth moved in a neat, terse, equivocal act of confirmation. He smoothed one trouser leg with broad, ringless fingers.

'Know all about me, right?'

'Sure, we do,' he said, injecting a curious note of modesty into his utterance. His voice was cultured, I thought, but his sensibility was deranged.

'Then you know all about Dennis Jackson, too.'

His face had set in a front of calm rigour. The look in his eye was not at all encouraging; I had the impression that he did not want this kind of conversation to take place with the scientists present. I considered this something of an advantage.

'Get him out,' I said, 'out of his difficulties, whatever they are. Get him out and we can do business.'

'Mr Jackson,' he said, 'is a malefactor. At the time he is serving a long sentence in a South American . . . ah, penitentiary. It is the natural conclusion to his chosen career plan.' His face ticked.

'Get him out,' I said, 'tomorrow. Make him safe, give him peace, pardon him.'

'What is Jackson to you?'

'My father in this world.' I said.

'I heard you had been told that this is not the case. He's not your father, didn't you know?'

'He is my father,' I said, 'and he's not. I choose him, as of now.'

It was the woman who replied to this remark. 'But you are very *artful*, Mr Clare.'

I looked at her in amazement; suddenly something was clear to me, yet I could not explain it, or describe it, even to date. But I think my eyes twinkled, the true Thayer twinkle for the first time in my life, because her inquiring, somewhat wry, cool smile grew in warmth so that she became beautiful and perhaps even loving as I looked at her.

'Yes,' I said, slowly. 'It's *occult* artful.'

'Pardon me?' she was hooked, and terribly keen to catch what I had said.

I said loudly and clearly, 'Occult artful, yes. What you might call a form of gnosis.'

'What's that you say?' The loud hateful noise of his voice radiated from the blue-blazored creature; he had tired of his loathsome machine sport and had sauntered back to where we sat. 'No sister? Is that all you guys ever say over here?'

'Piss off you half-brained bumptious turd,' I said to him. 'You may be a genius at modelling in silicon your own ill-evolved reasoning processes but you haven't got sixpenny-worth of human beingness, the true creative, compassionate intelligence of humankind. You might as well be dead, chum.'

'I guess,' said the older man, 'I guess that's blown it. You people won't be working together, I suppose.'

The computer man was standing there, staring at me.

I said to him, 'You think that computers can model human beings just because you are yourself no more, no better than a human model of a computer. You may be the present pinnacle of material evolution but you are the despair of being, the despair of anything that anyone might reasonably call God. It is as though the world had finally created its own virulent, baleful demi-urge. I look at you, *pal*, and I weep for all mankind.'

'Is that so, pal?' said the computer man, and he was remarkably untouched by my invective. 'I'm happy to talk to you if you think you can handle a dialogue. Maybe it's me and you who really should be talking. If it's true, that is, you know something that we don't. So tell me,' he sat back and folded his stubby fingers together across the silver-plated buttons of his jacket. 'Tell me.'

'My father was in Heaven,' I said, 'and I believe I was conceived there;

and I have a friend who is all fire and creative action; and I have another who is all compassion, humanity, and art; and I have a friend who is at one with the natural forces of the natural world; and I have a friend who has spiritual illuminations, who teaches me things; and me, well I'm susceptible to things in the air. I haven't the least particle of doubt,' I said, 'that I can tell you things that you really need to hear.'

'So,' said the older man after a moment's pause, 'what exactly are your terms?'

'Co-operation,' I said, 'subject to certain conditions.'

'More conditions? My,' he said, suavely, 'you are quite the entrepreneur. You know, Mr Clare, I'm not sure that we can help you.'

I turned to the woman and said to her, 'You know, those strange things that happened to me ... I could *feel* that there was something about them, something intimate, rooted in my own life, even in the past I did not know. I have so much to tell you about those moments. *And so much more besides . . .'*

The older man raised his hand a few inches and nobody spoke at all. After a further pause he said to me, 'I think you overestimate your importance in this field.'

'If I'm worth this cosy little meeting here with all of you now,' I said, thinking fast, 'then I must be worth more than it's going to cost you to meet my demands. With all your technology and your God-almighty dollar you can do any amount of evil anywhere in the world. I'm asking you to do a little good. That's all.'

'I make no promises,' he said, speaking I thought more for her benefit than for mine, although this new, concessive intonation was as music to my ears. 'But I will raise the matter with those concerned.'

'That brings me to my next point,' I said, firmly.

They stared.

'There are people in this country, officials, who are making it difficult for me to write my book. My book is all about the things that have happened to me since . . .'

'Since Thayer came back from Berlin?' the man finished for me. I nodded.

'It will include what little I know about the Disko, and of course your good selves, and the whole Commission thing. When I've written it I want it published. At the very least,' I said, 'I want it published in America.'

'We in the States have an open society, Mr Clare. I see no immediate difficulty in this request.'

'And that brings me to my last condition,' I said, relentlessly.

353

'Ah,' he said, with malevolent sweetness of regard, 'so soon the bottom line?'

'I want you to find my father for me. My real biological father. I want to know who he was and how he came to father me. And if you can't find him in person,' I added, 'I want reliable documentation. Otherwise there's no deal.'

'Very well, Mr Clare,' the man replied. 'We hear you. We'll do what we can. But maybe the most difficult part of it is saving Jackson's ass. Why do you bother about him?'

'Because I care,' I said. 'And Jackson is the most concrete way I can show it. If he didn't exist,' I said, 'I'd have to invent him. Make sure he doesn't have any accidents, now. I want him fit, pristine, good as new.'

Upon reflection I decided that I should share this new information with my grandmother, Omschka; but it was Liselotte who answered my phone call. She told me, fearfully and in tears, that Omschka was ill and was about to go into hospital in Hamburg. Would I please come and spend some time with her? It was March, 1984, just a fortnight after my meeting with the American scientists.

And so I went to Hamburg and learned from the doctors that Omschka's condition was critical and that she could not expect to live much longer. I sat with her, my mother's mother, and watched her grow shadowy before my eyes. In her strong, kind, withered face I saw my mother, phantasmal flower of youthful womanhood; and Omschka saw in me her daughter Eva. I sat with her all day and most of the night, holding her hand. She could speak but it cost her dear, and I too, at her bedside, found words difficult. And for all my burning desire to question her I held my tongue. It was the great moment of self-discipline in my life; for my urge, nay my lust to know, took second place to love. I turned my imploring attention to the void and begged for her to live. And when I left her a day later she was already out of crisis. The doctors, who were impressed, said to me, 'The old girl's heart is strong as a horse,' and I laughed almost hysterically. When I left the hospital I took with me back to England a package which she had brought with her into hospital.

For weeks I went in fear of the telephone; but the majestic old woman survived, and three months later she was able to return to her little cottage at Westergellersen. When she was well again she rang me to say that the day I had spent with her had been my actual birthday. It was a strange coincidence, and a revelation; or perhaps it was only Omschka's wishful thinking. Henceforth, however, I shall celebrate my birthday three days earlier than I have done in the past.

The package she had given me contained about twenty school exercise-books from the years of the nineteen-twenties and thirties. They had belonged to my mother, and spanned much of her school career; before my eyes I saw the painstaking handwriting of a child changing to that of a woman, and I looked for my mother there. I studied the loops, the fullness of the vowels, the high-minded consonants of her hand. When her schooldays ended she put away her exercise-books; but some years later she took one from a trunk and started to write a diary. It is the most moving testimony of a mother, for she turned to pen and paper when she came away from Heaven and learned that she had conceived there. And the embryo she was carrying in her womb was Robert Mark Clare. In her schoolbook turned diary I read against every entry that follows from that time the following words, repeatedly written, like a prayer:

We must hope Michael. We must hope always. As long as we live we must hope. He will be a boy and we will call him Robert. He will bring us together again. I know it. I know it.

The last entry of the diary, dated February 12th, 1945, reads:

How I have yearned for this news! I will see you again soon, my husband. Tomorrow I set out. Be still my child and walk with me through the woods to Ludwigslust. Do you see, my dearest love? Already he draws us together. Our still to be born dear son.

In July of that year I received a further communication from the Americans. They notified me that they had traced my father, that he was alive and well and living in a sub-monastic community in north-west Scotland. He was aware of my existence, they assured me, and expected a visit from me as soon as I cared to arrange it. They supplied a full list of biographical details: my father had been a Russian Jew, born in St Petersburg in 1899. His father had been a jewel-smith, his mother an English governess. So, I said to myself, not so much an Indian as a Jew — and Grandpapa was a Jew who made art of jewels. Indeed, to me it was like rubies, such knowledge. When my father was a little boy the family left Russia and emigrated to the United States of America. In 1925 my father had travelled to Germany and a few years later had fallen foul of the turbulent political situation and had been imprisoned on charges of anarchism. Once Hitler had acquired power, however, his prospective discharge from prison was annulled and his term was indefinitely prolonged. Should I have been suspicious, I ask the reader, that they had sent me a biography of the father I was at last about to meet? In the event it was a meeting which took six weeks to arrange, in a somewhat problematic exchange of letters with those who seemed to be in authority in the sub-monastic community in question.

On the first of September I took the overnight train to Edinburgh, and thence I pressed on in a hired car. The cold blue waters of Loch Lomond were choppy in the golden light and the terse white crests of waves flickered against the cruel blue background. All along the wavering shoreline the differing shades of green were fading to russet and amber. I drove fast when expectation overtook me, and I stopped frequently to let the scenery work its calming spell. At four o'clock precisely I arrived at the community house in Achiltibue.

It was a forbidding Victorian mansion set in thirty or forty acres of gently rolling land. I drove soberly up the long drive and passed men and women working the vegetable plots to my right and left. Long lanes of raspberry trees and strawberry plantations stretched away to either side of the road and the fruit trees in the orchards were crazily decorated with ladders. Here and there among the litter of bright red apples and golden pears stood patient home-made wooden wheelbarrows. Pickers moved intently among the trees.

A wide-open doorway led into a bleak, thinly carpeted hall. As I entered, a man came down the stairs towards me; there were several pieces of pine tucked under his left arm, and balanced on his right shoulder was a long heavy plank. I hesitated to bother such an emburdened individual and stood to one side to let him pass, but he stopped in front of me and asked me if I was all right. If I hadn't been so tense at the prospect of meeting my father I would have chuckled at the joke.

'I have come to . . . see . . . a man called . . .'

'Second floor, turn left and it's the last door on the right.' He looked like a marine but for his eyes, which were lustrous and kind.

'Thanks,' I said. 'Thanks a lot.' And then, because I was nervous, perhaps, and not entirely in control of my tongue, I said to him, 'Er, excuse me, have you ever been in the army, by any chance?'

'Active service,' he said, 'in Vietnam.'

Feeling as timid as a mouse I strode up the stairs to knock at my father's door. It was opened to me by a bulky male who had the most strikingly brilliant big round eyes. My immediate impression of him was of his good health. He looked at me inquiringly but did not speak so I too kept silent and stepped into the room. He indicated to me that I should remove my shoes, which he took from me and placed in a box by the door. It contained a few assorted pairs of working boots and some wooden clogs. I examined the man's clothes: he wore a cheap, baggy, unfashionable pair of jeans and a loose, smelly woollen pullover. On his feet he had thick, coarse socks with fibres waving in the air. There were two simple armchairs in the room.

'Are you Michael?' I asked. He had such kindness in his face; I was inclined to think he was my father. And there was something about him which suggested that he was considerably older than he looked.

'Please wait,' he said, and his voice was surprisingly quiet and soft. He opened an inner door and stepped out of the room, pulling the door to behind him. A moment later he returned, smiling from ear to ear.

'Please go in now,' he said.

It didn't strike me, for some reason, that he wasn't the man I wished to see, so I stood there in the middle of the room with a silly little smile on my face. I had the absurd notion that he was testing me. And I suddenly felt the compulsion to explain to him that there was some mistake . . . it was all very cloudy. With a curiously introspective insouciance he sat down in his chair and closed his eyes. After a moment I opened the connecting door and went through.

A very old man sat quietly on the floor. And this man, too, had remarkable eyes, brown and full of expression. His hair was snow-white and his skin seemed to be made of paper. But he had about him a quality of singular solidity and firmness, and he seemed to generate a considerable degree of heat for as I approached him I actually detected a rise in temperature.

'Won't you please sit with me,' he said. He spoke very quietly, almost without moving his lips; but his words seemed to resonate within me as though it was myself I was hearing, speaking in a dream.

I sat down on the floor and sorted out my limbs a little; and as I sat there with him, about three feet off, I became increasingly self-conscious so that I grew hot and bothered and began to redden.

'You worry so much,' he said. Again I wondered at his preternaturally clear voice. 'Bill said you came *squawking* up the stairs . . .'

'Because I don't know who I am.'

I was astonished at the raw quickness of my own response.

'There is nothing to worry about,' he said. This utterance had such a ring of truth that I thrilled to hear it. 'Do you know who I am?'

I let out a deep breath, and asked him if he was Michael. I stammered as I spoke.

'Yes, I am,' he said. 'And you are my son, Robert.' He extended his arms a little and his hands came towards me in a sort of embrace. I grasped at them in eager clumsy fashion and found instead that his hands were holding mine; they were very warm, and strangely communicative.

'Shall we drink some tea together?'

'Yes,' I said. 'That would be very nice.'

My meeting with Jackson had given me much-needed practice in singular meetings, especially with fathers I had never met in all my forty years of life. I was determined not to fall into the recriminatory state of mind that Jackson had so criticized. It was unfortunate that the thing I most wanted to know then was why he, Michael, had never tried to find me. Any doubt that he might not be my father had vanished from my mind.

'If you could know everything about your life at this moment,' he said, and I listened raptly, 'you wouldn't understand it. Understanding is one with time, but its true object is the past. Our feelings and ideas are bound in a wheel of time. What you cannot understand you cannot know the value of. Too many questions will only unsettle you.'

There was a smile upon his face such as I have never before or since encountered. It expressed unfathomable inner warmth.

For a while I sat very still and thought about what he had said. Presently he tapped sharply on the floorboards and a moment later the door opened behind me.

'Some tea?' a voice asked my father.

'Thank you, Bill,' he replied. And then he turned to me again and gave me his full attention. It was uncanny how he seemed to tune in to my thoughts.

'Is your grandmother still alive?'

'Yes,' I said, and I felt as though I had entered a new element, one which bore me up. 'She's alive and well and living in Westergellersen still.'

'I was born in the summer of 1899. Your mother was nineteen years old when we married. It was 1937. They made a bureaucratic error and let me out of prison by mistake. Without it we might never have married.'

He paused, and looked carefully into my face. 'I see your mother in your face,' he said. 'I hear her in your voice, and her touch is in your hands.'

'I never thought about her,' I said, 'before I met Omschka.'

'You are entirely possessed by her.'

'Is that a bad thing?'

'Only because we often run away from what possesses us. In life we should walk, not run.'

'Actually, Omschka told me that you had spent time . . . imprisoned. During the war years, I mean.'

'It was not a prison. I was in a camp for scientific research.' He smiled broadly. 'They called it Heaven.'

'Who called it Heaven, Father?'

'The guards, the men and women who lived and worked there.'

'Was it the camp at Ludwigslust?'

'Yes.'

'Were you a subject in that project? The Eigenmusikswesen?'

'Yes.'

'I learned about it from one of the scientists who was involved in the research.'

'Oh?' My father seemed very interested; and yet I could feel the effort it cost him, to attend to my prattle. 'What was his name?'

'Ernst Schwirrer.'

'Oh yes, I remember him quite well. A very pompous man. I remember he had no manners.'

'Father, did you . . . I mean, were you one of the people who . . . who, danced?'

There was a pause and I noticed that he was studying his hands, which were folded now in his lap. He was wearing a monkish-type habit, and as he sat there on the floor before me he seemed the very incarnation of the Buddha.

'Yes,' he said at last. 'I danced in Heaven. They called me the Original Dancer.'

I was dumbfounded. A deep silence descended on us. His smile grew broader as he watched me. He seemed to grow more content with it, so that to talk about it to me was no longer a burden for him, no longer an imposition. I listened with my heart.

'I would like you to imagine what it means,' he said. 'Please try. You see, I was a full-grown man and I used to dance before the SS and the dignitaries of the Party. Many of them wept. Yes. The SS men wept when we danced. But their faces were full of fear. Can you imagine it? Like children on the dangerous rides at the fair!' He laughed aloud. And I was completely unable to laugh with him; but I tried to picture them, the satanic, uniformed, misguided, weeping onlookers.

'How serious you are,' he said, and there was in his voice an intensely musical quality.

'But . . .' I struggled hard to find the right words, 'didn't it make you . . . well, after they'd played the Eigenmusikswesen to you a few times, didn't you . . . well, go all funny?'

'Here we call it *satori*.'

359

'Satori?'

'Enlightenment. Many were enlightened. Some danced only seven times at most. But you see,' he was smiling again, and his exuberance filled the room, 'I held out against it. I danced a hundred times.'

'Held out? Why?'

'They shot all those who danced out of their hands. I resolved to live. I had promised to live so that one day I would see your mother again.'

There was a quiet knocking at the door. Bill bore a tray into the room: a small teapot and a couple of tiny cups.

'One day in spring they took us away to America. At first we thought it was the SS who had come for us. But they were English soldiers. In America it all continued as before. The same faces, the same names, always the same people wanted to study us. They offered us large sums of money to continue with the research but I wanted to get away from it, and from them, from all the Germans. I came back to Europe and learned that Eva had died. And Erna too had died in a bombing raid on a train. Poor Omschka. How she suffered in her life. In the first great war she lost her husband, and in the second she lost her daughters. I came to live up here.'

'Why did you go to Germany in the first place? I mean, you could have stayed in America . . .'

'I wished to participate in the great political events of the time. I had principles, I was a socialist and anarchist. There was no room for such things in America then. The Nazis did not like my beliefs and they sent me to a labour camp. In 1939 I was sent to the research station at Ludwigslust. I was three years in prison and eleven in the camps.'

Then I said to him, before I could stop myself, 'Father, all my life . . . I have longed to meet you. Couldn't you have tried to find me?'

He passed a small cup to me. It was full of tea.

'I was always with you. I am part of you. Haven't you found me now?'

With trembling hand I raised his cup to my lips.

'When the war ended I was a stranger to myself, and to all men and women. Everywhere the war had left its mark. Every person, every child, every growing thing bore its imprint. I could not live in that world. I who had danced a hundred times in Heaven . . . I was as a child. They wouldn't have permitted me to raise you. They thought I was mad. I came to this house and devoted myself to a tranquil, simple life.'

'She gave birth to me all alone. In a snow-filled wood. Why did she have to do that?'

'She walked through the woods to visit me at Ludwigslust. In the five

360

years that I spent there she came to see me three times. She came when they permitted her to. She had to come, Robert. Each time was always for the last time. Can you understand how it was for her? For them it was an act of kindness. They wanted to thank me.'

'The scientists?'

'The administrators. I was a very good experimental subject.'

'Did she *walk* all the way from Westergellersen to Ludwigslust?'

'It was war-time. There was no fuel for vehicles. She had no horse, no donkey to ride on. She couldn't ride a bicycle in her condition.'

'Omschka said she was a wonderful woman.'

'She was a person of great courage and great inner strength. She was high-minded, gentle and kind. When I looked into her eyes I learned something about what it is to love. She was filled with love for all living things. I know I will meet her again.'

We sat together and sipped tea. The house was still and silent about us. It was just as I had hoped. I had come home to a quietness, to . . .

'Try to laugh a little at all that your life is,' he said. 'It is not right to be so serious. I am your father and I fought in the First World War. For six months I lived in the trenches in Belgium and there I lost my youth. And the Second World War I spent learning to dance at Ludwigslust. And that is where you were conceived. You see, my son, you were conceived in Heaven.'

'Yes,' I said, 'that's what the Americans said.'

'What is this place where you live now?'

'It is not a monastery, but it is a house of spiritual retreat. There are thirty-nine of us: seventeen men and twenty-two women. We attend to the good. We work in peace.

'Is it Buddhist? Christian?'

'There are Sufis here, too. Each finds his own way. It is our common aim to live pure, wholesome lives.'

I told my father about Dennis Jackson; I told him that it was Jackson, in a Waffen-SS uniform, who had liberated Heaven in April, 1945. My father seemed to remember him. And I asked him if he had ever heard of an Austrian by the name of Schorsch Bruedelmann. I was so keen to share my story with him that I forgot how tiresome it must be for him; he didn't know the individuals involved, he had no inkling of my own emotional weather in the ambit of The Commission. He laughed at my questions, and in a very mild tone of voice he told me that he seldom read the papers and hadn't watched television for seventeen years.

'There's one other person who helped me find you,' I said. 'His name is Hugo Thayer. But actually, the person who helped me most, I suppose, is a woman called Herta Geschwisterheim.'

I realized that I was boring him. He was looking at me quite intently but he wasn't interested in what I was saying.

I said, quickly, 'I would never have found you if Jackson hadn't thought that I was his son. And there was a painting, commissioned in the sixteenth century, which has some kind of connection with Disko 39. You know, that's the name . . .'

'Yes, I know.'

'It brought us together, that painting . . . but of course, it isn't really a painting at all.' I spoke hurriedly, breathlessly. I was under some inner compulsion to strike a recognition in him. I needed to take away with me a revelation, a gift of wisdom from my father. 'It was created by a man who worked as a spy for the English government about four hundred years ago. In Queen Elizabeth's reign.'

'There is always a story,' he said. He seemed to glow with joy. He was the most exuberant person I had ever met. My father.

'Story? I don't understand . . .'

'The story you have told me is very involved. But really, it's nothing but the circumstances of our reunion. The painting, the man Jackson, these other people you mentioned. They are merely the form of the thing.'

'But there's really something special about this painting, Father.'

'Ah.' He had spoken so quietly it was almost a sigh. Then he closed his eyes. After a couple of moments I decided to continue, hoping that he was listening.

'There are all sorts of people trying to find out the meaning of this painting. They want to decode it, Father, but actually there's nothing to decode.' I was babbling like an infant, but I could not stop myself. It was pitiful; and now, as I look back, I am touched by it. My father, I remember, had completely lost interest; I hastened to change the subject.

'How do you live here, Father? I mean, what do you do?'

'I walk in the fields of light, Robert.'

The fields of light. It was a phrase which had come to haunt me; it was the phrase that Schwirrer had used to describe the experimental psychosis; it was the phrase that Bartholomew had coined, that Henricus Wykzo had repeated, all those years ago.

I asked, tentatively, 'What are they like, Father, the fields of light?'

'I cannot tell you, Robert. Really. It's impossible to say.'

*

'Could I have a photo of you?'

He laughed delightfully. 'There are no photographs of me.' He made it sound as though such a thing was a logical impossibility. I found myself chuckling with him.

'Not even a passport photo?' I said, and now it seemed hilarious.

'I don't even have a passport,' he replied. 'Where is there to travel to? Everything is here. Now.'

We talked for a few minutes more and then he seemed to grow faint in my presence. It was a most curious sensation; I had the distinct impression that his voice grew fainter as I listened to him, and the clear definition of his form seemed to blur before my eyes. But these impressions were not strictly physical – perhaps if I had held up a mirror to him and recorded his voice on a tape there would have been no evidence of this withdrawal. However, I could not mistake his communication; it was time for me to go.

I said to him, 'I wish I could have you near me. I could visit you and hear your voice. I could draw strength from your experience, from your insights. You are just as I have always dreamed. You are gentle, and strong, and wise.'

'Not so gentle,' he said, 'not so wise.' He smiled. 'But you may come and visit me again if you wish.'

'I'll certainly come again. I feel that I really need to see you.'

'That may be true at the moment. But soon you will no longer need to visit me. And what a good thing that is.'

He seemed to be in a state of constant, unmitigated delight.

'Are you always as happy as this?' I asked him as I got to my feet.

'What is always?' he asked.

Then I embraced him and left his room. As I walked to my car I thought I heard a nightingale singing in the fruit trees.

But I did not leave without the revelation I had hoped for. As I climbed into the car Bill came running down the drive towards me. 'Please come back, Mr Clare. Michael has remembered something.'

He was shuffling about with his eyes closed. I heard little sounds coming from him, as though he was humming a tune. And with his hands and feet he was making uncanny, minimal movements. Suddenly a strange harmonious fullness was in the air. His face was both familiar and yet terrifying. And then he started humming, incredibly loudly, and my hair stood on end; it was the Eigenmusikswesen.

I crouched down on the floor and stared. When at last he spoke it seemed to me that his voice came directly from within myself; and yet it seemed to resonate around the room, like a bell tolling.

363

'When I danced for them I felt a strange power in me. It grew each time. We all felt it. When we danced together we saw that everything melted away. The walls swayed like flimsy screens and started to melt away. Inside me too, everything dissolved and I started to see. I had a vision. It came and went but it was always the same. Do you hear me, Robert?'

'Yes, Father, I'm listening.'

'I saw a creature coiled in a tree. It was like a snake, or a dragon. And somewhere nearby there was a woman. Her presence was everywhere but I could not see her. I could not see her but I knew her. I seemed to walk towards her. I came closer and closer to the tree and to the creature that was coiled in its branches . . .'

'Yes?'

'She was calling to me. Meech-a-el.'

Tears came into my eyes in a sudden flood, blinding me.

'She spoke to me. She was telling me something. It seemed to take a long, long time to tell it but I knew it was very simple. But I couldn't understand it. I longed to know what she said to me . . . I never understood her, Robert. I must tell you, that woman . . . it was Eva.'

He stood stock-still in the middle of the room and his eyes opened.

'Robert,' he said. 'Robert, my son, I didn't want you to be born. I didn't want you to be conceived there. Not in that place. I knew it would be with you for ever. You will never be free of it. Forgive me. I did it for Eva.'

'But I'm glad, Father!' I shouted. 'I'm truly glad I was born!'

'Are you?' he said. 'Are you really? Perhaps it was this she was trying to tell me.'

He sat down on the floor and rested his hands on the ground beside him.

'There was a man in Heaven,' he said, 'I have remembered him again. He was from Vienna, a restorer of paintings. He said he could send messages over great distances when he was dancing. Many of them said they could do it. They said they could change things by thought alone, when they were dancing together . . . dancing.'

'What was his name, Father? Was it . . .' I racked my brain to remember the name of Georges Bruedelmann's master, but I could not recall it. 'What happened to him? Do you know?'

'They shot him, the day before the liberation.'

'Father, before I go again, there's something I must ask you. It's about the hair-clasp, remember? The hair-clasp that you gave Eva. Did your father make it? It's really important to me.'

'I can't, Robert,' he said, and he sounded very tired. 'I want you to go now.'

'All right, I'll go, Father. But you do remember it, don't you?'

And as I looked at him then, sitting on the floor with his face averted, a terrible doubt passed through my mind. He felt it too, for he looked up at me, and his eyes were veiled.

'I came up here,' I started . . .

'You wished to meet your father. I know this.'

'But you *are* my father,' I said, making a rhetorical question out of an abyss of suddenly mounting dread.

'Without me,' he said, slowly, breathing heavily between words, 'your mother would not have been inseminated.'

What happened in that moment? Why had everything changed suddenly? Was he a man grown so spiritual in his perceptions and in his speech, so utterly detached from the world that he must talk like this to me of the moment of my own conception, and more particularly of his own participation in that act? Was it the dance, the Eigenmusik, that had wrought this ominous change in him?

'I don't understand what you mean . . .' I said, and heard myself speaking in sorrowful, grave tones, as if I had recognized something unbearably sad, or repugnant to all that I hoped and believed.

'We were in the camp,' he said, 'at Ludwigslust. It was nothing that you could ever imagine. It was not like the concentration camps, where evil was supreme. It was a place of compromise. It was very bad, and it had an atmosphere of . . . of happiness, of perverse delight. People were suffering in that place, starving, undergoing experimentation, receiving electric shocks, people were shot, and still there was something like happiness. Nearly all of us felt it.'

'Yes,' I said, 'I know. I know about the place from Schwirrer. And from my mother's diary. Did you know she kept a diary? She loved you so much . . .' And then I shut up, for he hadn't answered my question.

'Robert,' he said, and his voice had changed from something light and joyous to a dark heaviness that was close to despair. 'Robert,' he repeated, 'it is a lie. I have lied to you. They wanted me to do it. I wanted to do it. But I went too far and now I see that it is impossible. It is impossible and wrong.'

'Why do you speak like this? Why, Father? We were so happy a moment ago.'

'He said, 'We were *doppelgaenger*.' It was little more than a whisper. I clutched at my face; I didn't want to hear this. 'Once I saw his face, among a crowd of experimental subjects, and I knew at once what I should do in order to become a free man after the war. Because I wanted to escape my punishment I stole your father's identity. In the course of time I recreated him as myself. On paper at least. I created myself in his image. I kept him alive, and when the time came I starved myself and then . . . and then I arranged for them to kill him. You see your father's face before you, Mr Clare. But I am not him. He is not me.'

'No,' I said, 'no, don't do this. Don't deny that you are him. They assured me that you are my father. I don't resent the years of silence. Please don't be embarrassed. Please don't reject me. I am your son, Father. Don't deny me now.' My words came in a rush, my cheeks were hot, my eyes were misty with tears. He was unmoved.

'Your mother was Eva, such a beautiful woman. A truly beautiful person.'

'Yes,' I said eagerly. 'Yes it's true.'

'Your father and I, we had an understanding. I was chief scientist, he was an experimental subject. He was glad to help me. He was happy about it. I am not your father, Mr Clare, but I gave you life. He did not want you to be born. He said it would be with you for ever.'

A sickening pain swept through me and I felt the burn of acid in my throat. I didn't know whether to kill him, or hug him. My senses swam.

'I am deeply sorry to disappoint you,' he murmured. And now, more proudly, he declared, 'I am the one who made your existence possible. Without me you could not have existed. You see, I am a sort of father, Mr Clare. You are a sort of son.'

'Why do you keep saying it?' I started up, and suddenly I felt I could have strangled him, this poor, pale, kindly old man, sitting there calmly, stoically on the floor.

'I am an old man,' he said. 'Please respect the courage and good will which I show you now. I did not have to tell you. I promised your father that if I ever met you I would tell you about the tree, about the creature in the tree and the woman calling. But I could have continued to lie to you.'

'I'm sorry,' I said. 'I will control myself, I promise. Please tell me, everything. Everything.'

'Your father was one of the special subjects. Only a very few did not suffer the experimental psychosis. Only those few special subjects did not begin to love the scientists, the experimenters. We examined these persons with very great attention. I had long conversations with your father. He and I understood that we had together achieved something of very great importance. He had no bitterness towards us. He said we had done terrible things, unpardonable things, but he did not judge us. I arranged for him to see his wife; it was an understanding we had, do you see? I took a great risk in this situation. Your father was a Jew, you understand, and I made it possible for his wife to visit him conjugally. Through the observation window I saw how they embraced. When she left him we examined her. Her egg had been fertilized. We knew a child had been conceived. Without my personal intervention, Mr Clare, your mother would never have been inseminated. And you would never have come into the world.'

I staggered to my feet and found my way to the window. 'This is unspeakably repugnant to me. It is a disgusting, horrific . . .' I gagged into my handkerchief. How could they do this to me, I was thinking, those bastards? Why? Why?

'You have me to thank,' he said, quietly and firmly, 'you have me to thank that you exist.'

'Schwirrer told me,' I said, 'that some of the scientists were very influential. He mentioned names . . .' I was struggling to remember what Schwirrer had told me; it was so important now. And for some unaccountable reason I found myself, in that moment, thinking of Hugo Thayer.

'My name is Schaffer,' he said.

'Schaffer!' I almost shouted it. 'Yes, that's a name he mentioned.'

'I am Cosimo Schaffer,' he said.

'What's that? *Cosimo?* Where in God's name did you get a name like that?'

'My father was a student of the Renaissance. He loved its art, its humanistic ideas. He wrote learned articles in journals. He was creative and humane. He was an intellectual. He called me Cosimo to celebrate his love for mankind, and his reverence for God, and for God-in-man. But I never knew him. He died in the First World War. At the battle you call Passchendaele.'

'Cosimo Schaffer,' I said, deep in horror and yet filled with wonder. 'It means "creator of the cosmos", it means "creator of the world".'

'Yes,' he said quietly. 'That is so.'

'You are a true European,' he said to me, as I was preparing to leave. 'Your father was a Jew, a Russian, and yet he was drawn to the German experience. Your paternal grandmother was English. Your mother was pure German. You were raised in England. You see, I know all about you. It is for you to build the future. It is for you to break down the barriers between left and right, between East and West, between one ideology and the other. Only the Europeans can do this now. It is for you to do these things. Just as Germany must build the bridge between East and West, out of its own division, so you, out of your own division, must unify and make whole. And not just the divisions within the world must be made one by such as you.

As I went down the path towards the car I was muttering to myself like one distracted ... bastards ... nothing but nothing is bloody real, all fraudsters and trickery, tawdry bloody world ... and as I passed the rows of fruit trees on my left, I suppose I should have guessed, of course ... a voice hailed me from the thick of an apple tree's boughs and foliage. I looked about, took a few paces one way, a few the next. 'Hello?' I called out, quietly, unsure.

Above me, in the apple tree, the face of Hugo Thayer subjected me to otherworldly scrutiny. But he was fatter now, redder in the face, and altogether more at peace with the world than he had been on the film.

'Still pattering and muttering, muttering and pattering about?' he asked, in his fine studied, Oxford voice.

'You! But how do you know it's *me*?'

'Because all of us are me, he said.

'I don't think you should be here, Hugo. Or maybe you should ... this place is not as it appears. There are people here who are not what they appear to be.'

'But of course,' he replied, 'for what is not what it does not appear to be? Who is not so? That in itself is not the interesting thing; what interests me is the difference between the two.'

'There's an old bloke in there,' I said, and suddenly I did not know whether to laugh or cry — Hugo Thayer's intense personal energy seemed to push my feelings to pitch. I felt light-headed and heavy-hearted; hilarity buoyed me up, and a sharp acid ache began in my vitals. 'He's supposed to be my father.' I groaned aloud. I sank down on to fat, wet earth. 'Not my dad, Hugo, just a mean old Nazi turned holy man and sage. Hiding out here, in this place, with you lot.'

'Not hiding, but seeking,' said Hugo Thayer, his face framed in a laurel of apple leaves. 'He's probably looking for his dad. Just like you, Rob Clare. Everybody is.' He smiled, and his head shook delicately, almost imperceptibly, like a leaf atremble.

'It's all right for you,' I said. 'You've got it all sewn up.'

'There you go,' said Hugo Thayer, 'pattering and muttering about. What matter to you the missing pattern? Pattern the matter for yourself, Rob Clare. Isn't that what Jackson told you?'

'But you've got it all sewn up.' I repeated, more strident now. 'It's easy for you. You just tell yourself stories and wait for them to come true.'

'But that's precisely the secret of it,' said Hugo Thayer. 'We have to make new patterns. We have to tell ourselves stories and help them come true. Don't you know it's time?' He waved his hand at the house. 'In there,' he continued, 'is a world-famous physicist — he's hiding out too. He says we're all completely free. So free it's frightening. I believe him too.'

He had such conviction then, such peace and clarity. I smelt the damp cool earth under me; its rich, fat vapours filled my head. I clutched at tufts of grass. Again hilarity swept over me, I laughed like a poisoned thing.

'The painting is energy,' said Hugo, seemingly oblivious to my condition. 'It is the source of power. It is mind in the world . . . Will you please listen to me?'

'I'm listening,' I said. 'You're mad, Hugo Thayer.' There, I thought to myself, I've said it now.

'That's what we're moving towards,' he continued. 'The next century will discover the mind as a new source of energy in the world. No wonder they're all so keen on the painting, those people . . . but it'll still be only the secular version, because the true spirit is universal, undivided, unimpoverishable and undiminishable, endlessly returning to God. It's in me, and it's in you. It's in your old Nazi, who isn't your dad, it's in Jackson, in Georges Bruedelmann . . . all, all. All. It is everything that ever was, or can be, or will be, forever and always. Amen. But the painting is the more secular version, just one escape from the determinism of matter, the escape from heavy weight, from force. But it is only the secular version, Rob Clare.'

'They've conned me,' I said, and now that I was growing more self-possessed I felt rancorous towards them.

'It's funny you know,' said Hugo, 'that physicist . . . he says we're free — but he can't yet see how free we are because he hasn't got a paradigm. Don't you think it's beautiful,' he said, 'that in order to see that we are free, we have to be trapped in a paradigm? And then there's no freedom to behold. The paradox is the paradigm, that's our time for you.'

'You don't understand, Hugo. The Americans are doing research on the powers of the mind. Bruedelmann's master was at Ludwigslust. He transmitted his vision of it to the painting, by some kind of thought transmission. That's why Bruedelmann felt his presence in the pigment on the canvas.'

'And that's why I saw,' said Hugo Thayer, '. . . what I saw in the painting.'

'What did you see, Hugo? Tell me.'

'I saw a man dancing,' he said, 'and it was Jesus – my love, my friend, my family of mankind.'

And now he was coming down from where he sat among round ripe glistening apples; he was ungainly though, uncoiling from the branch and slithering down the trunk. Suddenly I was afraid.

'A pattern,' he was saying. 'That's what you want, Rob Clare. But can't you see that you are free? You can make your own pattern, make your own pattern in eternity. I can tell you right now, you don't need a father. Absolutely no. No father for you. No father for me. Not here, not now. No sir.'

And then he did it again, that dance of his, and he recited the words that the gnostic Jesus is said to have spoken to his disciples in the Garden of Gethsemane. And I took one hand and tried to join in with him; but it was futile.

I said despairingly, 'Hugo, I can't bloody dance!'

'Fusion of mind and matter, Rob Clare, that's what you've got to achieve. That's why you've got to learn the dance. Then you can change the world.'

My breathing was stertorous; my feet seemed set in concrete at odd angles; my skin itched; I was sweating like a man in fever. 'Hugo, let's stop now, I've got to ask your advice . . .' but he would keep dancing and so I started up again, abashed and clumsy. I noticed, in the corner of my eye, some half a dozen people in the orchard about us, slowly moving towards us, speculatively eyeing us. 'Hugo,' I said, 'they're connected, you know, Bartholomew's Commission and Disko 39 . . .'

'They think they've got a bomb there,' said Hugo Thayer, all the while dancing, celebrating his phrasal verbal particles with hand and foot and finger. 'They think they've got something like nuclear fusion. They're going to fret you know, thinking out ways to threaten, coerce and exploit populations – not with propaganda or with advertising slogans but with art – pure art! And we must undo them. We must frustrate them. We must slip past them where they watch for us from their towers . . . yes, it's fusion they've got in the painting, Rob Clare. But it's not nuclear, no, it's the fusion of matter and mind – and its spiritual, not nuclear. It's the very stuff of the dance. And this is the dance to do . . .'

'The very stuff of the dance,' I echoed, and for a glorious instant my feet seemed to find a rhythm and my breath seemed to find for itself in all the ocean of air.

'They've got being-in-the-world there. Just another way, Rob Clare, of talking about the dance.'

'My God,' I said, suddenly, as though waking from a dream. 'No wonder they're so excited about it!'

And now he was intoning, invoking, uttering prayer, '. . . When you make the two one . . . and make the inside like the outside . . . and the outside like the inside . . . and you make the above like the below . . . and when you make male and female one and the same . . . then you will enter the kingdom of Heaven.

'These are your new patterns, Rob Clare. It's your way, it's your path forward. And we'll take the archons with us. But don't you tell them yet, Rob Clare. Just remember – mum's the word.

'Mum's the word, eh?' he said, and he stopped dancing, and started to laugh, beautifully. My eyes filled with tears of joy, tears of laughter, and I shouted then, at the top of my lungs, 'MUM IS THE WORD!' It was just as Nolton had said it was; but somehow the meaning had changed, changed utterly, and we had slipped past the nets of it, the sense and referents of the archon's rhetoric. And I was jumping around, like a little boy, jumping about, jumping up and down for joy. 'Mum's the word,' I shouted, and I danced around the tree . . .

When my rapture had passed off I leaned against the narrow trunk and looked about for Hugo Thayer.

'Hugo!' I called out, 'Where are you?'

And the half-dozen people who were standing around and watching it all from twenty yards away gestured to me sweetly, pointing upwards . . .

Amidst a tangle of boughs Hugo Thayer was light and solid, fixed and free, floating and enthroned among the branches, each thickly studded with bright red fruit.

His voice, so fine, so much like a cleric, or a scholar of Oxenford, floated down to me. 'I have a vision,' he said, 'from Bartholomew's Commission. You and I are free; what we choose to bring into being comes into being as reality. But we don't know that we choose, deep down, right at the start of thought, even as we learn the steps of an infernal, fallen dance. It's a dance, yes, but that dance is a sort of tribal frenzy; it's madness – a twitching, stinging, lashing, ravening thing. We must learn to dance like angels: light of foot, harmonious, sustaining, loving. I look at you, Rob Mark, and you're muttering and pattering about; but that's not dancing, Mark Clare, that's not being.'

'But I can't dance, Hugo,' I retorted, 'because I don't know whether I'm coming or going. I don't know where left is, where right is, I don't know any more what's up or down, what's in or out . . .'

'That's fine,' he said, 'just fine. It's the first stage of knowledge in the dance. But if you really want to learn the steps you must seek your left foot where your right is standing . . . and you must find your head in the soles of your feet, in your toes . . . and you must find the centre in me, in them, in everybody. Inside is outside, do you see? And you must learn to flow along . . .'

'Hugo,' I said, and now I felt tense and unhappy, overwhelmed with a sense of doom. 'Hugo,' I said, 'I can't flow along. I don't know how to flow, I'm pattering, muttering . . . staggering, at odds, encumbered, stiff, unmothered, unfathered . . . alien.'

'All you have to do, Rob Clare, is write it all down. You're a man of words, only. So write it down. You are the little Indian and your leaves are pages – it's words that will get us to where we need to be.'

'Listen, Hugo, listen to me! I've got to tell you about the man I've just been talking to. Everything you said about gnosis, it seems to apply somehow.'

I stood there, hands clasped together in front of me, craning my neck to tell him, to unburden myself to the man in the tree. I told him about my mother's diary, and about my father's imprisonment at Ludwigslust. I told him about Cosimo Schaffer, who created himself in the image of my father, and created Heaven in the image of the world.

'But it doesn't add up,' I said, finally. 'It's not exactly as it should be. I mean, don't you think, Hugo, don't you think it's garbled?'

'Yes, it's garbled.'

'Why is it garbled?'

'Maybe the Logos is broken,' he said, 'or our meanings are awry. Maybe we've done to language what the archons did to Adam . . . botched it, made a monster of it. Or maybe we've changed the way things are . . . and the spiritual truths of our lives. My friend in there, the physicist . . . he says to me now and then, it's like a greeting, or a password: the quantum wave function collapses under the shadow of language.'

'Eh?'

'You don't have to worry about that,' he said. 'It's my latest project. I'm working on gene theory, quantum physics and the Sephirothic Tree of Life. I'm going to show how genes and archons are closely connected, and how words can create fields, and how in fields of light we can re-create the world.'

Later, as I walked to the car, Hugo Thayer walked with me, his arm around my shoulder.

'Listen, Rob Clare,' he said, 'I want you to tell me ... tell me, Rob Clare, who am I? Who am I to you?'

'You're Hugo Thayer,' I said.

And he replied, 'I'm Who Goes There. I go before you and I catch the light, and in the distance created between us truth is possible. Now listen, listen: on March 16th, Rob Clare, my dad died. It was my dad who made the posters possible. He slaved in the desert for half his life and then he gave me money. And with his money I created my posters ... I was there when he died. He said to me, "Hugo, I'm going now." And he gripped my hand with the last of his strength and he said to me, "Goodbye, and thank you for all your help." I said to him, "Dad, Dad — tell me what you see." And with his last failing voice he whispered to me, "pattern ... eternity".'

'I'm sorry,' I said. 'I didn't know. I wouldn't have moaned so much if I had known.'

And Hugo Thayer replied, 'Isn't my loss your loss? Isn't your pain mine? And if the father is dead, still the son lives on. And the son is the true self — mother, father, sister, brother, daughter, son — there's Anthropos for you, Rob Clare. Listen, I want to explain it to you, it's all you need to know: in the moment of his dying, my father, who was fiercely attached to the world and to his family, for the first time in his life became truly detached from family and from the things of the world. And for the first time he was able to see me, and to imagine me seeing him, in a detached way. And although he saw in me so much, so much of himself going on to live, he was nonetheless able, in that moment of his death, to put aside the bonds of family, those bonds of love that are based on blood, and he saw himself in me with true detachment and knew that my life would mirror in a thousand ways his own now ending one. And he knew then that it was a pattern that reached out to infinity, and he was at its centre and its centre was everywhere. A pattern that transcends the bonds of furious blood-love, the selfish interests of family; it is the pattern of the self which finds itself mirrored in the other, in that infinite mirroring that springs into being then. It is being-fathermothersisterbrother-daughterson; it is the father-mothering, the mother-fathering. It is to be the pattern of our time. There's only One Self, you know. That's why you had to write me — to make Hugo Thayer a fiction, so that I could be free. Don't you see, though, Rob Mark Clare, we're all of us a fiction; aren't we?'

*

373

One morning just a few weeks ago I awoke in the small hours to an overwhelming conviction: I must create a union – not forged, or welded, or stitched, but woven in the stuff of the self, woven in the stuff of the world – a weaving together of abstract, unknown entities.

And two or three hours later I was awoken by a telephone call. There was a woman on the line.

'Hello? Robert Mark Clare?'

'Yes.'

'Can you hold on a moment, please, Bill's just coming to the phone.'

'Hello Robert? This is Bill here, remember?'

'Hello Bill. I hope you're well . . .'

'Robert, it's your father. He died in the night. He was very comfortable. He had a peaceful death. He sends his blessings to you. We all loved him, Robert. He was such a good person.'

And some time later, perhaps it was just a minute or so, the letter-box slapped a summons. I went sluggishly down the hall; but when I pulled open the door, the breath rushed into my body. The man on the doorstep was about five foot tall, dark-skinned, broad-shouldered and wiry of build. His hair was jet black and hung thickly down. His hands were small and strong. I could easily have been dreaming. I spoke without thinking.

'Are you from . . . ? Are you delivering something?'

I seemed to hear him speaking. He seemed to say to me that he was a political refugee. An exile from home. And in a sudden welter of images I saw: destroyed Indian habitations, smouldering stumps of forest, churned earth and choked black waters. I found a package in my hands.

'Are you . . . returning?'

He put his hand on my shoulder and shook me; his strength was extraordinary. And on the instant I seemed to see it all, all in one long vista of the mind: Henricus Wykzo, whose fields of light were absorbed in the resins of a make-up case; Magdalene and Bartholomew; the mysterious littel Indyan; Jackson in a mantrap on Lueneburg Heath; Georges Bruedelmann's paint-stained palette; my father dancing in Heaven . . . I stood on my doorstep in the grip of an inner world.

When my vision ended the man had gone.

The package was from Georges Bruedelmann, whom I hadn't seen or heard from since our Santa Lucia reunion, although I had sent him a letter soon after, to a forwarding address in Iquitos, telling him about my mother's hair-clasp, which Dennis Jackson had taken from her hair as she lay in death upon the kitchen table. And I had written to him a second time, soon after my trip to the hospital in Hamburg, when I thought

Omschka was dying; and I had told him about my mother's exercise-book diary. Bruedelmann's parcel contained a book entitled *Fragments of Lost Cosmogonies: An Anthology of Myths Collected in the Amazon Basin*; and tucked into the flyleaf there was a postcard from Georges himself, published by the Society for the Preservation of the Planet. It showed a sweep of Amazonian rain-forest: glittering green and russet-golden as far as the eye could see. On the back of the card Georges Bruedelmann had drawn his own sketchy version of a tree. It had its roots in the earth and its branches in heaven; and draped among its branches and snaking to its roots were the toiling curves of a dragon. And next to his drawing he had written, perhaps in answer to the letters I had sent him, a short inscription from the writings of Lao Tzu:

> He who knows the masculine and keeps to the feminine
> Shall become a channel for the whole world.
> If you are a channel to the whole world
> The constant virtue will remain with you
> Then you will be as innocent as a babe.

And in the index of chapters he had marked in pencil the cosmogonic myth from which I have quoted at the beginning of each of the main parts of this book; and lying flat on the page which began the chapter in question was a small sealed envelope. With trembling hand I opened it ... to remove a scrap of canvas; a scrap of precious substance of infinite and endless possibilities.

There could be no mistake; I looked at it and felt at once that presence I had met with when Bruedelmann had first shown me the work in his Normandy château. 'It's the real thing,' I said, as though there was someone with me. 'He's cut a bit off. Just for me. But it's different now ...' And indeed it was; and I felt stirrings of wonder and excitement. Now, as I looked at the scrap of canvas, it was as if I could hear a voice.

I turned it over, and on the back of it I read the following scribbled, ill-written words:

> Put away your photographs.
> There is no family album for
> the likes of us. Instead you can
> put this in your wallet, Robert.
> Or maybe you should put it
> in your make-up case. It's not

a mirror. And it's not a
pattern. But it mirrors the past
and you can shape your future
in it. Take care, son.

Consanguineous

And as I worked to finish the book it seemed to me, sometimes, that there supervened upon the landscapes of my dreams a certain compassion, a softening: the beginnings of wisdom. I told myself it was Eva calling to me, just as she had called to my father as he danced. In gnosis, too, it is Wisdom who speaks to Adam; and it is Wisdom no doubt that the children of the Amazonian tribe distilled for themselves in their ritual of sacred leaves.

Or perhaps it was the subjects of the new research, the new wave dancers of 'enhanced positive affect', who had an 'enhanced capacity for ... well, I guess it's *agape*'; perhaps it was their imaginings that so supervened upon my dreaming world. She had said, 'Really, it was my baby.'

I wonder, too, if my imaginings may supervene upon their own, as Hugo Thayer had suggested. Wasn't I conceived in Heaven, after all, where my father danced and dreamed?

And now it is finished; and Cosimo Schaffer is dead, but I'm not too sure about God. God, who is love, who is compassion which is infinite. Let me, with all my life, without and within — let me mother and father it forth, else there is nothing.